# A CAT'S CHANCE IN HELL

## SHARON

## HANNAFORD

# DEDICATION

If it were not for one specific person, this book would never have got past chapter 3. It would have fallen by the wayside as one of those "projects I'll get back to one day". He nagged, suggested, coerced, encouraged and finally, quite literally, put his money where his mouth was.

So this one's definitely for Tim – brother in a million!

# ACKNOWLEDGMENTS

As with any endeavour this one was not accomplished without the help of many people in my life. Some helped in big, quantifiable ways and others in smaller, less definable, but equally meaningful ways.

So thanks must go to the usual suspects; Brian for the practical advice and encouragement, Mel for being the core of my crit group and for doing wonders for my writing ego, Mom, Dad and the rest of the family for the support during the tough times.

Appreciation must also go the rest of my test readers for their insightful input and unerring support, and the BFFs in the 'Naki who dragged me away from the computer for a cup of coffee, a chat, a movie or a girls' night - you definitely kept me sane, and I'll never forget your unwavering support when life threw a small, ugly mountain in my path.

I was lucky enough to work with a fantastic editor who was patient and encouraging, who tolerated my uncontrollable need to rewrite every word myself with good humour, and was willing to let me learn from her as we went. Big thanks to Pauline Nolet.

Garth and Robert you are the reason I get up every morning, the reason I scramble over every obstacle in my path, the reason I'm determined to succeed. Even when you drain my last drop of patience and get on my very last nerve I still love you both insanely.

# CHAPTER 1

The nightclub was packed for a Thursday night. "Just my luck." Gabi thought sourly, wondering how many more times she was going to be hit on before she tracked down her target. Between the men, the flashing lights and the pounding music her annoyance gauge was on max and her patience gauge was on zero. Not a good combination. She casually swirled the whiskey and ice around in her glass as she swivelled on her barstool, doing another sweep of the writhing mass of dancers with her supernatural senses. She growled in frustration. Zilch again. She drained her glass and was considering a refill when she felt a small vibration against her left breast. She surreptitiously reached into her bra and pulled out the tiny phone, flicking it open to read the message. She sighed, the message wasn't good news, but at least it meant a reprieve from the sensory abuse of the club. She quickly wound her way through the throng of barely-clothed revellers, deftly avoiding groping hands and drunken invitations.

When she finally burst out the door into the crisp night air she paused to drag in a few deep breaths and adjust to the sudden lack of light and noise. The bouncer leaning against the outside wall looked her up and down appreciatively.

"Summin' I can help you with Sugar?" he drawled, pulling another drag from the cigarette held semi-concealed in his huge paw of a right hand. She surmised his boss didn't like him smoking on the job. He was tall and broad-shouldered, overly muscular, your typical, garden variety nightclub bouncer. She watched his gaze travel over her high-collared bolero jacket, her form-fitting, black mini dress that showed off her toned thighs and all the way down to the four inch heels of her patent-leather, black boots clinging lovingly to her shapely calves, and then slowly back up again, this time taking in her lustrous, auburn curls cascading in gentle waves onto her shoulders.

"I'm off duty in twenty." He hinted with a grin, his teeth seeming very white against the dark, chocolate brown of his skin. His eyes finally met her own emerald green ones and she worked to keep her expression flirtatious. He didn't need to see the real Gabi Bradford; he hadn't committed the kind of crimes that her elusive target had. It amused her to think of how quickly his sexy leer would switch to astonishment if he got close enough to touch her, close enough to feel her concealed accessories. She contained her dark humour and instead gave him a smile of apologetic regret.

"Sorry, big boy, I have business elsewhere," she gave him a wink, "but I might be back later." He sighed gustily as she sauntered away from him down the dimly lit side-walk. As soon as she was around the corner she dropped the sultry sway and quickened her stride, heading swiftly for a parking area around the back of the

2

club. There was a short cut to the lot, but it was a dark, unsavoury alleyway that most people would avoid at this time of the night. As she stepped into the alley her internal radar pinged. She wasn't alone. She didn't know whether to sing hallelujah or curse like a sailor. After spending three hours in Club 'Hell on Gabi's Nerves' her mark had been hanging around outside in a back alley. Adrenaline surged but she controlled her physical reactions, not showing any outward sign that she knew he was there. She strode briskly down the uneven tarmac, keeping her head down and exuding an aura of distracted vulnerability, directly into the path of the dark shadows hunching between rows of garbage bins where a tall, trench-coated figure waited with inhuman stillness.

The tall, pale stranger lounging in the shadows may have been surprising in his choice of hunting ground, but there was nothing surprising about his method of attack. As soon as Gabi drew level with him, he detached himself from the shadows and in an instant was just behind her left shoulder. Gabi feigned a gasp of shock and spun to face him, flicking a hand to the back of her neck as she did so. The speed of her movements must have startled him, because as she held the curved blade of her sword, aptly named Nex, pressed against his cool, untanned skin he froze, staring at her with his mouth slightly open, two grossly elongated canines gleaming dully in the dingy glare of a distant streetlight.

"Angeli Morte," he gasped in a bare whisper, his eyes wide with sudden fear. Gabi snarled in annoyance, her face no longer calm and composed.

"Yes," she growled, "I've heard some use that name for me." The pressure of Nex against the place where his pulse should beat increased minutely. "I'm told you've been a bad boy, Thomas," she hissed, "I've heard you like to make your meals scream."

3

She watched as the realisation of his fate crossed his face. He knew he'd already been tried and found guilty, that was when the pleading usually started. Thomas tried the 'go-down-fighting' route instead. He spun away from Nex and came at her from behind, lunging for the back of her neck with a speed and force that would have sent most people flying across the alley, but Gabi had spun with him, levelling her blade at his chest. He surged forward, unable to break his own momentum and Nex slid easily between his ribs bisecting his heart before his brain registered his mistake.

Gabi grimaced and yanked Nex out of the Vampire's chest as the body slid to the ground in a graceless heap. As she bent to wipe Nex on the bloodsucker's trench coat she caught the faint trace of a familiar scent coming from the far end of the alleyway. A man stepped out of the shadows, a cocky grin on his face. He was tall and lean in an endurance-athlete sort of way, though his shoulders were broad and muscular enough to make him look slightly out of proportion. His tousled, sandy blonde hair gave him an approachable, 'boy-next-door' look, but Gabi knew better than to be fooled by outward appearances.

"Thanks for the help," she said, her voice heavy with sarcasm, as the new-comer approached at a gentle lope.

"I didn't want to spoil your fun or deprive Nex of another notch in her sheath, Angeli Morte," he said with a wicked grin. Gabi rolled her eyes and shook her head with a long suffering sigh.

"Drat," she cursed, looking down at the Vampire again. "This shithead's a young one; he's not going to turn to ash. We'll have to stash him somewhere until a clean-up team can get to him." The body had already taken on the shrunken, desiccated look of a long dead corpse, but didn't appear to be decomposing any further.

4

"Make yourself useful, Wolf," she said, toeing the body and making a shooing motion with her hands towards the industrial sized garbage bins clinging like overgrown limpets to the grimy brick walls. He gave her a disgustedly reproachful look, but grabbed the collar of the trench coat and dragged the body away without further comment.

While he stashed the body safely out of sight Gabi made a call to the clean-up team. As Kyle straightened and wiped his hands against his denim covered thighs she remembered that he'd called her away from the bar with a text message. He'd said it was urgent.

"Now tell me Kyle dearest," she said, advancing on him with Nex still held loosely in her right hand, intrigue warring with annoyance. "What was so important that you had to pull me off a job?"

"Put that thing away," he grumbled, grabbing her sword hand as she got close enough to touch him with the tip of the blade. "Where do you stash her in that outfit anyway?"

Gabi arched one eyebrow arrogantly and, in a movement too quick for the human eye to follow, slid the blade back into the sheath nestled between her shoulder blades. She shook out her hair to hide the tip of the hilt which protruded ever so slightly from the top of her jacket. She didn't know what difference it made to Kyle, he knew that she could kill with her bare hands, but maybe he was thinking back to the last time someone saw her holding the sword and called the cops. It was a tense scene when they arrived and tried to disarm her. Only Kyle's calm head had kept the damage to a minimum until a clean-up team arrived and one of the Magus crew was able to wipe the memories of the whole event from the cop's minds.

The air was suddenly tinged with the scent of adrenaline. Gabi's body responded instinctively to Kyle's tense excitement as he elaborated on his message.

"The Magi surveillance team has picked up a huge power shift near the old sports stadium. There is some weird anomaly with the ley lines running under there. They predict as many as six or seven Demons will try to cross the Void at the same time," he reported, all hint of teasing chit-chat now gone.

"Shit. That many? How long have we got?" She was all business now. "I need to pick up some weapons on the way," she looked down at herself, "and some clothes."

Kyle turned to head back down the alley towards the parking lot, a superior grin on his face. "I've got you covered," he threw back over his shoulder. "I figured you'd need some other work clothes, and I brought a selection of your favourite weapons, as well as some proto-types from the geeks in the Tech department. Byron says the Veil will be thinnest in around..." he glanced at his watch, "Forty-five minutes. My van is just here."

She raised her eyebrow as they strode into the lot. "My car is faster."

"But I saw it parked three blocks away and my van has work clothes and weapons," he countered.

"Fine," she conceded impatiently. "But I'm driving. And if my car gets towed you're going to get it out of hock. The last time I went into a police station they tried to arrest me for weapons smuggling!"

Kyle had to stifle a chuckle. Her last trip into the police station to retrieve her car was unforgettable; when she'd walked through the metal detectors the cops didn't know whether to chat her up or arrest her. Springing the car would've been easy if she'd decided to use her charm on them, but she was so pissed that the towing of her car had caused her to lose track of her mark that she took her temper out on the officers instead. Kyle was glad he'd been there to calm everyone down before things escalated to actual violence. Even though there'd been over half a dozen cops in the station at the time he knew where his money would've been, and it wasn't on the boys in blue.

He'd left his van close to where they exited the alley. It'd once been a people mover, of the sort that families with lots of kids drove around in. He'd ripped out most of the interior, blacking out the windows and giving it the appearance of a camper van, complete with bed and mini bar. What the average inspection wouldn't uncover was the hidden compartments under the bed and in the floor, concealing a mini arsenal of weapons. He'd personally replaced the original engine and upgraded the suspension, tyres and braking system. It was one of the great loves of his life, so it was with resigned reluctance that he threw Gabi the keys. The stadium was a good half hour drive from the City centre, so there was no time to waste arguing with her.

Gabi drove the suped-up van like a sports car, speeding through red lights and crossing intersections without slowing. Kyle would swear she took some of the corners on two wheels instead of four. He was used to her driving, but winced every time she red-lined the engine. Suddenly she slammed on the brakes almost hurling him nose-first into the dashboard; only his inhuman reflexes saved his boyish good looks. He grimaced as he smelt the burnt rubber from what was left of his almost new, low-profile tyres. A tabby cat stood frozen in the middle of the road directly in front of them, its eyes turned almost completely black by the onslaught of the van's headlights. Gabi stared at it for a half second and Kyle could feel the slight whisper of supernatural power tickle the hairs on his arms, then the cat hissed loudly and bolted off into the darkness.

"Bloody hell," she cursed, flooring the accelerator and sending them hurtling down the street again, the engine whining in protest.

"What exactly did you say to it anyway?" he asked curiously. Gabi's ability to communicate with animals was the stuff of legends, but he was one of the few people who knew the true extent of her gift.

"I told him to go home and stop chasing cute little pussy tails around at night, or a big bad monster was coming to get him," she replied with a stern huff. "That should keep him off the roads for a couple of nights." Kyle grinned, shaking his head. That was the Gabi he knew and loved; as quick to save the life of an innocent, no matter what species, as to take the life of a monster. She was actually kinda sweet in that way, but nobody had the rocks to say that to her face, not even him.

"What're you grinning at?" she demanded, swinging the van violently onto the highway and rocketing past a road hauler rather than brake and fit in behind it. He didn't bother to reply, hanging onto the seat for dear life as she manoeuvred into the fast lane and headed out of the City towards the stadium.

To distract himself from the abuse of his van, Kyle ran over in his mind what he knew about the old stadium; it had been a top class sports arena not too long ago, but it had fallen into ruin after being abandoned. It would probably seem odd to out-of-towners that such a valuable piece of property had just been left to go to ruin without any attempt to re-develop it. You had to be a local to understand. The urban legends surrounding it were many and varied. Many centred around it being haunted; but by who, or what, was hotly debated. Some said dead sportstars, or a group of cheerleaders who'd died under the stands, and some were convinced it was an army of long-dead warriors or soldiers. Other urban legends claimed the place was cursed, and yet others said it was protected by aliens from another planet; but the one thing all the stories agreed on was that it was best to stay the hell away from it. Teenagers still dared each other to spend a night in it, and the so-called "Satan Worshippers" gathered to practice dark rituals (fortunately most of these didn't actually have a clue what they were doing), and it was sometimes used by drug lords and other criminals to conduct illicit business, but not as often as an outsider might expect. The police made a token effort to keep people out of it, but they rarely patrolled it anymore, most lawful citizens stayed away from it in any case.

The truth of the matter was known only to a select few; those who were Magi by birth and those who were trusted by the Magi High Council. The stadium had been built over an area where an unusual number of strong ley lines merged before fanning out again into individual streams. This convergence caused a pool of supernatural energy to build-up below ground until its effects could be felt even above the surface of the earth. The power manifested itself in bizarre phenomena at the stadium. It began with freak accidents and mysterious occurrences during initial construction. The Council of Magi tried to have the construction suspended, even claiming it was being built on an ancient burial ground to get the land owners to build elsewhere, but the construction went on as planned. Once opened, the stadium suffered one disaster after another; stands collapsed, the electricity was off more than it was on, kitchens caught fire, showers turned themselves on and off, and the injury stats for athletes were astronomical. Within months teams refused to play

9

there, staff refused to work there and contractors refused to keep repairing things. Two years after it opened, the stadium was abandoned. The only things still being maintained were the security lights, which were supposed to enable police to patrol it at night. There were eight foot security fences surrounding the perimeter of the stadium, but vandals, drug dealers and teenagers had long since cut holes in the fencing, so the place was essentially open to anyone who wanted to get inside. Tonight Byron; their boss and head honcho at the SMV, aka the Societas Malus Venatori, would've made sure that a police patrol, including one of their covert team members, would do a sweep of the place and clear out anyone loitering. The place would be deserted tonight. At least until the Demons turned up.

They left the lights of the City behind and sped towards the light industrial and agricultural area that surrounded the Stadium.

There was a parking area on the far side of the stadium which wasn't fenced off. Kyle directed Gabi to it and they found that some of the other members of the SMV had already gathered. The stadium loomed large and ominous in front of them; huge openings in the walls that once allowed public access to the interior and now looked like dark maws waiting to swallow unwary trespassers. Gabi parked the blacked out van near the others, turned off the engine and threw Kyle the keys.

"I'm going to get dressed and kit up. See what else you can find out," she ordered, climbing into the dark depths of the van. She didn't need any light, Gabi could see perfectly well in the dark.

"Yes, Ma'am!" Kyle shot back, throwing her a mock salute, and getting out of the van. He pretended to realign his neck, and check his arms and legs were all in one piece after the wild drive.

"Idiot!" she hissed from inside the van. "Don't think just because I can't see you I don't know what you're doing. Now get going or I'm going to spit on all your knives and make them rust!"

He sighed dramatically. "You can be a cruel, cruel woman Gabrielle Bradford. You know exactly how to poke at all my soft spots," he lamented mournfully.

"The only soft spot around here is your head!" Her retort was muffled by clothing.

He chuckled and sauntered off to join the others. A team of three was climbing back through a jagged rip in the fence and they quickly loped over to report the area clear. He touched base with everyone else who had already arrived; none of them had any more information than he did, so he headed back to the van to update Gabi.

When she emerged from the van, a bystander probably wouldn't have known it was the same woman. As she stepped into the dull light thrown by the security lights he could see why they called her Angeli Morte. Angel of Death. That was the name she'd earned for herself among the greater supernatural Community, though her fellow Hunters tended to use a different nickname for her, one that Kyle had been calling her for years. She was dressed in black, toughened leather pants, a tight-fitting Kevlar-reinforced jacket and black flat-soled boots and with her hair tied up in a severe knot. She'd made no attempt to hide the myriad of weapons attached to her body in every conceivable way. She appeared cold, ethereal and deadly. Kyle knew just how deadly. She was one of more recent additions to the Hunter squad but she'd already notched up the highest number of clean kills. She stepped out of the van and began pacing back and forth across the tarmac, stopping every now and then to stretch out or warm up her muscles, running through short sequences of complicated martial arts moves.

Gabi's hair-raising driving made them good time to the stadium. They had ten or fifteen minutes before they could expect any kind of action and he'd gone to the calm, quiet place he went to when a difficult fight was staring him in the face. He leaned back against the van and watched the members of the other Elimination Teams arrive and begin getting ready. There was a hushed, anxious kind of excitement running through them. Byron had called up everyone he could get hold of (and a few he couldn't); he was obviously going with the concept of 'throw the kitchen sink' at them. Mind you, half a dozen Demons coming out of the Etherworld at once, was something you would want to throw the kitchen sink at, if that kitchen sink happened to contain a nuclear bomb. Demons hated everyone, other Demons included. They very rarely, if ever, made any kind of attack in numbers over two or three, and generally attacked alone. He briefly wondered if the Magi at SMV Headquarters could've been mistaken, but shook that off. They'd never been wrong about an attack in all the time he'd been part of the SMV. Sure, they missed some attacks, it was impossible to monitor every inch of a city the size of this one, but when they said there was an attack coming they were right.

He looked around again counting the SMV members milling around in an ordered sort of chaos. Normal Elimination Teams consisted of two Hunters, one Banisher; a Magus capable of sending Demons back to the Etherworld, and a Clean-up Crew in a specially kitted out van. The Clean-up Crew consisted of an Eraser; a Magus gifted at wiping human memories, a Medic, and a

Driver/Muscle person to help with hauling bodies when necessary. The Driver was most often a Werewolf but occasionally a Magus or Shapeshifter. There were different team set-ups for captures and for street patrols, but those details he left to Byron and the rest of the SMV Council, it wasn't for him to worry about, and as long as they teamed him and Gabi together as much as possible he didn't interfere. Tonight he greeted all three of the other Hunters; Douglas, a tall Shapeshifter who knew more about weapons than he and Gabi put together; Matthew, a Werewolf, particularly welcome tonight as Werewolf saliva was fatally poisonous to Demons; and Lance, a very powerful Magus who could launch fireballs at you as easily as he could set you alight where you stood, he was affectionately called Zippo by the rest of the Team, and nobody tread too hard on his toes – not even Gabi. Kyle didn't know all the other members who'd shown up; he knew a few of the 'Offensive' Magi, the ones who had some kind of gift that could be used in a fight, and most of the Banishers he'd worked with before, but the Clean-up crews he rarely interacted with and they were switched out on a regular basis, he knew some faces but not many names. The Medics he knew intimately of course, both of them had patched him up more often than he cared to remember. He blew out a deep breath, hoping that the Medics wouldn't be needed tonight.

Gabi had resorted to muttering and cussing to herself and Kyle glanced back at her. He almost grinned, but thought better of it and bit it back at the last second. Her vocabulary got more inventive in direct proportion to her adrenaline level. She'd had a short temper and florid vocabulary for as long as he'd known her. He turned back to the van as memories finally cracked through the controlled mask he'd tried to cover his grin with. He started to get various weapons strapped to his own body as an excuse to keep his face turned away from her, as he remembered their very first meeting.

# CHAPTER 2

Saying that he switched schools a lot as a child was rather like saying the Pope prayed a lot. In fact, he couldn't remember spending more than two terms at any one school. His mother was a single parent, and they lived on the small wage she made from casual work on farms or in factories or restaurants, moving on once work dried up or his mother felt it was time to go. When he approached his teens he finally put his foot down and threatened to drop out of school if they moved again. It was the incentive she needed to settle down and keep one job. She found work as a housekeeper for a wealthy family in one of the better suburbs on the edge of a rural, forested area. She and Kyle were given the use of a small, self-contained apartment above the garage. He'd been enrolled in the local High School, which was full of rich snobby types, along with a few poorer souls who were allowed in from lower class suburbs because they excelled either academically or in sports.

It'd been important for Kyle and his mom to settle down near a rural area. Werewolves needed access to a large forested area during the time of the full moon, and his mom had been a Werewolf since shortly before his birth. Werewolves were often volatile creatures who struggled to contain their tempers, and were forced to change to wolf form over the three days of the full moon. Fortunately, the need to change was strongest at night, once the moon rose. So as long as his mom wasn't expected to work in the evenings, and managed to keep her temper during the day, the housekeeping work suited her perfectly. Her supernatural strength made the daily chores easy and she was generally finished with everything before the bratty kids arrived home from school, minimising the chance of them igniting her temper. To Kyle's utter astonishment, it had worked out amazingly well.

A few weeks after he started attending Parkhurst High he met *her*. Kyle had certain abilities that no one else in the world possessed, or so he thought. These abilities stemmed from the fact that when his mother had been infected with the Lycanthropy virus she had been over eight months pregnant. She'd survived the attack of the Werewolf, as well as the attack of the virus, and had given birth to him a few days later, shortly before she underwent her first change. She never told him the exact details of how she coped those first few weeks and months; it had obviously been an extremely difficult time for both her and his father. Kyle seemed to be a perfectly healthy baby and didn't seem to be affected by the lycanthropy virus. His mother had hoped that somehow the womb had protected him. Kyle's father hung around for a year or so and then vanished, leaving her and Kyle to fend for themselves. Kyle still had no idea where his father was, or even if he was still alive.

As Kyle grew, it became apparent that he had been affected by the virus, but not in the usual way. He possessed heightened senses of smell, hearing and eyesight, and an uncanny ability to move absolutely silently. He was fearless and agile and often astounded other people with his physical coordination and ability. His mother began to tell people he was older than he actually was, for fear that someone would begin asking uncomfortable questions. She kept him well away from doctors and hospitals, terrified of what they may find. Fortunately he never got so much as a cold or flu, and with their frequent moves, no-one became suspicious of his incredible abilities and growth spurts. She taught him from a young age how to disguise his extra abilities, but he found it difficult to "play dumb" when he could smell and hear better than any normal human. He never experienced a need to change as his mother did, and didn't seem to have the volatile temper innate in all 'made' Werewolves. But the fact remained that he was a supernatural anomaly. Lycanthropy renders males sterile and females unable to carry a child to term. This startling fact meant that all Werewolves are made by surviving a Werewolf bite – Werewolves are not born. He was something no other Werewolf had ever heard of, abnormal in Werewolf society, and certainly outcast in human society if anyone ever found out the truth. He'd felt like an outcast in life. He would've had no shortage of female company with his looks and physique, but he tended to brush them off when they tried to strike up any kind of conversation with him, he was too nervous of unwittingly revealing his true nature. And so he assumed the persona of a quiet loner, albeit one who was never picked on or bullied. Until the day *she* walked past him in the school corridor.

He was walking to Science class when a peculiar scent caught his nose. He was used to sifting through a million different smells every day, everything from deodorant, perfume and shampoo, to bad breath, dope smoke and teenage hormones. This scent triggered an instant adrenaline surge through his body. He'd never experienced anything like it. He froze on the spot, his mind going blank as students jostled him in their rush to class. He shook himself aware enough to shove his way to the corridor wall, putting his back against it and looking around anxiously to locate the source of the scent. He closed his eyes and concentrated on that individual smell, following it to its strongest point. When his eyes flashed open they were looking directly into the eyes of a petite, auburn haired girl on the other side of the corridor. She also seemed to be frozen in place, staring directly at him, as a tide of children surged around them.

He couldn't believe this strange, alarming scent was coming from this tiny slip of a girl. It wasn't even a bad smell, just different, but it was making his senses scream 'Danger'. His breathing quickened, his pulse sped up, and his muscles tensed in response to the fight or flight instinct suddenly controlling his body. Then a student clipped him with her bag, breaking his intense concentration on the girl and his rational mind kicked back into gear. As he breathed in deeply, reaching for calm, he realised, that although this slip of a girl, barely into her teens, was standing in the middle of the flow of students, no one touched her, no one jostled her, no one cussed her for standing in the way. It stuck him as extremely odd.

Her eyes suddenly narrowed, and her face took on a predatory look. She stared directly into his eyes and then flicked her head to one side; her auburn curls bouncing, and looked pointedly at the exit door at the end of the corridor. He glanced at the door and then back to the girl, but she was gone. A second later he found her looking at him from just outside the open door, a small, condescending smile on her lips and open challenge in the slight raise of one eyebrow. He didn't give himself time to think, he simply reacted to the dare. Curiosity killed the cat, not the wolf after all.

He slipped quickly to the open door and out onto the concrete path, closing the door behind him. His breathing was still coming too fast and his heart was pounding in his chest. She was standing under a tree almost behind the gymnasium building. Anyone looking out of a classroom window wouldn't see her, but he was going to have to get really close to her if he didn't want to be spotted by a teacher. He decided to ignore his base instincts and go with the cocky self-assurance of a youth who hadn't met anyone who would be a danger to him; semi-werewolf that he was. He should probably have trusted his instincts. He melted into the shadows of the building and slipped quietly through their protection to come up a few feet behind her. The next instant he was lying face first in the dirt with both arms behind his back and a slight weight in the very centre of his spine. He was stunned. His muscles bunched to throw her off when her voice came from just behind his left ear.

"If you move I will break your spine," she said from between clenched teeth. Her bony little knee pushed further into his vertebrae to illustrate her point. "Hold still and we can talk."

Her hands had his wrists in an unnaturally powerful grip. His wolf instinct howled to get away from her immediately, by any means necessary, but his human intuition overrode that. She wasn't actually hurting him; if she meant him harm she could've hurt him already. He considered the possibility that she was actually scared of him. Then he realised it was likely that she too had never smelled anything like him, and was just as curious. Years of dealing with his mother had taught him that violence rarely solved anything, so he lay passively underneath her. Now that he was calmer he could hear her heart racing, could taste the slight tang of fear and adrenaline coming from her, her breathing much too fast.

"What *are* you?" She growled in her little, feminine voice. Her words confirming his suspicions.

He raised his head a little, cautiously, spitting out dirt. "If you let me up and stop acting like a little animal, I'll tell you," he admonished. "There's no need for all the theatrics!"

She let him up after some assurances that he wasn't going to retaliate for her unprovoked attack. They moved further away from the school into a nearby thicket of bushes and spent the rest of the school day talking.

He'd never thought he would meet someone else with a story as bizarre as his own. He'd never thought to meet anyone aside from his mother that he could open up to about his life without fear of rejection, revulsion or horror, and with total understanding. What were the chances of the two of them meeting, how astounding that they'd found each other. How ignorant he'd been, thinking that Werewolves were the only supernatural beings wandering the planet, the only creatures from human myth and legend that actually existed.

Her name was Gabrielle and, like him, she was an anomaly and had been from birth. Gabrielle had the blood of a Vampire running in her veins. Her mother had also been attacked when she was already pregnant, although it was so early in the pregnancy that she hadn't known it at the time. A lone Vampire had attacked her one night and dragged her into a back alleyway. Unbelievably, a second Vampire had appeared in the alley and, instead of joining in the meal, had attacked the first Vampire. With the fighting Vampires blocking her escape route, Gabi's mother had been forced to witness

20

the vicious battle at close quarters. As the two Vampires ripped into each other, Vampire blood sprayed directly into her face and she'd reflexively swallowed the blood in her fright. The second Vampire had ultimately beaten the first one, but seemed badly injured himself. He left the scene without a word or a glance her mother's way. Weeks later her mother discovered she was pregnant and had been already at the time of the attack. Her parents kept this terrifying story from everyone except her father's close friend Byron who had his own reasons for believing and understanding the outlandish tale.

Gabi was born a few months later, premature but healthy. As Gabi grew, there was little unusual about her, aside from extraordinary good health and being quick to walk and talk. There was nothing that couldn't be explained by good genes and conscientious parenting.

That had all changed shortly after her seventh birthday. Her parents found her sitting on the grass in the back garden surrounded by wild animals. When they called to her in alarm, she calmly told them that she liked talking to the animals and they liked talking to her. This had been the first of her powers to manifest. She could literally talk the birds down from the trees, or soothe the most vicious dog. Not long after that she developed amazing eyesight and hearing, and then an incredible sense of smell. Her parents had forced her to hide these extra abilities from other people, and she'd only been allowed to "talk" to animals when she was safely alone at home, or around Byron, who was privy to all the new developments. She hated the restrictions, but acquiesced to her parents' wishes.

Life turned tragic for her at age ten, when her father was killed by a Vampire. Her father and Byron, who was Magi born, had co-founded the Societas Malus Venatori (Hunters of Evil); a secret organisation of Shape-shifters,

21

Magi and humans that monitored supernatural activity and silently dealt out punishment to supernaturals who attacked others with apparent impunity. When a supernatural went rogue the body count could quickly get out of hand. The SMV routinely hunted down rogues and eliminated them, disposing of evidence of the kills and using Magi to erase the memories of any humans involved. Gabi's father had been on a hunt for a particularly brutal Vampire when he was killed.

Gabi had had to grow up fast, she'd assumed many of the responsibilities of running the household, as well as looking after her mother. Byron and his wife spent as much time as they could helping out, but many tasks still fell on Gabi's slim shoulders. Between her duties at home, her mother's erratic behaviour and her own feelings of abnormality, Gabi had no close friends and few casual friends. She comforted herself with animals, and amassed a small menagerie to keep herself sane.

Kyle and Gabi became firm friends after that first meeting, both finding immense relief in having someone they could be completely honest and open with. Kyle was the perfect foil for Gabi's fiery temper, and the passionate loves and hates of her life. He was strong enough to not always give in to her, and resilient enough to put up with the explosions that followed when he didn't. Gabi was Kyle's first real friend and she also presented him with a goal to work towards once she told him of the existence of the SMV. In time most kids at school assumed they were involved in more than a platonic relationship, and though they had actually given it a try, it hadn't worked out. He was the big brother she'd never had, and nothing could change that.

When Kyle left school he'd been accepted immediately into the SMV as a Hunter Trainee. But a few years later when Gabi left school Byron dug his heels in about Gabi joining the Hunter ranks and insisted that she take time to mature and to get a tertiary qualification, perhaps hoping she'd give up the idea in a couple of years.

Things became very strained between her and Kyle after that, she'd felt hurt, betrayed and abandoned. It changed something between them, their relationship no longer as easy-going and as defined as it had been before. When they did meet up during her university days, she seemed dispirited and demoralised. She felt that she was letting down her father by not being a Hunter. It was Kyle who convinced her to learn how to fight properly, pointing out that if she got her degree and proved capable of holding her own against an enemy, Byron would have no more reasons to keep her from joining them. Kyle had underestimated how much she would take his advice to heart.

She threw herself into her study of Animal Behaviour and Ethology and in her spare time began practicing an array of martial arts, studying both fighting styles and the history behind them. She immersed herself in Korean, Japanese and Chinese fighting styles and learnt to use their weapons. Her training choices proved to be the perfect preparation for a Hunter.

It took her four years of blood, sweat and tears to get to the point that she felt ready to demonstrate her abilities to Byron. To prove herself, she took on two of the best Hunters of the SMV at the same time, and wiped the floor with them. Convincingly. Byron had been forced to admit she could handle herself and had finally welcomed her into the fold, inducting her as the first ever female Hunter. He'd also incorporated much of her martial arts training into the training routines of the existing Hunters, and into initiation training for future Hunter hopefuls.

With guns outlawed in the City, her choice of weapons was as considered and unusual as her choice of martial arts training. Her weapon of choice was her sword, Nex, appropriately meaning Death. Nex was a Kris, an Indonesian short sword with a cruel and distinctive appearance. Renowned for its curved, wave-shaped blade, it was designed specifically for stabbing and sliding easily between ribs. Perfect for hitting the heart of any target. Not everyone got to wield one of these swords. The makers of these blades firmly believe that the blade has to choose the wielder, not the other way around. After Gabi had been successfully matched with Nex she'd had the maker embed a gemstone from her father's signet ring in the hilt. She was rarely without the blade, and it did indeed seem to have magical qualities in her hands, Nex had tasted heart's blood many, many times.

She also introduced the rest of the Hunters to Butterfly swords. Kyle himself liked to carry these as back-up weapons. Short, single edged blades roughly as long as a human forearm, easy to conceal and perfect for close quarters fighting. Sporting a D shaped hilt, they allowed the wielders hand some measure of protection, and could be wielded in pairs. Being designed to be carried two to a sheath, meant you could carry plenty of them. It wasn't often you ran out of butterfly swords in a fight.

Gabi's degree paid dividends too, and she'd built a small but thriving business for herself, helping people with problem animals (or animals with people problems, as she liked to put it), as well as training and managing animals for TV and Film shoots. Working for herself left her plenty of free time to dedicate to the SMV while still maintaining the all-important illusion of a normal life for the rest of the world.

"Have you suddenly become a doddering old man?" Gabi's voice broke into his reverie. "Are you getting those blades strapped on or are you just going to sit the whole thing out tonight?" Her words were slightly slurred as she sucked on a lollipop while bitching at him. The lollipop was one of the special ones that Byron had made up for her by a pharmacist friend. She had some strange vitamin and mineral deficiency which no one had been able to explain, it was assumed it was part and parcel of the Vampire blood thing, but no one knew for sure. She was so bad at remembering to take tablets that Byron had resorted to having the supplements made into lollipops to get them into her; Gabi was also renowned for her sweet tooth.

He mentally shook himself, and snapped back to reality. "Hmm, I thought maybe I should just sit out and see how you cope on your own for a change," he teased. She glowered at him, knowing better than to rise to his bait, and settled for throwing her lollipop stick at him.

"What did the geeks send? They better have tested whatever it is properly this time!"

Kyle leaned into the van and picked up a pair of handgun-shaped weapons. He threw one at Gabi, who caught it easily and stared at it with astonishment. "What the hell is this supposed to do?" He threw a strap at her. "But wait… it even comes with its own solidly constructed holster," Kyle mimicked the overly enthusiastic voice of someone on one of those idiotic TV infomercials.

"I could just test it out by shooting you with it," she threatened, turning it over and pointing the barrel straight at him, her finger on the trigger. "Stop messing with me Wolf, I'm not in the mood."

"Chill Hellcat, I'm just trying to lighten the mood before we all go off to be eaten or ripped apart by Demons." They had a small audience by this stage, and a nervous chuckle rippled through them. Many of them had never seen the aggressive banter that sparked between Kyle and Gabi before a fight; those that knew them well just ignored them.

"You're going to be ripped apart before the Demons get a chance at you, if you don't tell me the point of this absurd weapon," she growled. Literally. There was a reason he'd nicknamed her Hellcat. He'd seen her face down full grow lions and win the pissing contest.

"You're no fun when you're psyched up for a fight," he muttered presenting his own weapon with a flourish. "This is the newly patented Werewolf Saliva Dart Gun. It's pre-loaded with five saliva filled ampoules and is like having five mini Werewolves on your side. One dart should be sufficient to slow down a Demon enough to finish him off, or to kill him once he returns home. Two should kill him in minutes." Kyle pulled the gun apart to show the tiny ampoules inside. "Needless to say, it is best to avoid shooting anyone on our side with one of these, as they will have the same effect as a real Werewolf bite – death or turning furry at full moon." He drew in a breath to continue when a shout went up from a group near the edge of the stadium.

"Heads up," a male voice yelled. "The gateway is opening."

The air between the parking lot and the stadium began to turn hazy and everyone began scrambling into position. Kyle and Gabi strapped on their new dart guns and ran for the fence line to push through with the other Hunters.

# CHAPTER 3

Gabi felt the air around them grow bitingly cold as a thick, throat-clogging mist roiled up out of the ground. The five Hunters stopped just on the other side of the fence, fanning out into a defensive line, the five offensive Magi hovered slightly behind them. Even though they were standing over a hundred metres from the place where the roiling mist was bubbling out of the earth, the cold was bone numbing and a gag-inducing stench threatened to choke them.

"Alright," Doug called in his deep, urgent baritone. He was the most seasoned Hunter among them so the others deferred to him. "Let's see what comes out of that, then we'll split them up amongst ourselves." He turned to the Magi. "Banishers and Trackers, you can pick up any that get away from us, but stay behind us as much as possible. We're relying on you to send back any we can't kill outright. Give us a chance to strike a deathblow first, but the priority is to keep them from leaving the area. The Clean-up teams have orders to follow any that do escape us, at a safe distance, and we'll catch them once the rest are destroyed. Don't be tempted to attack any that escape on your own, don't forget how easily these things can poison you, wait for back-up and do not engage one alone. Am I clear on that?" he roared like an army sergeant.

Gabi had to bite her lip to stop herself saluting and yelling back, "Yes, Staff Sergeant!" Doug would not be amused.

The Magi murmured agreement and moved apart into a loose line, their expressions calm and resolute as they began their own internal preparations for the battle. Gabi was quietly cursing the fact that she'd run out of sweets, and took to pacing in a small circle as she tugged on a pair of fingerless gloves. Lance was playing idly with a small ball of fire, tossing it casually from one hand to the other, while Kyle was rechecking his weapons and Matt was stretching out muscles, a grin of anticipation on his rough, unshaven face.

Gabi suddenly became aware of another change in the air, an electric charge seemed to crackle angrily across her skin, and a thick, oily darkness descended into her brain. She looked quickly around at Kyle and the others, they were looking uncomfortable too, and she heard a quick, hissed intake of breath from the group behind her. The Demons had made it across the void.

"Buckle up boys," Gabi drawled loudly. "Time to kick some fucking Demon ass!" Her last words came out as a scream of defiance. A snarl broke from deep in her throat as she ripped Nex from her sheath, a look of vicious determination on her face. The darkness swamping her brain immediately dissipated, and her outcry seemed to have the same effect on everyone around her as they all drew weapons and issued war cries of their own.

The Demons emerged from the mist; a motley group of repulsive aberrations from the darkest depths of hell. Four grotesque creatures lumbered into sight, and the group collectively breathed a sigh of relief. The relief was short-lived as another smaller Demon flew out of the fog and hovered a few feet above the others, and then another wraithlike being floated out and to the right of the gathered hoard. The Hunters froze in tense expectation, wondering what exactly they were pitting themselves against, and how many more were coming.

"That's all of them," a small, hushed female voice said from just behind Gabi. "The portal has closed. No more can cross tonight."

"You're sure?" Doug demanded from the slightly built Magus.

"Positive," she squeaked.

"Trinity knows what she's talking about when it comes to portals," one of male Magi quickly backed her up.

"OK then," Doug continued quickly, "let's see what we have to deal with."

The Demons had started to get their bearings and the wraithlike one raised a tattered sleeve and pointed towards the group of Hunters standing ready and waiting. The Wraith was wearing a heavy, dark cloak that covered its entire body, if it even had a body. Nothing could be seen except for glowing, yellow-green orbs floating around in the depths of the cowl.

Matt, the tall, heavily muscled Werewolf, was the first to stake his claim.

"I'll take the skinny, green giant," he said, referring to the tallest of the Demons. It was over eight feet tall and covered in bits of leather armour which sprouted vicious metal spikes. Its skeletal arms and legs were covered in flaky pea-green skin and its hands ended in three inch, dagger-like claws; dripping with a dark, oily substance that hissed and spattered when it came into contact with the grass at its feet. It turned its human-shaped head to look at them and Gabi realised it had no discernible mouth and only holes for nostrils. Three large eyes, completely black, were situated just below a ridged brow of dark green spikes protruding from its forehead.

"You're welcome to that one," countered Lance, "I think I'll take Godzilla over there. Weapons aren't going to pierce its armoured skin easily, so let's see how it takes to being slow roasted inside its shell," he finished with an evil smirk. This Demon was also tall and hulking, though not as tall as the first one. Straight out of a B-grade monster movie, it was mostly reptilian in appearance, though standing upright on thickly muscled legs. It was covered in large, metallic scales all the way down to its massive tail, which was easily as long as Gabi was tall. Its gaping jaws were more like those of a crocodile, and were filled with thousands of razor sharp teeth which oozed with slimy, black saliva.

Doug interrupted quickly as Gabi and Kyle started to claim their targets. "I'll take the birdman," he said, jerking his head upwards towards the stick thin, avian Demon hovering in mid-air. It had motley yellow and brown skin and no feathers, but leathery bat-like wings that were far bigger than the rest of its emaciated body. It had scrawny human arms and legs, but instead of a mouth it sported a vicious looking hooked beak sprouting from its humanoid face. It was carrying a crudely fashioned crossbow. "I can change to something with wings to chase it down if it tries to run."

"You'll need to watch out for that crossbow," Lance cautioned. "If I get the chance I'll try to set fire to it."

"OK, but don't lose your concentration on Godzilla." Then Doug steeled himself, Gabi wasn't going to like what he was about to decree. He drew in a deep breath. "Hellcat--"

"Yeah, yeah, I know," she interrupted with an annoyed sigh. "I get the short one." The shortest one of the bunch was around Gabi's height or a little shorter. It was squat and heavily muscled with huge hairy feet and long coarse fur sprouting out all over its body and head, including its face. It flashed a macabre grin baring rows of needle sharp teeth from its overly large mouth. It carried an odd assortment of weapons, all medieval in nature; maces, clubs, spears and battle axes. Gabi knew it made sense that she took on the one closest to her in size, the men would have to change their fighting style to accommodate the difference in height, and there was no room for egos in a fight like this one. "But once I'm finished with Shorty I get to go after the Wraith!" she declared triumphantly.

"I think we'll all have to go after the Wraith," Doug declared, but didn't bother warning Gabi off. "Keep it busy until we can help you finish it off."

"Well, I guess that leaves me with the brick shithouse," Kyle said. The only unclaimed Demon was a hugely built, seven foot tall creature with an extra pair of arms and several eyes spaced a few inches apart in a ring around its head. It had no lips covering its shark-like teeth and a wide, flat nose which flared as it sniffed the air. Metal armour covered its torso and legs and it was holding two wooden war clubs and a spiked flail. It was definitely built like the proverbial brick shithouse.

"Don't worry Wolf," Gabi teased, "I'll rescue you if he gets too much for you to handle."

Kyle gave her a withering look.

"They're advancing," a voice called from behind them, dragging their attention back to the horde. The Demons had spread out into a rough line and begun moving towards them. The Hunters also spread out, angling closer to their assigned targets, giving each other room to fight. The Magi moved back slightly and clustered together, touching each other lightly. Alone, they each had formidable powers. Connected, they could combine powers and become an astronomical force, which could withstand the strongest offensive magic and overcome the most stubborn defensive magic. They would watch closely and render assistance to the Hunters when needed. Their magic couldn't kill Demons, but could banish them back to the Etherworld. Unfortunately, at times when the Veil was thin, a banished Demon could always return to the place it had been cast back from. It was best to kill them on this plane, so there was no chance of a revisit.

Savage screams rent the air as the Demon onslaught began. Gabi streaked towards her target, quicker than any of the others. Nex tasted Demon blood before any of the other Hunters had even engaged their targets. She'd drawn a butterfly sword as she ran, she knew she would be sacrificing this sword; Demon blood ate through any metal it came in contact with, unless the metal was magically protected by a complex spell. Each Hunter carried one protected sword or knife. Nex was protected; the Kris had met with Demon blood many times before and was impervious to the corrosiveness. The other sword would only draw blood once on a Demon, but it would be enough if she could get it into the heart of the beast. As she darted in to take another chunk out of Shorty's upper arm and sidestepped to avoid the spurt of blood she heard the others clash with their targets and smelt the distinct, acrid stench of burning Demon flesh. She ducked, narrowly avoiding a spear hurled with immense force straight towards her head, pivoted around in a semi-crouch and sprang forwards driving Nex directly into the Demon's right eye. She danced backward, hissing as a drop of blood splattered the side of her face. It burnt like molten lava and she quickly wiped it off with the back of her gloved hand, and then bent to wipe her glove on the grass before the blood ate a hole through the toughened leather. She dropped the butterfly sword that had started to disintegrate, and grabbed another one out of a thigh sheath while the Demon bellowed, lurching around uselessly with Nex protruding from its eye. She darted back towards the Demon, and, using every ounce of her considerable strength, drove the butterfly sword directly into the Demon's chest, cutting downward to open its chest cavity and expose its internal organs. It started to collapse to the ground, grabbing at her with huge, hairy hands as it did so, but she was as quick as a cobra. She ripped Nex from its eye, kicked the Demon onto its back, dropped the other sword and, using both hands, plunged Nex straight into its black pulsating heart. She leapt back as black gunge spewed from its chest cavity, and stood watching as the body of the repulsive creature begin to liquefy. Soon it would only be a puddle of foul smelling, acidic jelly. The Clean-up crew would deal with the remnants of the Demon later. She snatched Nex out of the rancid mess, cursing as the Demon blood seared her exposed fingers. She quickly wiped the blood off with a strip of cloth from a pocket and threw it into the jellified remains. It was a hard-learnt trick of the trade to include scraps of tough cloth in your battle gear for times like this.

She did a quick scan of the four other fights; her blood was boiling with adrenaline, her breathing was quick and deep, her eyes bright and her face flushed with excitement, she revelled in the thrill of the fight. Lance had Godzilla careening around in agony, though his thrashing tail was posing a danger to anyone in the vicinity, the reptilian Demon was too overcome with the internal fire to really try and cause Lance any damage. Demons typically didn't react in pain, they didn't seem to feel any, the exception to this rule was pain caused by fire, and Lance's fire in particular seemed to cause them agony.

Doug had shifted into the form of an enormous condor and had ripped huge holes in the hide and wings of the Birdman Demon; they were now circling each other warily. The crossbow was lying blackened and smoking on the ground. Zippo was living up to his reputation today. Matt was still in human form facing off against the thin green Demon, so he obviously didn't feel too overpowered. Matt had the rare Werewolf ability to change to his wolf form in seconds. If he found himself outclassed as a human fighter he simply retreated, ripped into his wolf form, and hurtled back at the, usually astounded, attacker in a blur of teeth and claws. Kyle was the only one looking like he could do with some help, the four-armed Demon was swinging the cruel looking flail at an alarming speed, making it almost impossible for Kyle to get anywhere near it. The Demon's extra eyes made it difficult to rush it from any side, and even if he did get past the flail there were the three foot long war clubs to contend with. She knew he would be pissed at her later for intervening, but it was going to take more than one Hunter to take that Demon down.

She was just heading in Kyle's direction when she heard the Magi cry out in alarm. "Shit," she thought. "The Wraith." She skidded to a halt and cast about seeking the ghostly Demon when an icy chill suddenly passed over her, freezing her in place. She knew instinctively that the Wraith was directly behind her. With a huge mental wrench she freed her immobilized muscles, and spun around to face the new threat. Now, standing only a few feet from the Demon she could see that it had no substantial form. It seemed to be made up of smoke and fog. As though air particles had been condensed and moulded into a vaguely human shape. Spectral hands protruded from the ends of its ragged sleeves, but no feet or face was visible, only glowing orbs suspended in the dark space of its cowl. It radiated pure, undiluted malevolence.

Gabi didn't hesitate; she lunged directly at the creature, aiming Nex at the glowing orbs. As Nex pierced the air inside the dark cowl she felt a sharp jolt, like an electrical current. She felt herself picked up off the ground and flung backwards like a ragdoll, landing in a crumpled heap several metres away. She lay on the ground stunned; gasping for air, her limbs refusing to move.

"Holy Shit. Gabi!" Kyle yelled, taking his eyes off the four-armed Demon momentarily to assess Gabi's situation. It was a mistake. The spiked flail caught him across his left side, pounding into his ribs and gouging strips of flesh and muscle as it tore free. Agony ripped through him, and he stumbled backwards falling on his backside. The fall saved his head from being concaved by the huge war club that hurtled through the air, directly where his head had been only a millisecond before. He'd lost his main sword, and was groping desperately for another weapon when his hand closed around the dart gun. The Demon rushed him, drawing back the flail once more. Kyle drew a gasping breath, steadied himself and fired the dart gun three times into the beast's face.

The Demon tossed its head in annoyance at the bite of the darts, sending the flail down slightly off target, Kyle managed to wrench his body aside but the cruel, spiked head of the weapon caught a glancing blow off his upper thigh, tearing through the leather and lacerating the flesh beneath. The wolf inside him howled in fury, it wasn't going to lie quietly and let him be flayed alive. The power of the wolf brought him to his feet, forcing him to move his agonised body away from the crazed Demon. It was floundering around, swiping at mid-air and roaring madly at unseen attackers. The Werewolf saliva was working through the Demon's body; it would be incapacitated in seconds. Matt and Lance both streaked in towards it and plunged knives and swords into it, finishing it off quickly and efficiently.

"Gabi," Kyle yelled again, clamping his left arm down over the bloody gashes in his side to try and staunch the flow of blood. She was slowly picking herself up off the ground, but she seemed unsteady and confused. She was blinking her eyes wildly, rubbing at them with her hands as the Wraith moved menacingly towards her.

"Shit, something's wrong with Gabi," he yelled to Matt and Lance. He started staggering painfully towards her, but then he felt Matt's steely hand suddenly grip his shoulder.

"We've got her Wolf, get yourself to the medics," Matt ordered and then sprinted after Lance towards Gabi and the Wraith. Kyle knew he wasn't going to be any help in a fight, but the wolf wouldn't let him just curl up and wait for the medics, he couldn't shake the feeling that there was something off about the way Gabi was reacting. Lance and Matt placed themselves between Gabi and the Wraith and Lance began tossing fire balls at it, aiming for the eyes inside the cowl. The Magi had moved closer to the fight as well and were gesturing wildly to the other Hunters. Doug flew into the middle of the melee and changed back to human form, shouting at the Magi to start the Banishment spell. Kyle had managed to drag himself close enough to call to Gabi.

"Gabi, are you alright?" he shouted anxiously. "Gabs, you need to get back from there," "The others have got it under control." "I hope," he added under his breath.

"Tell them not to touch it," Gabi yelled frantically. "They mustn't touch it!" There was an edge of hysteria in her voice.

She put her arm out towards him as though feeling for him, stumbling in his direction. It was in that instant he realised she was blind.

Gabi felt the air whoosh out of her lungs as her back hit the ground with a bone jarring crunch. The force had felt like huge electrical charge exploding through her body. She lost track of time while her lungs remembered how to breathe. She groggily opened her eyes, but the darkness still clouded her vision. She shook her head trying to clear the black fog from her eyes. Her limbs were shaking and she didn't seem to have any control over them.

"Holy cow!" she muttered to herself, "what the hell is that thing?" In the distance she heard Kyle yell her name. She knew she had to get to her feet, had to clear the blackness from her eyes and prepare to face the Wraith again. She could smell the dry, musty odour of it, it was coming for round two and she wasn't sure she had another round in her. How was she supposed to fight this thing? "Distract it until helps arrives," she told herself sternly. "Get up!" She fumbled around until her hand closed around Nex's hilt, then managed to get her feet and legs into some kind of order and dragged herself upright; swaying as she tried to lock her legs in place and take a confident stand. She wondered briefly if this was what it felt like to be drunk or stoned; her metabolism burned through alcohol and drugs so fast that she'd never experienced either. Maybe she was blind drunk she suddenly thought inanely, almost letting out a hysterical giggle. She started rubbing furiously at her weeping eyes, they were burning and itchy. Nothing she did seemed to clear the black fog. She couldn't see anything, and she knew the Wraith was edging around to her other side, hoping to take her unawares. But she had other senses to rely on; she concentrated on those and tried not to think too hard about the loss of sight. She took in a steadying breath and was about to turn and face the creature when she heard Kyle call out to her again; asking if she was alright, telling her to move away, that the others were close enough to take over the fight. A surge of panic shot through her. They didn't know what the Demon was capable of. She shouted at him to tell them not to touch it, but she wasn't sure they'd listen in the heat of battle. She reached out blindly towards Kyle's voice, and took a few steps in his direction. She could smell blood, Kyle's blood.

"They've got it under control,' he repeated, "the Magi are almost done with the spell." At that moment she felt his hand take her outstretched arm and guide her into a warm, reassuring hug. She collapsed into his chest, not saying anything as she took an unsteady breath and put her arms around his waist. He flinched involuntarily, grunting softly; she could feel warm, sticky wetness under her arm where it touched him.

"Shit, Wolf," she exclaimed. "You're badly hurt. I could smell the blood, but I didn't know it was this bad. We need to get you to the medics." She quickly sheathed Nex and began pushing him in a direction, but then realised she didn't actually know which direction they needed to head in. The stench of Demon blood and burnt Demon flesh obscured the other odours around them, so she couldn't even smell where the Clean-up teams were parked.

Kyle pulled her back to face him, put a finger under her chin and brought her face up towards his.

"You can't see me can you?" he asked softly. He was trying to keep the horror out of his voice, but it leaked through, and its presence sent a wave of icy cold fear cascading through her veins. She shook her head quickly, not trusting her own voice. He ran his thumbs over her eyelids and took her face in his hands.

"We'll sort this out, don't worry. It's probably something magic related, the Magi will know what to do." He sounded like he was babbling, trying to mask his fear for her.

She cleared her throat. "Yeah, of course they will," she agreed in a cheery, business-like voice. "It's just a temporary thing, my body is still feeling the effects of the zap too, it'll probably just wear off." She wasn't sure if it was him or herself that she was trying to convince, but bravado was better than collapsing in hysterics. She tried not to think too deeply about what the permanent loss of her eyesight would mean.

"Now," she continued with her false air of cheeriness, "point me in the right direction and we can get you to the medics." She turned her body so that she was supporting him on the uninjured side. "Can you walk or do you need me to carry you?" she asked snidely.

He chuckled lightly then groaned, grabbing his torn side. "Don't make me laugh Hellcat, I think I cracked some ribs," he complained.

"That'll teach you to take your eyes off a Demon with four arms," she said without sympathy.

They had just begun their slow, painful hobble back towards the parking area, when an enormous wave of elemental power crashed into them sending them both to their knees. A deafening roar, followed by a gale-like rushing of air signalled the end of the spell and the return of the Wraith to the Etherworld.

There was an excited hum as everyone gathered in the parking lot, mostly standing in small groups near the medical van. Gabi was sitting on the rear tailgate of one of the Clean-up vans while Melinda, a Healer Magus, applied a salve to the burns on her face and hands. She could hear Kyle a short distance away hissing as they patched him up. She could tell by the sharp intake of Harry's breath that whatever injury Kyle had sustained, it wasn't a pretty sight. Harry, even though a full human, was a seasoned vet at patching up Hunters after a fight. If Harry thought it was bad, then it was really unpleasant. It was a good thing that Kyle healed quickly; so quickly in fact, that it was a constant sore point between him and Gabi.

Melinda told her calmly that she had already patched up some cuts, scrapes and burns on Doug; nothing too serious, and the other two Hunters had come out unscathed. Kyle was by far the worst off, but with his speedy healing he'd be good as new in a few days. She didn't say anything about Gabi's blindness; it was hanging over all of them like an oppressive cloud. Some of the Clean-up crew had been sent off for coffee and food from a near-by gas station, and the rest were disposing of the Demon remains using the specialized equipment Byron and the Tech Geeks had developed for exactly these situations. She could hear Doug and the Magi discussing the assortment of Demons that had come through the veil. The Wraith was the hot topic of the night, and there was some heated debate as to what kind of Demon it was, and why it seemed so powerful.

"It must be some kind of mix between a Cheitan and a Shalbriri," one of the male Magi theorised.

"You could be right, Christian," a female voice answered. "The Cheitan is the traditional Wraith-type: born of smoke and air, but I've never heard of one with the power to cause an electric shock and blindness. The Shalbriri has the ability to cause blindness, but they are traditionally a solid-form Demon. This is something we've never encountered before. A combination of powers," she drifted off thoughtfully.

"The researchers are going to have their work cut out for them tomorrow, trying to make sense of this attack," came Christian's voice again.

"Nothing was normal about this attack," a different male voice chimed in. "We need to start liaising with other groups around the world to see if anyone else has experienced this kind of deviation from the norm."

"And what about the Birdman?" This was the female again." Do you think it was a Lanithro or an Arachula?"

This question sparked a whole new debate and Gabi grew bored of listening; she tuned them out and cast about for something else to grab her attention. The tailgate sank down as someone joined her; Doug, she recognised by scent.

"Coffee?" he asked. She held out her bandaged hand wordlessly. A polystyrene cup was pressed into it. She brought it to her nose and breathed in the warm steam appreciatively. It wouldn't be the best coffee in the world, but at that moment in time it would taste fantastic. She wrapped her other hand around it and took a tentative sip.

"I hear the Birdman took a few chunks out of you," she teased him.

He ignored her attempt at deflection: "I've spoken to Byron and Athena," he said carefully, referring to a young Magus that Gabi didn't particularly like.

"And what did the great and powerful Magus Liaison have to say about my predicament?" she asked savagely.

41

The last person she wanted informed of her weakness was Athena.

Doug sighed as though he'd known his statement would raise Gabi's hackles, but also knew he hadn't had a choice. They both knew the truth; Athena was one of the most powerful Magi in the City and even Gabi realised that if her blindness was magically induced, Athena would be the best person to try to reverse the damage. She just didn't like to think of owing Athena anything.

"She was very concerned about you; as we all are," he ploughed on. "Byron is, obviously, rather distressed as well. He wanted to come through and collect you immediately." He interrupted as she started to protest. "I told him you would be fine with us for now, and you would call him if you wanted him to collect you."

She could hear footsteps approaching them on her other side. Kyle. He silently sat down on her left side and put a comforting arm around her shoulders. Her tough ego self wanted to shake him off, but her practical inner self intervened and told her that she needed his solid familiarity to keep from going to pieces.

"Did they have any ideas on what to do for Gabi?" Kyle's carefully neutral voice asked.

"Their recommendation is that we wait at least twenty-four hours to see if the effects wear off on their own."

Gabi and Kyle both instantly started to protest.

"Yes," Doug cut them off loudly. "I know that sounds really harsh, but their reasoning is sound. Athena feels that if they interfere unnecessarily, they might do more harm than good. If the blindness doesn't wear off on its own, then the risks of intervening are worth it. Waiting twenty-four hours is not going to make the situation any worse, and all going well, Gabi may not have to let Athena into her mind and body to fix the problem," Doug quickly played his trump card.

Gabi knew she had been painted into a corner. She capitulated with a low growl and resorted to finishing her coffee without another word.

"OK then, we'll do it that way," agreed Kyle on her behalf. "I'll get her home. Can you arrange for someone to collect her car and drop it at the house?"

Doug agreed and after reminding Gabi to call Byron he strode off, probably to chase everyone home. It had been a long night, and dawn wasn't far off, they needed to be clear of the place before the first workers arrived in the area to start their shifts.

"Your place or mine, babe?" Kyle teased her.

"Mine," she said tiredly. "What time is it? I must get back to feed Razor and Slinky."

"It's just gone four am." Kyle answered.

Well that explained the chill in the air she thought, then another more panicked thought rippled through her. "Oh, shit!"

"What?" Kyle asked, instantly alarmed.

"I didn't leave any extra food out for Razor before I went out. He's gonna have wrecked the place!"

# CHAPTER 4

Kyle was still chortling at Gabi's concern when they rounded the bend in the road and turned up her long paved driveway. At least he'd got to drive his own van this time.

"It's not that funny Wolf," Gabi groused. "The last time I left him this long with no food he destroyed my sofa *and* my bed. The sofa I can live without, but my bed is sacred! I had to wait three weeks for a replacement last time."

She was ranting now, and Kyle felt a ripple of relief that she was acting more herself. Earlier when she hadn't shaken him off for hugging her, he'd felt a strong sense of disquiet; it was completely out of character for her to show that she needed anything from anyone, especially emotional support. It'd exposed the depth of her distress.

She'd called Byron on the way home and had, very convincingly, reassured him that she was fine, not concerned and didn't need babying. She'd sounded believable enough to keep him from driving straight to the house to check on her, but Kyle knew the older man would be there before lunch.

"Well you only have yourself to blame," Kyle said sanctimoniously, purposefully trying to rile her up. "Firstly, you have a cat the size of a mountain lion, with an appetite like a hyena's and the patience of a stampeding bull, and secondly you forget to feed it before going out on an assignment." He knew he was looking for trouble, but it seemed worth the pain if it kept her out of the funk she'd been in earlier. He was wrong. The backhander from her hit him full force on the shoulder. She'd carefully avoided his injuries, but it hurt like a bitch anyway.

"Geesh Hellcat. Take it out on the injured man, why don't you?" he retorted indignantly, flexing his numb shoulder.

"If you don't want trouble, don't look for it," she countered.

Kyle stopped the van in front of her little house. Well, it was more of a bungalow, but a smart, stylish bungalow. Not that he could see much of it in the pre-dawn gloom, but he knew the place almost as well as he knew his own. It was set against a backdrop of huge oak trees and the large garden had a wild, yet somehow structured look to it, as though mother nature had had a day with an A-type personality. Ordered unruliness was how Kyle would describe it, a bit like Gabi he realised. She loved the overgrown flower beds, an odd assortment of herbs dotted in amongst the flowers, the uncut lawn sprouted wild flowers haphazardly and the little pond that sported so many water lilies that the goldfish could hardly breathe. Now he wondered, in a quiet corner of his mind, if she'd ever see it again. No, he pushed the thought away; they would sort this problem out. He knew that the SMV had some of the best Magi brains in the country at their disposal, as well as the best researchers money could

45

buy.  If it didn't come right on its own, someone would figure out what to do.

"Well, at least I won't be able to see the devastation," Gabi muttered darkly, opening the van door and sliding out.  Kyle loped quickly to her side as she fumbled to close the door.

"One guide dog at your service," he said officiously, putting his arm under her hand.

"Does that mean I can change your nickname to Mutt instead of Wolf?" she asked snidely, but took his proffered arm and allowed him to lead her up the steps and into her sanctuary.

"As long as you don't expect me to eat kibble," he countered.  "Or sit up and beg," he added quickly, before she got any ideas.

As they walked in the door they were instantly set on by a ball of fur the size of a retriever.  The hugely overgrown cat—thought to be some kind of Maine Coon mix but Kyle privately thought it was probably mixed with Bengal tiger—ran straight up to Gabi and launched itself directly into her chest, complaining furiously in cat language all the while.  She managed to catch the furry monster in both arms, having expected the assault, and began apologizing sincerely for leaving him with no food, and for getting home so late.  She buried her face in his three inch long ginger and brown coat.  Kyle knew she was also reassuring the stripy furball mentally, as the cat immediately curled into her arms like a baby and began purring outrageously.  It was only Gabi's supernatural strength that allowed her to carry the cat unassisted, normal humans would have struggled to hold the enormous animal, he weighed over forty pounds.  Kyle put his hands gently against Gabi's back, ignoring the baleful glare he got from Razor, and steered her towards the kitchen.  She allowed him to do this without comment.

He turned on the lights, though Gabi couldn't see them and he didn't need them in the dim light of dawn, it was more force of habit and maybe a form of comfort. He seated her and the furball on one of barstools on the far side of the kitchen counter and went around into the kitchen to turn on the coffee maker. Her housekeeper, Rose, had left it ready to go for Gabi when she got up in the morning.

Rose was grandmother to several Shape-shifters and several more non-Shape-shifters; the ability had skipped two generations, but had kicked back in with the youngest generation. She was well aware of the strange and dangerous things that lurked in the shadows of our world. She knew what Gabi did, though she wasn't actively involved with the SMV. Several years ago Rose had been sent by Byron to help Gabi around the house for a few weeks when Gabi had been severely injured in a fight with three Vampires. The weeks had passed and Rose had just continued working for Gabi; now years down the line, the two had developed a close bond and Rose had become like a second mother to Gabi. It was Rose's touch that ensured there was food in the fridge, coffee in the cupboard and the house was always clean and tidy. Gabi would not have won any awards for domesticity; it was definitely not her forte.

Rose deserved Sainthood, Kyle decided as he surveyed the scene in the open-plan lounge, from the safety of the kitchen. Razor had indeed decided to make his displeasure known, and the sofa was another write-off, as was one of the wingback chairs. It looked as though a pack of rabid dogs had attacked the place. Fabric and stuffing lay over every square inch of the carpet, lamps had been knocked on the floor, side tables overturned and ornaments lay scattered and broken on the stone hearth of the fireplace. He shook his head and glared at the unashamed culprit

"If it were up to me you wouldn't get fed for a month, you bad tempered monster," he grumbled at the impudent cat. He was tempted to wave an accusing finger at the animal, but decided he liked having all his fingers intact. He knew Razor was as fast as he was enormous; if he decided to swat you for being irritating he could give you lacerations that required stitches, if he bit you he could probably take your hand off. He was named Razor for good reason; Kyle had the personal experience to back that up.

Gabi sighed. "How bad is it this time?" she asked resignedly.

"Let's just say I'd better feed him before I tell you about it. I wouldn't want him starting on me."

"Raz, you're a bad boy!" Gabi admonished without any real rancour. That cat could get away with murder when Gabi was around.

Kyle hoped Rose would give him a dressing down of momentous proportions later. Rose was the only other person Razor had more than bare tolerance for. Though she lectured him, chased him outside when the sun was shining and wouldn't tolerate him destroying things like Gabi did, the cat seemed to actually like her. The same could not be said for Kyle, who Razor delighted in harassing at every opportunity. Maybe it was the age-old Cat versus Dog, or in this case wolf, thing. It was for Gabi's sake not Razor's that Kyle opened a cupboard and took out two tins of the most expensive cat food on the market, opened them and emptied both into a large ceramic bowl on the kitchen counter. Razor gave Gabi one last, big kitty smooch across her face, making her wince from the sting in the burn on her cheek, and walked languidly over to devour the food, pointedly ignoring Kyle.

Gabi reached out patting at the counter until her fingers found the sweet bowl. She delved into the bowl pulling out a toffee, unwrapping it and shoving it in her mouth, then she began to unstrap the multitude of sheaths and holsters from her body and lay the weapons in a heap on the counter.

The smell of fresh percolated coffee began to permeate the kitchen and Kyle opened another cupboard to pull out two large mugs with pictures of kittens and puppies on them. No wonder she didn't invite other people over, Kyle thought slyly, if some of their SMV or her work colleagues saw these, her tough girl reputation would be in ruins. He poured coffee into both, added milk and sugar to one and pushed it over to Gabi, directing the fingers of her unburned hand to it. She gratefully breathed in the warm aromatic steam and quickly finished her sweet to take the first sip.

"Hey," he called cheerfully as another furry body galloped into the kitchen, "here comes Stinky, oops, I mean, Slinky!" he pretended to correct himself.

He took a large slurp of his own coffee and bent down to pick up the ferret that had scampered in, blinking and half asleep, to see what the commotion was. At least the bandit-faced, little animal seemed to like him.

Gabi had rescued the orphaned ferret from some illegal animal traders a couple of years ago. She'd brought him home with the intention of getting him healthy and finding him a suitable new home, but obscurely enough Razor seemed to quite like the other animal and had even deigned to keep the little mite warm during the cold winter months that followed his arrival, so Slinky had become a permanent member of the household. Slinky grew up with no real idea that he was a ferret, and, as Razor was his only animal companion, Slinky acted more like a cat than anything else. He did still have a distinct ferret odour to him though; hence Kyle's continued mispronunciation of his name.

"Come here baby,' Gabi crooned to the wriggling animal, "don't let Kyle be rude to you. He's just a Mutt in any case, and have you ever smelled a wet dog?" she continued conspiratorially, trying to keep a wicked little grin off her face and failing.

"Hurmph," Kyle snorted, letting Slinky climb onto the kitchen counter and scamper over to Gabi. "Just remember who's making your coffee at the moment. If you're rude I'll take it away," he threatened.

"Ok, Ok, anything but the coffee." She scooped Slinky up and let him nuzzle her cheek and ear, then he climbed onto her shoulder and, weaving around her neck and under her hair like a live fur stole, the ferret settled down in his favourite spot.

"The painkillers are in the cupboard above the oven," she told Kyle. "Take what you want and give me a double dose; I'm getting a headache of gargantuan proportions."

Gabi was, as a rule, resistant to the effects of most drugs, including painkillers, so her cupboard contained some really strong medications. Through their SMV medical contacts they could get hold of most medicines, even the prescription only ones. Kyle took down a bottle of morphine based tablets and shook out a dose for her, then took out some milder painkillers for himself. He healed far quicker than she did, and he wasn't resistant to painkillers, so those would be good enough to dull the pain in his side and thigh while he healed. He handed her the tablets and a glass of water, took his own tablets and then went off to inspect the rest of the little house for Razor damage.

"Well, there is one piece of good news this morning," he told her as he returned from his once-over of the house. "The destruction was limited to the lounge this time. The bedrooms are still intact."

"Oh, thank all the gods of ancient Rome," Gabi proclaimed with feeling. "I feel like I could sleep for a week."

"I've got sad news for you if you think Byron's going to stay away past ten o'clock," he reminded her.

She groaned at the thought.

"Do you know where the rubbish bags are?" he asked her. "I can start clearing up the lounge while you go and shower." He wasn't relishing the thought of bending to pick up couch shrapnel but Gabi wasn't going to be able to do it.

"Don't be absurd," she grumbled at him. "You're hurt and just as tired as me. Rose will be here in a few hours, it'll give her something to grouse at Raz about for the next few weeks. You hit the shower first, I'm sure the spare bedroom is ready for you, and you know where the towels are. I'm going to soak in the tub once you're done."

"OK," he capitulated, trying to keep the relief from his voice. A shower and bed was exactly what he had in mind right now. He would normally drive back to his pad now, it was only ten minutes away, but he didn't want to leave Gabi alone, even though she was trying to pretend not to feel the same way. Usually it took them both a couple of hours to wind down after a good fight, but the unexpected consequences of this one seemed to have drained the adrenaline straight out of them. They were both exhausted and missing the usual post-battle high.

"Do you want me to take you to your room?" he asked, trying for a casual tone.

"I do know the way around my own house," she said reprovingly. "I'll find my own way once I'm finished my coffee. Now, scat before I send you home, Mutt."

"Woof, woof," Kyle responded obligingly, and, grabbing his coffee, headed for the shower.

A few minutes later she popped her head into the bathroom. He was already standing under the flow of hot, soothing water, trying not to wince as the water washed over his lacerations. Nudity didn't bother either of them and they had long since stopped worrying about the societal norms for opposite-sex best friends. Slinky was still wrapped around her neck and Razor was winding himself between her legs.

"Do you need new dressings?" she raised her voice to be heard over the noise of the shower.

He looked down at the wounds to see how far the healing had come.

"Hmm," his voice floated back. "Yeah, probably a good idea if you don't want blood on the sheets."

"I don't think Rose needs that much extra work; come to my room when you're done, and I'll help," she called retreating from the bathroom. "The emergency kit is in the hall closet, bring it with you," she yelled over her shoulder as she headed down the corridor to her bedroom.

A while later they clumsily redressed Kyle's wounds. He grimaced seeing the nasty slashes down his side, eternally grateful for the werewolf blood that would heal him in a matter of days. If he'd been full human he would've been out of action for weeks, if not months.

Twenty minutes later Gabi sank into stingingly hot bath water in her large en-suite bathroom, wincing as she submerged her burned fingers, and then sighing as the heat began seeping into her stiff muscles, easing the tension in her neck and shoulders. She wondered how bad Kyle's injuries looked. By the size of the dressing pads he'd given her to hold in place they were not little scratches. He would be appreciating his Werewolf blood right about now. Before leaving her to her bath she heard him draw her bedroom curtains closed, and wondered if it would make any difference to her when the sun rose in a few hours. She doubted she was going to get any sleep; although utterly exhausted, her mind was whirling, tormenting her with thoughts of being permanently blind. She tried using the meditation techniques her various martial arts instructors had tried to drum into her, but she'd never been particularly good at them, even in the best of circumstances. Eventually the water cooled and she reluctantly got out, towelled off and crawled into her huge comfortable bed, snuggling up with Razor sprawled out on one side of her and Slinky on the other. Somehow the exhaustion won, and she slept.

She slowly became aware of voices somewhere in the house, trying to stay hushed, but clear to her hearing anyway. She didn't even bother opening her eyes; she hadn't had nearly enough sleep yet, so she resorted to burying her head under a pillow. As the pillow came in contact with her cheek the burn mark stung, and memories of the previous night flowed back like a tidal wave. Now, having not opened her eyes on waking, she was extremely reluctant to do so and discover whether dark fog still blanketed her sight. In fact her stomach began churning anxiously at the thought. Like a little girl hiding under the bedcovers because she thinks there's a monster in the room, she berated herself. She hadn't been scared like this since she saw Byron's face when he came to the house to tell them of her father's death. She knew she'd have to do it eventually, she wasn't going to be left alone for much longer. Still procrastinating, she began picking out the individual voices, so that she knew what she was up against when she did venture out.

Kyle's voice was clear but muted; Rose answered him now, in very quiet, worried tones. Then Byron, of course, she knew better than to think he wouldn't be here already. She idly wondered what time it was. So, it was the usual suspects out in the kitchen discussing her. Then another female voice spoke up, not attempting to keep to her tone low and hushed like the others. Gabi's emotions flashed from fear and worry to rage in an instant. What was Athena doing in her house? She thought furiously, her eyes snapping open instinctively as she sat up, tipping a disgruntled Razor onto the floor and rolling Slinky half way across the bed. She had the covers off and was almost standing before she realised she could see.

She sat back down with a thump, for once ignoring Razor's annoyed grumbling, her hands tentatively going to her eyes. Well, "see" was probably a strong word for it. Her vision was still far from perfect, it had gone from a pitch black fog to a light grey fog, but she could make out shapes and see the sunlight streaming in through cracks in the curtains. She was still blinking and doing ridiculous eye contortions, trying to clear her vision when the door opened a crack and Kyle peeked in. Razor stopped languidly scent marking her legs and deliberately moved to place himself between Gabi and Kyle, facing Kyle with what Gabi knew would be a 'give me an excuse' expression on his face.

"Uh, hi," he greeted. "I thought I heard movement in here. Can I come in?"

"As long as you don't bring the witch in with you," she said in a steely tone, almost hoping Athena would hear her.

"So you heard her, did you?" he asked, coming in and closing the door.

"I could be rude and say I smelt her, or heard her broomstick touch down," she said archly.

Kyle tried to stifle a chuckle. "Now, now," he reproved, "put the claws away and play nice! She's here to help."

"So she says," Gabi countered, "she's probably just here to gloat."

Kyle ignored that. He made to start moving across to the bed but Razor took an even more aggressive stance and hissed menacingly at him.

"Call your damn guard cat off, he won't let me near you."

She smirked condescendingly. "Raz, come here you big, bad boy, and stop scaring Mutt." As she bent to pick him up, Kyle started across the room and must have noticed her tracking his progress.

"Gabs, can you see me?" he asked in barely leashed excitement. He rushed the last few steps, crouching down in front of her and peering into her eyes, ignoring Razor's attempt to slash him. She promptly planted a foot in the middle of his chest shoving him backwards to land on his butt in the middle of the thick carpet, chuckling at his pained expression.

"Not my fault you're getting slow in your old age," she said, still grinning wickedly.

Kyle put on his long-suffering face. "Now that you've had your laugh for the morning, can you answer the damn question?" He didn't bother getting up off the floor.

Sighing she sobered her attitude. "Yes, I can more or less see you," she said, squinting slightly as she peered at him. "Well, I can see a big, blurry blob that I imagine must be you. So at least it's an improvement."

Kyle heaved a sigh; she imagined it was a sigh of relief that he wouldn't have to play guide dog forever.

"That is really good to hear, I guess it'll come right on its own then. No Magus interference required."

"Yes, and you can go back to being Wolf, instead of Mutt," she teased, stroking Razor absent-mindedly.

"Aaaawww," he drawled in mock disappointment, "just when I thought that the new nickname would bring the ladies running. All chicks love a cute puppy." He was probably making cute puppy faces too. "But, more to the current point, you do realise you can't hide in here all day. You're going to have to come out and face everybody at some stage." He hauled himself up off the floor, wincing slightly. "So stop delaying and get dressed. I'm running out of scintillating conversation out there."

She pulled a face at him. "I don't see how that's my problem."

"I'll pour you some coffee, get dressed," he reiterated, walking out and closing the door behind him.

Gabi made herself presentable and reluctantly prepared to face Byron, Rose and Athena. Walking down the corridor to the kitchen, using her fingertips on the wall to guide her, she steeled herself for a conversation with Athena. It was not going to go well. She was tired and grumpy, and she didn't appreciate Byron bringing the witch into her home. No one came in here without her express invitation, that's just how it was. Only a select few were welcome in her private little refuge, and the damn witch was definitely not one of them. And on top of that she hadn't even had her first cup of coffee yet. She was sorely tempted to encourage Razor to take a piece out of the witch, but that would just be plain childish.

She rounded the corner into the kitchen and was instantly set upon by Rose, fluttering worriedly, patting Gabi's sore face, smoothing her hair and touching her all over as though to reassure herself that Gabi was indeed in one piece. She prattled away at break-neck speed, admonishing Gabi for frightening the life out of her, and vowing to not let her out Hunting again.

Gabi smiled wryly, accepting all the fuss, and reassuring Rose whenever she could get a word in. Then Razor announced his presence, jumping on the kitchen counter and loudly demanding breakfast, so Rose had a new target for her attentions. She instantly switched to berating him for his appalling behaviour; but at the same time reaching for two tins of food, and emptying them out for him as he favoured her with a huge kitty smooch to the face, almost knocking her over.

Kyle rolled his eyes. "I say again, that monster gets away with murder," he declared, holding a steaming cup of coffee out to Gabi. "Byron and Athena are waiting for us in the dining room, I figured you could use a shot of caffeine before seeing them."

Kyle knew her too well, she thought, reaching carefully for the coffee mug, which she could smell better than she could see. She took a long sip and then mentally braced herself.

"Alright," she said, feeling like she was being led out to the gallows. "Let's go."

As they entered the dining room Byron immediately stood up and gathered her into a strong fatherly hug. Although Gabi couldn't see him clearly at that moment, she knew what others would see when they looked at Byron; a distinguished looking man in his mid to late forties, a few inches taller than Gabi, with the lean, toned look that suggested a man who looked after himself. Very few people would have guessed that he was already in his sixties; only the slight greyness visible in amongst the dark brown hair above his ears gave away any sign of his true age. The grace of his aging was due directly to his Magi parentage. Byron had chosen not to take up his Magus heritage, an option for any Magus-born child, and so had no special powers or supernatural talent, but the Magi blood still worked its own brand of magic on him. If full blood humans ever found out about what Magus blood did for the signs of ageing, well, that didn't really bear thinking about. Byron's face, now marred by a worried frown, still hinted heavily at the strikingly good-looking man he'd been in his youth.

Everyone at the SMV knew that he could have his pick of eligible, and some not so eligible, women anytime he chose, but he hadn't shown any inclination to take another partner after his wife died in a freak car accident some five years ago. If he felt he needed a female partner along with him at a social function he often took his daughter, Lara, or Gabi, but otherwise he attended alone. He was immensely proud of both his children, who had each become involved in their own way within the SMV, even though neither of them had any supernatural talent. Lara was a well known attorney in the city, having made a name for herself in the male-dominated world as both hard-nosed and compassionate, and she often took cases for Werewolves and Shapeshifters. His son, Ian, was a doctor at one of the largest hospitals in the city, his work was absolutely vital to the SMV as he could spot a Were or Shifter, and have them patched up and discharged before any of the other staff became suspicious or got to draw blood for testing.

Byron was officially retired from his job as a city councillor, but he still did consulting work for them, and still regularly attended government meetings and assisted on various committees. His involvement with government and local councils had been invaluable to the SMV over the years, and he was still able to get the inside track on many issues which affected the supernatural community. He exuded calm self-assurance which inspired trust and respect from others. No one in the human world would ever have suspected his thorough involvement in the supernatural world.

His parents; both alive and well in their nineties, as was common for Magi, and living out their retirement in a small seaside village, respected his need for secrecy and never let slip about their own extraordinary talents to the general public.

"Gabrielle, honey," he said in his warm, comforting voice. "How are you holding up?" He moved back slightly to hold her at arm's length and have a good look at her.

They usually kept a careful façade of polite friendship when in the company of others, besides Kyle and Rose. There was politics involved even in a group like the SMV, and Byron and Gabi didn't like to advertise their personal relationship to everyone. The longer-standing members knew, of course, that Gabi was like a second daughter to Byron, but they rarely saw it demonstrated outwardly.

"I'm fine, Daddy Fuss Pants," she teased him. "My vision has cleared a lot since I went to sleep, I'm sure it will be back to normal in a few more hours. So you were right to wait and see what happened." She heard her own voice change suddenly from teasing reassurance to cold annoyance. "Athena really didn't have to drive all the way out here before I even woke up."

The implication was clear; Athena wasn't welcome in her house, and anyone who had invited her in was in trouble. The Magus in question was sitting at the dining room table with a steaming cup of tea in front of her; trust her to be different, Gabi thought sourly. She was looking steadily at Gabi and Byron, a deadpan expression on her face; if she was surprised by Byron's actions away from the normal SMV environment, or by Gabi's obviously displeasure, her face didn't show it.

"Er," Byron seemed to know he was in trouble, but ploughed on, trying to ease the tension in the room.

"Athena was very worried about you," he explained, ignoring the sarcastic quirk to Gabi's eyebrow. "She thought you may feel like we weren't taking your condition seriously enough, after our advice last night. We both know it must be a horrible feeling thinking that your eyesight may be permanently affected. So Athena suggested we be here when you wake in case there hadn't been an improvement."

Gabi knew anything she said now would just sound ungrateful and childish, so she bit her tongue and kept quiet.

"Come and sit," Byron pulled her gently towards a chair at the table. Kyle was already lounging in one of the chairs on Gabi's left, Athena the only one on the far side of the large rectangular table. "Kyle says your vision is still quite fuzzy, tell us exactly how much you can see. Are you in any pain or discomfort? I spoke to Ian earlier, and he insisted that you stop in at the hospital and let him check you over too."

"We're also keen to hear your impressions of the Wraith and its unusual abilities," Athena spoke up for the first time. Her voice was calm and businesslike. If she was really concerned for Gabi's well being, she wasn't letting it show in her voice.

Well, at least she wasn't acting the distraught best friend, Gabi thought as she looked over at the fuzzy, cream coloured shape that was Athena. She didn't need to see the slim, fair-haired woman to picture her clearly. Athena was close to Gabi in both true age and apparent age; they both were heading towards thirty, but appeared closer to twenty. That was where the similarities ended; in both looks and attitude they were polar opposites. Athena was the liaison between the Magi council and the SMV council, facilitating the flow of information and supervising the use of Magi within the SMV organisation.

She was one of the Head Councillors of the Magi High Council, and was, by far, the youngest person to ever hold one of the coveted positions. Only those who had passed the top level of proficiency in Magi training could put themselves forward for one of the five positions, and then they still needed to be voted in by the majority of the Secondary Council. Athena was more than proficient in many aspects of Magic, but she was exceptional at counter-magic; the talent that allowed a Magi to counteract the effects of another's spell or power. It was a rare and valuable gift, and the reason that she'd been consulted about Gabi's loss of eyesight. It was a pity she seemed to have such an intense dislike of anyone not Magus-born.

Gabi hadn't managed to get Athena to squirm even once during the long seconds of staring at her, so she turned to Byron to give him an account of the previous night. With Kyle's occasional input she clarified the events up to, and including, the shocking encounter with the Wraith, and ended by explaining how her vision was still clouded, but apparently improving, she didn't think she would need to bother Ian. Athena asked a few polite but probing questions about the Wraith and the effects of its power on Gabi, and Gabi answered equally politely, getting to the bottom of the Wraith's power was more important than her dislike of Athena.

Sometime during the discussion Razor had wandered in, Gabi had automatically pushed away from the table to allow him to climb on her lap, though he was far too big to sit there comfortably. He was just trying to get comfortable when he noticed Athena across the table. He went dead still for a quarter of a second, and then lunged onto the table directly towards Athena. Gabi made a wild grab for him, missing completely, and Kyle's face took on a horrified expression. But Razor stopped dead a few millimetres from Athena's shocked face, sat down and stared into her eyes with baleful malevolence.

Athena sat back very cautiously, as though confronted by a wild tiger, and asked out the corner of her mouth, "What. Is. That? And is it going to eat me?"

It was the first time any of them had ever heard Athena sound anything except controlled and businesslike. She actually sounded terrified.

"Razor!" Gabi called sharply, "Don't torment strangers, its not polite." She was careful not to use the word guest, as that would exclude Razor from tormenting Kyle.

"Meet Gabi's cat, Razor," Kyle said sardonically. "Though we use the term 'cat' loosely around here. He may take a chunk out of you, but I don't think he'd actually eat you."

"I doubt he would enjoy the taste of witch anyway," Gabi muttered under her breath.

"In that case, I don't think he likes me very much," Athena said stiffly; ignoring her comment, and drawing in a deep, steadying breath as Razor disdainfully made his way back across the table to Gabi. He gave her a loving head butt, before hopping to the floor with a grace that belied his incredible size, and exiting the room with an arrogant swish of his tail.

"Don't worry about it," Kyle commented mildly, breaking the tension. "He doesn't like anybody, except Gabi, and maybe Rose. He takes a piece out of me any chance he gets."

Gabi was hard pressed to keep the smug, satisfied expression off her face. She wondered to herself if she had sub-consciously transmitted her feelings to Razor, or if the cat had taken an instant dislike to the witch on his own. She decided it was time to get her house back to herself so she could give him an outrageous reward. She stood up, yawning.

"Well, I think I could do with a few more hours sleep. I completed last night's assignment, so I can join Patrol tonight, unless there's another assignment for me. Kyle, are you up for tonight, or do you want me to pair with someone else?"

"Gabi," Byron said sternly, also standing up. "You are NOT going on patrol tonight. In fact I've called off all patrols tonight, everyone could do with a night off to recharge. Matt and Lance are on stand-by if the Magi sense any signs of trouble. You must go and see Ian; you're not going back on duty until he clears you. Kyle will be keeping an eye on you for me, and he can drive you in when you're ready." He ignored her outraged expression and pulled her into another big hug. "Honey, I'm glad you're alright, and I want you to rest and recover. You too Kyle," he said looking over at the younger man.

"We'd better get back to work," he said extending his arm to Athena, who was still looking a little shaken. "We have loads of research to do on these new Demon powers and their unity. Gabi, Athena brought your car back this morning, we've left the keys in their usual spot." With that he guided Athena out of the room and left Kyle to deal with the fallout.

# CHAPTER 5

Kyle sat calmly through her ranting and raving about the witch being not only allowed in her house, but also allowed behind the wheel of her car. Then, adding insult to injury, she was banned from going out on patrol tonight. His vague amusement only served to annoy her further. Even Rose bringing her a second cup of coffee wasn't doing much to improve her mood. Kyle tried another angle, trying to mollify her.

"You've been moaning for weeks that all you ever do is work and Hunt, that you've forgotten what a normal person does at night. Why don't we make the most of an official day and night off and do something normal?"

She scowled at him, the idea actually held some appeal but she wasn't going to accept defeat gracefully.

"Come on," he cajoled. "We'll do something we haven't done for ages. Maybe go to a movie or a show, and then hit the city for dinner and drinks. It'll be fun; we haven't done anything like that for months."

"Fun, huh?" she sounded doubtful. "I've probably got work to do anyway." she said thinking about the fact that she didn't know what animal work she had booked for today.

"No you haven't," he announced. "I checked your diary and your e-mail already. You have nothing urgent on, just a whole day and night of R and R."

"Fine, Smartarse," she finally capitulated, "if it'll stop you badgering me. We'll do a 3D movie or something equally mindless and then we can go out drinking and looking for trouble. Tomorrow morning we're going to see Ian first thing and we'll be back on patrol tomorrow night."

Suddenly the gentle sizzle and delicious smell of frying bacon wafted in from the kitchen and Gabi saw Kyle react as instantly as her. They both perked up and headed for the kitchen as if tugged by their noses.

"Oh, Rose, you know how to make a person feel better in the morning," Gabi sighed, taking a stool at the counter and pulling another one out beside her.

Kyle pulled the next one out, knowing that the one next to her was reserved for Slinky or Razor, whichever one got there first.

Rose chuckled cheerfully. "I've spent many years feeding Shifters, I know how to fill bottomless pits." Then she sighed, "if only I had the same metabolism as all of you, then I wouldn't have to avoid all my favourite desserts and sweets." She patted her ample hips before whisking up some eggs in a glass bowl.

Gabi smiled and shook her head. Rose was always going on about her weight, and trying every new exercise machine that came on the market, but she somehow always seemed to stay the same build. Not that she was excessively overweight, just on the voluptuous side, with an ample bosom and curvaceous hips.

"Rose, you know real men like a bit of 'junk in the trunk' and cleavage big enough to hold a beer can. That man of yours is as happy as a drunkard locked in a brewery; he'd go off you if you ever got as skinny as me," Gabi reassured the older woman.

Rose giggled girlishly at the mention of her husband's preference for meat on a woman; although married for over thirty years Gabi knew they still thoroughly enjoyed each other's company, and 'other' things. Rose covered her blushing cheeks by turning away to pour the egg mixture in a pan. She bustled happily around the kitchen, enjoying having the two younger people to cater for. She put the mounds of food on the counter and plates in front of each of them, adding a smaller plate next to Gabi for Slinky, who'd arrived for breakfast too. Kyle scooped some scrambled eggs onto the smaller plate, and added a few pieces of lean bacon, the Ferret's favourite, placing it close to Slinky's whiskery face. He then snagged Gabi's plate, piled on food and handed it over to her before doing the same for himself, smilingly appreciatively at Rose as she brought yet more coffee.

"Thanks Rose, you're an absolute gem!" he enthused. "Anytime Gabs mistreats you or you get tired of cleaning up after Razor, you know you're always welcome in my house," he teased.

Gabi smacked him on the shoulder with the back of her hand over Slinky's head.

"Watch yourself, Mutt," she warned with a mock growl around a mouthful of hot sausage. "I'll revoke your breakfast privileges and set Raz on you."

"Hey," he protested, "I just fed Stinky for you. I'm earning my keep," he said nodding towards Slinky who was happy scoffing his morning treat.

They bantered until the piles of food were all but gone and their appetites sated, then Kyle got up to help Rose clear away the dishes and pack the dishwasher. They both steered Gabi away when she attempted to help, joking that she was bad enough when she could see clearly, Rose didn't need any broken crockery to clear up.

"Fine," she pretended to fume. "I know when I'm not wanted. I'm going back to bed." She hefted Razor off the floor as he came wandering in and stalked off down the corridor to catch up on sleep.

Rose woke her mid afternoon, to say she was on her way home. She had left lunch for Gabi in the fridge, and Kyle had gone home to change and would be back soon. Gabi thanked her sleepily and considered going back to sleep until Kyle got back. Her anxiety about her eyesight overrode the need for more sleep, and she forced her eyes open to assess their current condition. She was pleasantly surprised to find the grey fog almost gone; though things were still a little out of focus, almost like she was wearing a pair of someone else's prescription glasses. When she got up and went to the bathroom to look at herself in the mirror, she was met with a somewhat blurry, but unclouded view of herself. It wasn't a pretty sight. Her hair was a jumbled mess of knotted curls and the burn mark on her cheek was an angry red blister with slight puckering around the edges. She grimaced. Shower first, burn cream second, lunch third she decided.

By the time Kyle got back she was dressed and eating sandwiches at her computer, squinting hugely to try and make out the printing on the screen.

"The vision that much better?" he asked surprised, plonking down into the spare office chair and kicking his feet up onto her large mahogany desk.

"Good enough to take you on at some pool after the movie," she challenged.

"You're on, Babe," he declared, "but don't cry foul when I whip your ass."

"In your dreams, Wolfboy!" she taunted.

She gave up trying to read the print on the screen, it was giving her a headache. Kyle followed her out of the office and lounged in one of the undamaged armchairs in the now sparsely furnished, but tidy sitting room, while she filled up Razor's food bowl to over-flowing and slapped some cover-up over the angry red mark on her face. The blisters on her fingers weren't as serious; they were almost healed but still tender. Then she slid Nex into her sheath down the back of her shirt, rearranging her hair and collar to cover the top of the hilt. Lastly she tucked two butterfly swords into a sheath hidden by her black, leather boots; a discreet slit in the jeans gave her easy access to them in a pinch.

Kyle shook his head sadly.

She quirked an eyebrow at him.

"What?" she demanded. "Can't a girl go out prepared? You know I feel naked without some protection."

He rolled his eyes, but held his tongue. She knew he would have at least three weapons hidden in various places on his body as well. No Hunter ever went out unarmed. They all still cursed the law banning handguns in the city; it was far easier taking out a Rogue from a distance, than hand-to-hand, but they knew the penalties for using a firearm. The alarms raised by someone reporting gunshots resulted in far too much interest from the police. Then she remembered that guns did little to stop Demons and Ghouls, and to a lesser extent, Vampires, and was grateful for her swords and daggers.

"Let's go, Warfare Barbie," he teased her, laughing wickedly, then ducking as she hurled her cars keys at his head with deadly accuracy.

She threw a black, knitted wrap over one arm and stalked haughtily out to the car. Her car was a Ford

Mustang Shelby GT500, the new model, red, of course, with black Le Mans racing stripes. Gabi pretended to have no real interest in cars and machines, not deigning to enter discussions about things like torque and horsepower, but she loved the power and handling of this supercharged muscle car, and she had a friend who was a pro-racing driver who'd made sure she knew how to handle the wild beast. She rarely let anyone else touch it, let alone drive it, which was why she'd been so pissed off at the thought of Athena getting her paws on it. Kyle couldn't contain his grin at the prospect of getting to drive it.

It was during their third game of pool that Gabi spotted him the first time. She'd felt the tingling presence of a Vampire when she automatically cast out her supernatural sense as they entered the bar. It was one her of special talents, this ability to feel the presence of other non-humans. But with so many people moving around in such a relatively small area it was difficult to pick out the Vamp from the humans, so she couldn't pinpoint him right in the beginning. She decided to adopt a wait and see approach, not all Vampires were up to no good.

She sent Kyle to the bar for drinks while she racked up the balls on a pool table. Both of them played atrocious pool; between her sore fingers and poor vision, and his not-quite healed injuries they were both at a disadvantage, but as they were fairly evenly matched they continued to play, ragging each other as they progressively played worse and worse.

Suddenly Gabi glanced up, instantly on the alert, she'd felt the power of a Vampire brush the edge of her senses. That was strange; Vamps normally did their utmost to blend in, rarely using their power so blatantly in a crowded place, in case another supernatural was present. Gabi noticed Kyle had gone on the alert as well. The ability to sense the use of supernatural power wasn't just a talent of Gabi's, most other supernaturals could feel when that kind of power was being used, though Gabi seemed to get a better sense of it than most. She followed the tendril of power back to its owner and found him watching her from near the bar.

He was tall and blonde, appearing to be in his mid twenties, his features a little too boyish to be considered handsome. By the brush of his power as he tried to mind roll her, he was a relatively young Vamp, still a little clumsy in his attempts at rolling humans. He was probably wondering why the hell she wasn't already making her way over to him, begging for his attention. She hadn't met a Vampire yet who could mind roll her; it seemed to be another of her talents. She figured that one day she would meet her match, but this Vampire definitely wasn't it.

Vamps used the mind control to call humans to them, using a kind of hypnosis to convince their target of their trustworthiness, sexual appeal or harmlessness. This allowed them to feed regularly, while maintaining their cloak of secrecy. Most Vamps took what they needed, and left the human with memories of an erotic encounter with a seductive stranger and an unusual lethargy the following day, but no other negative side-effects. Some Vamps however, were thrilled by the taking of blood involving fear and violence. The theory was that some liked the taste of blood saturated with adrenaline as it gave the Vampire a high of sorts. Once a Vamp decided this was their drug of choice, they would do anything to increase the high, often resorting to more and more brutal methods of creating fear in their victims. These were the Vamps that the SMV took out of circulation permanently.

She looked away from him, pretending indifference, but fastened her senses onto his 'scent', unobtrusively telling Kyle to keep an eye on him. During their next game of pool Kyle and Gabi noticed him heading out of the bar with a cute brunette stumbling along drunkenly beside him. He was met near the door by darker complexioned man, who looked the brunette up and down appraisingly before giving a curt nod to the blonde Vamp and grinning malevolently as they preceded him out through the doors.

"That second one was a Vamp too," Gabi told Kyle as they watched them leave. "I have a bad feeling about this. Two Vamps on one girl. That story just doesn't seem to have a happy ending for the girl."

"Let's go," Kyle agreed, figuring that they could at least scare the Vamps off, if necessary. The Hunters could clean up properly another night; Gabi and Kyle knew them by sight and scent now, they wouldn't avoid the Hunters for long. They put up their cues, leaving their drinks on the table, and hurried out after the trio.

As they exited the pool bar they heard the girl scream from the alley behind the bar and took off at a dead run, Gabi drawing Nex and Kyle unsheathing a dagger for each hand. As they rounded the corner into the alley the two Vamps whipped around, their eyes completely black and their fangs fully extended. The girl held between them was still screaming in terror. The Vampires faced the Hunters for a second, then looked at each other, and with matching growls shoved the screaming girl right at them and took off down the alley at Vampire speed. Kyle caught the girl and held her against him stifling her screams. Gabi took off at full throttle after the escaping Vampires.

"Gabi. No," he shouted, cursing when she didn't even slow. He pushed the girl down onto an overturned crate, and pulled a phone from his pocket as he took off after Gabi and the fleeing Vamps. As he got to the end of the alley where it split onto a main road he could see Gabi running to his right, the Vamps a short distance in front of her.

"Gabi," he yelled again, trying to get her to quit the chase. The next second one of the Vamps split off the main road heading down another alley while the other continued straight. Gabi sent him a hand signal telling him to follow the one who had split off, weaving between late night party goers. Kyle sighed in exasperation and took off after the blonde Vamp, as he explained to the Magi who answered his call, where to find the girl.

Gabi kept up her pursuit of the darker Vampire without actually engaging him; they were jogging now, keeping to an acceptable human speed. She didn't want to start anything with him while there were potential spectators, and he seemed to be counting on that; staying in the main streets and heading deeper into the city centre. Abruptly he disappeared down a side street, Gabi checked around briefly before following him; they were kilometres from the pool bar already, and Gabi wondered how Kyle was fairing with Blondie, or if he'd gone back to take care of the girl. She tracked her target to the end of the side street, he was moving quicker again, there were no pedestrians on these streets, and not a vehicle in sight. She lost the Vamp for a few seconds, but picked him up flitting down a dark side alley; he was obviously hoping to give her the slip in the darkened streets. She sped up heading for the entrance to the alley; this would be as good a place as any to take out a Rogue, she figured as she rounded the corner.

"Oh. Shit!" she thought, coming to a dead halt in the grimy alley. "I knew there was something odd about that

72

fucking Vampire's behaviour" she muttered to herself, while sizing up the six Vampires who were steadily moving in on her.

The two from the pool bar now stood calmly in front of her, another two moved out of the shadows behind her, and two more from dark entranceway to her left. She fell into a defensive stance and cast out her senses, searching for more, but that seemed to be all of them. More than she'd like to take on alone.

Damn, there were disadvantages to a city, not even a stray owl that she could use as a distraction. Nex was still in her right hand, but with a twitch of her left arm she hooked a butterfly sword from her boot. Then she took a deep breath, "Well, what do you know," she sneered at the two closest Vampires, "the Rogues have friends!" She casually moved to position her back against the right side of the alley, now she had all six in her immediate view. The two coming up from the entrance to the alley were the closest to her now, less than twenty metres away, they were both male and heavyset and muscular, one was slightly taller than the other, but besides that they could've been twins.

The taller one spoke "There is no need for bloodshed tonight," he said in a deep rumble. His voice had an odd formal cast to it, which seemed wholly out of place in this reeking alley. "Our Master would like to meet with you, and he sent us to extend his invitation," Deep Voice continued in a slow measured way.

Gabi blinked, mentally thrown sideways. This was a first in her books. "If this is supposed to be friendly, then I suggest you ask your friends to stop crowding me," she suggested evenly, eyeing the other four Vampires moving closer.

Two of them were the males from the bar, another was a shorter, skinnier male with a darker complexion. The last was a female.  She was inordinately beautiful; tall, graceful and platinum blonde, but there was a cruel set to her crimson mouth and emerald green eyes, and her whole body spoke volumes of disdain for the Hunter in front of her.

Deep Voice gave a miniscule toss of his head towards them and they stopped, standing dead still, only the female appearing unhappy about it.

Gabi was feeling decidedly outnumbered, and was trying desperately to calm her racing heart; a bright beacon of her anxiety level to the Vamps' sensitive hearing.

"I'm still feeling rather crowded," Gabi stated flatly.  "If we're going to have a civilised conversation we can do it one-on-one, no need for a conference."

There was slight movement from the group of four, as the female took another step forward.

"I don't think you're precisely in a position to give orders," the female spat in Gabi's direction.  Her accent seemed to have a touch of French in it, well that explained a few things.

"Genevieve!" Deep Voice cautioned with an increased rumble in his voice.  "We are not here to intimidate her."

"Angeli Morte – Phuh!" spat the female, with a sneer thrown in Gabi's direction.  "She is just a pitiful scrap of semi-humanity, what good can she do anybody?"

Deep Voice drew himself up to his full height and turned towards the female with exasperation on his face, but Gabi simply ignored the female.

"If you are not here to intimidate me then why did he send six of you?" She directed her question at Deep Voice and his brother, acting as though the female did not exist.

Deep Voice threw one more threatening glance Genevieve's way, and then visibly calmed himself before replying. "The Master simply wanted to get your attention without any bloodshed. He felt extra numbers would make you less likely to attack us on sight."

"Six against one?" she asked incredulously.

Deep Voice inclined his head slightly, almost respectfully. "Your reputation precedes you, Miss Bradford."

Gabi raised one eyebrow. These Vampires were well informed. Members of the SMV tended to keep their identities as secret as possible. She was no longer holding a fighting crouch, but she hadn't relaxed her defences; she still held swords in both hands, her wrists crossed loosely in front of her.

"Perhaps it would be more civilised to introduce ourselves first." Deep Voice used that odd formal cadence again. "I am Liam, and this is Nathan." He inclined his head towards the Vampire next to him. He was purposefully making very few movements, Gabi noted, obviously trying not to startle her. "You have met Genevieve...."

"Well, I heard a dog bark anyway!" Gabi interrupted.

Genevieve shrieked and launched herself straight at Gabi in a fury of fangs and nails.
When was she ever going to learn to keep her big mouth shut?

"NO!" Liam growled, leaping forward. "Stop!"

He was too late, by a fraction of a second. Genevieve blew past him and launched herself directly at Gabi. Gabi's arms raised and her swords flashed outwards in a single fluid motion. The two of them flew backwards as Genevieve collided with Gabi and they landed in a tumbled heap against the far brick wall. The fight was over in seconds, both of them using every ounce of strength and speed to rip into the other. When they suddenly broke apart Genevieve was still shrieking, but this time in disbelief. She reared away from Gabi, her eyes wide and her hand clutching at the blade sunk deep into her chest. She stumbled several metres backwards, for once completely ungraceful. Her body suddenly stiffened as a single drop of blood trickled from the corner of her mouth, and she collapsed to the ground. Gabi was already picking herself up off the street, leaning on the wall assessing her own body, but there was no time to do more than make sure she could stand. The other Vamps, shocked into stillness for the briefest second, leapt into action. The blonde one from the bar broke from the pack and streaked towards Genevieve. Inhumanly fast.

"No!" He roared hoarsely as he reached her. He watched in stark disbelief as her corpse began to mummify in front of him. Gabi hadn't been formally introduced to this male yet, but he obviously cared about the very beautiful, but now very dead, Genevieve. Then he looked up at Gabi with rage twisting his pale features.

"You bitch!" he screamed, baring his pale, glistening fangs viciously. He began to stalk towards her.

Liam and Nathan threw themselves into the small space between the pissed off Vampire and Gabi, while the other two hung back, seeming bemused by the turn of events.

Gabi pulled in a ragged breath and switched Nex to her left hand, her right arm wasn't following orders and the butterfly sword was still sticking out of Genevieve's decayed corpse. She could feel blood seeping down her right arm, not a good thing when surrounded by excited Vampires. Time for Elvis to leave the building she decided.

"Stephan, No!" Liam ordered in a stern voice. "The Master has offered her his protection. To attack her means death."

"She hasn't accepted his offer yet, has she?" Stephan bellowed back. "Get out of my way. I will avenge Genevieve's death."

"Genevieve attacked first. There is nothing to avenge. Angeli Morte had the right to defend herself." Liam moved towards Stephan, apparently trying to force him to step back. Stephan suddenly cowered down slightly, appearing to acquiesce. Liam relaxed minutely, and then Stephan leapt into the air and soared over their heads, somersaulting before landing inches from Gabi in an aggressive crouch. He didn't pause for so much as half a second before diving straight towards her. Time almost stood still as Gabi took one quick step to the right, spinning herself away from the enraged Vampire like a matador, changing the grip on her sword so that she held it pointed downward in her fist in the same instant. She noticed the other Vampires rushing forward, but they would be an instant too late. She continued her spin like a dancer, and brought the short sword up in a backwards thrust. She used all the force of her weight and spin to drive the sword deep into Stephan's back.

She didn't wait to check that she had hit his heart, she yanked Nex out of his body, hissing as pain lanced through her right side, and took off in a dead sprint back down the alley.

She could sense them following as she raced through the dark, empty streets. Only four, so Stephan was either dead or severely injured. Her breath was coming in ragged gasps and the pain in her arm and chest was sharpening with every stride. Two of them suddenly streaked ahead slightly to the right of her. So they thought they could ambush her again, fortunately she knew this part of the city well. She made an abrupt left turn into another side street, there was a well hidden fire escape just a few hundred metres down, this would get her onto the rooftops. Hopefully it would take the Vampires a couple of minutes to realise she was no longer on street level.

She stopped at the ladder to catch her breath, and to steel herself for the climb up the ladder. Her right arm still wasn't working right, she was guessing at dislocation, and she had definitely heard something crack when she'd been crushed between Genevieve and the brick wall. Arm? Collar bone? Probably a few ribs too. She took one more shallow breath, slipped Nex back into her sheath and grabbed hold of the ladder, hoping she'd have time to pull her phone and call Kyle once she got to the top. She scanned for the Vampires, and felt a huge surge of adrenaline as she realised two of them were at the entrance to the side street, she didn't bother trying to find the other two, she just threw all her concentration into the cumbersome task of climbing the ladder one handed.

She reached the top and rolled onto the flat roof, biting back a groan as she stood up. She could now sense the other two Vampires coming from the right at roof level, the first two almost at the ladder. Gabi crouched down and ran for the nearest shadows, there was another building with a flat roof about three metres jump from this one, she angled for a spot that she knew was the easiest to jump from. Normally this would be an easy jump for her, but she wasn't feeling particularly confident right now. She was out of options, however, so she left the shadows and started towards the edge of the roof, resisting the urge to let out a groan. She stopped dead in her tracks as she became aware of two Vampires appearing on the roof of the adjoining building. Then, a very masculine voice spoke from the dark behind her.

"Good evening Miss Bradford," the husky male voice said, strangely polite. "Or may I call you Gabrielle?"

She turned around very slowly, realising she was once again surrounded. A tall man stepped out of the shadows and walked with noiseless grace towards her.

"Oh, shit. Shit. Shit. Shit. Shit. Shit!" Gabi thought desperately. Her inbuilt 'Vamp-meter' was telling her this Vampire was enormously powerful.

As he stepped into the light cast from a taller building she could see more of the newcomer. He was very tall, well over the 6 ft mark, his broad shoulders were emphasized by a full length leather coat, that she couldn't help thinking must have been tailor-made to fit him. His hair was slightly longer than fashionable, in varying shades of dark blonde and brown and curling softly into his collar. His face could easily have been on the cover of any one of a dozen fashion magazines. He was the epitome of maleness in the hard angles of his cheek bones and jaw, and his dark eyebrows; offset by a sensual pair of lips and eyes framed by thick dark eyelashes that most women would give their first born child for. He was, quite simply, the most strikingly attractive man Gabi had ever seen in her life. Her heart felt like it stuttered a few beats while she took him in, before she forced her usual mask of haughty, nonchalance back into place.

"You have me at a disadvantage Mr...." She left it hanging. She purposefully stared straight into his eyes, though she was by no means sure she would be immune to such an immensely powerful Vampire.

He flashed a brilliant smile, clearly displaying his pearl-white fangs, his expression taking on a sardonic edge. "Of course, I am being rude. Forgive me, as I am not often in the company of one with such an esteemed reputation."

Gabi raised her eyebrows but decided to keep her mouth shut for once.

He continued, "My name is Julius, and I would very much like to make your acquaintance." He was still smiling mildly at her, keeping very still, and watching her reactions closely.

"I take it then that you are the uh, Master, that Liam was referring to," Gabi asked, trying to keep her voice steady. "The one who wanted to meet with me?" She tried to keep her voice even, and not show any sign of her injuries. She resisted the urge to cradle her injured arm to her body. Openly displaying weakness in front of an aggressive Vampire was courting a short trip to hell.

"Yes, indeed," he replied. "I hope my envoys were clear and polite in their extension of my invitation." He spoke slowly, with measured words, his voice low and husky.

She wondered if he knew how utterly mesmerising his voice was. She mentally shook herself, scanning again and realising that the Vampire numbers had now grown to over a dozen, her heart jolted with a new surge of adrenaline, and she suddenly became highly aware of the blood seeping down from her shoulder. The Vampire in front of her suddenly stiffened and her left hand flashed to Nex's hilt.

"No," he said in a flat, dead voice. "It would seem they were anything but friendly." He was now radiating fury, but oddly it didn't seem directed at Gabi. He didn't even seem to notice when she slipped Nex free of her sheath. He looked over her head and bit out the words, "Why is she bleeding?"

Gabi knew instantly why this Vampire was deemed Master of the City. The power rolled off of him in waves. It was like standing too close to a bonfire. A male Vampire stepped out of the shadows to her right, he had his head bowed deeply, but Gabi recognised Liam's voice as he spoke.

"Sire," he began in a rough voice. "My deepest apologies. Genevieve's temper got the better of her, and the rest of us were not quick enough to intervene in time."

The cold fury on the Master Vampire's face didn't change as he demanded. "Where is Genevieve?" His eyes scanned the roof quickly.

Liam's head didn't lift as he answered. "Miss Bradford defended herself against Genevieve's attack Sire."

"So she is gone?" Julius demanded.

Liam gave a quick nod of his head.

Gabi tightened her grip on Nex, no way was she getting out of this one alive if the Master considered Genevieve's death malicious, but she would take a couple more with her, she thought fiercely.

"And Stephan?" Julius demanded again, irate but controlled.

"Stephan tried to avenge Genevieve's death. Nathan and I tried to talk sense into him, but he was incensed, out of his mind." Liam shook his head sadly.

"You and Nathan took him down?" Julius asked, sounding completely matter of fact, as though it was a normal occurrence

"No Sire." Liam seemed to hang his head a little more. "He managed to get past us. Miss Bradford took him down too."

Julius's eyes flashed with something that seemed a little like surprise as his concentration flicked back to Gabi. A muscle twitched in his jaw as he spoke through slightly clenched teeth. "I should never have given in to Stephan's suggestion that Genevieve join the operation. I will speak to you and Nathan later. I expect a full debriefing." The threat in his voice was implicit, and Gabi could almost feel sorry for Liam, if she wasn't feeling so utterly exposed herself.

Gabi felt her body beginning to shake and knew that the adrenaline high was about to wear off. She closed her eyes for a brief second while she tried to collect herself, and when she opened them again he was standing mere inches from her. She flinched back automatically, but held her ground, tipping her head back to see his face. He looked to be assessing her, probably noting her hammering heart and quivering body. He seemed oblivious to Nex held tight in her left hand. He reached for her right arm, he could obviously smell the blood seeping down from the bite Genevieve had inflicted on her shoulder. As he brought her arm up, as if to inspect it, pain slammed into her. She pulled back from him, letting out a gasp and collapsing to her knees, her head reeling and nausea threatening to overwhelm her. She dropped Nex and wrapped her left arm protectively over the right; cradling it. She closed her eyes and fought the nausea down, trying to breathe evenly, feeling a cold sweat pop out on her forehead. Too late to hide the extent of her weakness now. If she'd been in any less pain she would've been very surprised to hear his voice sounding apologetic as he crouched down in front of her.

"I am sorry," he said, sounding almost contrite. "I was not aware you were that badly injured. You hide pain well. Too well for your own good it seems." He sounded like he was musing to himself now. Then he suddenly became businesslike. "It seems my original plan for our meeting has gone completely awry, we must see to your injuries first, most pressingly the dislocation of your shoulder."

Gabi wondered disjointedly how he knew it was dislocated, he'd hardly touched her. She brushed the thought away, trying instead to concentrate on getting to her feet and finding a way out of this mess. She briefly considered trying to bring in some bats to create enough confusion for her to escape, but quickly banished the idea, realising that these Vamps weren't going to be put off by a handful of flapping mammals.

As she started to try and rise, Julius put a cool, strong hand under her left elbow. She flinched and had to work hard not to rip her arm out of his grip. She steadied herself and allowed him to help her upright, Nex once again in her left hand. Then she moved back from him. He watched her move away with a brooding, pensive look on his face.

"I'm guessing you're not going to want to come back to our headquarters with me, so that we can get your injuries attended to and then continue with our meeting." He made it a statement of fact, rather than an actual question.

Gabi quirked one eyebrow upward. "That would be a safe assumption to make." She was trying for polite, shooting her mouth off earlier had got her hurt, but it was her natural defence when she felt cornered. "How about we all go home, and think about things, and we can try this again another night?" She tried to smile winningly. A girl could always live in hope. If she got out of this one alive, she vowed she would never, never, never run off alone after a Vampire again. Well, at least not for the next few weeks anyway.

"Hmm." Julius mused. "I thought you might feel that way. Fortunately I brought this with me. It'll make the whole thing much more painless. For all of us." And when he brought his hand up in front of him, there was a small black device in it.

Gabi heard a sharp whistling noise and as she tried to spin herself out of the way she felt a sharp sting in her uninjured shoulder. She looked down in surprise at the small dart and realisation arrived too late for her to do anything about it.

Her limbs began turning to jelly as she ground out the words "You BASTARD!" through clenched teeth. She felt him take the curved sword from her numb fingers. The adrenaline and the fury coursing through her couldn't hold back the darkness. She expected to feel the impact with the ground as she collapsed, but instead she felt cool, hard arms catch her and lift her up. The last thing she heard as she slipped from consciousness was his deep, sexy voice saying, "It is the easiest way, trust me."

# CHAPTER 6

Julius sighed and threw down the pen onto his paper strewn desk. It was pointless trying to even pretend to get any work done while she was lying unconscious on the chaise longue across the room from him. He was confident she would start to come around in the next few minutes anyway, so he needed to be ready when she did. They'd needed to give her another dose of tranquilizer on the trip, as she had started to come around too quickly. She was going to be like a cornered lioness when she woke up, cagey, mistrustful and more likely to attack him than listen to him. He'd deliberately put her in his office rather than one of his many spare bedrooms, hoping she would feel less threatened in the businesslike surroundings.

He was relieved that Jonathon, his resident doctor, had been at the estate when they came in with her. Jonathon had been able to put her shoulder back into place with relative ease while she was still unconscious. They'd bound her ribs, which Jonathon suspected were broken, and stitched up the bite wound. The doctor was reasonably certain that she had a fractured collarbone too, but it didn't need resetting, so they'd strapped her arm into place against her chest to prevent further injury. It was up to Julius to keep her calm and still when she came around, but he wasn't sure how successful he was going to be. It was obvious that she didn't heal as fast as a Vampire, but rumour was that she healed faster than the average human; she'd never been off street patrol for longer than two weeks as far as his informants knew.

He frowned. She looked so small and helpless lying asleep on his couch, and she'd felt so fragile as he helped Jonathon take care of her injuries. He'd only seen her in surveillance photos before tonight. In those she looked proud, self-assured and utterly capable of ripping someone's heart out without a second thought. She always had her russet hair tied back and a purposeful, arrogant expression on her face, and the ready tension in her body was visible even in those grainy images. And she had taken out Genevieve and Stephan, both Vampires over a hundred years old, without apparent difficulty.

Yet now, lying with her features calm and relaxed, she appeared very young and vulnerable, almost childlike. Her hair had come loose and was framing her face and neck in gentle, mussy waves. In the clear light of his office he could see a sprinkling of freckles across her cheekbones and the dark mark of a bruise slowly spreading across her right jawbone. There was also what appeared to be a burn mark streaked across her left cheek, though this must have happened prior to tonight, as it was still partly covered with make-up. He could sense the pulse of blood through the main artery just below her ear, and he felt his incisors lengthen instinctively. She smelled utterly delicious. Proof, he thought, that she was far more human than supernatural.

He found himself fascinated by her; something he hadn't expected, it had been many years since he last found something so captivating, and it startled him. He wanted to know more about her abilities and capabilities, and how exactly she had come by her supernatural talents. The speculation was that she was part-Vampire, but he knew that was impossible unless she was ingesting Vampire blood, and that seemed unlikely. He'd heard many rumours and second-hand accounts of her feats, not too many first-hand accounts of course, though he had spoken some with Liam earlier. He knew she worked with animals as her daytime career, and he wondered how far her control of animals extended, and if she realised that this was a Vampire ability. Utterly intriguing.

On the whole, he'd never found women particularly interesting. Simone had been one of the exceptions, of course, intriguing him to the point of utter stupidity. Why was he only attracted to the dangerous ones? Death wish? He wasn't sure. He took a deep breath and mentally shook himself out of the old memories.

He fervently hoped he'd made the right decision by approaching her. He'd been unable to dig up the names of any of the so called High Council of the Malus Venatori; it was much easier for them to hide themselves than it was for the Hunters themselves. Thank all that was holy for technology like facial recognition software and a loyal Clan member who knew more about computers than Einstein knew about physics. They'd waited weeks to get the chance at her alone, knowing that two Hunters together on patrol would probably fight to the death. They'd been ready to act the moment they could get her on her own. It was pure chance that she and her Werewolf friend had turned up tonight in one of his pool clubs and his barman had recognised her. His informants had confirmed that she was truly off duty, not just on an undercover job, and they'd put the operation into effect. It had seemed like it would work out so beautifully when they'd been able to separate her from the Wolf. And it had, right up to the point where Genevieve had attacked her.

He'd selected her to approach for two reasons; firstly, he had, apparently incorrectly, assumed that she would be the weakest link in the group of hunters, but secondly, and more importantly, he knew from his informants that she had some kind of special link to the SMV Council. They didn't know exactly what the connection was, only that she had a direct line to them. So he was counting on that connection to be able to get things smoothed over enough to convince them of the need to work together with him and his Clan.

He'd allowed the Society to continue to function in his City because they took some of the responsibility of hunting down rogues and miscreants off his hands. Their misguided sense of honour kept them honest enough that they rarely took out anyone who didn't deserve it, and as long as they stayed away from him and his immediate Clan members he saw no reason to put an end to them.

Now he was facing a threat that seemed too big for even him to deal with on his own. He was hoping that by combining forces and resources with the SMV he could prevent outright war. He'd known it was only a matter of time before he was challenged like this, but he hadn't counted on this particular nemesis making new and dangerous friends so quickly. The entire City was going to pay the price if he couldn't find a way to resolve this. He had to get her to listen to him, accept what was coming and then convince the Council to side with him against his rival for control of the City. But first, he would have to gain her trust, and that could prove to be more difficult than the fight itself.

She stirred slightly, turning her head away from him and baring her neck invitingly. He almost groaned, closing his eyes and clamping down on his lust for a taste of her. What was wrong with him tonight, he usually had unwavering control over his thirst. He wondered briefly if he needed to find a quick snack before she woke. But it was too late. Her breathing suddenly changed, becoming uneven. She groaned slightly and then went completely still. He could almost follow her thoughts. He could see her body respond the moment she realised she was in strange territory.

She became aware of a burning ache down her right side and into her shoulder as the dark mist began to dissipate from her brain. Had she been hit by a bus? She heard herself groan and took in a quick breath to steady herself. As the air hit her nostrils she realised she wasn't in her room at home, or in a hospital, or anywhere else that smelled familiar. She stiffened, instantly on guard. Something wasn't right. She cast out her senses and hit a wall of Vampiric power. It all came rushing back to her. Shit. He was here in the room with her, wherever 'here' was. She kept her eyes closed, trying to slow her heartbeat and keep her breathing even, hoping he hadn't yet realised she was conscious. She concentrated on her environment again. It was quiet. She could hear the purr of a computer, his breathing – huh, so Vampires did breathe - some footsteps and quiet conversation somewhere in the distance, behind walls. No immediate danger. The more conscious she became the more intense the pain seemed to get. Her shoulder was on fire now, her ribs in agony. She clenched her teeth against crying out. She was going to have to move soon to try and relieve the pain, but she wanted a few more minutes to collect herself. His low, husky voice broke into her indecisive thoughts.

"When you decide to stop pretending you're asleep I have some painkillers for you," he said with, what sounded suspiciously like, amusement in his voice.

So much for fooling the Vampire. She cracked open one eye, and then the other and turned her head towards where she sensed he was. She was in a room which looked incongruously like an office. Since when did Vampires have offices? The lights had been dimmed, so she didn't need to squint while her eyes adjusted. She was lying on a suede covered chaise longue, with a small pillow tucked under her head and a light blanket covering her. She was surprised to find that she didn't seem to be restrained in any way. She was still wearing her denim pants, but her shirt had been replaced by a man's black silk dress shirt, and she could feel her boots still on her feet. Her right arm was in a sling and strapped to her chest, her ribs were strapped too by the feels of it, besides that she couldn't tell much about her own state of health, beyond being in minor agony.

He was sitting in an office chair behind a desk a few metres away from her, he had his arms folded across his chest and he was watching her with an intense, hooded gaze. He seemed almost expectant. She wondered what he was expecting her to do. To be honest, her instincts were screaming at her to get her back to a wall and a weapon in her hand. Perhaps that was what he was waiting for. Unfortunately her body was not in any state to be doing anything like that, so she settled for trying to get into a sitting position without sounding like an utter wuss. She slowly swung her legs to the floor and used the momentum to pull herself upright, biting her lower lip to hold back the groan. She was breathing in quick shallow gasps but she was upright, now she felt more ready to face the Vampire the rest of them called Sire.

The two of them appeared to be alone in the office. He was no less beautiful to look at now than he had been in the dim light of the rooftop earlier. Her eyes definitely hadn't been playing tricks on her in the dark. She briefly and silently celebrated the fact that her vision now seemed to be back to normal and she could see him in clear, sharp focus. The broad expanse of his shoulders seemed even wider in the confines of the office, not the huge overly muscled shoulders of a body-builder, more the toned athletic look of an Olympic swimmer. The dark blue shirt fitted him snugly and hinted heavily at the toned muscles sculpting his chest and arms. And while his glorious face remained passive, his dark eyes glittered with a mixture of emotions she couldn't quite separate out. She realised now that his eyes were an exquisite shade of sapphire blue ringed by a halo of age-darkened gold. She'd never seen a more remarkable pair of eyes. She'd previously taken them to be completely black, and she wondered if they changed hue with his moods. She'd always thought of Vampires as cold and vicious; the dead Genevieve was to Gabi the epitome of the Vampire race as a whole, but there was something smoulderingly passionate about the Vampire sitting across the room from her. His skin was unusually pale, like someone who didn't tan easily, but other than that he seemed, in many ways, almost....... human. Which was actually laughable, as he was the single most powerful Vampire that she'd ever encountered. This last thought reminded her that she really needed to get the hell out of there.

"You said something about painkillers," she rasped, clearing her throat and swallowing against the dryness in her mouth. If he wanted to kill or torture her he was going about it in a very unusual manner. Then again, who knew with a Vampire, they weren't exactly known to follow human norms.

He nodded. "The doctor left some tablets for when you came around." He unfolded his arms slowly and leant forward in the chair. "I will bring them to you, please stay calm; I'm not going to harm you." He was using the same tone of voice she used when trying to calm a frightened wild animal. "It would be best if you didn't move your arm too much as our doctor wasn't certain of the full extent of your injuries without X-Rays," he said as he rose smoothly, at human speed, and turned to a table behind him with a carafe of water and some glasses standing on it. He carefully poured a glass of water and picked up a small bottle from the table. "He suspects a fractured collarbone and some fractured ribs. We got your shoulder back into place relatively easily, but the wrong movement could pop it out again," he continued as he walked slowly and lithely over to her with the bottle of tablets and the water. He watched her closely, as though expecting her to jump up and run away, or leap up and attack him.

"Vampires need Doctors?" she asked him, slightly incredulously. She needed to steer him away from thoughts of her injuries; he must never guess that while she was healing she was almost as helpless as a full human. That was one of the secrets she held very close to her chest, only Kyle and Byron knew of that weakness. It could prove disastrous if that became common knowledge among the supernatural population, especially the Vampires. Fortunately it only applied to serious injuries, but that was bad enough.

He smiled slightly but ignored her question; instead he shook two tablets into his palm and held them out to her. "Oxycodone. Jonathon assured me they are very good for pain relief. I would have to take his word for it, of course," he said with a wry tilt to his lips.

Gabi wasn't quite sure what to make of his odd humour. "Water first. Please," she asked. See, she could be polite when she needed to. She would've been polite to a Demon right now if he was holding the painkillers. Well…. maybe not a Demon. She took a deep drink. "Make it a double dose." She took another sip of water as he shook out two more tablets.

"You're resistant to painkillers?" he queried, not seeming to take offence at her demand.

She didn't answer but handed him back the water and took the tablets from his large, cool hand, tilting her head back and swallowing them quickly. When she looked at him again his eyes had gone dark; the deep blue irises almost swallowed by his dilated pupils, the gold halo all but vanished, and his face hungry. She flinched back minutely and adrenaline surged through her. Before she could move he spun abruptly way from her. He was back at the small table without her having seen him move. Freaky Vampire, she thought, annoyed. She was instantly on her guard again, searching the room for something to use as a weapon, for the quickest escape route, but when he turned to look back at her a second later, his face and eyes were back to normal. A sardonic smile crossed his face.

"My apologies. Again. I didn't mean to startle you. I'm not used to being around humans anymore. Or mostly-humans as the case may be," he added when he saw the protest on her face. "Oh, yes. You are far more human than supernatural, my lovely Hunter, even with your unnatural resistance to human drugs."

A growl rose in her throat. He thought he knew so much about her. "Firstly, I'm not *your* anything.

Secondly, I am anything but lovely, and lastly what makes you think I am so human?" she demanded testily.

He walked two steps towards her, a dark, predatory look on his face. He closed his eyes for a moment and took a deep breath. "Oh, your utterly delicious smell gives you away as mostly human, Gabrielle, you smell positively and irresistibly edible." He smiled darkly, making sure that she got a glimpse of his elongated fangs, starkly white and glistening. Nothing like a flash of fang to remind you that someone is higher up the food chain than you. "But don't worry," he went on conversationally, "I've resisted more delectable morsels than you in the past. I have other plans for you."

Gabi was caught on the back foot, no Vampire had ever gotten the chance to tell her how edible she smelled, and she found the chill sliver of fear running through her deeply disconcerting. She could hear soft footsteps nearing the office, her senses told her it was two Vampires. Julius looked up at the door as the footsteps slowed and stopped. His face suddenly went completely still and she felt a surge of power flow from him, it tingled over her skin like a million electrified butterfly wings. She was expecting the other Vampires to open the door, or at least knock, but instead she just heard the footsteps hurrying back the way they just came. The power rolling off Julius instantly subsided, leaving Gabi feeling like someone had just closed the door on a sandstorm. She looked at him in awe, a stirring of unease building in her stomach.

"What the hell *are* you?" she muttered more to herself than him.

He smiled, slightly arrogantly, obviously revelling in his own power. "What do your senses tell you?" he taunted, crossing his arms and leaning back against the desk. "I have it on good authority that you can sense a Vampire from miles away. Don't tell me you can't get a read on me."

She couldn't take her eyes from his face, and it wasn't Vampire thrall that was holding her there. "My senses do say Vampire," she said hesitantly. "But they also tell me that you are to the rest of them," she indicated the rest of the building with a tilt of her chin, "as a tarantula is to a common house spider."

His eyebrows lifted quizzically. "And that would be…?" he left the sentence hanging.

"The same species in principle, but the tarantula is a whole lot bigger, a whole lot scarier and a whole lot more deadly than the house spider," she explained.

"Ah," he said. "Well, then, your senses are quite possibly as good as they say."

She once again experienced an almost uncontrollable urge to get the hell out of there. Julius had the ability to seem quite human and reasonable one minute, and then remind her forcefully that he was powerfully Vampire the next. She was tired and sore and starting to feel a little light-headed from the painkillers. She wasn't sure that she was up to any kind of altercation with him, either verbal or physical. By the number of Vampires in the immediate vicinity she knew they were in some kind of Vampire stronghold. Fighting her way out probably wasn't a viable option. She was going to have to talk her way out of this one.

A single set of footsteps approached the door now.

"Enter," Julius said, without raising his voice and without looking at the door.

He was still looking at Gabi when a slim female Vampire entered the office carrying a small tray. The smell hit Gabi instantly and if it wasn't for the broken ribs she would've sighed when she caught the whiff of fresh coffee. A double-shot, caramel latté with extra cream.

Her instant cure for all ills. And in the bag she could smell baked apple Danish, her mouth was already watering. Julius moved towards the other Vamp and relieved her of the tray.

"That will be all Claudia. Make sure we are not disturbed again," he said in a tone that brooked no argument.

"Of course, Sire. I will be nearby should you need anything further," she replied with her head slightly bowed. Then she turned and was gone closing the door behind her soundlessly.

Julius picked up a small side table and placed it close to Gabi's left hand, placing the tray on it. "I took the liberty of ordering you some refreshment, I hope we have your preferences correct," he said.

"You've done your homework Jules," she drawled, watching his eyes flash with annoyance at her shortening of his name. There was just something about poking dragons with sticks that she couldn't resist, no matter how dangerous she knew the dragon to be. "I trust if you were going to drug me again, you would have just used the dart gun like last time."

"That's starting to sound like an attractive prospect,' he retorted, but then caught himself, and took a calming breath. "The food and coffee have nothing added to them. I would offer to sample them myself, but as human drugs have no effect on us, it would prove nothing. Please trust me in this case, they are perfectly safe."

Gabi couldn't possibly resist the smell a moment longer. She picked up the coffee, trying to hide the slight trembling of her hand, and took a long sip, closing her eyes and revelling in the sweet, aromatic taste as it washed down her throat. It was still hot and made exactly as she liked it. Then she set the cup aside and dug into the paper bag, pulling out a warm, crusty pastry. She tried to take small dainty bites while wanting to devour it in two mouthfuls. Byron didn't have any sound theories on why she craved so much sugar, so the simplest answer was to indulge it as often as possible. Not even Kyle could keep up with her when it came to sweet treats. Julius leant back against the desk watching her in utter fascination; it had obviously been a while since he watched a human eat. Or at least she hoped that was the reason for the fascination. She brushed a few crumbs from her lips and washed the first pastry down with more coffee. So far Vamp hospitality was better than she'd expected. Her hands were steady now, and the painkillers had kicked in, it was time to get this meeting under way.

"Now perhaps you would like to explain what exactly I'm doing here," she said, pulling a second Danish out of the bag.

Julius took a deep breath and folded his arms. "I believe that you are aware of the increase in the number of Demons entering the City lately."

She looked up sharply at him. As far as everyone at SMV HQ knew there was no association between Demons and Vampires, but in truth, they didn't know very much about Vampire society in general.

"Yes, there has been an increase in Demon activity recently," she said around a mouthful of pastry. "What do you have to do with it?"

"I would like to say I have nothing to do with the increase," Julius said tightly, "but I would be kidding myself if I did."

He pushed away from the desk and began pacing up and down the length of the room in front of the heavily stocked, floor-to-ceiling book case. He reminded her of a racehorse walking the ring before a race. He was trying to contain his movement, trying to rein himself in, but his desire to move, to let rip, was oozing through his tight self-control. "How much do you know about the way Vampire Clans are run, how our hierarchies work?"

"To be honest, not much," she replied. "My experience is that there are Vampires that try to blend in and feed themselves without resorting to terror and violence, and there are Vampires who revel in the horror of attacking and killing humans to feed. The former I ignore and the latter I kill. There aren't too many hand guides out there explaining the intricacies of Vampire life," she quipped.

"I guess that is true. We are secretive by nature and by necessity. But I would have thought that the esteemed Societas Malus Venatori would have gathered more intelligence on the supernaturals that they hunt".

She raised a sceptical eyebrow. "Are you actually trying to tell me that you would prefer us to know more about you?" she asked dubiously.

He let out a low growl. "No, that is not my preference, but it would take far less time to explain our situation now if you had some background information. What is currently happening in the city is intrinsically linked with the hierarchy within the Vampire Clans."

"You mean the increase in Demon activity has something to do with Vampire politics?" she asked, somewhat bewildered.

"In a nutshell, yes," he replied. "But it is also far more complex than that. I think a short history lesson in Vampire politics would help you understand my current position. Will you bear with me while I try to make this clear to you? You should also understand that this would be a large show of faith on my part, as we keep this kind of information secret in order to protect ourselves. There are those of my kind who would kill you simply for having the knowledge I am about to give you. You would need to accept that threat to your own safety, and to anyone else you impart this knowledge to in the future."

"You mean you're not going to swear me to some kind of Vampire Code of Silence?"

He looked at her with a "be serious" expression on his face. "No, there is no 'Vampire Code of Silence'. If you agree to what I will be asking of you, you will need to impart this knowledge to some of those on your Council in order to gain their support. I just want to be sure you know the danger you are putting yourself, and others, in when you are party to this information."

Both her eyebrows rose in incredulity now. "Whoa there, let's back up a few steps, I'm not sure I want to be the proverbial messenger who takes the bullet for your political agenda, Sire Jules."

He closed his eyes and took a deep breath. She remembered the same expression on the faces of some of her school teachers. "Will you just listen to me for a few minutes? Please. I'm not going to ask you to make any rash decisions now. I just want you to have all the information you need to make a rational choice. I don't expect you to make that decision on your own. There is a war coming, and the Malus Venatori will need to choose a side if they want to keep down the number of human victims in that war!"

She looked at him in silence for a few seconds. Then she sighed and nodded. "Alright, I'll listen. I'll even try to keep an open mind." Then she added, "But you better rustle up some more coffee if you want me coherent."

A slight smile lifted one corner of his mouth as she felt a slight surge of power. "Your wish, my command" he said, only slightly sarcastically.

# CHAPTER 7

Claudia had been dispatched for another round of coffee and pastries, and Julius had given Gabi back her mobile phone and left the office, giving her some privacy to call Kyle and reassure him that she was alright. Gabi guessed Julius would stay close enough to hear her side of the conversation. The phone had been turned off, so she assumed he knew that she could be tracked via her phone, and by giving it back to her he was either confident she would stop them from coming to get her, or he reckoned he had enough time to complete their meeting before the cavalry arrived.

She stood up cautiously and stretched out stiff muscles in her legs while she made the call. It took several minutes of reassurance to get Kyle to calm down, and not to come searching for her with every member of the SMV he could contact. She didn't bother telling him about her injuries, just that she'd been ambushed and darted with something to knock her out, and was about to engage in a meeting with the Master Vampire of the City. Finally, to give him something to do, she told him to arrange an urgent meeting of the SMV Council for the following morning. She assured him that Julius had guaranteed her safety and that she would be dropped off at a place of her choosing before sunrise. She would call him from there to collect her; she wasn't letting Vampires anywhere near her house or Kyle's. She didn't use her emergency word, and she hoped he noticed in his anxious state. They had long ago decided on a word they could use in an emergency situation that would alert the other that they were speaking under duress. They had never had to use the ploy, but it was there, and she hoped Kyle got the message and didn't try anything stupid.

When she was finished the call she sank into one of the comfortable leather office chairs near Julius's desk, choosing the one that allowed her a view of both the door and windows, and waited for Julius to return. She didn't have to wait long, he arrived moments later with her second coffee and a bag of pastries, placing them on the desk in front of her, and retreating to his chair on the other side of the desk.

"So," he began, leaning back in his leather chair and looking at her speculatively, "how long do we have until they arrive to rescue you?" he asked, confirming her earlier suspicions.

"What makes you think that I would need rescuing?" she challenged archly. "And in any case, I thought we were having a civil conversation, after which I would be safely deposited back in the City. Are you implying I have something to worry about after all?" Her voice was calm and precise, but there was steel in the undertone.

"No, not at all, I have guaranteed your safety; you will not be harmed while you are here." Julius reassured her, "but I would imagine that the Wolf was not too happy about our kidnapping you. If I were in his shoes I would probably be chafing to get you out of the clutches of a nest of Vampires, and would do it by any means necessary."

"Wolf may not always like my decisions, but he does respect them," she said. "He'll wait for my call." She left it hanging there, not specifying when she was expected to call Kyle. Let him believe that the cavalry were just a moment away if she didn't check in at the required time. Though oddly she felt she could trust Julius not to harm her tonight. If he had ulterior motives they didn't seem to include torturing or killing her; so, for now at least, she'd give him the benefit of the doubt. Nonetheless, she slipped her phone into her front pants pocket where she could reach it easily if she needed to; Julius wasn't the only Vampire in the building after all. "Now, can we get to the point of this meeting," she finished bluntly, pain and tiredness washing over her.

"Yes," he said, apparently satisfied that they would not be interrupted. "Firstly, would you be prepared to tell me what connection you have to the Council of the Malus Venatori?"

"I am a Hunter," she replied evenly. "The Council decide when a Rogue needs to be eliminated, and the details are passed to me or another Hunter."

"Yes, I guessed that much of the operation," he said carefully, "but I'm also aware that there is a deeper connection between you and a member, or members, of the Council."

"I'm not discussing that with you," she replied flatly, her expression clear that the topic was closed. Under no circumstances would she put Byron at risk, he was their most treasured and respected member and their most closely guarded secret. Only the Council, the Hunters and few of the office staff knew his true identity, and they were determined to keep it that way. Other members knew his first name, but they were unaware of his real identity, they knew him simply as a voice on the phone that gave them their assignments, or called them up for emergencies. They had no idea that he was a respected member of the City Council, a founding member of the SMV Council, a born Magus and Gabi's second father. Gabi sat tensely waiting for the explosion, but to her surprise he simply nodded, a wry smile tweaking the corners of his mouth.

"I guessed that would be your answer, but I had to try," he said calmly.

Gabi suddenly realised that he had probably read more than she wanted him to at her response to the question. She would have to be more careful how she answered his questions. She also found herself wondering how he was even aware of her relationship with Byron, and how he'd known where to find her and Kyle tonight? This was something else she'd have to discuss with the Council; it seemed they had a leak.

"I need to tell you something of the Vampire histories in order to explain our current situation. I will try not to bore you with too many details, but please stop me if you feel I am giving too much or too little information," he began, sitting forward and crossing his pale long-fingered hands on the desk. She nodded her assent and picked up the fresh coffee, settling into the big chair and tucking one leg up under her, getting as comfortable as she could while still tensed to react if another Genevieve barged through the door.

As he started speaking, telling her the beginnings of Vampire culture as it existed today, how the Vampire cleansing in Eastern Europe in the early 18th century, the so called 'Age of Enlightenment', had decimated the strong Vampire presence that existed in the world at that time, she found herself studying him in minute detail. A small part of her concentration started trying to analyse his voice, his mannerisms, the way he spoke. She was trying to place him geographically as well as in a time period, intrigued with trying to work out where and when he'd been born. He appeared to be close to her age; her true age, of twenty-nine, maybe a little younger. He was well built and looked as though he'd had good nutrition growing up.

She didn't know much about Vampires, but she did know that their height and build was carried through the change, although deformities, physical abnormalities, excess fat, hair loss, wrinkles and skin damage were often repaired. Once a Vampire had changed they were stuck with their build and height; a short, skinny human became a short, skinny Vamp, and a large, muscular human became a well-built Vamp. She'd never encountered an older Vamp with the muscle and bulk of Julius however, or for that matter, his power. Those born in the years before decent medical care, good nutrition, and gym membership were mostly on the short and skinny side, and appeared older than their human age. She had no idea of the exact correlation between power and age in a Vampire, but she did know that the younger ones had far less mental power than the older ones, and her internal 'vamp-meter' always gave her an idea of the supernatural capabilities of a Vamp. Julius was a very powerful Vampire, but why he was so tall and so muscular, was a mystery to her. The general consensus among the Hunters about Vamps was; 'be careful of the little ones'. Julius was most definitely an exception to that rule.

His accent was almost impossible for her to pinpoint exactly. He had a carefully neutral accent, probably English, but not one of the broader British accents. In fact, it reminded her of the accents of those from the

British colonies; a clean upper-class accent without blatant inflection and slang, but also without the clipped, pompousness of royalty. She could imagine him speaking several languages without altering his basic accent at all. Perhaps that would explain his neutral accent; if he had been around for as long as she suspected, then he probably had learnt several languages and lived in several countries over the course of his lifetime.

Then there was his name; she wondered if it was the name he had been given at birth or if he had assumed it somewhere along the line. It was obviously a popular name in ancient Rome, but she doubted he was actually that old, maybe it had made a comeback at some stage and become popular again sometime in more recent history. His build and colouring suggested an Anglo-Saxon bloodline in his background, but not knowing his exact age was making it almost impossible to be sure of anything about him.

If he was aware of her scrutiny he pretended ignorance, continuing with his chronicle of Vampire history. He explained that the remnants of the Eastern European Vampires had scattered into the rest of the world, many to Western Europe and the British Isles, but some adventurous ones took on the 'New World'. They concentrated on keeping a low profile and quickly dispensed with any Vampire who threatened to expose them again. For a while they shunned the company of humans, only coming into contact with them to feed, but there were so few Vampires left that loneliness eventually drove them to resume the dangerous process of Turning humans. Slowly Vampires began rebuilding their decimated numbers, creating families for themselves.

The first 'family' of any note was one in Scotland in the mid eighteenth century. A female Vampire, named

Ilyana, had fallen in love and Turned a Scottish nobleman into a mate for herself, and between them converted most of his direct family into Vampires. Several other older Vampires latched onto her idea and they also Turned a number of other Scottish and English families. Ilyana became the 'Matriarch" of the McCullum Clan, taking on her mate's name, and this blueprint for a new type of Vampire Family quickly spread throughout Britain and Europe. Vampires were now living a similar existence to their Eastern European heyday, but spread out in solid family groups, each ruled by a powerful Matriarch or Patriarch, known as a Master Vampire. The Master Vampire was expected to keep tight control over all members of the Clan, enforcing secrecy and curbing Vampire related deaths, ensuring humans didn't learn of their existence. It was after a number of Clans had been formed all over Europe and Britain that they began forming mutually beneficial bonds with Werewolves and in some cases even Magi and Shape-shifters.

"Of course over the past century the Clans had started to become more like business enterprises than true families," he said, "businesses that employ the majority of the Vampires and many of the Werewolves in each city. Cities are regarded as territories, and generally only one major Clan lives and rules in each city. Positions of Master Vampire in the larger cities are highly prized, and only the strongest Master Vampires get to hold these positions. It has, in short, become a political game. He or she with the biggest influence and the strongest supporters wins. If a Master slips up there are numerous others waiting to take him down and replace him."

Now the story had begun to interest Gabi.

"So you're telling me you had to fight to be Master of the City?" she interrupted him for the first time.

"Yes," he replied solemnly, "in more ways than one."

"What do you mean?" she asked.

"Well, for the most part only the oldest, most powerful of us get to a point where we can challenge another Master for a prime position. If we aren't considered powerful enough to maintain order in the Clan, other Masters will join forces to eliminate us as possible contenders. A Master first has to prove himself strong enough and ruthless enough to control a Clan, before he is allowed to challenge."

"Let me guess," she drawled, "you weren't considered 'old' enough for the position."

Julius seemed startled that she'd reached the correct conclusion; she realised that most people would've automatically assumed he wasn't powerful enough. She, of course, knew better.

"Yes, as a matter of fact I *was* considered too 'young' by Vampire standards,"

"So, what are the Vampire standards for a Master Vampire?" she queried. "Is there a certain age, a kind of test, what exactly makes a Master a Master?" She decided to push him and see how far he would go at divulging intimate details of Vampire Society. Any information she could gather was more than they had now, and she was sure that Byron would find it fascinating.

"There aren't really any specifics involved. It has more to do with mental power and strength, as well as ruthlessness and experience in playing political games. A Master is a Vampire who reaches a point where they can do things that other Vampires aren't capable of. Such as," he continued as he saw the demand in her expression, "not having to sleep through the daylight hours," Gabi's felt her eyebrows shoot up at that piece of news, "not needing to feed as often, being able to mentally compel another Vampire to do something and having control over Werewolves and other animals."

He said the last few words with a discreet look at her, as if watching for her reaction. She felt her eyes narrow in contemplation, and quickly concealed her interest by burying her nose in the coffee cup.

"Go on," she said in a carefully neutral voice, filing away that enlightening piece of information for later consideration.

"Not all Vampires have the ability to become Masters. Many can live to be a thousand years old and not ascend to that higher level. It's something innate, the ability is either there or it isn't. Something like an Alpha wolf; if you concentrate on the ability and have the determination to strive for that higher level you'll eventually be able dominate others, but if you're not quick enough, strong enough, powerful enough, clever enough, another will take you down before you hit the top. Survival of the fittest."

Gabi nodded, it made a lot more sense to her once he compared it to the Alpha ability.

"What made you a Master before the rest of them thought you were..." she paused looking for the right word, "experienced enough."

"I had, shall we call it, a certain advantage over others of a similar age to me," he said cryptically, leaving her to ask him the obvious question.

She simply raised an eyebrow and waited, refusing to be baited.

He bit off a slight smile and gave in. "I have been able to compel other Vampires to do whatever I want them to since I was first turned. And I have very strong mental defences against the ability in other Vampires."

"So, in short, any other Master with you in their 'Clan' would always be looking over their shoulder, wondering when you were coming for them," she surmised almost to herself.

He smiled wryly.

"Yes," he confirmed. "That's the main reason I was allowed to challenge for my own Clan at such a comparatively 'young' age."

"So," she took her eyes off him to study the pastry she'd pulled from the bag and nonchalantly asked the question that was burning a hole in her, "how old are you really?"

He actually let out a burst of laughter, which startled her more than anything else he could have done. "That is personal information, and not relevant to our discussion," he said, "but I might be tempted to divulge the answer for some personal information from you in return."

Gabi's expression turned instantly wary. "Maybe another time," she said, her voice implying that he had about as much chance of that as a Vampire had of surviving five minutes in full sun.

A teasing grin touched his masculine features. "You don't even know what I would ask you. Aren't you even the slightest bit curious to know what I would like to know about you?"

The curiosity was gnawing at her like a million termites, and she had a thousand questions she wanted to ask him, but she wasn't going to admit that to him.

"Are you going to get to the point of the meeting sometime before the sun comes up?" she asked instead, stifling a yawn. "Some of us do have work in the morning." Weariness was starting to make her crotchety, probably not the best attitude to have when trapped in a building full of Vampires.

The grin disappeared from his face. "Yes, of course. I forget sometimes that others do not keep our hours. I will try to summarize this as much as possible." He took a deep breath, reminding her of another question to add to the growing list in her head. "There is a challenger for my position as Master of the City. This of itself would not normally be a problem to the citizens of the City. For the most part fights for this kind of position take place only in the presence of a select few, along the lines of the 'duel at dawn' scenario. They would rarely affect anyone in the contested city, besides the top level of Vampires associated with the two Masters. This case, however, is not a normal contest." He paused for a moment, as though fighting down anger, but before she could interrupt with a question he continued. "The challenger to my position is something of a radical in our world. He has not been 'approved' by the other Masters to challenge me, but they will not stand against him either."

Gabi was confused. "But everything you've told me so far indicates that the Masters as a whole will not tolerate anyone overstepping their given authority. So why is the challenge against you any different, and why would this affect the rest of us?"

A number of emotions crossed his face as he looked down at the desk for a brief moment, and Gabi's heart rate jumped as she recognised unease and guilt as two of them. Abruptly his face went passive, as he exerted rigid control over those emotions and looked back at her.

"The challenger has some unique talents, and some unique allies; making him a virtually unstoppable force. The other Masters wouldn't be overly distraught to see the end of me, as I don't play the political game the way they think I should, and I'm too powerful for them to force me to play it their way. They're also hoping, of course, that once he takes the City from me he'll be content to stay and play here rather than challenge them for their cities. If I defeat him, they're no worse off than before; if he defeats me they believe he'll leave the rest of them in

110

peace, so either way they win in the end. They've decided to be Switzerland in this case, and won't interfere or assist either side."

"So spit it out," Gabi demanded, "why is he such a threat? Why are you all scared of him?"

Julius looked her straight in the eyes. "His biggest strength is the ability to control Demons. He has power over them like I have power over other Vampires. He also has a Magus allied to him." Gabi's blood ran cold as she knew intuitively what he was going to say next. "She is one of the very rarest types of Magi; one you would call a Dark Mage, one who can open gateways in the Veil; pathways for Demons to cross the Void to our world. I believe he is planning to attack us with an army of Demons at his command."

Gabi sat in stunned silence. She realised the implications of this challenge to Julius's position without him having to lay them out for her. She'd already had a taste of what would be sent against them. A number of things clicked into place in her head at the same time. This revelation explained the unusual behaviour of the Demons, their willingness to work together, the appearance that they had goals in mind, the sheer number of them appearing in the City. She tried to clear her chaotic thoughts, filtering out things she could discuss with Byron later, and figuring out what other information she would need from Julius before her meeting with the Council.

"The Masters who make the decisions, the old ones..." Gabi said.

"We call them the Princeps," Julius supplied helpfully.

"Alright, the Princeps," she continued, "you said they are adamant that secrecy is maintained, that it's one of the oldest and most unbreakable rules. If this contender..."

"Dantè," he supplied again.

"Ok, if this Dantè is bringing hordes of Demons against the City, it's going to be obvious that there's something supernatural going on here. You can't hide dozens of Demons from the human population for very long. Why are they going against one of their oldest rules and letting him attack you? It doesn't make sense to me."

Julius sighed broodingly. "It doesn't make sense to me either, and I can't give you a straight forward answer to that. I can only surmise that they assume they can limit the fallout, somehow keep it contained within the boundaries of the City, and later, once the dust settles, find a way to blame it on some other source. Mass hallucination, rabid animals, tainted water, something like that. They seem actually scared of him. Of Dantè. Their main concern at the moment seems to be to keep him from challenging the rest of them. They seem to think he will be content with my City; they don't realise he has a much bigger plan in mind. They don't realise how much of a radical he truly is. And they don't realise he is almost completely insane." Julius's voice had a morose edge to it.

Gabi frowned. "You sound like you have personal knowledge of him, like you know him well."

"I do," he confessed bitterly. "I had the chance to kill him, to give him true death, and I didn't," he bit off angrily, leaning back in the chair and closing his eyes.

She sat still in the ensuing silence; digesting the latest revelation. Then the common sense side of her kicked in. "So, what if you simply stood aside for this Dantè? Let him take control of the City. You could go off and find another city to challenge for. Why are you so determined to fight him?"

Julius didn't open his eyes when he replied. "Two reasons," he said quietly. "Firstly, he will destroy life in the City as we know it. He sees humans as sheep or cattle, simply a food source. He doesn't understand why we hide from them; he sees it as cowardly, to live as we do now. He wants to live in a world where he is openly the top of the food chain, and humans cower in his presence. He is humanity's worst nightmare come to life; he is what humans make horror films about. Secondly, it wouldn't matter what other city I took control of, he would want to take it from me. He's determined to destroy me, as he knows I'm one of the few true threats to him, and he knows I'll stand against him in his quest for a new order of Vampire Clans."

He sat forward now, looking at her again, his sapphire eyes boring into hers. "You and the Malus Venatori have three options here. You can try to continue the fight on your own to the best of your abilities, you can flee the City and save those you love the most, or you can join forces with me and we can try to bring Dantè down together."

He stood up and walked around to stand in front of her. "This is what I need you to present to your Council. I will fight this war with or without you, but I know you have strengths that would be valuable to me. I think the best chance we have of bringing the City through this without major human casualties is to stand together." He paused briefly. "If you choose to stand with me, and we defeat Dantè, I will give the Malus Venatori my full support in the future. I will provide staff to assist you and information that will help you in your dealings with Rogues, and your protection of friends and relatives."

Gabi stood as well, though he still towered over her, she needed to bring them back to some kind of level. She moved to place the chair between them; having him stand so close was playing havoc with her heartbeat, and she knew it had nothing to do with fear and everything to do with the sudden surge of primal lust as she watched him move. It had been a while since she found a man this sexually exciting, and she was angry with herself for having those feelings for the Vampire standing, looking pensively at her from the other side of the chair. She knew Vampires could have that effect on humans, it was one of the weapons at their disposal that helped them draw in prey, but she'd always thought of herself as immune to that, as well as to their mind control. Maybe it was just a combination of her exhaustion and injuries that had her defences down. She fervently hoped so. She needed to get away from him before her body betrayed her feelings in a way he could detect.

His eyes had taken on a speculative gleam, but he continued as though nothing had changed. "Is there anything else you need to know before you leave?" he asked, his voice, deep and sultry, vibrated through her body.

She deliberately took a deep breath, making a small groan when her ribs sent a sharp protest ripping through her side. Anything to curb her body's current desires.

"No," she said through gritted teeth. "I think I have enough to take to the Council. I can't tell you how long it will take them to reach a decision though. You'll have to give me a way to contact you."

She felt herself sway slightly and gripped the back of the chair. Julius's face instantly took on an expression of concern.

"Do you want some more painkillers? Or shall I get the doctor back to look at you again." He started to move around the chair towards her, his hands ready, as though to catch her if she collapsed.

Gabi waved him away, and retreated from him again. "I'm fine. I just need some rest. I've had worse."

Julius didn't look convinced but backed off, giving her some space. "I'll give you a number to call. You can

114

leave a message for me. We can meet in a more neutral place to discuss the Council's decision. Perhaps a club or restaurant. You are welcome to bring the Wolf if you like, but I would prefer to keep it to just the two of you at the meeting. You name the time and place."

"Can I trust you not to try anything stupid?" she asked bluntly. "Wolf and I will be armed, and we won't take kindly to being disarmed by a Vampire."

Julius sighed, "No, I won't try to disarm you or the Wolf, none of my Clan will touch you, and I expect the same of you and yours."

Gabi looked sceptical. "You don't have any more Genevieves in your closet?"

Anger flashed across his face and his voice turned so deadly she had to suppress a shiver.

"There will not be a repeat of that. I will make sure of it," he ground out through suddenly extended fangs. Then he took a deep breath and calmed himself. "And speaking of weapons," he moved back to his side of the desk in a single fluid motion, and opened a drawer. He pulled out Nex and two of her butterfly swords and laid them on the desk. "I believe these belong to you."

Gabi's eyes lit up at the sight of Nex. Gods alone knew how that sword kept finding its way back to her, but she was unbelievably glad to see it. Her hand itched to close around the solid comfort of the hilt, but she held her ground, waiting to see what Julius would do. He reached into another drawer and pulled out a piece of black satin, Gabi found herself wondering what kind of person kept pieces of black satin in their desk drawers. He spread the material on the desk and carefully laid the three swords on it and began wrapping them up.

"This is a truly beautiful sword," he commented as he carefully laid the cloth over Nex, "A one of kind, and obviously bonded strongly to you, it is a priceless piece of

115

weaponry. There are not many bonded Kris in the world anymore; the two of you are a good match." He finished binding the swords and looked up at her, "I hope I never come up on the wrong side of the two of you," his expression turned musing, "but it would be an interesting fight."

Then he sent out a short spike of power. Seconds later a Vampire knocked quietly on the door. "Come," Julius called. Nathan, Liam's brother, entered the room.

"Sire," he said deferentially, his head bowed. "What can I do for you?"

"Gabrielle needs to get back to the City. She'll tell you where to take her. I trust you will ensure she gets there safely." The deadly tone in his voice left no doubt as to Nathan's punishment should he fail again.

"Of course, Sire," he was practically grovelling now. "Thank you for giving me the opportunity to make up for our previous errors. I will not fail you again."

Julius picked up the black bundle containing the swords. He held them out to Nathan. "These are to be returned to Gabrielle in the car. Bring a car around to the rear entrance; I will bring her down to you in a few minutes." Nathan took the bundled swords carefully and bowed his way out of the office, disappearing on swift, silent feet.

Great, Gabi thought, a few more minutes to keep her treacherous body from betraying her. The damned Vampire exuded confidence like a pheromone. Maybe she could test the fractured collarbone this time.

Julius couldn't help himself; that hint of sweet, musky arousal lacing the air earlier had called to him on a base level. It had been a long, long time since he had found a female this enticing, this exquisitely tempting. He knew he had to have her, even if it was just to end the itch he

116

could feel building deep inside his body. It would be an interesting hunt. He knew he'd have to be patient and cunning to seduce her, but it would be a delectable distraction from his current situation. The challenge was an even more formidable one, in that she seemed to sense when he used his power, so he was down to his own natural charms to win her, the victory would be all the sweeter that way, he smiled languidly.

"So have you reconsidered my offer to exchange personal information," he almost purred. It felt good to try out his rusty flirtation skills again; he'd never had much trouble attracting the opposite sex, even before he was turned, but it didn't hurt to know how to best utilise the tools you had been given to work with. He was rewarded almost instantly with a return of the scent he had been hoping for. Rape was definitely not his thing; he would only pursue a willing victim. This little cat was about to be stalked by a much bigger predator. But the little cat still had claws and teeth, and he figured she wasn't going down without one hell of a fight.

"You're not that interesting," she declared airily, but he could see her left fist clenching like she was driving her fingernails into her palm, and she broke eye contact with him.

Julius's smile turned predatory as he reached down into a desk drawer again and drew out another piece of black cloth. He knew she wasn't going to like this one bit.

"I'm afraid I need to bind your eyes on your way out of here. Until I'm sure we have an agreement of some kind, I wouldn't want you to be able to find your way back here and do away with all of us while we sleep. You understand I'm sure, just as you would not want us knowing where you or the Wolf sleeps."

Gabi's breath hitched in her throat at his statement, and Julius was perplexed by the jolt of fear he detected washing from her as he held up the blindfold, but as suddenly as it appeared, it vanished, and was replaced by a much more enticing fragrance, as though some other course of events had suddenly occurred to her. He filed the confusing snippet away in his mind, determined to discover its meaning eventually. He moved unhurriedly towards her again with the blindfold. She held out her hand imperiously as he closed the gap between them.

"Give me the damn blindfold," she groused, but as she said it he saw the realisation that there was no way she could tie it herself with one arm strapped in a sling.

He saw the weary capitulation in her eyes and wordlessly moved closer to blindfold her. He leant over her and tied the binding firmly, but gently behind her head; tilting her chin upwards and touching her face to pull the fabric into place over her eyes, careful to avoid the healing burn mark on her cheek. Then he casually brushed a small dusting of icing sugar from the corner of her luscious mouth, which was currently fixed in a stern, annoyed line.

She jumped back from him as though scalded, haughty disdain on her face. "If you're quite finished," she huffed, "I'd like to get home for some sleep."

Julius held his tongue as he took her hand in his to lead her out of the office; she deliberately pulled out of his grasp and put her hand on his arm instead, muttering unintelligibly. Julius smiled enigmatically; the answer to his question drifting tantalisingly off her body. The poetic words 'Will you walk into my parlour, said the spider to the fly' flashed through his mind as he led her down the corridor to the waiting car, and his smile grew wolfish.

# CHAPTER 8

The drive to the drop-off point was a largely silent one. Nathan asked her where she would like to be taken, and after about ten minutes of driving informed her that she could remove the blindfold. She did so immediately. She was being chauffeured in a BMW SUV, being a Master Vampire seemed to be a lucrative business. Looking out the darkened windows of the large car, nothing appeared familiar at first, but then she started to pick out few recognisable landmarks and got her bearings. She pulled out her phone and called Kyle, telling him she would be at the pick-up point in a few minutes.

The quiet time in the car had given her a chance to digest what Julius had told her. She'd sifted through all the information he'd given her and tried to figure out how she was going to put the proposal forward to the Council. She knew there was going to be instant distrust of Julius and his motives. They were going to want some kind of proof that it wasn't him summoning the demons himself, or that this wasn't just a personal vendetta against a rival. Gabi thought the key to finding out the truth may well lie with what the Magi High Council could tell them about the Dark Mage, who Julius claimed was working with Dantè. Julius only knew her first name, Mariska, but that may be enough to obtain some information.

The Magi Council governed all Magi-born and was what Gabi considered a 'busy-body' organisation, they kept records of all Magi born, those they knew of anyway, and tended to keep tabs on those with pure Magi blood throughout their lives, whether they practiced the art or not. The High Council oversaw all the city and town based councils and kept a central records department in a highly secret location, protected by numerous spells and wards. They'd been keeping information on Magi for over three hundred years. If information about this Mariska existed, they would have it. Now all Gabi needed to do was convince the high and mighty Athena to request the information. Maybe she should take Raz with to the meeting, she mused with a malicious grin.

Her musings came to a halt as they rounded a bend and came within sight of Kyle's van parked outside their current gym. There were no other vehicles in the parking lot yet; it was still a couple of hours before opening time, so Nathan stopped the car a few metres away.

"Miss Bradford," he rumbled in a slightly lighter bass voice than his brother's, turning in his seat to face her. "I would like to apologize again for the way things turned out tonight. You were never supposed to come to any harm, and I was taken completely by surprise by Genevieve's attack."

Gabi paused in her reach for the door handle. "Alright," she said evenly. "Why have you found it so important to tell me that?"

Nathan pursed his lips, "I don't want you to get the wrong impression about Julius. I know this looks bad, perhaps like he set the whole thing up, but he genuinely did give us the order to bring you to him unharmed, and also to make sure the Wolf was left alone and unharmed." He paused for a moment chewing on his lower lip and then seemed to come to a decision. "You see. I probably shouldn't be telling you this. But I think you may need to look at the situation from another perspective. Julius has only been Master of the City for a few years. In that time he's made many changes and not all Vampires in the clan are happy with the new regime. I'm afraid there are those who don't agree with his decision to try and join forces with you."

Gabi suddenly tensed, ready to fling herself out of the car.

Nathan just smiled apologetically. "No, no. You've got nothing to worry about from me, I'm with him on this. I trust Julius with my life, and I think the changes he's made are for the betterment of all of us." He shook his head. "Even if I didn't agree with him, I would never go against his orders. But you should know that there are others who think less of him for asking for your assistance. In Vampire society asking for assistance is seen as showing weakness. If he's asking for your help he's serious about the threat that's heading our way."

"I'll try to take that into account," Gabi said diplomatically. Kyle had lost patience waiting for her and strode over to rip the car door open and poke his head inside.

"You coming?" he asked brusquely, glaring darkly at the Vamp in the driver's seat.

Gabi reached over and picked up the bundle containing her swords and thrust them at Kyle.

"Take these," she ordered, pushing them into his hands and pushing him backwards so she could get out. As she eased out of the car Kyle took in the fact that she was only using one arm and his lips twisted in an angry snarl. She sighed tiredly. Leaning towards the car she said "Thanks for the ride, Nate," and slammed the door closed, turning back to face Kyle as the car pulled smoothly away.

The expression on Kyle's face was caught somewhere between concern and anger.

"What's wrong with your arm?" he demanded. "You didn't tell me you'd been hurt."

"Because I knew how you'd react," Gabi's temper flared instantly. "I'm a big girl. I can look after myself. And we have much bigger concerns than my arm," she finished darkly.

"What? I'm not allowed to worry about you now?" he demanded, but she saw the slightly hurt look in his eyes.

She sighed heavily and her ribs protested. "Sorry. It's been a long night. I'm tired and sore and confused. Let's just get in the van and head home. I'll fill you in on the way."

Kyle grumbled but moved to the van, opened the door and helped her in, dumping the bundle of weapons on the floor at her feet. He got in, started the van, checked for potential tails, and then headed out of the City towards Gabi's house. He was silent for the most part as Gabi filled him in; first on the fight with the Vampires and then the meeting with Julius, only asking the odd question when she didn't give him enough detail. His expression went from tight-lipped fury at the kidnapping, to incredulous disbelief over the reason for the meeting, and finally to deep thoughtfulness coupled with vague suspicion as he tried to work out what other motives could lie behind the proposal from Julius.

At home, Gabi side-stepped the assault by Raz when she walked in the door and left him to walk, stiff-legged in haughty disgust, to the kitchen on his own four legs, tail twitching. He seemed to forgive her though when he jumped on the counter and allowed her to give him a rough, one-handed petting. She switched on the coffee maker and took down some mugs as Kyle took a stool at the counter and they continued their discussion. Slinky galloped into the kitchen and patted imperiously at Kyle's leg until he lifted the squirming animal up and onto his lap. The little critter promptly curled up, contented, and went to sleep.

"The most obvious possibility," Gabi said, "is that he needs our help to get rid of this Danté, but Danté isn't actually as dangerous to the rest of us as Julius is making him out to be. Julius could well be using a Dark Mage himself to bring the Demons into the City to scare us into helping him." She leaned back against the kitchen counter and unwrapped a lollipop using her teeth, sticking it in her mouth as she looked to Kyle for input.

Kyle raised his eyebrow speculatively. "Or it could be some kind of trap for the SMV. Get us to trust him, expose our numbers to him and then he wipes us out as soon as he sees where our vulnerabilities are."

Gabi couldn't really fault his distrust. They knew so little about the Vampire race, and she knew that the same prejudice would probably be shown by the Council at tomorrow's meeting. She personally had more than enough reasons to hate them.

"I honestly don't think we're that much of a threat to him," she disagreed, talking around the lollipop. "He is the single most powerful Vamp I've ever been anywhere near. What would he have to fear from our little organisation, which takes care of the dregs of supernatural society anyway? He didn't come across as the type with such a fragile ego that he would need to eliminate us simply to prove he can. He was very self-assured, very self-confident, but not in the way that it felt like he needed to prove anything. Not like one of those who is so insecure that they have to do powerful things to prove to everyone that they are the strongest, the most ruthless, the most powerful." She paused to pour the coffee into the mugs and took them, one at a time, over to where Kyle sat. "You know, something that Nate, the driver, said to me also makes sense now," she continued. "He told me that Julius has been their Master for short time now, and that he's made some unpopular changes. Think back to the number of violent crimes that have been Vampire related in the past year, as opposed to the previous three or four years."

Kyle sipped his coffee, looking studious as he gave that some serious thought. "Hmm. That is a point," he conceded. "There've been very few Vampire incidents that we've had to clean up recently. A few years ago there would have been several a month, but now we're mostly dealing with Weres and the recent increase in Demons and Ghouls. So you think he's been keeping a tight rein on them, and that proves his power."

"I think it proves that we're not really a threat to him," she replied. "Why would he go to such extremes to wipe out the SMV when we're no danger to him and his?"

"Maybe he has something big planned, and doesn't want us around to interfere once he implements his nefarious scheme," he suggested.

Gabi smiled tiredly at Kyle's attempt at drama and realised that they were just talking themselves in circles. She looked at the clock on the microwave, it was after 4am, no wonder they weren't making sense anymore. "How about we sleep on it for now. We can tackle it in the morning with the Council, maybe some fresh minds will help make sense of it."

Kyle got up and took the empty mugs to the sink while Gabi dished out food for Razor and Slinky.

"Do you want to crash here again?" she asked him. "It'll save you having to come and collect me in the morning."

Kyle agreed; he had fresh clothing in the van. He went out and grabbed his overnight bag and Gabi's weapons from the van and locked up the house before heading for the shower and bed.

Gabi didn't bother to do more than brush her tangled hair and clean her teeth before stripping off and heading to bed as well. She decided the strapping could just stay where it was, she would worry about it in the morning. She collapsed gratefully into her warm covers – Raz made a great hot water bottle - and was asleep in minutes.


An incessant knocking roused her, if she'd had a gun in her hand she probably would've shot whoever was making the damned noise. She groggily lifted her head to peer at the bedside clock. Eight thirty. Lord and Lady, what would make the noise go away so she could go back to sleep?

"Gabs," called Kyle's voice loudly. "You alive in there?"

"Go away Wolf," she growled threateningly.

"I'm coming in with coffee," he warned. "No attacking on sight, and keep that monster cat of yours under control." The door clunked open, as he used his elbow to manipulate the handle; he had a steaming mug in each hand. "Rise and shine, sleeping beauty, we have a meeting in an hour and a half." He plunked a mug down on the table next to her nose and sat on the edge of the bed blowing on his own mug. Raz awoke under the covers and issued a warning growl, Gabi patted him quiet.

Gabi pulled a face. "Damn. Council meeting. Did you have to make it so early?" she groused, stiffly pushing into a sitting position. She felt like she'd been run over by a truck. A large truck. The whole right side of her body was one big ache; she was going to be black and blue. The bite on her shoulder was throbbing, and she could feel the pull of the stitches. The coffee made warm, comforting trails down her throat and the groggy, hung-over feeling began to recede.

"Ten am is not early in most people's books," he said in mild rebuke.

"Most people don't get to bed after four am," she muttered, "Why do you look so damned chipper this morning." She hated the fact that Kyle could get away with a few hours sleep and still function normally, while if she got less than her obligatory eight hours she was like a zombie until at least her third cup of coffee.

Kyle just let her grumble away until they'd both finished their coffee.

"Do you want some help getting the strapping off before you shower?" he asked.

"No, I'll manage," she replied quickly. She hadn't come clean about the bite yet. "I'll call you if I need help. Just make sure there's some breakfast ready, or I'll be forced to snack on you when I get out."

Kyle chuckled wryly as he left with the empty mugs and Slinky draped over his shoulder.

Getting the sling and the strapping off was a slow, painful process. One look in the bathroom mirror was enough; she closed her eyes and climbed under the steaming flow of water, wincing as it hit the waterproof film covering the stitches. She could move her right arm a little, but it was weak and slow to respond. She guessed that meant Julius's doctor was right about the fractured collarbone. She clumsily managed to get clean,

126

dry and dressed, not bothering to put the strapping back around her ribs. She'd go and see Ian later at the hospital if it was still bothering her; he was a lot calmer about seeing her battered and bruised than Kyle, Rose and Byron. She put the sling back on, over her long-sleeved shirt, and slipped her right arm into it. She felt almost ready to face the world now.

Kyle was busy making pancakes when she came through, Rose wasn't coming in today with it being Saturday, but she'd left pancake batter in the fridge. Gabi couldn't remember how she'd coped before Rose came along. They quickly glutted themselves on pancakes drowned in maple syrup, washing them down with a second mug of coffee. Gabi popped some painkillers and then they headed off to the meeting with the Council.

The Council didn't have one set place that they convened at; they moved between several locations at random, depending on who was calling the meeting. Today they were gathering at Byron's house, no one in the neighbourhood would think it unusual that he had a few friends over for an early lunch on a Saturday. After all, he often had "Book Club" meetings with the same group of people who were arriving today. His housekeeper, Meryl, was Rose's sister-in-law and completely trustworthy. Gabi knew she would have a light lunch prepared for them all, as well as snacks for morning tea; Meryl was nearly as good at feeding people as Rose.

Kyle found a spot to squeeze the van into in the large, paved parking area and Byron's four dogs came charging out to greet them. As usual they lavished licks all over Gabi, and whined in frenzied delight when she patted and rubbed each one in turn. Three of them were enormous Rottweiler crosses and the last was a small pavement special, which could have been a mixture of four or five different terriers and toy poodles. Kyle only got wary glances and general avoidance. All dogs saw Kyle for what he truly was – Wolf. And no ordinary dog with its head screwed on right challenged a wolf the size of Kyle, but they also didn't seem to feel the need to grovel before him either, perhaps because they felt he was cheating by using his human form. So Kyle ignored them and made his way to the front door, going in without knocking. Byron would know they'd arrived; he had surveillance cameras linked up to the parking area, installed at the Council and Gabi's insistence. Gabi disentangled herself from the mob of canines and followed him into the spacious house. Byron met them in the hall, giving Kyle a warm handshake and stopping himself mid-way into the act of hugging Gabi, as he noticed the sling, settling instead for kissing her forehead.

"Gabrielle, Honey. You were supposed to be resting and recovering, and now you come in with your arm in a sling." He was in instant worry mode. "Kyle didn't tell me you'd been hurt." He looked questioningly at Kyle.

"Don't blame Kyle," Gabi sighed, wondering if Byron would ever stop fussing over her. "When he contacted you he didn't know I was injured. I didn't tell him I'd been hurt because I didn't want anybody trying anything stupid in an already volatile situation. That's all. Besides it's not that serious. I've had worse."

"You'll go straight to Ian once the meeting is over, he'll be on duty from midday today," Byron's tone brooked no argument.

"Ok, fine. If that'll make you feel better," Gabi capitulated, trying to sound more put out than she really was. She knew Ian wouldn't blab about how bad the injuries were. They had an understanding; she would follow his medical advice when she came to see him, and he wouldn't baby her, or rat her out to Kyle and Byron.

They both pushed the boundaries of the agreement at times, especially Gabi when it came to getting back to work, but it worked pretty well.

"And your sight too, Ian can check that while you're there," Byron insisted.

Gabi pulled a face but agreed to that too.

"Now, everyone is here and we're all on tenterhooks wanting the details of this whole incredible story," Byron continued. "You being kidnapped to have a meeting with a Master Vampire has got everybody positively buzzing with speculation."

"Yeah, incredible is a good way to put it. Let's go through and I'll explain as best I can," Gabi said.

Byron led the way through to his games room at the rear of the house, where the billiard table had been converted into a conference table with an easy slide-over panel. Comfortable chairs were arranged evenly around it, pens and pads of paper sat in neat piles, and a glass of chilled water stood on a coaster at each chair. The Council members were scattered around the tea table in the far corner of the large room. Meryl had outdone herself in the snacks department; scones, muffins, a cheesecake and a pecan pie all called invitingly to Gabi from the little table. All the Council members were present and accounted for.

Athena was dressed, as usual, in a neat, businesslike suit, this one in a pale grey, with a lilac blouse and shoes. She already had her cup of tea and a single muffin on a plate and was heading to the table. She nodded an icily polite greeting to Gabi and Kyle, and sat down, opening a slim leather briefcase to pull out a PC tablet and ignoring everyone around her.

The others were far more enthusiastic in their greetings and concerns over Gabi's injuries. Margaret was a Shapeshifter Elder; having reached the venerable

129

age of eighty-three she rarely shifted anymore, but she was as sprightly as any fifty year old Gabi knew. She was warm and grandmotherly, and she showed genuine concern for the Hunters and Crews in their dangerous work, but she had a backbone of steel, an uncanny ability to unravel any mystery, and a memory for detail that rivalled a computer. She fussed over Gabi and asked how her eyesight was, and then checked up on Razor and Slinky, like she was asking after someone's children.

Irene was standing next to Margaret. She was a quieter type who wasn't given to social chit-chat; when she spoke it was generally to say something quite profound. The tall, slender, middle-aged brunette was also a Magus, a powerful one. She was the Senior Magus of the City, and one of the people who had voted Athena onto the High Council. Gabi knew that this woman saw more than you really wanted her to. Irene had the ability to see auras and she also seemed to have some innate sense that told her when someone was lying or glossing over the truth. She quirked one eyebrow when Gabi told Margaret that she had a simple shoulder strain. Gabi prayed she would leave well enough alone and silently thanked Kyle when he pushed a cup of coffee into her hand. She was grateful she'd shoved a container of painkillers into her pocket; she'd need them before the meeting concluded.

Rounding out the members of the Council was Alistair, a Werewolf. He was in his forties now and had been infected by an ex-girlfriend in his late twenties. He was an unassuming, but oddly attractive man, with a lean, wiry build and a shock of dark blonde hair. His position as Head of the Department of Prisons proved vital for the SMV cause. He could get imprisoned Weres into isolation cells over full moon, and was able to exert some kind of control over them while in prison, even going as far as getting them released if they were proving too much of a problem inside. Of course those who were released early by Alistair were never seen or heard from again. It had only taken two of those to convince the rest to behave; the stories travelled and grew more sinister with every telling, which served Alistair's cause perfectly. He would normally have given Gabi a rough hug or a punch in the shoulder by way of greeting, but today settled for roughing up her hair as he made his way to the table with a mound of food on his plate. Gabi mock growled at him before following his example and heaping her own plate full of cake and pie. She hastily carried the plate back to the table where she'd left her coffee as Byron called everyone to their seats. She ate quickly as Byron called them to order, gave a short welcome and thanks, and then gave her the floor.

"Morning everyone," Gabi said, rising out of her seat and quickly brushing crumbs off her mouth as the small group gave her their full attention. "Thanks for agreeing to this meeting on such short notice." Sometimes it paid to be polite, she knew how these Council things worked, the less she antagonised them the better. "If you don't mind I'm going to take a seat while I explain this, as it is a somewhat lengthy story." When the others murmured their assent she sank gracefully into a chair, pulling it close to the table and leaning forward to rest her good arm on the mahogany surface.

Gabi told the story, breezing over the initial ambush, but stating that she killed two of them who'd attacked her. She then related the story that Julius had told her, trying to keep as close to his exact words as possible. Finally she related what she had felt about Julius's powerful abilities and the sense of loyalty some of the other Vampires had shown for him, as well as her and Kyle's observation that Vampire related crimes had diminished since his rule as Master of the City. The others had interrupted occasionally with questions, but for the most part they made notes on their pads of paper, and Gabi guessed that 'a hundred and twenty questions' would be their next game. Kyle had added in a few observations of his own, and backed up several of Gabi's assessments of the situation.

Finally Gabi sat back. "So the decision needs to be made as to whether you are willing to accede to his request for a meeting with him, and if you are, how and where we can accomplish that without either side feeling too insecure."

She reached for her glass of water to relieve her parched throat, and prepared for the onslaught. Everyone began talking at the same time, voices ranging from excitedly agitated, to grumpily suspicious. Athena was sitting primly upright in her chair and studying Gabi from across the table.

"Alright everyone," Byron called loudly, getting them to quieten down. "Obviously we have many questions for Gabi, let's do this in a calm, ordered way. I think we'll do a lap around the table, each of you can ask Gabi two or three questions. Once she's done with those we'll take a break lunch, and then we can let Gabi get some rest while we discuss the situation further."

Gabi could've kissed him at that stage. She just wanted to have her say and get the hell out of there, she'd been dreading that Byron might keep her and Kyle in the session until a decision was reached.

While the others were reading through their notes and preparing their questions, she shifted to get Kyle's attention and then peered forlornly at her empty coffee cup. Kyle shook his head wryly, rolling his eyes, but got up and poured her a fresh cup, taking it to her at the table and muttering "you owe me big time!" into her ear as he bent over her.

She smiled mischievously, "I'll tell Raz not to bite you for a whole month," she offered in a low, teasing tone. Kyle snorted and returned to his seat with a martyred look on his face.

"Everyone ready?" Byron asked. He received nods from the other Council members. "Good. Athena, how about you get the ball rolling."

Athena nodded, leaning forward to pick up her neatly written notes. As she looked up Gabi realised that she wasn't going to like what Athena was about to ask, the witch had a nasty glint in her eye. She steeled herself.

"You sound like you're quite impressed by this so-called Master Vampire," Athena said in her clear, clipped voice.

Gabi waited for her to go on, but she didn't. "Was that meant to be a question?" Gabi asked in a flat tone, "or are you just airing your personal views?" Gabi bit back a smile when she noticed the slight flush rise in Athena's cheeks.

"I'm just noting," Athena ground through stiff jaw muscles, "that you don't seem to be upset with this Vampire for ambushing, assaulting and kidnapping you. My actual question is whether you're an impartial witness in this thing, or if he has managed to infiltrate your mind and influence your emotions and reactions."

"Athena!" Irene's calm, strong voice admonished sharply. "A question like that is uncalled for."

Athena switched her glare to Irene, eyes flashing warningly. "It is a perfectly legitimate question. What if she's been sent in by the Vampire to trick us into trusting him? He can apparently control other Vampires. Gabrielle has Vampire blood, so there's a strong possibility that's the reason he chose her to be his messenger. He knew he'd be able to control her." She spat the last sentence out.

Gabi almost laughed out loud, if Athena actually knew exactly how Gabi had reacted to the impossibly good-looking Vampire, she'd have had a far bigger leg to stand on. As it was, Gabi slowly rose to her feet, put her good hand on the table and leaned across towards Athena, her eyes glittering dangerously. She could hear the hissed intake of breath from the others at the table and felt Kyle tensed to react. As Byron started to rise to calm the situation she froze him with a look.

"If that is what you suspect,' Gabi drawled softly, "then how about we prove you wrong quickly, and after that you sit down and shut-up. Your question time will be over." She had to give it to the witch, she didn't back down, even though her heart was racing and her breathing was coming in short, sharp bursts. "Irene, will you check my mind for any extraneous presence, please," Gabi ordered quietly, without taking her eyes from Athena's.

"I don't need to check your mind, Gabrielle dear," Irene stated emphatically, shaking her head. "I can see quite clearly that there is no disturbance in your aura. Besides your injuries, which are worse than you let on, your mind has not been tampered with." She turned her attention to younger Magus. "Which Athena would have known if she had bothered to look for herself." She paused for a second letting her reprimand sink in, and then directed her next comment to Athena in person. "Athena, you can't let your prejudices rule your common sense in a Council session. That kind of conduct is not becoming of a member of the High Council."

Athena looked shattered for a second, her face as pale as a Vampire's, and then a haughty mask settled over her features and she threw herself back in the chair and folded her arms, anger flicking the taut muscles in her jaw.

Wow, thought Gabi, looking with new respect at Irene. She knew the older woman had a back-bone of steel, but she never thought to see her bring the witch down to size like that. She took a careful, relieved breath and settled back into her own seat as Byron stood up to restore order.

"Please everyone; let's not forget that Gabrielle has been through a lot in the last few days. We're not here to shoot the messenger, so keep it relevant, and try not to repeat each other's questions. Margaret what have you got for Gabrielle?" Byron waved to the Shapeshifter who was sitting nearest Gabi and took his seat.

Margaret shot a displeased frown Athena's way, before smiling gently at Gabi.

"Gabi, my dear, we all know you have as much reason to dislike and fear Vampires as anyone, so I would like to know if you feel there is any merit to us meeting with this Julius. You were the one in his company, and I know you to be a very good judge of character. What reservations would you have, and do you think he would have any reason to try to destroy the Malus Venatori or its members?"

Gabi considered the questions carefully before answering. "As I've said before, he is a particularly powerful Vampire. Kyle and I discussed this a little last night, and I see no reason for him to want to destroy the SMV. We are simply no threat to him. I think his request for a meeting to set up some kind of unified group is a genuine one. Whether his need for our help is purely selfish though, I can't tell you. Perhaps Danté is of no threat to us directly. For what it's worth, my own gut instinct said that he meant me and the rest of the SMV no harm."

Margaret nodded thoughtfully. "Thank you, my dear. You did very well in difficult circumstances. We appreciate and value any input you give us," she finished off giving Gabi a warm, reassuring smile.

Gabi resisted the urge to glance Athena's way and see how the witch was taking the indirect dressing down from the other Council Members.

Alistair was next with questions about Julius's powers and Danté's abilities, which Gabi couldn't really add much to besides what she had already shared. Then he and Byron called up information on a laptop to check Kyle's premise regarding the decrease in Rogue Vamp activity over the past eighteen months, and declared that it was indeed true.

Byron asked about the information that Julius had about the SMV, and agreed with Gabi that there must be an information leak somewhere. Gabi told him she felt it was a person, rather than computer leak, but nothing major seemed to have come from it, and Julius was apparently oblivious to Byron's involvement.

Irene went over the conversations Gabi had had with the other Vampires, and tried to build a clearer picture of Julius from their point of view. Of course, it could all have been an act, but it seemed unlikely they could've pulled it all together on the one night they would happen to catch Gabi without a Crew.

It was after midday when they broke for lunch. Gabi immediately went to the bathroom, and swallowed some painkillers, before heading back to enjoy Meryl's splendid lunch spread. She and Athena stayed out of each other's way, and after lunch, at Byron's insistence, Kyle drove her to the hospital for Ian to assess her injuries.

# CHAPTER 9

Ian concurred with Julius's doctor and sent Gabi straight to radiology for x-rays. Gabi had tried to shoo Kyle from the room before Ian examined her but he stubbornly sat in a chair and refused to budge. Gabi knew he was glaring holes in her when he saw the size of the dark purple and black marks on her ribs and the stitched bite wound, but she pointedly ignored him. Ian double checked Gabi's shoulder joint and the stitches, and did a full examination of her eyes while they waited for the results of the x-rays. Her eyesight seemed perfectly normal, and the x-ray results confirmed that she had a fractured collarbone and three fractured ribs, but nothing needed resetting, so Ian prescribed strapping and rest. Ian declared her officially off duty for two weeks, and when she grumbled loudly over that he simply raised an eyebrow and reached for the phone. Gabi knew he would call Byron and tell him to take her off the roster for four weeks, so she snatched the phone away quicker than Ian's human eyesight could track.

"Alright, two weeks!" she capitulated grumpily, "but don't expect me to like it." She plonked the phone back in its cradle a little harder than was strictly necessary.

Ian bit back a smile and wrote out a prescription for more pain meds.

"Kyle, Rose and Byron will all be keeping an eye on you, so don't make me book you off longer," he warned. "Keep your arm in that sling, and get Rose to help with the strapping on your ribs, she's done it before."

"Can I do some normal work, at least?" she demanded. "I do need to make a living somehow."

Ian and Kyle both snorted at her last comment. They both knew it was more her inability to sit still than any need to earn money.

"Yes, you can do some normal work, but nothing handling large animals. Consulting only, nothing hands on, and someone else will have to drive you to appointments," Ian said, closing any loopholes quickly.

He was beginning to know her too well, she thought, resisting the urge to stick out her tongue at him, and instead fished a lollipop out of a jar on his desk and snatched up the prescription. She went around to the other side of Ian's desk and gave him a kiss on the cheek, making sure to leave some sticky lollipop residue behind.

"Thanks, Brother Fusspants," she teased him impishly before stalking out the door.

Kyle gave him a sympathetic grin and raised him a quick mock salute before following after her, Ian's wry "Good luck" drifting after him.

Gabi was alone in the house, catching up on e-mails when Byron called later that afternoon. He reported that the Council had decided to do further investigation before making a decision. They specifically wanted to substantiate Julius's claims regarding the Dark Mage,

Mariska. If they could find information that Mariska was indeed a Dark Mage, and had gone renegade, they would agree to the meeting with Julius. Meanwhile, Byron had a few ideas of where and how the meeting could be set up. He couldn't tell Gabi how long it would be before they heard back from the Record-keeper of the Magi High Council, but thought it may take a few days.

Gabi chafed at the delay; instinctively knowing that Julius was not going to be pleased, but she also knew that the Council was right to be cautious. At least they hadn't flat out refused the meeting. She was also pretty sure that Julius wasn't going to talk to her over the phone about the matter and would insist on their planned meeting, but Byron didn't need to know that. The less he had to worry about the better. Gabi worked on the principle of 'it was easier to ask for forgiveness than to ask for permission', not that she made a habit of asking for either, but the basic principle was there. She rang off from Byron after he assured her he would keep her updated on any developments. Then she pulled out the small, white card Julius had tucked in with her swords and called the number hand-written on it. There was no answer and no message; the call simply went straight to a beep prompt. This threw Gabi for a moment, but she recovered quickly enough; what else would you expect when calling a Vampire?

"This is Gabrielle Bradford," she said in her most professional voice. "I have some news from the Council. Call me," she added her mobile number, though she figured he probably had it already, and hung up.

She rubbed her eyes wearily and wondered if she'd have enough time for a catnap before she heard back from Julius. There were still a couple of hours until full dark, so she decided to take the chance. She tucked her mobile into her sling, snagged Razor off the sleeper couch in the corner of the office, and went to catch up on some sleep.

An annoying buzz woke her. Her phone was vibrating on the table next to her bed. She glanced at the clock; it was a little after six pm. Probably Kyle checking up on her she thought testily. She picked up the mobile; the message icon flashed merrily on the screen, an exact counter-point to her cranky mood. She touched the icon, and was surprised to find the message was from an unknown number. It read; "Gabrielle, thank you for your quick response. I would like to discuss in person. Name your favourite restaurant. I will book for 9pm. One person each as discussed. Julius."

She sighed; she'd known he would find a way to force a meeting. She should've waited until tomorrow to call him, at least she would've been able to have an early night tonight. She knew the perfect restaurant though, so she immediately sent a message back. "Olivella. Old Mill Rd. Make it 8:30."

Her mood immediately lightened as she pictured a huge, rare rump steak with a mountain of chips and a bottle of good Italian Red. Olivella belonged to a Shifter who was a friend of hers; they made the best steaks in the City, had an eminently noteworthy wine list, and their chocolate mousse was positively ambrosial. It had the added bonus of being in a largely residential area, so Gabi would easily be able to monitor any extra Vampire presences, and if push came to shove, Shawn would be in his office in the back, so she had extra back-up without Julius knowing it.

Her mobile chimed again. "Agreed" was the short reply.

She made a call to Kyle and was pleasantly surprised when he didn't even bother trying to talk her out of it. He just asked what time he needed to pick her up and hung-up.

It was eight thirty on the dot when Kyle stopped her car a few blocks from the restaurant; Gabi had refused to drive in the van this time and had once again tossed him the keys to her car. He waited quietly while she scanned the area, casting her senses out to feel for the ominous, vibrating spots that indicated Vampire presences. There were just two; Julius radiating like a miniature supernova, and another fairly strong presence quite close to him. When she was sure it was just the two of them, she nodded to Kyle to drive on to the restaurant. They parked the car and Gabi checked the area again. The Vampires were already in the restaurant and there were no signs of any others nearby.

As she stepped out into the slight drizzle and grimaced up at the starless sky she wondered if the Vampires would be eating or drinking tonight – human food that was. She only knew the common folk lore that stated they survived purely on human blood, and she was intensely curious to find out the truth. She and Kyle made a quick dash for the welcome shelter of the doorway, being careful to keep to human speed. The maitre d' quickly came forward to open the door and welcome them into the fragrant warmth of the cosy but chic little restaurant.

"Ah, Miss Bradford," the maitre d' greeted her enthusiastically. "It's wonderful to see you this evening. And Mr Robson, it's been too long since we last saw you." The short, swarthy man helped Gabi out of her leather jacket, clucking when he saw her arm in a sling. "What this time Miss Bradford?" he asked with a slightly exasperated tone. "Not an out-of-control lion again, I hope."

Gabi grinned, remembering the last time she came in bashed up and blamed it on a rogue lion. It hadn't been a huge lie; there wasn't that much difference between a rogue Werewolf and a rogue lion. At least her job as an animal trainer made it easy to come up with excuses for injuries.

"No, Jorge, not a lion this time," she said, quickly wracking her brain for a new excuse. "Just a frisky thoroughbred stallion, managed to pop my shoulder out of joint, nothing too serious," she explained, trying to keep her thoughts about Julius in the proper compartment in her mind as an image of him prowling his office popped into her head.

Jorge tsked as he hung up their jackets in the coat room. "You really must be more careful, Miss Bradford, perhaps you need to stick to little kitties and puppies, they're much safer to deal with," he fussed.

Kyle barked out a laugh. "You've obviously never met Gabi's cat if you think they're safer," he muttered darkly.

Jorge shook his head, as though knowing his concerns wouldn't change this young lady's mind. "Your friends are here already; let me take you to the table. Shall I let Shawn know you are here? I'm sure he would love to see you," Jorge babbled on merrily as he led them through the candlelight tables to a private alcove on the far side of the restaurant.

"No, that's alright Jorge," Gabi said quickly. "I'll pop in and see him in his office once I've greeted my guests." She didn't want to expose her little advantage too early.

Julius rose lithely as she came around the edge of the partition which had been used to create a small private alcove. She watched his eyes skim her body, taking in her black hipster dress pants and deep maroon blouse as well as the black silk scarf she'd converted into a sling.

He seemed to study her unbound hair a little longer than strictly necessary and she wondered if he could make out the hilt of her sword nestled into the nape of her neck. She pasted a cool, businesslike expression on her face as she acknowledged him.

"Gabrielle," he greeted in a low, smooth purr. "Thank you for meeting us this evening." He turned slightly to indicate his companion sitting at the table. "This is Alexander. One of my most trusted friends."

The other Vampire had a barely concealed scowl on his face. He had a much slighter build than Julius and Kyle, with mussy, pale blonde hair and a face straight off the cover of a Mills and Boon romance. The image was so strong Gabi had to gulp back a disbelieving giggle, covering it with a discreet throat clearing and moving aside to introduce Kyle. She nodded a greeting to the disgruntled looking Alexander.

"Hey Jules," she said cheerily. "This is Kyle, as I'm sure you are already aware. Kyle this is Julius."

They nodded warily at each other; no one reached to shake hands, and Alexander's face grew more surly by the second. Gabi sighed, lamenting the fact that males of all species felt the need to size each other up. She took the lead and sat down in the seat opposite Julius, leaving Kyle to take the one across from Alexander.

There was an open bottle of Chianti standing on the table, and before she could reach for it Julius was holding it above her glass, a questioning tilt to his eyebrow.

"Can I pour you a glass?" he asked politely.

She glanced around the table. There was a half full glass of red in front of Julius's seat and Alexander had his hand around a short glass which smelled like it held bourbon.

"I trust it's a decent bottle?" she challenged.

"One of the best, according to the maitre d'," he answered smoothly, pouring before she could think of another smart ass comment. He offered Kyle, who declined in favour of waiting for a beer.

Julius settled into his seat just as a young female waiter appeared to take orders. She seemed flustered. As Gabi looked around the table she realised why. Kyle had the kind of face and physique that drew attention from women (and men) wherever he went, and tonight he was possibly the least attractive man at the table. With Alexander doing his best James Dean bad boy impersonation, and Julius exuding dark, brooding predator, Gabi could almost pity the girl, but she was having her own problems trying to keep her traitorous mind on the business at hand. Alexander brusquely ordered a refill of bourbon and Kyle ordered a beer and two platters of antipasto for himself and Gabi. Julius asked for another bottle of wine. Neither of the vampires ordered any food, Gabi noted with interest. The flushed girl left to collect the drinks and Gabi reached for her wine glass, savouring the first sip slowly. Julius's eyes tracked her every movement.

"How are your injuries?" he asked Gabi.

"Fine," she answered flatly, ignoring Kyle's annoyed frown. At least he was holding his tongue; she'd warned him if he couldn't be polite to keep quiet, obviously he was finding it difficult to be polite. Perhaps that was Alexander's problem too; the hunky blonde Vampire had yet to say a word to anyone at the table.

"I would like you to forward any medical bills to my office," Julius continued, "and let me pay for a driver until you are healed. It's the least I can do."

Gabi was thrown for a second, and somewhat amused. Not often you got beaten up by a bunch of Vampires, who then offer to pay your doctor's bills. She allowed a small amused grin to appear as she dropped her gaze from his.

"No, that's not necessary. My bills are covered already," she drawled, tipping the wine glass and inhaling the pungent bouquet, "but, if it makes you feel better, you can owe me a favour." She took a mouthful of wine and looked him straight in the eye to gauge his reaction. His mouth tightened, but she thought it was in amusement rather than annoyance when she noticed the cocky glint in his eye.

"Alright," he agreed smoothly, "I owe you a favour. Do you have a specific favour in mind, or is it to be an open-ended one?" He leant back in his seat, bringing his own wine glass to his lips and appearing to savour the taste as he swallowed.

"Oh," she threw back nonchalantly, "let's go with open-ended." She was enjoying the repartee.

"So, we are agreed," Julius affirmed. "I owe you a yet-to-be-determined favour, at a yet-to-be-determined date, and you will forgive me for indirectly causing you harm."

Gabi's eyebrows quirked as he added the last part; but she decided to continue the charade. "I can live with that," she declared. A low growl issued from the right of her; Alexander apparently wasn't happy with the arrangement. Gabi had had about enough of his Neanderthal-like attitude. She leaned back in her seat and dropped her left hand down beside the chair; her fingers now millimetres from the knife strapped to her left calf, and she turned her attention to the taciturn Vampire.

"Lex Boy, are you always this cranky, or is it just a show you put on for pretty girls?" she asked him. Sticks and dragons, one day she was seriously going to regret poking a dragon. She felt Julius and Kyle both tense, waiting for Alexander's reaction.

He leaned forward in his seat, giving Gabi a venomous glare.

"My name is Alexander," he ground out in a clipped, aristocratic, British accent, "and I'm cranky because I'm hungry, and Julius won't let me snack on you!" he finished in a hard, sharp hiss, snapping his fully extended fangs at her aggressively. Fortunately their little alcove was completely private, and the hum of the other diners drowned out anything they said to each other.

"Alexander," Julius snapped warningly, but Gabi wasn't about to be cowed by an angel-faced bully, no matter how close he was to Julius. She leant slowly towards the angry Vampire, no hint of fear in her, keeping her eyes locked on his.

"I wish Julius had allowed you to try," she said in a deceptively calm, quiet voice. "That set of fangs would make a really nice necklace." She enunciated the last three words carefully, drawing them out. If a Vampire could spontaneously combust, then Alexander would probably have burst into flames on the spot, his expression threatened death by small increments. Gabi felt the swell of Julius's power; he was obviously worried that this was about to get out of control.

"Gabi," Kyle growled warningly just as the waitress appeared with their drinks and starters.

Gabi relaxed her stance and went back to innocently sipping her wine, as the waitress placed the platters of meats and cheeses in front of her and Kyle. The freshly made-up and newly perfumed waitress breathlessly asked for their mains orders, her disappointment obvious when Julius and Alexander declined, saying they'd already eaten. Gabi and Kyle made up for it by ordering huge rare steaks with all the trimmings. The interlude seemed to calm Alexander, or perhaps that was Julius's influence; either way, the obnoxious Vampire had lapsed back into a sullen silence. Gabi regretfully decided to leave the dragon alone for now.

"I apologise for Alexander's behaviour," Julius addressed Gabi, as though none of it was her fault for stirring up the angry Vampire, "he's somewhat annoyed with me for seeking out the assistance of your organisation. He feels it undermines my authority in the Clan. Makes me look weak," he explained. He pursed his lips and shot a sidelong glance at Alexander. "He has yet to understand the severity of what we're about to come up against. Alexander hasn't had much experience with Demons, so he's convinced we can deal with them on our own. He's forgotten that while Demons can only cross the Void at night, they are quite capable of moving around in sunlight if they escape detection for that long." He sounded like he was trying to drum the lecture into Alexander's head for the hundredth time.

As he said the last sentence a few more pieces of the puzzle clicked together in Gabi's head. She glanced surreptitiously at Kyle, wondering if he'd made the same connection. The Vampires needed the SMV's help because Danté had minions who were able to attack during daylight; this exposed Julius's Clan in the most dangerous way, they could be slaughtered without even being able to defend themselves. Kyle nodded minutely, acknowledging the connection; the request for an alliance was beginning to finally make sense. Julius leaned over to re-fill Gabi's glass before filling his own.

"You said in your message that you had some news for us from the Council. I trust that means you presented my case to them," he asked Gabi, watching as she shovelled the thinly sliced meat and cheese wedges into her mouth.

"Yes," Gabi answered between mouthfuls. "I met with the Council this morning. They've agreed to consider

147

your request for a meeting." She winced and shook her head slightly. "I know that sounds extremely bureaucratic, but at least they didn't dismiss the idea outright."

If Julius was disappointed he hid it well, his expression remained bland, even though Alexander snorted derisively.

"Alexander, perhaps it would be better if you waited for me in the car," Julius said in a deceptively mild voice, a muscle tightening in his jaw. Alexander finally seemed to realise he was pushing Julius a step too far.

"No, I'll restrain myself," he conceded, dropping his gaze from Julius and burying his nose in his drink. Julius took a deep breath watching Alexander for a long moment before addressing Gabi again.

"Did the Council give you a time frame of any kind?" he asked. "I understand the bureaucracy involved in any kind of Council, but we're running out of time. I think Danté is preparing some kind of assault as we speak."

"They want to try and verify some of the details you've given us; mostly the ones about the Dark Mage. They've sent an inquiry to the Magi High Council for any information they have on her. If they can establish that she is a dark mage, and that she is working with Danté, they'll meet with you."

Further conversation was stalled by the arrival of Kyle and Gabi's main course. The waitress fussed at the table for a while, hovering, until Gabi felt a slight brush of Julius's power and abruptly the girl seemed to realise that she had something else to do and scuttled off. Gabi raised a questioning eyebrow in Julius's direction. He smirked back at her, unrepentant, like a school boy caught cribbing on a minor test.

"She won't be back to bother us for a while," he said, as though that excused him.

148

A CAT'S CHANCE IN HELL

"Useful talent," Gabi remarked blandly, "what other tricks do you have up your sleeve?" She pretended she wasn't particularly interested in his reply as she gingerly slipped her right arm out of its sling to cut into her juicy chunk of red meat. Kyle and Julius simultaneously leant forward to offer assistance. She glared them both back into their seats, but ground her teeth as she used the injured arm to hold the meat in place with a fork and sliced off bite-sized chunks with her left hand. She caught Julius and Alexander both watching her with an odd intenseness as she devoured the succulent meat.

"What?" she demanded. "A girl has to eat." She was a tad sensitive about her enormous appetite, she knew it wasn't considered appropriate for a woman to eat like she did, and she often got incredulous stares when she ate in a restaurant.

Julius shook his head, and Alexander actually cracked a hint of a smile. "Sorry," Julius apologized quickly, "we're not passing judgement. It's just been too long since we actually watched a human eat. It brings back memories, makes us yearn for the variety of tastes." He got a distant look in his eyes.

"So, the legends got that bit right then," Gabi nudged, "you can't eat any human food?"

"Yes," Julius confirmed. "We can't digest solid food. We could eat it if we had to, but we would have to purge ourselves soon afterwards. It also doesn't taste palatable to us, so to appreciate to the taste of a good rare steak we have to taste it vicariously through your reactions. We can, obviously," he indicated their glasses "drink liquids, and as some of us get older we develop the ability to taste some of them like we did as humans; hence my appreciation of red wine and Alexander's inclination towards bourbon."

Gabi found herself enthralled, and even Kyle was paying close attention as Julius's discourse about the abilities and disabilities of being Vampire continued. The tension around the table gradually started to ease, and Alexander even added in the odd snippet of information. Julius confirmed that while breathing was not necessary, they still did it to both appear normal in human company, as well as to be able to smell their environment, a sense essential to a Vampire. Julius sent out a thread of power to summon the waitress back to clear the table and take dessert orders from Kyle and Gabi. Julius then turned the tables on her.

"Would you tell us something, now that we have been open with you?" he suddenly asked.

"I guess that depends on what you want to know," she said, suddenly wary.

"Your exceptional...." he paused searching for the right word, "abilities," he settled with, "are they Vampire in nature?"

"Why would you say Vampire?" she hedged.

He smiled but answered her. "Well, firstly the word on the street is that you are half Vampire, and secondly you have a very subtle but very definite Vampire scent."

Gabi concentrated on taking a large sip of her Irish coffee, contemplating her answer. He waited her out patiently. Finally she made up her mind.

"Yes, they are Vampire in nature," she said, only answering his direct question; she was going to make him work for his answers. His eyes narrowed and she thought he looked a trifle disturbed.

"But that's impossible, unless you are ingesting Vampire blood on a regular basis," he said slowly.

Gabi kept a calm face and looked directly into his eyes. "No, it's not impossible and no I'm not drinking Vampire blood," she said holding his gaze.

He'd gone dead still, he didn't even appear to be breathing.

Gabi flinched when Kyle's mobile suddenly vibrated. He glanced at the incoming number and immediately pushed away from the table to take the call. The others turned their attention to him, and as he listened to the voice on the other side of the call, his expression turned serious.

"Shit," he swore roundly. "When, where and how many?"

As he listened again Gabi knew instantly what was happening. She glanced at Julius. "Call the waitress. We need the cheque," she said tersely, looking regretfully at her bowl of chocolate mousse, knowing it was heading back to the kitchen.

"What's wrong?" Julius asked, instantly on full alert. The air was saturated with the scent of adrenaline by the time Kyle disconnected the call.

"I gotta go," he stated simply. Gabi grabbed his arm as he went to stand.

"How many?" she demanded.

"Too many," came his brusque reply. "Can you catch a cab home?"

"No chance. I'm coming with you," she declared.

"Don't be stupid," he responded curtly. "You're already injured; you'll only make things worse."

"I can see it on your face, they need every sword we've got. My perfect good health is not worth the life of innocents."

Kyle shook his head, realising he didn't have the time to get through to her. "OK. Fine. Whatever."

Julius spoke then, "You're talking about a Demon attack, aren't you?"

"Demon attacks," Kyle asserted, emphasising the plural. "At least three different locations, multiple

Demons. It's not going to be pretty. We have to go. Now." He stood drawing Gabi up with him.

"We're coming with you, give me co-ordinates and I'll call for reinforcements," Julius announced. "Alexander call Nathan, tell him to get a team together we'll call him with the details soon."

Kyle started to protest, but Gabi quickly stopped him.

"It makes sense; why not let them help if they're willing?" She looked at him challengingly. When he didn't argue further she turned to Julius. "You'll have to stick with us though; I can't guarantee the other teams will see you as allies instead of enemies."

He nodded, standing as Alexander pulled a phone from a pocket and began dialling. He drew a wad of notes from his pocket and slid them under an empty wine bottle. "Let's go. We'll follow you."

# CHAPTER 10

"We need more weapons," Gabi muttered darkly around a lollipop. "I have some extras in the trunk, but not enough."

They were in Gabi's car and Kyle was pushing the car like a racing driver. Julius and Alexander were right on the Mustang's tail, having no trouble keeping up, but then they were in an Aston Martin V12 Vantage. Master Vampire was obviously a very lucrative profession.

"The Clean-up Crew is bringing more from HQ," Kyle said. "I still don't think you should be fighting."

Gabi ignored him; it was pointless getting into an argument over it. "Where are we headed?"

"Central City Train Station."

"Shit! Keeping this one under wraps is going to be fucking impossible." She texted the location to Julius's phone as she spoke.

"Byron had a gas leak called in, he should be able to keep civilians clear for a couple of hours."

"How has he spread out the Hunters?"

"Matthew and I are covering the train station, Douglas has the old stadium and Lance is heading for another weak spot behind the City Cathedral."

She felt her eyebrows shoot up at the last one.

Kyle grinned wryly. "Go figure, huh?"

"I'll call Byron, tell him we have Vampire back-up and he can send Matthew to help Doug."

"Are you sure this is a good idea?" Kyle asked earnestly. "What if this is some kind of set-up by Julius, we could be playing directly into his hands."

"I can't tell you why, but I trust him. Alexander's behaviour certainly didn't suggest someone trying to charm us into letting down our guard, and I can't feel any deceit in their actions or emotions. If there is something more going on we'll figure it out after the Demons are dealt with."

Kyle finally caved, trusting Gabi's instincts. "OK. Call Byron, I think you're right, Doug will need the help at the Stadium."

Gabi dialled. It took her several minutes to convince him that she trusted the Vampires, and they would cope without Doug. She promised to stay out of the main fighting if she could, and hoped she could keep her word. As she ended the call Kyle pulled the Mustang into a parking space across the road from the train station. There were two vans pulled right up to the main entrance, both with Hazmat warning signs on them. Gabi had to smile, what didn't Byron have up his sleeve? The Clean-up Crew, dressed in Hazmat uniforms, were already evacuating the handful of late night travellers and pointing them in the direction of the nearest bus station.

Julius stopped in the space behind them and both Vampires were out the car in the blink of an eye. Gabi grimaced as she reached to pull open the centre console, she didn't really want an audience for this. She quickly pulled something out and slid it up her sleeve before throwing the lollipop stick into the console and getting out. Kyle opened the trunk and hefted out a large, black nylon bag.

"We'll gear up inside, out of sight," Kyle said. "Let's go."

Gabi hung back. "Go on, I'll be there in a second," she caught the keys Kyle tossed her way and turned back to the car, leaning inside and pretending to search for something. As Kyle hurried away she pulled the filled syringe out of her sleeve. It was her emergency stash of Morphine, and it had come in handy more than once. Good thing she couldn't get addicted to drugs, she knew it was easy to get hooked on Morphine if you were full human. She undid the button on her right sleeve and popped the lid off the needle, as she started to push up her sleeve a voice behind her said, "Can I help you with that?"

Gabi bit back a yelp, nearly banging her head on the door frame of the car as she spun to face Julius.

"Bloody hell," she swore, "I thought you went with the others."

"Obviously," he had a slightly smug expression on his face.

"I have another option for you," he said inscrutably. "That," he indicated the syringe with a nod, "will only dull the pain, making it easier to further injure yourself." He paused a moment as if weighing his next words. "If you take blood from me it will not only accelerate your healing, but make you stronger and faster, less destructible and more deadly." He fell silent, waiting for her response.

Gabi was stunned; her mind whirling with the possibilities and the implications. Then she realised there was no time to debate the issue. "Thanks for the offer," she said carefully, "uh, maybe next time." When she had

SHARON HANNAFORD

more time to find out the full extent of the side-effects of taking his blood, and to decide if she trusted him.

Julius simply nodded, "Then allow me to help at least," he said reaching for the syringe.

Her immediate reaction was to snatch it back and tell him she was quite capable of doing it herself, but then she realised she was going to be trying it left-handed, and she was bound to make a hash of it, so instead she pushed her sleeve up and offered him her arm. He took her arm gently and deftly slid the needle into her vein, she barely even felt the prick. After he drew the needle out, he rubbed the tiny pinprick of blood away with his thumb.

"The offer stands if you change your mind," he said with an uncharacteristic rough edge to his voice.

Gabi could've sworn his fangs seemed slightly longer than they had been a moment ago. She winced as she pulled off the black scarf she'd been using for a sling, and used it to tie up her hair. Then she flexed her shoulder a few times and inclined her head toward the station.

"Let's go kill some Demons," she said, tossing the empty syringe into the car and slamming the door.

"After you Angeli Morte," Julius intoned.

She threw him a withering look and took off in a sprint across the road.

The rest of the Crew were already gearing up in the main foyer. Civilians had been evacuated, trains had been diverted to other stations, and the usual emergency crews had been sent to the other side of the huge complex of buildings and told not to enter until the all clear was given by the Hazmat squad, i.e. SMV Crew in drag. Gabi introduced the two Vampires to the other members of the crew, giving them stern looks when they threw suspicious glances at the Vampires. Alexander and Julius both had their own long swords, but strapped on throwing knives and butterfly swords from the supply in one of the vans. Gabi and Kyle both added a Werewolf dart gun to their arsenal and Gabi grabbed a compact crossbow as well. She wasn't keen to go hand-to-hand with Demons tonight. She caught Alexander glancing at her out of the corner of his eye; he seemed amused by the sight of her kitting up.

Kyle and the Magi were discussing their options and making contingency plans when the rest of the Vampires arrived. A murmured ripple washed through the other crew members, fear and anxiety tainted the air around them as the five male Vampires came through the doors. The crew had rarely been this close to live Vampires before.

Gabi quickly stepped forward. "Hey, Nate," she called good naturedly to the burly Vampire. "Looks like you're gonna get your chance to make it up to me." She tossed him a short sword out of the pile, and he caught it easily by the hilt. She hoped her easy acceptance of their presence would help ease tension. "Gear up with whatever you're comfortable using and then we'll go over the plan of action. We don't want to be tripping over each other or letting any of these bastards escape."

Nathan nodded curtly at her and looked at Julius; waiting for his quick nod, before introducing the other four Vampires.

"Marcello," he indicated a slightly built, dark haired, dark eyed male with an easy smile, who gave Gabi an elegant bow as she recognised him as Stephan's accomplice in the bar charade. "Quentin's on the right." A tall, lanky male with shoulder length hair and a serious expression, inclined his head. "Charlie's the one in the stupid hat." A shorter male with broad shoulders, a Stetson and cowboy boots gave them a mock salute. "And Fergus," Nathan moved aside to expose a muscular male in combat trousers and a black vest. He was as muscular as Sly Stallone in his young days, but the first thing that struck all the onlookers was the terrible scar running across his face. It was an angry red line as thick as a pencil, and it slashed his face from his left temple, over his eye and down to the left corner of his mouth. It gave him a macabre and savage look, enough to frighten Freddy Kruger, Gabi thought absently; but as he stepped forward he cracked a huge incongruous smile and his voice boomed with a rough Scottish accent.

"Point me to them Demons! I been itching fer a good fight."

Gabi grinned viciously; something told her she and Fergus were going to get along just fine.

"Right, can someone give us an ETA on the Demons?" she called to the trio of Magi standing in a huddle to one side. Gabi recognised the two women from the fight two nights ago, and the third was a short, older male. It was the man who answered her.

"HQ says the Veil will be thinnest at just after eleven pm." The man paused and his eyes grew distant. Gabi started to ask another question, but one of the women held up her hand to cut her off. Gabi gave the woman a flat, unfriendly glare and received a wide-eyed, apologetic look in return.

"Sorry," the slim blonde whispered nervously, "but he's scanning. Neil should be able to pinpoint the location of the gateway."

So the group waited; most shifting impatiently, but the Vampires stood inhumanly still in a cluster near the entrance. Neil suddenly shook himself, a quiver running from his head to his feet, and blinked rapidly a few times.

"The gateway will open on the platforms, somewhere between platforms five and six," he announced.

"Ok," Gabi lifted her voice to get the attention of the whole group. She glanced at her watch. "It's five to eleven, so let's go over the plan of action quickly. There are only two exits from the platforms, clean-up crew split into two groups, one at each exit. You know the routine; whatever happens, do not tackle one. Magi, you come in with us, stay as close as you can to the fighting without endangering yourselves, banish only if there is no other choice." She then turned towards the Vampires, but addressed Julius. "Our usual method of attack is to wait until the Demons have exited and assess their strengths and weaknesses, we try to match up Hunters to Demons so that we don't trip over each other attacking the same one or letting one go unnoticed. If you finish off the one you've claimed you can help anyone else who looks like they need it." She looked askance at Julius, knowing instinctively that his Vampires weren't going to take orders from her, so he needed to decide whether he was onboard with them, or fighting his own fight.

"You are the Demon hunters, we are here to help," Julius turned his head slightly to look at his men, "and to learn. We'll follow your lead."

Some of the Vampires looked at each other, but no one said a word and their expressions were carefully neutral. Gabi was sceptical of their acquiescence but ploughed on anyway.

"It's better if we can double up two hunters to a Demon," she said raising her voice, though she probably didn't need to for the Vampires' benefit, "but we may be outnumbered if the last attack was anything to go by. We'll need to eliminate the most dangerous ones first if that's the case, and run down the others later. Demon blood corrodes anything it comes into contact with, including metal, and the best way to kill them is sword or knife to the heart, if you can find it. There was a particularly bad one at our last encounter, a Wraith-like creature I would recommend staying away from. The Magi will have to deal with that one, as it has no physical form to damage." She tried to suppress a small shudder at the thought of her encounter with it. She lifted the compact crossbow to her shoulder and gave them all a small nod. "The rest you'll have to learn the hard way. Let's go." With that she stalked off towards the platforms, Kyle next to her and the pack of Vampires moving on silent feet close behind. The rest of them scurried to get into their assigned positions.

Julius couldn't help but enjoy the view of Gabi's curvy backside as she strode down the corridor ahead of him. She may take charge like a man, appear to be tough and fearless like a man, but she was all woman when she moved. The minute trace of blood in the air when he injected her earlier had awoken a thirst in him. As he watched her become the ice cold, deadly Angeli Morte in front of his eyes, his thirst had ignited into a fierce desire.

The Hunters and the Vampires gathered half-way down platform four, having left the Magi clustered closely together on platform one. They were arrayed in a loose line, all looking closely at the area that Neil had indicated to them as the likely entrance point. Gabi took a moment to assess the new Vampires. She was relieved to see the hardened, anticipatory look of seasoned warriors like an aura around them. While most of them stood in alert stillness, Fergus was openly excited, a joyful, predatory gleam in his eye. Julius watched her appraisal of his warriors with a carefully blank expression.

"Ready?" she asked him.

He gave her a short nod.

"Good, 'cause here they come." She stepped back and loaded her crossbow as the familiar prickle of malicious energy washed over her. A thick, putrid smelling fog rose up from the ground under the train tracks and began to fill the large enclosed space. From the stinking fog, grotesque forms began emerging one by one. This time they didn't pause before attacking; as they emerged they launched themselves straight for the defenders. Gabi let the men charge in, standing back to try and assess the situation, trying to count heads, but gave that up as she realised two of the Demons had more than one head. She thought there were no more than seven Demons, so at least they weren't outnumbered, and she hoped like hell the portal had closed.

The Vampire group was fighting well as a team, though she could see, even in the dim lighting and hazy air, that Alexander and Marcello's faces reflected a mixture of shock and revulsion. She began scouting the area for flying Demons when she realised that a small group of troll-like Demons was using the cover of fog to try and leave the main fight and head towards the far exit.

"Kyle," she shouted into the din of clanging metal, and grunts and roars. She pointed at the retreating figures when he looked away from the huge, two-headed monster he was tangling with. She saw him nod briefly and then duck to avoid a blow from the Demon. She cursed; he had his hands full, after a moment of indecision she took off after the escaping Demons; a butterfly sword in her weak hand, and the crossbow resting on her other shoulder. Putting on a burst of speed she managed to get ahead of the misshapen group, planting herself firmly between them and the exit.

"Where do you think you fuckers are going then?" she challenged, lifting the crossbow into position. "We can't have you leaving the party yet." She casually shot a bolt directly into the single eye of the front Demon. It fell over backwards and clumsily took down the other two Demons behind it. She reloaded the crossbow and, as it started to rise, shot it in one of its large, leathery ears. It shook its head like a dog with a fly bugging it, and batted at the bolt, dislodging it. It lumbered to its feet and lunged blindly for Gabi. She leapt backward and drew the dart-gun, firing into the creature's ear again, now that she knew she could pierce the skin there.

The other two had got to their feet and were heading for the exit again. Annoyed, she shot another dart into big-ears and sprinted to intercept the escapees. Another presence materialised on her right, she knew without checking that it was Alexander, but she had no time to express her surprise as they leapt down onto the train tracks to face the Demons. As he stood shoulder to shoulder with her, sword at the ready, his eyes had a distinctly wild look to them, he had a burn mark down one cheek, and his fashionable leather jacket was in shreds down one arm. She didn't get a chance to comment, as the two Demons attacked without slowing.

Gabi danced back, pumping the last of the darts towards their faces, a few thudded into soft flesh. Alexander lunged in to slash at them, taking chunks out of their arms where armour didn't cover them, but that wasn't even slowing them down. Gabi growled, tossing the spent dart gun aside and drawing Nex with her left hand, awkward but doable she knew from past experience. Alexander yelled and flung himself backward as a huge war club suddenly hurtled towards his head. He landed heavily on the metal tracks and was forced to twist out of the way as the club smashed into the ground where his body had been an instant before. Gabi spared a glance his way as she whirled and ducked in front of the other Demon and realised that his sword had begun to disintegrate. She spun around, and flung the sword in her right hand towards Alex, yelling "Heads up," as she did so. She gritted her teeth against the pain flaring in her shoulder and ribs, but was relieved to see Alex catch the sword as he leapt to his feet. "Hamstrings," she yelled at him as she neatly avoided the Demon's wild swing at her with its battle axe. She quickly side-stepped the Demon, darted forward a step and spun again, drawing Nex viciously across the unprotected tendons at the back of the Demon's legs. The monstrosity swung around wildly, trying to find her, but as it took a step forward it crashed to the ground in a pile of hairy, leathery limbs. Alexander's one collapsed almost on top of the first, but they both started flailing around and trying to drag themselves towards the exit.

Suddenly the air was full of Vampires as Fergus and Julius arrived in a whoosh of swirling mist. It only took them seconds to finish off the two hamstrung Demons, and they all stepped back to watch the bodies turn to black goo. Gabi leapt onto the nearest platform and started back towards the main fight, pausing for a half-second to make sure the first Demon was a black puddle, the Vampires half a step behind her.

A sharp grunt of pain suddenly emanated from the fog around the main fight. Gabi recognised it instantly. She sprinted forward, searching the mist and shouting, "Kyle, Kyle, where the hell are you?"

She could see Charles in his Stetson still battling with a lizard creature, but holding his own, and Nathan and the tall Vampire tag-teaming a two headed freak with rotting flesh hanging off its humanoid arms. She suppressed a shudder as she ran.

"He's over there," Julius called out, and she looked to see where he was pointing. A large trollish creature with four arms was silhouetted in the dissipating mist; it was lifting two of its four arms over its head with a large mace grasped in them. The dark shape crumpled at its feet had to be Kyle.

"NO!" Gabi shrieked and lunged towards them.

Julius and Fergus beat her there, Fergus throwing his mighty long sword in the path of the descending mace, and Julius grabbing Kyle's limp body and dragging him out of the way, depositing him on the platform at Gabi's feet before heading back to help Fergus finish off the Demon.

Gabi automatically crouched over Kyle's body protectively, while surveying the area for other danger. It was then that she noticed the Wraith. She knew deep in her gut that it was the same one she'd encountered two nights before. It was some distance away still, as though it were merely a spectator to the battle, but suddenly seemed to notice her huddled over Kyle, and began moving towards them.

"Holy fucking hell, what next?" she cursed looking around quickly to see who was nearby. "Alex, Julius!" she yelled hoarsely. "Get to the Magi, bring them here to deal with that," she spat tossing her head towards the Wraith that was slowly, but inexorably, floating in their direction. She dragged her attention back to Kyle, trusting Julius to follow her orders. She knew Kyle was still alive, she could hear his heart beating, but his pulse rate was erratic and his breathing uneven. She quickly ran her hands over him, checking for injuries, noticing Fergus unobtrusively standing guard over them from the corner of her eye. She soon found the cause of Kyle's insensible state. A lump the size of a coconut on the side of his head, the thin skin of his scalp split open and blood pouring into his hair. As she grabbed a piece of linen from one of her pockets to press to the open wound he groaned and opened his eyes.

"Idiot!" Gabi cursed him instantly. "No more four-armed Demons for you, they get you every bloody time."

"Whaa?" Kyle said blearily, unsuccessfully trying to make his eyes focus on her face.

Gabi sighed. "The fight's not over. I'm going to put you here out the way." She'd spotted a thick pillar a few feet away. "Stay there until we come and get you."

Between Gabi and Fergus they managed to get Kyle sitting upright against the pillar, holding the cloth to his head, as the Magi rushed into view. The Magi were already chanting as they neared the scene.

The Wraith, who had been slowly bearing down on the trio, suddenly stopped and turned its burning yellow gaze on the Magi. Six Vampires suddenly materialised out of the darkness, forming a guard around the Magi. Gabi realised that all the other Demons had been destroyed; only the Wraith remained. The ghostly thing swept its robed arms upward and pointed towards the two groups. Suddenly the air seemed to grow heavy and putrid; breathing became an effort and moving an impossibility. The Magi's chanting grew louder and Neil stepped forward out of the protection of the Vampires and made a throwing and covering motion with his hands towards the Wraith. The Wraith abruptly stopped its forward motion, and the cloying thickness in the air disappeared as suddenly as it had arrived. Everyone, Vampires included, drew in a deep relieved breath. Gabi looked at Neil in amazement; the Magi had somehow managed to magically contain the Wraith while the two women worked the Banishment spell. Thank all the Gods of Olympus for the occasional miracle, she thought.

The Wraith was standing frozen, surrounded by a pale blue, glimmering veil. Neil was sweating profusely, the strain of keeping the containment intact clear on his

165

reddened face. Trinity and Bianca were furiously mouthing words in synchronisation, building the spell as fast as they could. The Wraith's glowing eyes seemed to bore straight into Gabi's as she watched the scene, mentally willing extra strength to the three Magi. Suddenly a hollow, inhuman voice echoed around them, rebounding off the walls of the train station.

"The human who isss not human, and the wolf who isss not wolf." The voice had to be coming from the Wraith, it sounded like the dry rustling of autumn leaves and hungry crackle of a log fire. "The Dark One wasss right," the omnipresent voice continued, "we should have killed you both inssstead of toying with you," it rasped, then focused its attention directly on Gabi. "My new Massster underessstimated you, didn't believe the Dark One. You thwarted hisss little attempt at asssassination. It was a pity I was under different orderss at our last meeting; perhapsss next time he'll let me have you insstead of trussting hisss other petss to do the job."

The glowing orbs then moved within the cowl to fasten on Julius as he stood holding what was left of his long sword. "Ah, The Baron," it said with apparent satisfaction. "I am pleased to sssee you here; you have sssaved me the trouble of hunting you down to deliver the messsage from my Massster. Though your alliance with the human and the wolf meansss I now have to accept the Dark One'ss predictionsss asss true, and that irkss me."

All other sounds had ceased; everyone's attention was on the Wraith. "Danté iss prepared to negotiate the termss of your sssurrender. Of course, he cannot let *you* live, but he iss willing to ssspare sssome of your Clan if you sssurrender now. If you continue to defy him we will dessstroy every lasssst member of your family. I persssonally would prefer it if you didn't sssurrender, but that isss your decision. I will return sssoon for your anssswer." The thing's last words had become an almost inaudible hiss as the voices of the two chanting Magi rose in a rhythmic crescendo, growing louder and stronger, and Gabi could feel the air grow heavy with the Magi's power.

A sharp female voice suddenly rang out, "Now, Neil!" The shimmering cocoon around the Wraith suddenly disappeared, and the stout male Magus fell to his knees. A shockwave of power burst from the two female Magi and the Wraith shrieked briefly before it disappeared in a flash of blue light. Everyone standing staggered as the force of the Magic hit them on the rebound. A few lost their balance and Kyle, who had been unwisely trying to stand up, collapsed back onto the cold cement.

The ensuing silence was deafening. Gabi had never thought to see Vampires look shell-shocked, but as she looked around trying to figure out exactly what had just gone down, most of the blood-suckers gathered near Julius definitely looked stunned. She ran back to Kyle, putting a hand on his chest to stop him getting up.

"Whoa there Wolf Boy, let the world stop spinning before you try and move. Julius," she yelled sharply trying to snap him out of his apparent daze. "Send someone for the medics, and tell the clean-up crew they can get started." Julius blinked and seemed to realise they were all standing around looking like idiots.

"Yes, of course," he answered snapping to attention. He turned back to his men, but before he could speak Alexander and Marcello took off for the closest exit. Gabi snorted, well would wonders never cease, Alexander doing something without a direct order from Julius; Gabi guessed their meeting with the Demon horde had been a bit of an eye-opener for the stubborn English blood sucker.

Soon the area was awash with people and Vampires, cleaning up, bandaging, collecting damaged weapons and bits of shrapnel. Kyle was declared concussed, and Gabi wearily accepted the responsibility of watching him for the next twelve hours. The bloody wound on his head was already starting to heal, the blood flow had all but stopped, and the medic taped a clean compress over it.

As she sat with him, Gabi surreptitiously took the scarf out of her hair and re-made it into a sling for her arm. She caught Julius glancing her way as she did it, he still looked unnerved, an expression that didn't sit well on his normally confident face. She wondered if it was the message from the Wraith that had him so off balance. She got up, pulling Kyle with her, and waiting until he stopped swaying and his eyes managed to focus on her. She pulled his arm around her shoulders, making sure she had a good grip on him with her left arm, and together they staggered over to the Vampires.

"We can get outta here now," she told Julius, "the crew will clean up and re-open the station." She suddenly felt a hundred years old. Then the big, scarred Scotsman came forward and put a huge, muscular arm under Kyle's other armpit.

"Aye Lassie, ye look about beat. Let me help the Wolf before ye both fall over," he said in his loud Scottish brogue, taking all of Kyle's weight without straining in the slightest. "That was a good fight, that was. I havna had such fun in many a year. We'll havta hang with your crowd more often," he said with a huge fang-filled grin. The Scottish Vampire was clearly totally unaffected by the shell-shock cocooning Julius and the others. Gabi gave Kyle over to Fergus with a grateful sigh; Kyle was so out of it he didn't appear to notice that she'd abandoned him to a Vampire. As she started trudging toward the exit she felt a cool, solid hand slip under her left elbow, and she knew without looking that Julius was beside her. She didn't have the energy to shake him off, and, having heard the words from the Wraith, she now knew for certain that everything Julius had told her was absolute truth.

The unlikely assortment of Hunters and Vampires spilled out onto the road and headed towards their respective vehicles. The extra Vampires had arrived in two identical vehicles, some kind of Range Rover 4x4, Gabi was too tired to bother identifying further. Julius barked out a couple of orders to Nathan's group and Alexander took over holding Kyle upright. The others each nodded a respectful goodbye to Julius and Gabi, and quickly climbed into their vehicles, speeding off as the sounds of multiple sirens approached the scene.

"Let's go before the cops get here," Gabi prodded, pulling away from Julius and starting across the road to their cars. Julius caught up to her silently, leaving Alexander to haul Kyle across the road.

"Neither of you is in a state to drive," Julius said quietly, "would you let us drive you home, or maybe somewhere that other friends could collect you from, if you don't feel comfortable with that?"

He was being polite, but he still had a strange distance in his expression. Gabi would've loved to tell him that she was perfectly capable of getting them both home, but truly she wanted to discuss the message from the Wraith with him, she quickly came to a decision.

"Let's go to my place," she said. "I'm sure you know where I live anyway." A slight grin lifted one side of his mouth, and he had the decency to look moderately guilty. She sighed and rolled her eyes, surprisingly happy to see a glimpse of his usual character.

"Alexander," he ordered, tossing the other Vampire a set of keys, "you take Wolf in my car and follow us, we're going to Gabrielle's house." He caught the set of keys Gabi threw at him, but walked around to the passenger side to open the door for her first.

She raised an eyebrow. "A Vampire with manners, what will life throw at me next?" she muttered sardonically, and climbed in, collapsing into the comfortable bucket seat gratefully.

An instant later he was in the driver's seat and bringing the Mustang to roaring life.

# CHAPTER 11

As Julius navigated the dark roads in the Mustang, Gabi pulled out her phone and called Byron.

"Gabi!" Byron's voice was full of relief. "What's happening on your side? Are you alright? Do you need any help?"

Gabi smiled despite her exhaustion. "Calm down, you'll give yourself a heart attack one of these days," she teased him. "The fight is over, we got every last one of them. I'm fine; Kyle has a concussion, but he's conscious. We're heading home now, and the clean-up team will probably call you in a few minutes to re-open the station."

"What happened with the Vampires?"

"Well, that's a longer story. The short version is that without them we'd have been in deep, deep shit. Julius is driving me home now."

"Gabi," Byron said, concern darkening his voice. "Are you sure that's wise?"

She sighed. "It's not like he doesn't already know where I live," she shot Julius a sidelong glare. "We have a lot to discuss. Something happened at the train station, and I now have no doubts that Julius is telling us the truth about the war with Danté. You'll have to call another Council session; you have to meet with Julius." There was a moment's pause on the other side of the phone, then with a sigh he relented.

"Alright, Honey. I trust your instincts. I'll call them first thing in the morning and arrange it," Byron agreed.

Gabi was quiet on the other side.

"Gabrielle?" Byron's voice called softly. "Are you sure you're alright?"

Gabi bit her lip, and then decided to lay it out for Byron. "There's a war coming ByBy," she said tiredly, unconsciously using the nickname she'd given him as a little girl, "and it's not going to be pretty."

"Don't you worry about that, Sweetheart," a protective steeliness entered Byron's voice. "We have a lot of allies and plenty of resources. We'll find a way to protect our city and our loved ones. Now get yourself home, eat something and get some rest. We'll tackle this all in the morning."

Gabi managed a weak smile. "Yeah, ok Daddy Fusspants."

"Call me if you need anything."

"I will." She ended the call and tossed the phone onto the dashboard.

"That was your contact in the Council?" Julius asked, smoothly guiding the car around slower vehicles on the highway. He was speeding, but not pushing the car to its limits. The calm had returned to his face, though there was still a hint of tension to the set of his jaw.

"Uh huh," she answered, pulling a chocolate bar out of the glove compartment.

Julius flicked a glance her way, watching her devour the sweet. She studied him in return, wondering if he'd shaken off the shock yet. His eyes had returned to their normal exquisite gilded sapphire and she found herself caught in their astounding depths.

"He's more than just an acquaintance then?" He pushed for more information.

Gabi blinked, dragging herself back to reality. She forced her brain to concentrate on his question instead of his effect on her. She pursed her lips speculatively, gathering her addled thoughts. "I answer yours, then you answer mine," she finally challenged.

"Fair enough," he conceded after a moment's consideration.

"Byron was my father's best friend," she began, watching closely for Julius's reaction to what she'd just disclosed. "He was a member of parliament in his younger days, and he still consults for the City Council. His parents are both Magi, and he is one of the founders of the SMV."

Julius's eyebrows rose abruptly, in what appeared to be astonishment. "So he is the famous Byron Reeves? The man you regularly accompany to social events in the City?" he asked, genuinely surprised.

Gabi grinned archly. "You mean you really didn't know? Our all powerful Master Vampire had no idea who ran the Malus Venatori?"

"That information is an exceptionally well kept secret," he conceded.

"Yeah, and it needs to stay that way," Gabi's tone suddenly changed to one of warning.

Julius nodded. "I will keep the secret, I promise," he vowed, looking steadily into her eyes as he said it.

"Uh, the road?" Gabi said pointedly, not sure she would be able to drag her gaze away from his again. They were travelling at high speed on a dark highway and Julius didn't seem too concerned with keeping his eyes on the tar in front of them. "You crash my car and I'll be forced to hunt you down and kill you." She hoped the threat didn't sound as hollow as it felt.

"Don't worry. Modern men may have a problem doing two things at once, but those of us who've been around a while do eventually learn to multi-task," he replied dryly, finally blinking and switching his gaze back to the road. "Nice car, by the way. It suits you."

Gabi decided to ignore that comment and avoid the dangerous places it could take the conversation.

"My turn now," she said. She was silent for a moment while she went through the hundreds of questions that she had stored up to ask him.

Julius waited patiently, still paying more attention to her than the road.

"Why did you seem so shocked at the train station?" she finally asked.

He glanced at her looked slightly confused.

"After the Wraith said its piece," she clarified.

"Ah," he said, understanding. He looked back at the road, as they turned off the highway and began to navigate through street lit suburbia. His face became a tightly controlled mask; as though he was straining to erase any trace of emotion from his expression. "I guess it was that the truth of situation had finally become reality. What I told you the other night was the truth, but I don't think that I had actually accepted it."

The mask started to slip, and frustration and anger tightened the muscles of his jaw, narrowed his eyes, and etched his cheek bones even more prominently across his face.

"I was holding out the hope that some sanity remained somewhere in Danté's mind, and that he would come to his senses. That he would make some threats, and throw his weight around but back off once he was faced with a

174

strong challenge. That was the main reason for the unity between us and you; a show of force. It was meant to make him back down."

"And now?" she prompted.

Julius's pale hands clenched the steering wheel so hard Gabi wondered if he was leaving permanent finger impressions in it.

"Now, I know that he will not back down for anything," he said with savage certainty. "What he's put in motion is impossible to stop. He has gone further than I ever thought him capable of. He has become truly evil." Julius paused for a moment, calming himself before continuing. "I think that's what shocked me the most; that someone I once trusted with my life, someone I thought I knew inside and out, can have become such a mindless, power-hungry monster." He turned to look at her again, his eyes flashing, now dark and angry; the colour of deepest ocean on a moonless night. "The plan has changed. I no longer need help from the Society. You can call Byron back and cancel the meeting"

"What?" she exclaimed in bewilderment. "You were there when the Wraith threatened to take us all out. You've just acknowledged that the threat is worse than you expected. How can you now decide you don't need our help?" She was utterly confused.

"Yes, I *was* there when the Wraith threatened your and Kyle's lives," he growled, his voice low and dangerous. "The creature made it clear that you were targets, and you would be taken out. I want you to pack up and leave the City until we can take care of Danté."

"You're insane!" she almost shouted, irritation replacing confusion in an instant. "You need every ounce of help you can get. And, Hunters do not run from a fight, especially one that threatens the whole city and all its citizens!"

"Gabrielle," he said, now in a frustratingly reasonable tone. "This is not your fight. I'm sorry I got you involved, it was never meant to go this far. I don't need your death on my conscience. I brought this here; I will deal with the consequences."

Gabi snorted derisively. "You underestimate us. This is our city and we will not go down without a fight. I can't speak for every member of the SMV, but I'm not leaving. So deal with it!"

Julius let his head roll back onto the headrest, closing his eyes and exhaling deeply. "You don't understand," he growled, all pretence of calm reasoning gone again.

"Then explain it," she challenged furiously.

He opened his eyes and took a deep breath, still not looking directly at her. "There is another reason I looked shocked, though I think perhaps you misread anxiety for shock," he continued quickly before she could interrupt. "I have very occasional flashes of clairvoyance, and before you ask, no, I don't know why. While listening to the Wraith I had a very clear vision." He paused, steering the car into her driveway and bringing it to a sharp halt outside her front door, then he turned to look at her with a brutal, almost tortured look on his face. "It was a vision of you lying dead at my feet, my hands covered in your blood."

They were still arguing when Alexander came into the house a few minutes later, half supporting Kyle.

"It was probably a vision put there by the Wraith to get exactly this reaction," Gabi growled in exasperation.

"The Wraith was contained by magic; it wouldn't have been able to project a vision."

"How do you know? It was obviously able to project its voice, why not a vision?"

"I know my own visions when I get them," he threw back, his voice rising savagely. "You need to get out of the City and stay away from this fight."

"The future is not set in stone. If it was a genuine clairvoyant vision then we've had fair warning, and we'll know to be more careful. I'm. Not. Leaving."

"Hey, guys," Kyle groaned. "Can you keep it down? Man with a titanic headache over here!"

Gabi stamped over to the fridge and hauled an ice pack out, wrapping it in a clean tea towel.

Julius followed her into the kitchen. "And what did the Wraith mean when it spoke about your last encounter? Did you fight that thing?" he asked, horror tingeing his voice.

"How am I supposed to know what it was talking about?" she grumbled defensively. "It was at the Old Stadium a few nights ago when we fought off a whole horde of those things, the Magi took care of it that night too." She stalked out of the kitchen back to Kyle. She pushed him down on the brand new couch and pressed the ice pack to his head.

"Hold this while I put on the coffee," she ordered almost tripping over Julius on her way back to the kitchen. He reached out quickly to steady her, strong, cool hands on her waist. It was in that moment that Razor made his appearance, and all hell broke loose.

It took Gabi several minutes to calm Razor down, even once she got him into her bedroom and closed the door. With all his hair standing on end he looked massive, taking on the proportions of a snow leopard. He'd still been hissing and spitting when Gabi hauled him in and shut the door. Once he had finally allowed Gabi to soothe him back to normal size and even managed to give her a few apologetic head butts, she left him on the bed and quickly slipped from the room, closing the door securely behind her.

Back in the lounge Kyle and Alexander were mercilessly teasing Julius about the attack.

"You better hope those heal before we get back to the Estate," Alexander snickered devilishly. "I would hate to have to explain that a pet cat did that to you."

"That," she heard Julius's voice rumble in reply, "was no pet cat. That, was a bloody rabid tiger!"

Gabi rushed guiltily back into the kitchen, grabbed another clean tea towel from a drawer and ran cold water onto it before heading into the lounge. She walked over to Julius, who seemed to have regained his composure and was sitting in an armchair inspecting his arms and hands for damage. She cautiously pressed the damp cloth to the deep scratches gouged down the left side of his face, half expecting him to pull away from her, but he sat dead still, allowing her to wipe the blood away.

"I'm sorry," she started to babble; "he's not normally quite that vicious towards guests. Apparently he felt you were some kind of," she trailed off, embarrassed.

"Some kind of what?" Julius prompted her, curiosity overpowering annoyance.

"Wow, these are healing already," she exclaimed as she finished cleaning the blood away from his face. She reached for his arm, going down on her haunches and peeling away the ripped pieces of his sleeve to examine the damage. The undamaged skin on his arm was smooth and hairless. Though it was pale, it wasn't unhealthy looking or ashen as she had expected, but seemed to radiate with a faint pearlescence.

"Vampire healing. Definitely one of the best benefits of undeadhood," Alexander commented wryly, snapping her out of her scrutiny of Julius's unusual skin.

She hoped they hadn't noticed her lapse. She mopped up the worst of the blood from the wounds, trying not to take any more time than was absolutely necessary, before moving to the other arm. She didn't need to move the remains of his shirt sleeve from that one, most of the sleeve was missing up to the elbow.

"Oooh, that's a nasty bite," Gabi said, grimacing as she saw one particularly vicious wound, flesh and muscle torn and exposed, reminding her of the stitched wound on her own shoulder.

"Just what that cat needed, a dose of Vampire blood," Alexander lamented sarcastically. "Like it's not enough of a terror without the addition of vampire speed and strength." The English Vampire was clearly enjoying the uncomfortable situation.

"Do you really think it will affect him?" Gabi asked worriedly, as she carefully began cleaning the blood from the wound. She suddenly realised that his blood had a very unusual scent; not like a human's but closer to human than animal or Were, it actually smelled vaguely appealing to her, she hoped that was just the exhaustion talking.

"No, it shouldn't affect the cat," Julius growled, glaring warningly at Alexander. Then his attention shifted back to Gabi. "You still haven't explained why you think the cat attacked me."

Gabi squirmed uncomfortably as she wiped the last of the blood away from his lacerated arm, amazed that the lacerations had stopped bleeding already.

"He thought you were some kind of," she broke off again trying to find the right word, "suitor, I guess. Potential… mate," she caught herself just before she used the word lover, but she could feel the blush spreading across her cheeks anyway. "He appears to think I belong to him, and him alone. He saw you as the

179

competition, and reacted like the idiotic alpha male that he is."

All three of the males in the room were deadly silently for a moment and then Alexander suddenly collapsed back into the couch roaring with laughter. Abruptly Kyle was laughing too. As Gabi glanced up at Julius, she realised by the twinkle of mirth in his eye, that even he was amused by her embarrassment. She quickly stood up, whirling around and stomping off to the kitchen again. She brusquely turned on the coffee maker, throwing the bloodied towel into the sink to soak; if Rose came in and saw all the blood on the towel, she'd have kittens thinking it was Gabi's.

She became aware of Julius's presence a millisecond before she bumped into him on her way to the fridge. Her irritation vanished as soon as she looked up and saw the healing, but still vicious, slash marks on his face.

"I really am sorry," she started to apologise again.

He raised a hand to cut her off. "It's fine," he said soothingly, "really. As you can see, I heal fast. You couldn't know he'd react that way toward me."

"Thank you for not hurting him," she said softly, busying herself with mugs and teaspoons. She knew that Julius could have broken Raz's neck in an instant, but as soon as he understood it wasn't a Demon, he'd simply defended himself against the cat's attack until Gabi could get him under control.

Julius smiled slightly, his features softening and a slight dimple carving the lean lines of the undamaged side of his face as he leaned back against the kitchen counter to watch her prepare the coffee.

Gabi's heart suddenly did a strange little double beat.

"I wouldn't want to find myself on the business end of Nex, and somehow, I imagine hurting one of your pets would put me there pretty quickly."

Gabi snorted a little laugh. "Yeah, probably. Coffee?" she asked as she reached up for the mugs. She grimaced as she automatically tried to use her right arm and switched surreptitiously to using the left one. She'd slipped off the sling sometime during Razor's spectacular entrance.

"No. Thank you," he answered. "It's not one of the tastes that have returned to either of us."

He seemed a tad morose about that, and she glanced at him curiously. The sight of him; tall, powerful and sinfully attractive, lounging so casually against her kitchen cabinet, was playing utter havoc with her ability to form coherent thoughts.

She shook herself slightly, dragging her eyes away from the liquid marble ripple of his chest, just visible through the shreds of his shirt, and trying to focus on the conversation.

"There are a couple of bottles of red in that cupboard," she indicated one behind him, "but I'm afraid I don't keep a stock of Bourbon, so Alex is outta luck."

"Serves him right for having such extravagant tastes," Julius said, reaching into the cupboard for a bottle and a glass.

Gabi finished stirring two coffees and pulled out a small tray placing the mugs and a packet of choc-chip cookies on it. Before she could attempt to pick it up Julius moved in, settling his glass of wine on it and whipping it away from her with a graceful flourish. Gabi pulled a face at him, but didn't comment. She didn't trust her voice not to betray how much his close proximity was affecting her.

Julius suddenly stiffened as Kyle called out from the lounge, "Watch out. Incoming."

Gabi instantly scooted in front of Julius, wondering how Razor had escaped from her bedroom, but instead of a large, angry fluff ball charging through, a small masked face poked itself around the corner. Gabi heaved a sigh. "Don't worry, it's only Slinky. He's not dominant."

Julius didn't relax his stance immediately, eyeballing the small creature warily. But, true to form, the little critter scampered in, gave Julius a cursory once-over at shoe level, and went to see what was in his food bowl. Julius visibly relaxed and followed Gabi back to the lounge.

After coffee and biscuits she got Kyle settled into the spare bedroom, leaving the door open so she could hear if he needed her. She knew the drill for concussion. Check on him regularly and wake him up every couple of hours to make sure he knew his own name. She sighed; it was going to be a long night, or morning, as was now the case.

The two Vampires had been having a low conversation while she was seeing to Kyle, it was too low even for her to pick out many of the words. She'd only picked up the odd one spoken with more vehemence by Julius. They were words like 'safety', 'responsibility', 'madness' and 'killed'. She heard the conversation break off as she walked out of the spare room, and by the time she walked back into the lounge they were both pretending to be intrigued with her collection of coffee table books and photographs.

Julius was standing near the fireplace, studying a framed black and white photo of Gabi lying in long grass under a tree with her head on the belly of a lioness while two cubs playfully gambolled about on top of her. It was one of her very favourite photos, and she found it very unsettling to have him looking at it. She thought again about how she liked having her own private space that no one, except for a privileged few, ever dared to invade. She found herself wanting to yank the photo out of his hands and throw the pair of Vampires out the door. But, before her instincts could overpower her, he carefully set the picture back on the mantle and turned to her, his face tense but resigned. The skin on his face was perfect again; all traces of Razor's attack had completely healed. She suddenly became aware of the throbbing in her shoulder and the aching in her ribs and she was abruptly envious, thinking how much easier life would be if she healed as fast.

Julius's eyes narrowed then and his expression became hooded, unreadable. "It's time we left you to get some sleep," he stated shortly.

Gabi raised one eyebrow. "As much as I would love to agree with you," she said "we still have a few things to discuss."

Alexander looked up from the book on African landscapes with an evil twinkle in his eye. "Didn't really think you were going to get away that easily did you?" he asked Julius, grinning.

Julius threw a narrow-eyed warning glare at the other Vampire. "She is exhausted and in pain. We can discuss things tomorrow."

"Yeah, right. And give you enough time to come up with a way to keep us out of the fight. No chance! We're discussing this now. As you just noted I'm tired and sore, that makes me decidedly irritable, so sit down before I'm forced to let Raz out again!"

"You'd dare to set that cat on me again?" he demanded, outraged. That did it, her fuse had been lit – and it was never a very long fuse.

"You dared to set your Vampires on me, and you heal a shitload quicker than I do, so I think I still owe you," she responded angrily, through gritted teeth, trying to keep her voice down for Kyle's sake.

Alexander watched the sparks fly for a moment then stood up to get in between them, still grinning. "She's got you there, mate," he told Julius in mock seriousness. "I should actually hold you down and let the cat get a bigger piece of you."

He turned to Gabi. "You want me to hold him down? Or you do you want to do the holding and I'll let the cat out?"

Gabi stomped over to her favourite overstuffed chair, that had miraculously escaped the worst of Razor's wrath, and plonked down, wincing in pain at the over-zealous move. She grumbled something that sounded like "Tempt me" but the worst of the tension drained from the air.

Julius gave up glaring at Alex, and strode off to the kitchen, coming back with the open bottle of wine, a glass of water and a bottle of painkillers. He put them on the table within Gabi's reach. She sat forward, quickly swallowing a couple of pills down with the water. Julius poured wine into his empty glass, and was about to take it from the table when Gabi reached out and snatched the glass from his fingertips. She took a deep swallow, and sat back sighing and then found Julius looking at her in utter consternation. She raised one eyebrow at him archly, mischief replacing anger in her emerald eyes.

"You know where the glasses are. Get yourself another one!"

When the Vampires left an hour later, Julius was still opposed to the SMV becoming involved in the war, but had accepted that their help and knowledge could an invaluable asset to him. Gabi had agreed to call them as soon as a time and place for the meeting with the Council had been arranged. After they'd gone, she secured the house, let Razor out of her room and took a long, hot shower. She checked on Kyle again, and set an alarm for two hours time; setting it far out of reach so she'd be forced out of bed to turn it off, she knew her own tendency to slam the mute button and go straight back to sleep.  Then she crawled into bed and embraced the temporary oblivion of sleep.

# CHAPTER 12

The phone buzzed annoyingly. Gabi cracked one eye-lid and groaned; she felt like she hadn't slept in a week. The morning sun was filtering through the cracks in her curtains, and she could hear Rose humming to herself somewhere in the house, that meant it was already after eight thirty. She could also hear the rush of water from the shower in the spare bathroom; Kyle must be up and about. Trust him to be awake and chipper after the night they'd just had. The buzzing sounded again. Sighing, Gabi picked it up to see who was calling. 'Byron' the caller ID flashed. She immediately hit the answer button.

"Hey," she greeted him groggily.

"Morning Sunshine," he teased her gently, "Rose will be in in a moment with coffee. I called her before I woke you. I hate waking you after the night you've had, but I knew you would want the news as soon as possible."

Gabi sat up in bed, tumbling Razor off to one side and making him grumble at her before yawning hugely and beginning his morning grooming. Before she could ask

Byron what the news was, Rose tapped at the door and entered carrying a huge, steaming mug of coffee.

Gabi grinned at her gratefully. "Rose, you are an angel. Thanks," she whispered, tucking the phone between her left shoulder and ear to take the giant mug with both hands and breathe in the heavenly scent of Ethiopian Special Blend.

Rose gave her a fond but slightly worried smile. "Breakfast will be ready in twenty minutes," she said sternly, bustling out the room with Gabi's laundry basket under one arm.

Gabi focused her attention back on what Byron was telling her as she sipped the hot coffee.

"The council has agreed to the meeting with Julius," Byron said. "In fact we're quite anxious to meet with him. The Mage High Council came back very promptly with some disturbing news about the dark mage, Mariska. They've been trying to track her down for some time now, and having spoken to the Mages who were present with you last night, they are extremely concerned about the alliances she's made in the Demon world. They're taking this every bit as seriously as Julius seems to be." Byron paused to take a breath. "We're mobilising everyone, and calling in favours from other cities, we may need to fast track a couple of the Hunter trainees. I've convinced the rest that if we can have a strong Vampire Clan working with us as well, it may make all the difference to how quickly we can eradicate this threat."

"And to how many casualties we'll have," Gabi noted quietly, a small shiver going through her, as she suddenly thought about Julius's vision. She shook off the dark, disturbing thought and put down the mug to get out of bed and throw on a robe.

"Where and when?" she asked Byron. "I need to let Julius know." She took down the details of the location for the meeting and said goodbye to Byron. Then she steeled herself for another long day, so much for Sunday being a day of rest.

Gabi dressed in comfy jeans and a rude t-shirt, pointedly ignoring the sling lying on her dresser, her collarbone was stiff and uncomfortable but not terribly painful today, then she headed for her office. She wanted to make the call to Julius before she went for breakfast, even though the delicious smell of fresh pancakes was an almost physical pull to the kitchen. She powered up her computer as she put the call through to Julius. Kyle appeared in the doorway wearing only a pair of jeans and looking sickeningly healthy. His damp, dark blond hair was standing in spiky disarray and there was no sign of the deep gash in his scalp. She waved him in and turned on the speakerphone just as Julius answered in his distinctive, velvet voice.

"Gabrielle?" His voice was almost a purr, but Gabi thought she could detect a faint trace of weariness in it. Did vampires get tired, she wondered idly?

"Morning Jules," she drawled, only just suppressing a yawn. She heard him snort softly.

"Is Kyle alright this morning?" he asked, surprising both her and Kyle.

She sighed. "Yes, he's as healthy as a proverbial horse. He's just walked into my office, so I can give you both the news and save repeating myself later." Julius stayed silent, so she went on. "Byron called me this morning to say the meeting has been arranged."

Kyle glared at her warningly when she used Byron's name.

She waved him down. "They seem to have some information about the Dark Mage, which has made them sit up and take note. Byron has suggested we use the conference room at the Riverview Hotel. Do you know it?"

"The one owned by the Magi Council?"

"Yes. There are safety measures already in place there, and the staff are used to catering to non-humans and turning a blind eye when they have to. Though we would understand if you feel uncomfortable with the venue, I'm sure something else could be arranged." She didn't want him backing out now.

"No, I think it would be appropriate for the Council to meet where they felt at ease. As long as I may bring a few of my own."

"Yeah, I discussed that with Byron, he agreed it was only fair. How many would you like to bring?" She was a little hesitant; she remembered very clearly the looks of fear and anxiety his guard had elicited when they arrived at the station last night. Some of the Vampires were very imposing.

She could hear the slight smile in his voice when he replied. "I'll try and keep it to a minimum. Alexander will insist on coming along, and I'm afraid he's not the best company when he feels I may be in danger, as you noticed at dinner last night, but I will keep him under control. I will need to introduce the Council to Patrick, my daytime Chief of Security; he is a Werewolf and integral to my security force. And perhaps two of my personal guard; Nathan and Marcello would probably be best. They are a little less intimidating than some of the others, unless you have another suggestion?"

"No, I think that would be fine," she said, fighting a grin as she thought of the suave Italian Vampire charming all the Magus women.

Nathan looked like the bodyguard he was, and she had no idea of what to expect from Patrick the Security Chief, but no-one would begrudge Julius a little protection in a hotel full of other supernaturals.  Alexander would be Alexander no doubt; she remembered her last thought as she went to sleep earlier was wondering if the English Vampire had multiple-personality disorder, but in light of what Julius had just said perhaps it was just a defence mechanism.  Regardless, if he chose to be charming tonight, the females in the meeting would stand no chance of resistance.

They agreed on a time an hour after sunset and ended the call.  Gabi quickly perused her e-mail and then headed to the kitchen with Kyle and filled him in on what he'd missed between mouthfuls of pancakes, fried bananas, bacon and syrup.

After breakfast, Kyle headed home and Gabi shooed Rose out the door before she could find a reason to stay longer.  Rose came in on a Sunday so that she could take a weekday off to mind some of the grandkids, but Gabi never let her work the full day, only letting her come in to do the basics and cook breakfast, then chasing her home to spend some time with her husband.  Once Rose left, Gabi went into the bathroom and had a good look at the wound on her shoulder.  She decided it was sufficiently healed to pull out the stitches and set to work with a small pair of scissors and a pair of tweezers.  She winced as the threads pulled free of her flesh, talking to Slinky to distract herself from the disturbing task.  As many times as she did this, it always gave her the creeps.  When the stitches were out, she covered the wound with a waterproof wound plaster; reluctantly admitting to herself that Julius's pet doctor had done a good job with the stitching, though a scar was still inevitable.  She picked up Slinky and let him wind himself around her neck as she went back to her office to catch up on admin and e-mails. She needed to try and clear her diary for at least the next week or two; she had a feeling that things in the City were about to get nasty fast.

When she heard Kyle's van drive up late that afternoon, she was still yawning after catching a quick catnap. As he let himself in, she was settling Nex into the sheath down her back, a half-eaten chocolate croissant in one hand and cup of coffee on the counter next to her.

"Here, let me hold that for you," Kyle said, grabbing the croissant as he passed her on his way to the coffee maker in the kitchen. He promptly stuffed the remains of the croissant into his mouth as he reached for a coffee mug. He ducked the apple she threw at his head and caught it as it ricocheted off the cupboard, biting into it as he poured coffee.

"Do you not have a kitchen in your own house?" she grumbled, looking for something else to throw at him.

"Of course I do, it just isn't nearly as well stocked as yours." He threw her his trademark impish grin. "Besides, I can smell the rest in the warmer, so you won't go hungry."

"I knew you were coming so I had no choice but to warm up extras," she groused, elbowing him in the ribs with her good arm as she moved past him to pull the rest of the croissants out of the warmer. They quickly fuelled up on coffee and carbs as Gabi filled Razor and Slinky's food bowls, and just after sunset they drove out in the Mustang.

It was after midnight when the Council session was finally called to a close. Gabi was ravenous, the lone lollipop she'd found in her jacket pocket was doing little to ward off the feeling that her stomach was trying to digest itself. The members of the Council had seemed to drone on and on, and there was huge debate over every tiny detail that was brought up, Athena being her usual obnoxious self, but Julius had shown nothing but patient attentiveness throughout. She realised that it had probably explained the slightly deferential attitude the elders had shown him by the end. That, and his charismatic personality, she reluctantly admitted to herself. He really could be quite compelling when he turned on the charm. He was dressed in black pants, a midnight blue cashmere sweater and his black leather coat, his pale, iridescent skin in stark contrast to the deep colours.

The rest of his entourage were dressed almost completely in black and had been largely silent throughout the meeting. Marcello and Nathan had stood inhumanly still at positions either side and slightly behind Julius. Alexander and Patrick had taken seats either side of him, Alexander in his typical James Dean slouch, belying his absolute attention to every movement in the room, and Patrick obvious in his scrutiny of everyone and everything. Patrick had proved to be a tall, dark-haired, muscular man with short-cropped hair, a neatly trimmed moustache and goatee, and a posture that spoke of a military background. Alexander had again begun the meeting with a belligerent attitude, but had mellowed towards the end. He'd even shown a degree of enthusiasm when discussing offensive tactics with Kyle and Douglas, who was present in the capacity of Senior Hunter.

Alistair and Patrick seemed to know each other, by reputation at least, and there appeared to be a mutual respect between them which was unusual in dominant Werewolves and said a great deal about their characters. Gabi had caught Patrick eyeballing Kyle a number of times during the course of the evening, but Kyle had refused to rise to the bait, pretending ignorance of

Patrick's attention. Kyle had long since gotten used to the odd attention he drew from the rest of the Werewolf fraternity.

Kyle and Gabi had been handed the positions of liaison between the Council and Julius's Clan as they had already established a relationship with the Vampires, and Gabi had secretly both welcomed and dreaded the part she had been assigned, just as she was both attracted to and disturbed by being in Julius's presence.

Gabi was relieved that Julius hadn't brought up his vision of her death at the meeting, but slightly annoyed with Margaret for bringing up her previous encounter with the Wraith. Gabi sighed, she was being unfair, the elderly shape-shifter had no way of knowing that Julius had been kept in the dark about the blindness, it really wasn't her fault. But the look that Julius had thrown her way at the time told Gabi she was going to be grilled about the incident as soon as they were alone.

Julius had been open and candid with the Council, answering questions unerringly, only pausing when anger overwhelmed him during their discussion of Danté and his motives. Athena had been openly antagonistic, trying repeatedly to trip him up by firing question after question at him until Irene had finally laid a reproving hand on her arm reminding Athena of her manners. Athena had then lapsed into a hostile silence, and Gabi found herself wondering what the witch was plotting. Irene's acceptance of his answers without extensive cross-examination meant that she felt he was being honest with them, if anyone would know, she would, and she was like a pit-bull when it came to drawing out the truth from someone. Strangely, the topic of Julius's insider knowledge of the SMV was not brought up, perhaps that was what Athena had been working up to. Gabi had vowed to get to the bottom of that mystery soon, but didn't want to bring it up with Athena around to cause dissent in the ranks.

The information the Council had been given about Mariska was informative but not particularly useful. She was a powerful necromancer who had been orphaned at a young age and had been fostered by one of the Magi Elders. She had been a problem child, and as hard as they had tried to mould her to conform to the ethics of the Magi Council, she had always seemed to be on the edge of slipping to the dark side. It seemed all she needed was a tiny push in that direction and she had gone rushing off down the dark path.

They'd lost track of her several months ago and hadn't been able to find any trace of her since then. They had several tracking spells that hadn't been tried as they were very difficult to perform, but with the current news, a decision had been made to find her no matter the cost. The only bit of good news was that she hadn't been taught the dark spells, so she'd be muddling through things as best as she could on her own. She was also relatively young, by Magus standards, and wouldn't have come into her full power yet. She was at the top of the Magus Council's agenda along with trying to find a way to destroy the Wraith. Gabi was more than happy to be leaving that in their hands. The less she had to do with that thing the better. The Magus Council had agreed to share any relevant information or discoveries with the SMV Council immediately, and that info would then be passed on to Julius as a matter of urgency.

By the end, a precarious alliance had been forged. Many of the details of the alliance would be hammered out over the next few days, the two sides needing to find ways to merge their forces and best utilise their unique strengths. Julius had made it clear that his Werewolf contingent would follow directions from Gabi or Kyle if he ordered them to, but the Vampires would only take orders from him or Alexander as his second in command, it was one of the few points that he refused to elaborate and was unmoving on. The Council had respected his decision and had agreed to work around these issues. Phone numbers for Julius, Alexander and Patrick were to be included on the emergency call list for any Demon activity notifications from the SMV, and Julius would ensure that the Vampires either helped or stayed out of the way when it came to cleaning up and limiting media coverage. Everyone agreed Byron was the master of those situations.

As the meeting wrapped up, the Vampires were the first to exit the building, leaving as a unit in a silent, fluid wave. Gabi said a quick goodbye to Byron and the other Elders, promising to look after herself and then headed for the far exit. Kyle finished up his conversation with Alistair and Douglas and caught up with her just as she opened the door. The cool night air was crisp and refreshing. Gabi had always loved night time, and tonight was the perfect evening for a run in the forest. She sighed as she realised the pack of Vampires was standing at her car, no relaxing run in the forest for her.

"We need to talk," Julius purred quietly, stepping out of the group as Gabi and Kyle approached the car.

Gabi eyed him a little warily. His voice sounded as though he was barely restraining his temper. "So talk," she said flatly, "but make it quick, Wolf and I are starving."

As if to prove her point her stomach grumbled loudly; she just barely held off the blush of embarrassment and gritted her teeth as stifled snorts and chuckles erupted from the group of Vampires. The anger left Julius's face and somehow he managed not to crack a smile himself.

"So it would seem," Julius agreed wryly. "We can talk after you and Kyle have had dinner. Shall we meet at your place again?"

Gabi's embarrassment vanished instantly as annoyance surged through her. She definitely didn't need a whole pack of them invading her cherished privacy.

"No," she growled, her tone brooking no argument. "Not my place." And then a thought occurred to her. "But we can meet at your place. Wolf and I will grab some food from a drive-thru and then we can follow you to your domain."

Julius looked like he was about to protest.

"It would only be fair," she said in an innocently practical voice, "for us to know where you live, since you know where I live!" She ended on a dangerous note, making it clear that she didn't like them having knowledge of her private details.

Julius chewed the idea over for a few moments before glancing at Alexander, who also paused before slowly nodding. "Alright, but I do expect the two of you to keep the location to yourselves. What drive-thru do you want to stop at?"

Gabi and Kyle were making short work of a bag full of burgers and chips, washing them down with large sugar-laden, caffeinated energy drinks, when they drove up to the gates of the 'Estate', as Julius called it. They were in one of the most affluent suburbs of the City, the place where celebrities and eccentric billionaires bought houses. They had already passed several vans emblazoned with the words 'Security' doing slow patrols of the area. Apparently they weren't too concerned about the red mustang tucked between one of the 4x4 SUVs and Julius's Aston Martin, and she noticed all the security personnel they passed give the SUV a quick nod.

"Woah," Kyle breathed in blatant admiration as they followed the SUV through the electronic gates and along the tree lined driveway, lit every few metres by lights made to look like brass lanterns. By the light of the waxing moon, they could make out a number of cottages and bungalows set into a large copse of trees to their left and a running track, tennis court and swimming pool on their right. Then the trees opened up ahead and they could see what could only be described as a mansion.

"You didn't tell me his place was this spectacular," Kyle said, still awestruck.

They drove around to the rear of the main house and parked next to the SUV under an enclosed carport big enough for ten cars. To their right was garaging for at least another six cars and a ramp that looked like it led to underground parking.

"You're just easily impressed," Gabi drawled at him, hiding her own surprise at the sheer size and grandeur of the place. "Besides, I never saw the place the last time I was here," she continued as she climbed out the car. "I was taken in unconscious and brought out blind-folded," she growled, throwing Julius a disgruntled look and slamming the car door shut.

Patrick, Nathan and Marcello took their leave, heading off towards a large single story building partly hidden behind a thick hedge after giving Julius short, respectful bows. Julius nodded at them and then moved toward a large, beautifully carved, wooden door, opening it and waiting for Gabi and Kyle to precede him into the house.

"Welcome to my home," he said simply, "Perhaps I can prove to be a better host this time," he continued, giving Gabi an enigmatic smile.

She suddenly noticed his eyes had turned pitch black, the gold halo barely visible, and suppressed a nervous shiver.

"Alexander," Julius called to the other Vampire who was divesting himself of his jacket and a short sword, "will you show our guests to the bar area while I tell Gregory we're here. I'll join you shortly."

Before Gabi could blink he was gone.

Wordlessly, and with a long-suffering expression on his face, Alexander led them through the impressive entrance hall, past the sweeping mahogany staircase, down a wide corridor hung with stunning paintings, and into a large open-air entertainment area, complete with fully-stocked bar, pool tables and several comfy looking sofas. Large glass panels slid back on two sides to completely open the room to a beautifully manicured garden sporting a hot tub and a barbeque grill.

Gabi snorted in amusement. "Really, a barbeque, in a house full of Vampires? You've gotta be kidding me!"

Alexander looked up from pouring himself a bourbon from behind the bar. "Oh, is that what that thing is," he replied indifferently. "I guess the builder wasn't expecting to have Vampires buy the place." He placed a bottle of red wine, two wine glasses and a beer on the bar counter, added some ice to his own glass and sprawled gracefully on one of the large sofas.

Gabi walked back in from the garden and took the glass of wine Kyle offered her. Kyle seemed content to grab his beer and collapse on another of the couches, but Gabi couldn't find it in her to settle down, something was eating at her, keeping her tension high. It seemed that Julius was taking a long time informing his clan member they were here.

Alexander and Kyle started talking strategy; Alexander was grilling Kyle about fighting Demons. She sipped her wine, savouring the taste, Lord and Lady it was an amazing wine. She thought idly about setting up the pool table, but the thought started her shoulder aching and she decided against it. She was just about to slip out of the room and go exploring when Julius swept into the room.

"My apologies for the delay," he said, not explaining himself further. He quickly checked that they all had something to drink before pouring himself a glass of wine.

Gabi found herself marvelling at the change in him. It took her a few seconds to pinpoint the differences. The biggest change was in his eyes; they were back to being the deep sapphire pools rimmed in gold, but some of the tension was also gone from the muscles in his face and jaw, and there was a healthier colour to him. It wasn't until she watched him open his mouth to take a sip of his wine and she noticed the length of his canines that it all suddenly made sense. Her breath caught in her chest as she made the connection. Her mind raced. She turned away from him quickly before he could see the expression on her face; revulsion and horror warring with her natural, ruthless practicality.

She knew how they lived; she knew what they had to do in order to survive, but her natural human instincts wanted to shy away from the idea. She wondered if perhaps he drank bagged blood, that would make it a little easier for her to deal with. The thought of him drinking from a real, live person left her shuddering, but the thought of him drinking from a real, live, beautiful, warm, female person sent a completely different spike of emotion through her.

Was that actually a jab of jealousy? That last thought brought her up short, and catapulted her back into the reality of the moment. She knew he was watching her, his unnervingly beautiful eyes boring into the side of her face. She suddenly wished her hair was loose so she could hide her face from him for a few moments longer while she gathered her scattered wits.

No one had spoken, Kyle and Alexander had broken off from their discussion of various types of Demons when they heard Gabi's intake of breath. It was as though they were all waiting for the bomb to go off. Kyle obviously hadn't come to the same conclusion she had, he didn't look revolted or angry, just confused by the sudden tension in the air and ready for anything. She took a deep calming breath, wincing slightly as her ribs complained, and braced herself to face him.

She was saved from saying anything as a stockily built, dark-haired man bustled in. He had two trays in his hands; one was piled high with a variety of mouth-wateringly decadent chocolates, the other with a variety of savoury snacks. Though her Vamp sense told Gabi this was a fairly old Vampire, he appeared to be somewhat nervous. While he deposited the trays on a low table in the centre of the sofas and bowed respectfully to Julius and Alex, he kept a wary eye on the non-Vampires as though they were large, unpredictable dogs.

"Gabrielle, Kyle," Julius inclined his head to them politely, "this is Gregory. He is my steward here at the Estate and takes care of all the day-to-day details of the place. If you can't reach me for any reason, you can always contact Gregory and he will more than likely know how to contact me." He paused and turned to Gregory. "Gregory, this is Gabrielle Bradford and Kyle Robson. I want you to show them every respect while they are at the Estate. They are under my direct protection, and I need all of our staff to understand and respect that."

There seemed to be a lot more said than the relatively simple words he had spoken, as Gregory dipped his head sombrely and spoke as though he were taking a vow, "Yes, Sire. I understand, Sire. The staff shall be informed." He raised his eyes back to Julius, studiously ignoring Gabi and Kyle. "Is there anything else before I escort the young lady home, Sire?"

# CHAPTER 13

Gabi knew she'd been right earlier. The woman Gregory was talking about must have been the donor for Julius's 'dinner'. While Gabi may have initially felt fear or revulsion when she realised what he'd been up to, now there was no horror, no distaste, only annoyance, and the unfamiliar spark of jealousy. This wasn't something she'd anticipated and she didn't know how to deal with it.

"No," he addressed Gregory, "you can take her home now. We'll be fine."

Gregory departed in a hurry, clearly pleased to be leaving the room.

Alexander let out an amused chuckle. "Poor Gregory," he chortled, "You really are unkind to him Julius."

"I am?" Julius asked mildly, "In what way?" He moved to join them, leaning back against one of the pool tables facing the other men but positioning himself where he could still see Gabi's face. She knew that to humans she had a very good poker face, but supernaturals were different, a Vampire would detect every tiny twitch of muscle, the slightest tightening of her jaw, the smallest change in the dilation of her pupils, her breathing or her heart beat. She schooled herself not to betray any of her internal disquiet.

"You just brought the big, scary bogey monster and her Werewolf sidekick into his domain, and told him they are to be protected at all costs." Alexander stopped chuckling long enough to take a sip of his bourbon. "He's going to walk out and kiss the sun one of these days, and then where will you be?"

"He wouldn't dare." Julius disagreed shortly.

"Hey," Kyle said in an injured tone, "since when did I become the sidekick?"

"Since your name isn't Angeli Morte" answered Alexander sardonically.

"True." Kyle conceded. "To Hellcat," he raised his beer in her direction, "bogey monster to Vampires everywhere."

"Hellcat," Alexander repeated, "I like that. It suits her better than 'Angeli Morte. To Hellcat." He toasted as well, raising his glass and downing the rest of his whiskey.

"Drunken idiots," Gabi muttered, picking up a handful of chocolate truffles and throwing them at Kyle.

He caught most of them and shoved them in his mouth, munching cheerfully before washing them down with beer.

"Ugh!" Gabi pulled a revolted face at him.

"I have a question," Gabi declared, looking pensively at Julius.

"Only one?"

"For now," she replied. "Will you answer me honestly?"

"As honestly as I can."

"Who is your informant in the Society?"

"Ah," he said, apparently taken quite by surprise by the sudden change in subject. He paused, deliberating his answer. "I'm afraid need your assurance that punitive action won't be taken against them before I divulge that information."

"We can't allow the people close to us to betray our trust in them without some kind of disciplinary action. What if that same person is also supplying information to other sources? Like Danté for instance?"

"I understand your viewpoint, but I'm afraid I'm not telling you anything unless I know they won't be harmed." Julius was unmoving.

"Harmed?" she exclaimed, shocked. "We'd never hurt somebody for being an informant. They'd probably be dismissed, unless there were extreme extenuating circumstances; perhaps told to leave the City, have their memories erased, but never harmed." She was slightly offended at the thought. "Anyway, I don't have the power to make that decision; it would be in the Council's hands."

Julius moved to the bar counter, swept up the bottle of wine and returned, quickly filling Gabi's glass before his own, and going back to his position against the pool table. It was obviously a delay tactic while he mulled the question over.

"First, answer a question of mine," he said finally.

"Why not answer mine first?"

"I'm afraid we'll get sidetracked once I answer yours, and my question is weighing heavily on my mind."

Gabi sighed and rolled her eyes, annoyance getting the better of her self-control. "Well then, by all means, get it off your chest, Jules!" She had a feeling she knew what was coming.

"Why didn't you tell me the truth about what the Wraith did to you?"

"You never actually asked me what it did to me," she replied calmly, but even she could hear the slight defensiveness in her tone.

"That's because you conveniently forgot to tell me that you actually engaged it during a fight," he said, a muscle in his jaw twitching.

"Well, no one knew what the damn thing was capable of; it just seemed like another form of Demon. I figured Nex would do some kind of damage." She was outright defensive now.

"And what happened when you attacked it?" he asked brusquely.

Gabi chewed on her bottom lip, trying to think of a way to put it that it didn't sound as bad as it had seemed at the time. She noticed Kyle close his eyes, apparently reliving the memory, and he gave a quick shudder.

"It threw her thirty feet across the ground without so much as lifting an arm," Kyle recalled sombrely. "She was aiming for its eyes, and all it did was flick its head at her."

Gabi glared at him, warning him to shut it. Julius hadn't taken those deep blue eyes off her even though Kyle was speaking. She shifted uncomfortably under the dark accusation. "It didn't really 'do' anything to me; it was just like I'd touched an electric current, or a force field of some kind. It threw me backwards and," she paused, looking down, pulling at a thread on her sleeve and then continued in a rush. "When I managed to catch my breath from the fall, I realised I couldn't see anything, like I was in thick fog in the pitch dark."

The twitching of the muscle in Julius's jaw grew more pronounced.

"And that was it," she protested. "The Magi banished it, and my sight was back the following day."

"And you didn't think this was relevant to bring up after the Wraith's appearance at the train station last night?"

"Well, you were already freaking out about your 'vision', you didn't need any more reasons to try and keep me away from the fight." She was back to sounding annoyed. Annoyed was good, better than defensive, she decided.

"How many days ago was this?" he asked.

"Uh, I think I've lost track." She frowned, drawing her eyebrows together in concentration. "Oh yes, now I remember. It was the night before you kidnapped me," she recalled dryly.

"So your sight was back to normal in the morning?"

"More or less," she replied warily, a slight edge in her voice.

"I'm sorry," he said, surprising her completely. "I wouldn't have blind-folded you if I'd known." There was genuine regret in his tone. "The Wraith also said that you thwarted Danté's attempted assassination, but it obviously wasn't classing its own attack on you as deadly. So what other attempt has been made on your life?"

Gabi cocked her head and stared at him, her eyes narrowed in confusion. She hadn't actually given that part of the Wraith's diatribe much thought with everything else that was going on. She shook her head, mystified. "I can't think of anything that would qualify as an assassination attempt," she said slowly, trying to remember the exact words the Wraith had used.

"And you, Wolf?" Julius turned his attention to Kyle. "Can you think of anything?"

Kyle's expression turned thoughtful, he was chewing the inside of his cheek. "Well, I honestly have no recall of the conversation you guys had with the Wraith, are you sure it wasn't talking about time it sent Gabi flying?"

"Hmmm. Yes, you were suffering a severe concussion at the time," Julius said. "No, the Wraith said that it was 'under different orders' when it encountered Gabi at the previous battle."

"Yes," Alexander interjected now, "it also said something about its Master's other pets as though they were the ones who had failed. It implied earlier that it had been toying with the two of you instead of trying to kill you, but that Danté would fix that situation soon. It spoke of a Dark One, who I'm going to guess is the Dark Magus, who seemed to have some arcane knowledge of your and Gabi's involvement in all this."

"Oh," replied Kyle, even he seemed shaken for once. "Well..." he trailed off, for once unable to put a positive spin on what had transpired.

Gabi snorted. "Yeah, it was all doom and gloom and prophesies, reminded me scarily of Athena," she said rolling her eyes theatrically at the name. "We even had special names. I was the Human who is not a human, and apparently you were the Wolf who is not a Wolf," she said dramatically, emphasising the names with a deep rasp, trying to imitate the Wraith, then she chuckled darkly, "very original." Her eyes snapped to Julius. "That reminds me, why did the Wraith call you The Baron?" she asked, putting little air quotations around the title and popping a pastry into her mouth.

Julius sighed. "Because," he ground out between his teeth, "that was my title when I was human. Now, we were trying to work out what assassination attempt had been made on Gabi's life, ideas anyone?" he continued, promptly changing the subject.

Gabi filed the little snippet of information away for future questioning.

"Have there been any close calls in the past few weeks? Anything, it could be work related or during personal time, any odd occurrences," Julius prodded.

Gabi still looked baffled, and looked over at Kyle. "I can't think of anything out of the ordinary, can you?"

"Nope, aside from the previous two fights, which the Wraith is apparently not referring to, things have seemed relatively normal," he mused thoughtfully. "The only other odd occurrence is you being attacked by..." he trailed off, glancing quickly at Julius then back at her. "You know. The bunch who were supposed to take you to Julius."

Understanding dawned on her face.

Julius and Alexander both went rigid.

"No offence, I wasn't implying anything," Kyle said quickly, seeing their intense reactions. "It was just an observation."

The two Vampires looked hard at each other, as though conversing without words. Julius's eyes were burning with anger and trepidation.

Alexander recovered first. "It's possible," he almost whispered, his jaw clenched but his face carefully blank. "We spoke about it, things didn't add up at the time, but it just seemed like one of Genevieve's bizarre moods. She was too old for the Red Rage, volatile yes, but to attack over one small insult, it was extreme even for Genevieve."

Julius shook his head, not in denial but rather in disbelief.

"Do you think.....both of them?" Julius asked in a voice tight with rage.

Alexander looked off out into the garden, his eyes distant, not seeing what was in front of him. Eventually, he nodded, a single quick bob of his head. "Yes, I don't see Genevieve keeping something like that from him, and you know he was the one who was so adamant they both went on the mission. It all seems to fit. Is there any way we can be sure, though?"

"We must investigate this further. If it's true, there may be others." Julius looked as though someone had just punched him in the gut, as though his world had just been upended.

Gabi looked across at Kyle to see if he was making any sense out of the conversation, but he looked as confused as she felt.

"Yes," Alexander responded shortly. "Do you think Sebastian can help? He might be able to trace their movements, their correspondence, any outside contacts."

"Can he be trusted, do you think?" Julius sounded uncertain for the first time since Gabi had encountered him.

"Maybe this will be a good test. If you order him to find the information, he will have no choice but to obey. His findings could be very telling." Alexander had settled into a cold, hard rage.

"Call him, tell him to meet us in my office in half an hour," Julius ordered brusquely.

Alexander left the room in a rush of air.

Gabi's head was spinning. A few moments ago, she was about to find out who had been leaking information to Julius about the SMV, and now the two Vampires had gone off on a tangent about the assassination attempt on her life, which she hadn't even known about until Julius brought it up. She wasn't sure how she felt about that little fact either; grateful to be alive? Annoyed at the attempt? That the Vampires were blowing it out of proportion? She needed to slow everything down and let her brain catch up. What did Alexander and Julius mean about Genevieve, and who was Sebastian? Too many questions and not enough answers.

"Julius," Gabi finally snapped, "are you going to tell us what's going on or am I going to have to beat it out of somebody?"

Julius pursued his luscious lips. "Well, we can't be positive at this stage, but we think perhaps we have traitors in our ranks," he said calmly and clearly, but the clipped tone he used spoke volumes about his feelings on the subject. "The way that Genevieve attacked you on Friday has not sat well with me, it never made any sense. Genevieve has never had the most even temper, but for her to attack you like that, completely against orders, was not normal, not even by volatile Vampire standards. Alexander and I had discussed the subject before and wondered if there was more to it than simple temper." He paused for a moment as though he needed to steel himself for his next words. "We're wondering if they had been working for Danté, and if they were, are there others in my Clan doing the same thing."

Alexander walked back into the room and went straight to the bar to re-fill his glass, in the silence Gabi could hear the clink of the ice falling into the crystal tumbler and the splash of alcohol over it. It was Kyle who broke the ensuing silence.

"But why would Danté want Gabi taken out of the picture? How does he even know of her existence?" he demanded. "It doesn't make any sense."

The other three looked at each other, Gabi gnawing on the inside of her lip again. Kyle had been too concussed to remember the Wraith waxing lyrical about the prophesies made by the Dark Mage. He didn't know that Mariska had foreseen Gabi and him as pivotal players in the upcoming war; players that Danté needed to control or eliminate if he wanted the upper hand. Alexander walked over with another beer for Kyle and explained in short clipped sentences what the Wraith had said while

Gabi and Julius stared at one another; pensive frustration on both their faces.

Minutes later, Julius led them out of the entertainment area, up a sweeping flight of stairs to the first story and along a short corridor to his office. As the door opened, Gabi remembered her first visit to the room. It was as large and comfortable as she remembered it. The computer still hummed quietly on one side of his desk, and she again felt the strange sensation of trying to meld her idea of a Vampire lair with this office, which so obviously belonged to a business man who made full use of all available technology and gadgetry. She noticed so much more as she stepped through the door this time. Walking in with full control of her own faculties, and not feeling threatened or unsure of her immediate future, she took time to admire the smaller details.

There were some beautiful watercolours on the walls, a few Greek and Roman artefacts, and a shelf on the massive bookshelf behind the desk dedicated to old books, which would probably prove to be first editions. There was a shadowed alcove in a back corner of the room which she was sure had been vacant the last time she was in here. It was taken up now by a large, strategically lit display case full of ancient weapons. Gabi was mesmerised, weapons were one of her favourite things in the world. Aside from Nex, she'd started a collection of her own, but nothing to rival this exhibit. She knew why the case hadn't been in here the last time she was a guest in this office, she would definitely have found a way to get her hands on a few of them. Julius was a smart Vampire. She glanced away from the display to see him watching her with a little smile playing at the corners of his mouth. His thoughts obviously echoing her own.

"Please make yourselves comfortable," he said, indicating the chaise longue Gabi had woken up in and another up against the window wall. Alexander had taken one of the two guest office chairs and Julius settled himself in his chair behind the desk. The other guest chair sat waiting for the unfortunate Sebastian.

Gabi continued her investigation of the room, browsing the book collection. She still had too much nervous energy to sit still. She didn't turn from her perusal of the books as she said, "I've answered your question, now it's your turn." She heard Julius snort softly, apparently he was under the assumption she'd forgotten all about that question amid all the new developments. She turned her attention to him now, leaning back against the bookshelf and resting her left hand on her hip, she would've folded her arms to look more stern if it didn't still hurt to do that.

"All right, fair enough," he conceded, "but you have to understand that much of the information we have on you came from Sebastian, whom you are about to meet. Sebastian has no ties to the SMV, he is a computer whiz, who used all kinds of geeky computer tricks to find out things about you. You need to trust me when I say that my informants didn't give me very much information at all."

Gabi sighed. "Informants?" she asked sharply, emphasising the 's'. "There's more than one?"

Julius nodded. "And I ask that you entreat the Council to send them to me if they decide to dismiss them, I have places for them in my own staff. They won't cause you any harm, I assure you of that. Neither of them would've given me any information if they weren't completely convinced that I had no intention of harming you or anyone else in the organisation. And they were under Alpha's orders." This meant that they were Werewolves and their Alpha was under Julius's orders Gabi realised, once again intrigued by supernatural politics.

"Just spit out their names, and we'll take it from there."

"Ross and Rory. They gave me the information that you were close to one of the Council members and told me when you had a night off. They were to help me make contact with you."

Kyle sat up in surprise. "Ross and Rory the Werewolves? The team Drivers?" he asked, shocked.

Julius nodded. "They're part of the Blackriver pack, and the Alpha of the Blackriver pack works for me."

"Byron would've looked into that kind of link. He would've checked on their Alpha before bringing them into the Society," Kyle protested.

"Ah," Julius responded dryly, "but their Alpha does genuinely work as Head Security Officer at Flamingos Gentlemen's Club. Flamingos just happens to be owned by one of my holding companies."

Further discussion on the matter was brought to an end as they all heard a set of quiet footsteps approaching the office.

"Come in, Sebastian," Julius called when the footsteps hesitated near the door.

Gabi took a seat next to Kyle as a tall, gawkish young man entered the office. It took a few seconds before Gabi realised that the freckled, ginger-haired individual was actually a Vampire. His Vampire presence was so weak so as to be almost non-existent. And he moved with none of the fluid, confident grace of the rest of Julius's retinue.

"Sire," he greeted, almost tripping over his own feet on his way to bow jerkily in front of Julius's desk. "Alexander asked me to come to you urgently." He kept his eyes down except for a brief, worried glance at Alexander.

Gabi wasn't sure he was even aware of her and Kyle being in the room. Extremely unusual behaviour for a Vampire.

"Yes, Sebastian. I need you to find some information for me. It is of a very important and sensitive nature. I know if anyone can do it, you can." Julius spoke with a carefully toneless, but utterly authoritative voice.

Gabi felt slight wisps of power brush against her as it quickly filled the room and swirled around the geeky, young Vampire.

Sebastian nodded, with quick erratic bobs of his head. "Of course, Sire, anything I can do to help, anything at all."

Gabi had the feeling that if Vampires could sweat, this one would be lathered like a nervous horse. It was strangely unsettling to see another Vampire having this kind of reaction to Julius. It reminded her once again of exactly how powerful Julius was and precisely what different worlds they lived in. It brought back the memory of Julius's 'dinner' guest, and she barely suppressed a shudder.

Julius rose from his chair and inclined his head towards Kyle and her on the couch. Sebastian actually flinched when he noticed the two of them, apparently for the first time. Gabi wondered if Sebastian was just a really new vampire, or if something had actually gone wrong during his Turning. She'd never encountered such a feeble, nervous, inept Vampire before. She guessed that out on the streets, without the protection of someone like Julius, he would've simply been fodder for other Vampires.

"I would like you to meet Gabrielle Bradford and Kyle Robson," Julius said formally. "I'm sure you recognise them from your surveillance footage."

The gawky, young Vampire swallowed convulsively and his eyes grew huge and panicky. He looked quickly from the two of them back to Julius with a pleading look on his face. He seemed utterly incapable of getting any words out. Alexander actually started sniggering from his chair and Julius's expression suddenly became one of annoyed exasperation. Then he spoke slowly and clearly, as though explaining something of significance to a three year old.

"I'm not giving you to them, Sebastian. They didn't come here looking for revenge or retribution."

The ginger-haired Vampire's anxiety levels immediately went down a notch, but he still had a frightened, apprehensive look in his eyes. "Something has come to our attention, and we need to verify or disprove a theory. You are the most competent Clan member for this kind of investigation." Suddenly, Julius's voice took on that strange authoritative quality again, and whispers of power teased the hairs on Gabi's arms upright. "What we are about to reveal to you is not to leave this room and is not to be discussed with anyone besides the five people present here. Do you understand me, Sebastian? No one."

"Yes, yes, of course, Sire, I completely understand. You can count on me, of course. Anything I can help with," he stammered quickly.

"Good," Julius said shortly, his voice returned to normal and the power level in the room subsided. "Alexander will explain the situation and our requirements to you, while I see to our guests." A millisecond later he was in front of Gabi with his arm extended in invitation. "Shall we," he invited, slightly mockingly.

Gabi ignored his arm but stood and strode towards the door, casting a last analysing look at the young Vampire causing him to pull in a quick nervous breath. Julius seemed to have problems hiding an amused smirk as he trailed behind her out the door. Kyle loped out after them, giving Alexander a quick farewell salute.

Ten minutes later Gabi and Kyle were in the Mustang on their way home. Gabi had wanted to stay and find out if Sebastian turned up anything, but Kyle had pointed out that he'd hardly had any sleep in the past few days, and he was on duty the following day. Gabi had the feeling that he was only saying it to get her to go home and rest, but she couldn't really argue with the sentiment. She was practically asleep on her feet; it was nearly three am Monday morning, and even though she was officially off Hunter duty, she was bound to have some conventional work for today. So they reluctantly left the estate with Julius's assurance that he would let them know the moment he had any worthwhile information to share.

# CHAPTER 14

Her phone was ringing. Again. At least it waited until after sunrise she thought grumpily as she noticed sunlight peaking in through slits in her curtains. She grabbed the phone, taking in the bedside clock with sleep blurred eyes. 9:18 glowed in bright red numbers. She squinted at the caller ID — Donovan. Damn. Donovan was one of her oldest and most loyal clients; a film producer who often employed her services as an animal trainer. Usually, she was contacted by underlings on a movie, but Donovan always called her personally. They'd developed a good working relationship over the past few years, and she always tried to help him out if she could. He was openly gay, and a genuinely nice guy if you were on his good side, heaven help you if you pissed him off though. She sat up and cleared her throat before answering.

"Hey, The Don," she said cheerfully, assuming her brisk, teasing but professional voice that she used on clients. As a Hunter for the Malus Venatori, she was known as short-tempered, rude and abrasive; she allowed her natural temperament to show among her supernatural peers, but in her business she was all smooth, confident professionalism and after so many years of wearing it, her business mask now felt comfortable and familiar.

"Gabrielle, my Sweet," he greeted her, his natural effervescence clear even across a phone line. "How is my little ray of sunshine this morning?"

Gabi groaned; he knew full well that she was not a morning person.

"I haven't had my first cup of coffee yet, so tread carefully," she warned in a mock growl.

Donovan chuckled on the other side of the phone as she absent-mindedly petted Razor who head-butted the side of her face, almost giving her a black eye.

"And what was my little Tiger up to last night that she's extra grumbly this morning?" His tone suggested she had been up to something naughty and he wanted details.

Gabi let his imagination go wild at what she got up to at night that often caused such bleary-eyed mornings. Rather he thought she was a wild party girl, living the single life than he find out the monster-encrusted truth. She climbed out of bed, wrapping a robe around herself one-handed and grimacing at the uncomfortable stiffness in her shoulder and ribs. "Now, that would be telling," she retorted. "A good girl doesn't kiss and tell, now does she?"

Donovan chuckled even louder. "Not sure I would put you in the 'Good Girl" category," he retaliated.

Gabi stifled a yawn and headed for the kitchen where she could smell a pot of coffee on the brew. Rose had obviously heard her take the call.

"Oh, I'm good," she drawled, "I'm really, really good." She found Rose in the kitchen and gave her a quick kiss on the cheek as she headed to the coffee pot like a Magus who'd spotted a henge.

"I don't doubt that for a moment, Angel," he countered with a mock seriousness.

Gabi smiled wryly; Donovan was a wonderful flirt. "I take it you didn't just phone to check up on my personal life?" she prompted him.

"No, unfortunately there's no rest for the wicked as they say," he replied, sighing dramatically. "The script writer for my latest movie has sprung a fight scene on me involving a black panther, so I am in dire need of your rather unique talents."

Gabi took a much needed gulp of hot, strong coffee and headed to her office. "Let me just get my computer awake," she told him, hitting the power button and sinking into her chair. The computer purred to life as she opened her diary to today's date.

"Ok," she said, putting Donovan on speakerphone. "What dates are we looking at? Do you have animals lined up or do I need to track some down?"

It was standard practise to use more than one animal on a movie set. The animals could only be used in short bursts, and in the case of large animals, if one got particularly grumpy it was safer to give it a break and use another.

"It's a fairly short scene, so we're hoping to do it in a single day," Donovan replied. "We have animals available, but there is a catch." He sounded a little apprehensive now.

"Just spit it out, Don," Gabi said calmly, she was used to the film industry after working in it for the past five years, the word impossible was not supposed to exist in the movie world.

"Well, we need you today. I know what short notice this is, and I know you have other clients, but we can only have the panthers today, and their regular trainer was mauled by one of them over the weekend. He just got a bit scratched and a single bite, nothing serious, but no other trainer will go near them now. Our stunt man is prepared to go ahead with the scene if you take over as trainer. He appears to think, as I do, that you have an uncanny knack with big cats, and isn't worried about them mauling him with you around. He thinks the other trainer did something to piss off the cats, and they were just putting him in his place."

Gabi sighed. She didn't like to upstage other trainers; it just drew too much attention to her abilities, but he was right, the stuntman would be perfectly safe if she was there.

"Let me guess, the stunt man is Derek," she said with weary resignation. She could really do without dealing with Derek today. He was a really nice guy. In fact, he was the whole package; rugged good looks, charm, mouth-watering physique, he was even single and he had shown obvious interest in Gabi from the moment they met on a movie set two years ago. She couldn't deny that he appealed to her on many levels, most of them physical, but he had one major short-coming in her book; he was human. Fully, completely and unchangingly human. It made a relationship with him impossible.

"I'll owe you for a life-time," Donovan wheedled, obviously sensing her wavering capitulation.

"I hope you know that you are the only client that I would consider doing this for."

"You will have my eternal gratitude and undying admiration," he persevered, sensing victory.

"I'm sure I got those the last time you needed me on such short notice," Gabi replied archly.

"You can never have too much eternal gratitude and undying admiration," he intoned in a serious voice, but suddenly his voice turned victoriously mischievous. "But just to prove my sentiments, how about I throw in dinner at Olivella with unlimited choice from the wine list?"

Now that was just playing dirty. Gabi chuckled wryly; he had played his trump card, but she would make his credit card cry for mercy before she was finished with the wine list at Olivella.

"Time and place?" she asked, now resigned to the prospect of a full day's work. "Oh, and you better get Russell there too. I'm on light work for the next two weeks, so I'll need some muscle to help out."

"What did you do this time?"

"A frisky thoroughbred," she casually used the same lie she had fed the maitre'd at Olivella. "Bust ribs and collarbone."

Donovan didn't bother telling her to stay home if she was injured, he knew better. "I'll get Russell here come hell or high water," he promised and gave her the address of the film set downtown, asking her to be there as soon as she could make it.

Gabi signed off, telling him she'd see him in an hour. Then she drained her coffee, grabbed a lollipop from the jar on her desk and headed for the shower.

She made one stop-off on her way to the film set; at her local Dunkin Donuts, for one extra large caramel latté, two breakfast bagels and three dozen donuts — crème-filled, choc frosted, glazed, sprinkled, sugar-powdered decadence. She hoped there would be a few left for the crew when she got to the set. She seemed to have an even bigger craving for sugar today than usual, so big her whole body felt like one big itch that needed to be scratched. She wrote it off to the injuries and lack of sleep, but it still niggled something in the back of her mind. Much to her disgruntlement, all the donuts were still in the boxes when she pulled into the set car park.

She'd discovered that it was annoyingly difficult to eat and drive at the same time when you have a broken collarbone. She'd resorted to wolfing down her coffee and bagels when she got stopped at a red light. By a lucky hiccup of fate, Russell pulled into the parking lot a few seconds after her. She greeted him by depositing the three boxes of donuts into his arms, opening the top one and helping herself to a Double Cocoa Kreme Puff.

"Morning, Russ Bear," she said cheerfully around a mouthful of donut. She liked to tease the short, friendly looking man. With his unruly, wavy, russet red hair, he reminded her of that annoying range of fluffy teddy bears that was a requisite purchase for any new baby.

He was a Shifter by nature, and as such, appeared vastly younger than he actually was. Gabi knew he was well into his thirties, but he appeared barely twenty. They made a good team on film sets. As he knew her true nature, he was able to help her cover some of her unnatural abilities, and he was quick to warn her when she was over-stepping the boundaries of human capabilities. It made things much easier for her not to have to constantly hide everything from her assistant. He was also exceptionally good with animals; not that he had any kind of supernatural control over them, his talent stemmed purely from experience and a deep, innate understanding of animal nature.

"Hey, Archangel," was his wry riposte. Referring both to her Hunter nickname as well as to the belief of Magi and Shifters that the Archangel Gabriel, along with many other biblical figures, was actually female and named Gabrielle, before the Catholic Church stepped in and patriarchalized everything. Guardian Angel of Death; an interesting oxymoron, she mused to herself.

"Be nice," she warned, "or I won't let you have any of those donuts you're carrying."

"I take it the fantastical stories that have been flying around the Community are true then," he said with one russet eyebrow raised as he watched her tuck her right arm into the unobtrusive, black sling. The Community being the collective name given to the wider family of Shifters and Magi of the City, who all gossiped like fifth grader girls about everything.

Gabi pulled a face. "I'm not sure what fantastical stories have been flying around, so you'd have to tell me the stories before I confirm or deny them."

"How about you just tell me the story straight, and I can fill you in on the embellishments at the end?"

"Later," she said as they rounded a corner and entered the melee of people and cables and lights and sound equipment and props. "For now, the story is I was injured by a horse, no one has any real details, so I'll make it up as I need to," she told him in a low voice.

"Collarbone and ribs?" he asked astutely as he watched her grimace when a gaffer spun around to yell at a technician, and she had to dart aside to avoid a collision.

She grunted agreement.

"And the burn on your cheek, how are you explaining that one?"

"Shit," she swore softly, covering the offending mark with her hand. She'd forgotten about it. "I'll have to get to a bathroom with some concealer."

Russell shook his head pityingly. "You haven't been around humans enough recently. You're out of practice," he admonished. "But don't panic, head for the make-up caravan just over there. I have a friend there who'll help; she's part of the Community." They put their heads down, hoping to avoid anyone they knew and darted into the caravan marked 'make-up - extras'.

When Gabi and Russell emerged from the caravan five minutes later; no one would look twice at Gabi's cheek, and Jenny was happily devouring a donut. It didn't take them long to find Donovan, and for the boxes of donuts to be received with grunts of approval. Donovan greeted her enthusiastically with a kiss on each cheek, and she mentally thanked Russell again for reminding her about the burn mark.

Russell put the donuts on the catering table set up for the senior crew, grabbed one himself and headed back to the parking lot to collect his and Gabi's gear. Gabi would sit in on a quick set meeting between directors, actors, camera crew, and stunt crew to find out exactly what was required from the panthers for the day. Then she'd meet Russell at the animal enclosure and spend some time getting to know the panthers before shooting started.

She poured herself another cup of coffee from the catering table and was just stuffing a third donut into her mouth when her glance strayed across the set and met silver grey eyes across the room. Derek. She'd thought that perhaps having been in Julius's and Alexander's presence recently, Derek would be a pale, bland comparison, but there was just something so vibrantly alive within him; a spark of humour glinting in the liquid mercury depths of his eyes, a supreme, confident maleness about him, that he could never, ever be considered pale or bland. She could hear the females in the vicinity tittering among themselves as he strode through their midst; a few of the more confident ones stared at him boldly, trying to catch his eye. If he noticed any of them he didn't show it, his slow, easy smile was all for Gabi. Damn, she sighed inwardly, this was going to be a long day.

"Into the coffee and the sweet stuff already, Bradford?" he teased her in his warm baritone; one dark eyebrow quirked in amusement. A slight smile played at the edges of his sensual mouth, not even the slight scar running down to his top lip could detract from his blatant sex appeal. The smile vanished as soon as he got close enough to her to notice the sling. A frown creased his forehead and his molten grey eyes narrowed.

"Morning Bo," she greeted him cheerfully, interrupting whatever he'd been about to say. She'd been going for brisk and cheerful, why did it sound to her ears as though her voice had just come out low, husky and inviting?

He paused for a second, annoyance at the nickname narrowing his eyes; the Bo Derek thing got to him every time, but his easy smile was back a second later.

Gabi resolutely pasted her teasing, sardonic mask on her face. He was now standing less than a foot from her, and he smelled absolutely delectable. She found herself wanting to run her tongue across the smooth skin of his neck, just below his ear, to see if he tasted as good as he smelled. Arghh, she thought wildly, straining to keep her face impassive, what was wrong with her this morning?

"Ready to wrestle with man-eaters this morning?" she asked nonchalantly, forcing bored indifference into her tone. It was taking real effort with him this close to her. Was she really that tired, she wondered, or was her lack of a sex life catching up with her?

"First, I'm going to wrestle one of those sinful donuts into my stomach, and then I'm going to wrestle what happened to your arm out of you," he stated matter-of-factly, reaching around her to open one of the boxes of donuts.

After the set meeting, Derek was sent off to make-up and costume, and Gabi hurriedly escaped to the panther enclosure before he could stop and question her. When she got to the enclosure Russell had already laid all their

225

gear out and was talking to the panthers through the fencing. Gabi took some quiet time to sit in the enclosure with the panthers and get to know them.

Roughly petting the two panthers Gabi found herself wondering how supernaturals would be treated if they ever 'came out' to the general public. Would the world consider it type-casting to use a real Werewolf to play a Werewolf in a movie? How many computer and animatronics geeks would be out of work if producers discovered the existence of Shape-shifters and Magi? Would the world still consider supernaturals super villains and burn them at public stakes or lock them in a macabre version of a zoo, or would it welcome them and protect them, treating them like superstars and celebrities? It would create an uproar of unprecedented proportions, that was for sure.

She was enjoying the quiet time with the panthers; for her being around animals was like a warm, candlelit bubble bath for the soul. It washed away the grim reality of her other life. Interacting with them was the most beautiful part of her birthright, a counterweight to the ugliness of the violence and destruction necessitated by her crusade against evil.

The male, Tynan, was just coming out of adolescence and was trying to assert himself as dominant. It was Tynan who had bitten the other trainer, so it was merely a case of the panther testing his new power and maturity. Gabi had to put him in his place twice, but after that he settled down and submitted to her dominance without any further animosity. The female, Ciara, was a real sweetie and within moments of Gabi's entrance into the cage had settled down with her head on Gabi's lap, demanding attention like a domestic cat.

Although Gabi loved all the big cat species, lions had become her favourite after spending several months helping out at a lion sanctuary in South Africa. She still got regular e-mails from the sanctuary updating her on their lives and she celebrated every success they had, and grieved for every failure.

"Gabi." Russell's voice broke into her reverie. "The set is ready. We can take the cats through."

\*\*\*\*\*\*\*\*\*\*\*\*\*\*\*\*\*\*\*\*\*\*\*\*

Kyle was just warming up in the gym. He wanted to stretch out some kinks and then relax with twenty lengths in the pool before going into HQ to see what the roster was for the next few nights. As he got into position at the first piece of apparatus, his phone rang. He grimaced but jumped up to grab it, ignoring annoyed looks thrown his way by other patrons. He was surprised when he saw the caller's ID.

"Alex?" he asked by way of greeting. He walked out of the main gym area into a deserted corridor.

"Kyle." Alexander's clipped voice was unmistakable.

"You're still awake?" he asked, confused.

"I am indeed," the Vampire confirmed. Kyle could picture the accompanying smirk. "Actually, I was about to go and get some rest, but wanted to give you a heads up and see if you were free to join us on a reconnaissance run tonight."

Kyle felt the icy tingle of excitement flood him. "You found something?" He moved further down the corridor as a pair of women came out of the saunas and paused to chat.

"Sebastian has an address for us to investigate. It might not be anything exciting, but Julius and I will take a small group to check it out at sunset. You want in?"

"Of course I want in. I'll have to check with HQ though. I can let you know in an hour or so." Then he had

227

another thought. "What about Gabi? Have you called her yet?"

"No, I contacted you first. Julius was concerned that she needed rest and recovery time, but we thought we'd let you make the final call on that one."

"Hmm." Kyle chewed at his lip. "She texted me earlier to say she's working on a movie set today. She definitely hasn't had enough recovery time. If we can get things wrapped up early enough, she won't even know we've been out until it's too late." He said the words confidently enough to Alexander, but he knew she was going to be seriously pissed once she found out that they'd left her out of the mission. He would deal with that later.

"Fine," Alexander agreed, "If you're coming with us, be at the Estate before sunset."

***********************

After some discussion with Russell and Donovan, Gabi decided to use Tynan for the close up shots of the panther tracking and then springing off a ledge because he was bigger and looked more dangerous, and Ciara for the shots of the tussle between the panther and the hero, because she was the less dominant and more playful of the two, and because Gabi didn't want Derek and Tynan to have a male dominance standoff. She'd have to keep the two males as far apart as she could, and would still probably have to use subtle mind control to keep Tynan in check. Thank the Lord and Lady they hadn't tried this without her and Russell, she'd have to have a word with Tynan's owners and get them to pull him from movie work until he got over his teenage nonsense and settled into responsible adulthood.

Gabi let Russell do all the rehearsal shots with Ciara to make sure cameras and lighting were perfectly placed and everyone knew what to do and where to go. Derek practised his tussle with Ciara, and spent some extra time petting her and making friends, while Gabi occupied Tynan, making him practice his leap and trying out a selection of lures to find the one he liked best. They would use this to initiate his hunting behaviour for the 'stalking panther' shots.

It was well past lunch time before Donovan called a break, having got all the shots they needed from Tynan and most of the ones with Derek and Ciara. He would now go over what they'd shot, and they could fill in any gaps with Ciara after lunch. Tynan had begun to get belligerent and annoyed and Gabi was struggling to keep him calm, while Ciara took everything in her stride, an utter pro, Gabi decided, and a pleasure to work with. She'd found herself getting annoyed with Tynan towards the end of the shoot, which wasn't like her at all, normally the animals calmed and centred her even if they were being difficult. She was having to work hard at keeping a cool head today.

At lunch she headed for the canteen, immersing herself in a group of technicians and crew that she'd worked with before, they were all clamouring to know how she'd injured herself this time. She embellished her story a little, blaming it on a problematic thoroughbred stallion who'd thrown a fit about getting on a plane. She'd just about finished the concocted story when she detected the subtle, spicy, masculine scent of Derek moving up behind her. She stopped herself spinning to meet him and tried to carry on the conversation as though he wasn't there. It might have worked if the rest of the crowd hadn't taken the hint in his stormy grey eyes and suddenly remembered things they had to do elsewhere. Gabi turned around in resignation.

"A panicked horse, huh?" he asked sceptically.

"More stubborn and obnoxious than panicked actually," she correctly mildly. "You know the type."

Derek raised one eyebrow and without looking away from her eyes reached to grab her right hand.

"This doesn't look much like a rope or nylon burn to me," he said as he turned her hand over and brought it up to the light where they could both see the healing skin on the tips of her fingers. "And you don't normally wear so much make-up, what are you hiding on your cheek?"

Damn, she cursed silently, he was one of the most observant humans she'd ever met. She shouldn't have pulled off her gloves to have lunch. Not that anyone else on set would know the difference between rope burn and acid burn. Only Derek. He was still holding onto her hand waiting for an answer.

"Kitchen accident," she lied smoothly, "hot oil burns like Hades."

His looked turned even more sceptical. "Kitchen accident?" he asked incredulously. "Since when do you cook?"

"And now you know why I don't cook," she retorted sharply. He was just going to have to be happy with that, she couldn't exactly tell him the truth, though she always got the impression that he knew there was something else up with her. He was always suspicious of her injuries. He seemed to know she was always lying about them. Odd, but irrelevant. If she ever told him the truth he would probably have her committed to the nearest asylum.

His face turned pensive, as though trying to make up his mind about something. Gabi was searching desperately for Russell to help extricate her from this conversation.

"It's not a boyfriend who helped the "kitchen accident" along, is it?" he asked at last, his jaw set in a tight line. "If it is, you need to tell me now and stop protecting him."

Gabi was so thrown by the question that it took a few seconds for his meaning to dawn on her. She almost laughed, only the restrained anger burning in his eyes stopped her. She had to appreciate his concern. If she looked at the overall picture with an outsider's eyes, she would have to admit that her constant litany of injuries could well be taken as proof of exactly that, but honestly, did Derek not know her at all? The concept of a boyfriend lifting his hand to her was beyond ridiculous; Kyle would fall on the floor laughing at the thought. But Derek meant well, he was simply worried about her, so she couldn't be rude. She gently extricated her hand from his and laid it on his forearm.

"I don't have an abusive boyfriend, Derek, I promise," she assured him. "I don't have a boyfriend full stop." Ok, so maybe she shouldn't have told him that, but she needed to get some truth between them or he'd never let the subject go.

"You've met Razor," she reminded him. He had come to her house once to drop off some equipment she'd lent him, and Razor had kept him from entering the house until Gabi locked him in her room. "Do you really think he would let anyone hurt me?"

"What about that Kyle guy?" he asked, refusing to be pacified that easily. "I don't want to be rude about your friends, but there's something off about that guy."

Gabi sighed, tired of the subject now, her annoyance rising again. "Kyle is one of my oldest and most trusted friends. He's like a brother to me." She couldn't say that he would 'never raise his hand to her' because that would be lying again; they regularly hit each other during training sessions, so she had to try another angle. "And besides, do I really strike you as the type of woman who would take abuse from a man? Considering what you know about the martial arts I've studied, does it seem likely?"

Derek stared at her for a moment, looking deep into her eyes, and then he suddenly relented, nodding in agreement. "You're right. Tiny as you are, I can't see too many men getting the best of you physically. I just worry, you know?" His voice went a little quiet and distant. "I didn't see the signs early enough with my sister, only when the bastard put her in hospital." His eyes had turned sad.

"I'm sorry about your sister," Gabi said quietly. "Is she alright now?"

"Yeah, she's okay. Not much better than okay, but alive and healing. When that bastard gets out of prison in a few years he and I are going to have a long meeting in an isolated wood."

Gabi got an evil twinkle in her eye at his comment. "Let me know if you need any help getting him to that meeting," she said innocently. "I have friends in low places who would be more than happy to help."

The easy smile was back in place on Derek's face, the tension almost gone. "You bet," he agreed. "Might even be more fun to watch a woman kick his ass, than to do it myself."

"Now you're talking my language," she grinned evilly. "I might even leave a piece of him for you."

Their conversation ended with the call for them to return to set. Derek seemed far more at ease now that they'd cleared the air about her injuries, and the shooting went smoothly.

*************************

After checking in at HQ and clearing his involvement in Julius's mission with Byron, Kyle drove back to his apartment. He made some lunch, put his phone on silent and crashed on his couch to catch a few hours sleep before the sun set. He had a feeling it was going to be another long night. As he was drifting off, he remembered he hadn't checked in with Gabi since that morning, she'd probably be wondering what he was up to. He made a mental note to text her when he woke up. What he hadn't remembered was to set an alarm. When he woke hours later and realised it was only a few minutes to sunset, he grabbed the van's keys and dashed out of the apartment, completely forgetting his phone.

*************************

The rest of the afternoon went by in a blur, and Gabi was surprised to note at five o'clock that she hadn't had any contact from Kyle or Byron or Julius. She'd checked her phone regularly, but only a few clients had left voicemails or texts. She excused herself quickly from the set after wrapping up with the cats, kissing Donovan affectionately, and threatening to take him up on his offer of dinner very soon. Russell helped her drag all the gear back to the cars, and she thanked him profusely for the help, promising to keep in touch. She wearily climbed into the driver's seat and brought the Mustang roaring to life. Then she activated her hands-free kit and dialled Kyle's number.

Half an hour and half a dozen phone calls later, she had ascertained that neither Kyle nor Julius were answering their phones, and that Kyle had asked off Hunter duty tonight for business with Julius. Strange how no one had bothered to let her know what was going on. She felt tendrils of anger blossom inside her as she pulled the Mustang into her driveway. She checked her answering machine and e-mail quickly to make sure Kyle hadn't left her a message, then fed Razor and Slinky and made herself a cup of coffee and a sandwich. She ate her snack quickly, trying to contain her irrational fury.

After an hour of waiting and wondering what the hell was going on, she decided she couldn't stay in the house another second. She went to change out of her professional work clothes, pulling on jeans, boots and a black halter neck top. She was just strapping on Nex's sheath when she caught her reflection in the hall mirror and noticed how the top showed off the spectacular bruising on her collarbone. She grimaced and added a lightweight leather jacket to her ensemble, grabbed her car keys and phone, and left the house.

# CHAPTER 15

As Kyle and the Vampires poured out of the vehicle at the Estate, an air of easy camaraderie surrounded them. Kyle and the warriors who made up Julius's elite guard were good-naturedly taunting each other. Julius was a few steps ahead of the guffawing group when a faint, unusual noise froze him, his hand still raised to touch the door handle. The rest fell instantly silent responding to his tension. A loud crash resounded from one of the upstairs floors, followed by a vicious growl and then a howl of anger. More crashing and the sound of broken glass followed, then a slight pause and a splintering crack. The group flowed into action as naturally as water flowing down river, weapons out and ready for anything. Julius waited for Alexander's nod before slamming the door open and surging through into the large, open downstairs hallway. The guard followed; flowing out around him in a defensive formation.

A small group of Vampires stood at the bottom of the large staircase, their eyes large and worried. They whirled around like a single entity as Julius and the fighters burst into the mansion, battle-ready. Claudia and

Gregory were amongst the group, and Claudia appeared to be wringing her hands in concern, while Gregory was biting his lip and looking equally as worried, but not in quite the way Julius was expecting.

"What the hell is going on?" Julius demanded tightly, quickly scanning the building for foreign mind patterns or scents, but finding nothing unfamiliar.

Claudia and Gregory's expressions instantly turned to relief, even though the sounds of destruction from upstairs had not diminished in the slightest. The other Vampires quickly moved away, melting into the shadows and away from Julius's angry questions. It was Gregory who moved forward to explain, while Claudia stayed near the stairs, wincing at another loud smashing of something glass or crystal.

"Uh, Sire," his steward started uncertainly, "I'm glad to see you are all back unharmed. You can relax your weapons, we, uh, are not under attack."

"Gregory," Julius growled impatiently, "just spit it out. What is going on upstairs?"

"Sire. Angeli M.… urh, Miss Gabrielle. She arrived at the estate about twenty minutes ago," he said, as if that explained everything.

"What do you mean about Gabrielle?" Julius demanded, confused. "Has someone dared to pick a fight with her against my orders?"

"No Sire, of course not, no one would dare." He assured his Master.

"Then what's going on?" Kyle demanded, patting his pockets, looking for something.

"She was very angry when she arrived. She wanted me to tell her where you had gone," the steward hurriedly explained. "I told her you would be back soon and that she could wait at the bar, I extended her every courtesy," his voice took on an edge of indignation. "She refused to calm down and ran upstairs to your office. Then the crashing started, but because of your orders no one wanted to go and confront her. We just didn't know what to do, Sire." Another crash punctuated the end of his sentence.

"What?" Julius bit out impatiently, although the reality was gradually sinking in. "Gabrielle is up there breaking things by herself?"

Gregory held his breath as he squeaked out the words, "Yes, Sire."

"Damn," exclaimed Kyle, now finished his personal pat down. "I forgot my phone at home, and I haven't called her since this morning. I knew she'd be pissed at being left behind, but that," he paused, his eyes going to the ceiling as something large hit the floor with a loud thud, "sounds extreme, even for her." He made a start up the stairs but Julius grabbed his arm stopping him.

"It's my office she's trashing, I'll deal with it," he said, a little grimly.

When Kyle started to protest Julius cut him off. "If she hurt you in a temper she'd feel horrible afterwards, I'm almost indestructible." He glanced Alexander's way. "I'll call you if I need you," he told him, dismissing the others with a wave and running up the stairs.

He slowed as he approached the doorway to his office. The door stood ajar and in the sudden silence he could hear her heart beating rapidly, her breathing rough with exertion, he could taste her anger in the air. He could also smell the faint trace of her blood; she had obviously hurt herself. He felt a wash of exasperation. He stalked silently through the doorway and stopped, taking in the scene with wide-eyed amazement.

She hadn't noticed his entrance; she was too busy trying to find something unbroken in the mess, her temper not yet satisfied with the degree of devastation in the

237

room. He was suddenly quite pleased that he'd resisted to the urge to put some of his more ancient pieces of art in his office. Nonetheless, there were still a few pieces in here that were irreplaceable, if not terribly valuable. The destruction was virtually complete. It was on a level with a small hurricane having started up in the centre of the room – nothing had been spared. Yet, despite his shock at the state of his private space, he still couldn't help admiring the destructive force that was Gabrielle Bradford.

She was dressed in snug-fitting demin jeans, a tiny, midriff-showing halter-neck, black knee-length boots and Nex's sheath. Though her back was mostly to him he could see a clean slice running across her right cheek bone, a trickle of blood running down to her jaw line. Nex was clutched securely in her right hand and her knuckles were cut and bleeding. Her hair was loose and as wild as her temper. If he hadn't believed what she'd told him about her abilities being Vampire, there was no doubt in his mind now. Right now she was far more Vampire than human.

He realised in an intuitive flash that she was in the grip of the Red Rage. A condition common in young Vampires; a state of uncontrollable fury, usually ignited by severe anger, but sometimes needing no more than a spark of annoyance or irritation. It often happened if a youngster hadn't been feeding well enough. The only remedy was to restrain the Vampire until they calmed down and regained control.

He confidently decided that if she had this much Vampire blood in her veins, his power over Vampires would work on her too. If he could subdue her with mind control, there was far less chance of either of them getting hurt. He took another silent step into the ruined office and threw his power out towards her without warning,

wrapping it around her and commanding her to stillness.
As his power touched her, she spun around to face him,
blood red eyes blazing in fury, confirming his assumption.
It was called the Red Rage for a reason. She stood
unnaturally still for a heartbeat as his power wove around
her, cocooning and binding.

He moved cautiously into the centre of the room,
carefully picking his way over a piece of his office chair
and around an up-ended desk drawer without taking his
eyes from her. Glass suddenly crunched under his boot
and in the same instant Gabi's eyes narrowed. Julius
reacted only just fast enough to catch hold of her wrist as
Nex streaked towards his heart. Not only had she broken
his mental hold on her, she had moved every bit as fast
as a Vampire and caught him completely off guard. She
grunted with the effort of trying to wrench her wrist from
his grasp. He was thankful that she didn't have the full
strength of a Vampire, but at the same time was very
aware of the fact that she didn't heal like a Vampire. He
didn't want to hurt her, though he knew he'd already
bruised her wrists badly, and heaven only knew what
extra damage she was doing to her existing injuries. She
wouldn't feel it in her current state, but once she came
down from the Rage, she'd be in pain.

She swiftly changed tactics. Shrieking, she twisted
around, spinning into him, throwing her legs at his, trying
to bring him down and break his hold at the same time.
Julius kept his grip, falling as she intended but grabbing
her with his right arm, keeping Nex under control with his
left and taking her down to the glass strewn floor with him,
trying to keep her body on top of his, away from the
shattered pieces of glass and crystal he could feel slicing
into his own back. With a small portion of his mind Julius
could sense the other Vampires coming up the stairs, and
he sent out a sharp mental command for them to stop,

making sure one of them kept Kyle back as well. He found himself unusually grateful for his ability to think of numerous things at the same time, as he tried to keep Nex from his heart, Gabi from pulling free, and look for a spot on the floor without too much broken glass all at the same time. She attempted a head-butt to his nose and a knee to his groin at the same time, and he found himself hard pushed to keep his grip on her without hurting her further. The gash across her cheek was oozing blood, and the distraction of the scent wasn't helping his concentration.

He finally spotted an area of the room that was relatively free of glass shards and slackened his grip for an instant. She took the opening and quickly leapt back from him. He was ready and leapt after her, tackling her and throwing her down on a Persian rug. He grabbed for her wrists again, hissing as Nex caught his lower left arm and sliced him open from elbow to wrist. The wound didn't slow or hinder him though, as he forced both her wrists above her head and covered her slight body with his own, pinning her down. With her immobilised underneath him, he quickly found the ulnar nerve in her right wrist and pressed until her fingers slowly and unwilling released their grip on the sword. As Nex fell from her grasp, Gabi growled and hissed in frustration, throwing all her strength into heaving Julius off her body.

In the moment of abrupt clarity, she could suddenly see that it was a Vampire on top of her. His fangs were more fully extended than she had ever seen before; his face was a mask of strain, the muscles along her jaw writhing like angry snakes. The red mist hazing her mind began to dissipate, and she wondered what the hell was going on. She knew she was angry, she knew she wanted to cause harm; to rip, to tear, to break, but she had no idea why.

"Gabrielle," a deep, masculine voice called to her, it sounded strangely stressed. The voice continued, trying to be soothing, but she was in no mood to be soothed. "Gabrielle, I know you're angry, but I need you to try and be calm for a few moments. No one wants to harm you," the reasonable tone of the voice was grating on her nerves, "if you take a few deep breaths the mist will lift from your mind, and you'll start to feel more yourself."

She tried once more to heave the Vampire off of herself, but even as she tried, she could feel the red mist evaporating and the rage begin to drain from her. As her other senses returned, she could smell blood, her own as well as another's. She'd never thought that blood smelt like anything but blood before, of course, she could distinguish between human and animal blood, but this blood had an entirely different accent to it. It smelled...enticing. Somehow delicious. She found her mouth aching with the need to taste it.

"Ugh!" she moaned in disgust as her conscious mind processed that idea. She shook her head slightly, trying to clear the last of the fog. "Julius?" she asked cautiously, blinking as she focused on his tense face hovering above her.

Julius released a relieved sigh and loosened his grip on her wrists a little, his body softening slightly from the rigid cage it had formed over her.

She was suddenly extremely aware of the muscled length of his body nestled demandingly into the relative softness of hers.

"Gabrielle," he replied, looking down at her with a familiar tilt to his eyebrow.

"What are you doing on top of me, why are you bleeding and why are your fangs so long?" she asked in a husky voice.

Some of the tension seem to drained from his face, and he lifted some of his body weight from her, allowing her to move under him, though not removing himself from his disturbing position over the length of her body.

"My fangs are at full length, because you're bleeding." He said, though this made no sense to Gabi. "I'm bleeding because you sliced my arm open with Nex while I was attempting to subdue you, and I'm on top of you because that was the only way I could think of to subdue you without hurting you."

Gabi pulled her wrists free and brought them up to push at his chest, trying to move him further away. He winced slightly seeing the vicious red marks his fingers had imprinted on them. She stopped wriggling, looking bemusedly at her wrists and bleeding knuckles. As the haze continued to clear from her mind, a sharp ache began to pulse through her collarbone, and she stifled a groan.

"I'm even more confused now," she complained, starting to sound annoyed again. "What are you talking about 'subdue me'?"

"You probably want to try and stay calm right now. If you start getting angry again, I'll be forced to 'subdue' you for even longer. Not that I'd mind," he said with a devilish smirk on his diabolically handsome face.

The innuendo in his velvet voice sent a blazing hot zing roaring through her body, her nipples tightened in response and a breath caught in her throat. His head suddenly dipped with the swiftness of a striking snake, and he ran his tongue across the cut on her face, lapping up the trail of blood as he went. A shiver ran right through him as he closed his eyes and savoured the taste.

242

"You taste absolutely delectable," he purred in a rough voice.

She went dead still under him; he could taste her lust turn to uncertainty.

"Don't worry I won't eat you," he said dryly. "Not unless you want me to." He left the sentence hanging, his expression turning to sinful.

She snorted; annoyance replacing the anxiety.

"You idea of bondage sex is a bit too full on for my liking,' she responded, showing him her bruised wrists.

"My apologies," he said, instantly remorseful. "If I could've been more gentle I would have, but you were trying to kill me at the time," he pointed out, lifting his arm to show her the already healing cut, revealed through the tatters of his shirt sleeve.

In that moment her conscious mind was once again shoved into the back recesses of her brain. The sight and scent of Julius's blood, still seeping from the deep gash, drew her like a moth to moonlight. She lifted her head and caught several of the blood drops on her tongue as they slid down his arm. She distantly heard him draw in a quick, surprised breath. The taste spread across her tongue, burning like a trickle of neat whiskey, warm and sharp like a strong red wine. She wanted more; she could feel an uncomfortable ache in her mouth, as though her canines were trying to push further out of her gums. She gasped as another drop landed on her lip and sucked it in greedily. Gabi opened her eyes to find him holding his arm near her mouth; she felt drugged, without a will of her own, but couldn't bring herself to care.

"Run your tongue over the wound, Gabrielle, it will help to stop the bleeding." Julius breathed, his voice rough and unsteady, strangely accented by his fangs.

She found herself complying as though compelled, but not feeling any power flowing from him. She wondered, in a small, back corner of her mind, where the compulsion was coming from. As she licked the length of the angry wound, removing all traces of remaining blood, she realised that the cut was no longer oozing blood, she ran her tongue over it again, feeling almost disappointed that it was closing in front of her eyes.

"Thank you," he said in a deeply sensual voice, "now let me heal yours." He bent his head to her cheek where the cut was still seeping blood.

She willingly turned her head for him, gasping when his tongue gently lapped at the gash, carefully layering saliva over the area. The intense, burning pain of the wound immediately lessened into a warm, dull throb, and she sighed in relief. Even the escalating pain in her shoulder and ribs was subsiding, as though she'd just been given a shot of morphine.

Next, he slowly, languorously brought her hands up to his mouth one at a time and cleaned the blood from her knuckles and a few smaller slices on the backs of her hands. When he raised his face to look at her again, his irises had bled to deep midnight blue, and his breathing was hoarse. She could feel his body hardening where it still lay close against hers, her body tightened in response, a blazing need igniting deep in her core.

It was evidence of their total distraction that neither of them heard or sensed the Vampires in the doorway until someone cleared their throat. They both froze instantly.

"We, uh, came to make sure that you hadn't killed each other," a male voice said, sounding more than a little amused. "Apparently, you have it all under control though. Glad to see you're both alive."

"Yes, Kyle," Julius ground out from between his teeth, "as you can see we are both fine. We will be downstairs as soon as Gabi is feeling more herself." He moved slightly away from her to look at the new arrivals, but held her in place with one arm.

Gabi's cheeks turned a hot flaming red as she caught a glimpse of Marcello, Charlie and Fergus peering around the doorway, surveying the mess with appraising eyes and sending furtive glances at the two of them lying on the floor. They were all trying unsuccessfully to conceal grins. Gabi simply closed her eyes and prayed for the carpet to open up and swallow her.

"I distinctly remember telling the rest of you to stay away from here," Julius's voice had become hard and unfriendly. "I'm sure I can find some work for you if you find yourselves at a loose end."

The rest of the Vampires very quickly seemed to remember something pressing they had to do and vanished, though the sense of their merriment lingered in the air. Kyle gave them a quick amused salute and left too, sauntering back out the door, neatly avoiding a broken chair with an assortment of knives and short swords embedded in the head rest.

Gabi watched as Julius rolled off of her completely, rose lithely to his feet and adjusted his pants slightly, she assumed to accommodate his raging erection. By the heat of his glare at the now empty doorway, his guard were going to find themselves with the most gruelling training he could come up with over the next several days.

"I just remembered why I was so annoyed," Gabi muttered darkly.

Julius tensed immediately, as though he expected her to lunge for Nex, but she had no desire to even move, she just tracked him with her eyes.

"So, I'm not going to apologise for your office," she said defiantly, "but I am sorry for cutting you. I don't know what came over me. I have a nasty temper at times, but I've never lost control like that before."

Julius bent down to her. "Come on, let me help you up, I want to see what other damage you've done to yourself, there's a lot of glass lying around. How about I send someone to the coffee shop, and then I'll try to explain what happened." He deftly lifted her into his arms and began negotiating his way out of the room.

Gabi couldn't even raise the energy to argue with him about carrying her. She felt exhausted, languid and more than mildly frustrated, but also strangely vital, as though she had just had a two week holiday at a health spa. And her shoulder and ribs felt like there was nothing wrong with them. Weird.

"Are you talking about the temper tantrum, or what happened afterwards," she asked.

Julius snorted wryly. "Both, I guess. It's going to be a long night."

Julius took her downstairs back to the large room with the bar and deposited her on one of the couches. She'd felt a brush of his power as they swooped down the staircase, and she assumed he was 'ordering' coffee.

"Sit still," he said as he went over to the bar counter and came back with a small glass bowl.

She looked at the empty bowl in confusion, but he just smiled a tiny lift of his lips, and told her to lean her head back towards him. She gave him a dubious look but shifted so her head was closer to him. Realisation dawned when she felt his deft fingers in her hair and heard the plink of glass shards falling into the bowl. He continued running his fingers through her hair long after the sound of glass dropping into the bowl had stopped. Gabi found the feel of his fingers running through the strands of her curls so calming, so mesmerising and so

246

sensual that she just couldn't bring herself to tell him to stop. It just felt too damn good. Now she knew exactly why cats loved to be stroked over and over again, and why they purred, she felt like purring herself.

They were interrupted by a timid knock at the door. Julius flinched slightly as though he too had been on another plane of existence.

"Come in, Claudia," he said, his tone slightly husky, and got up to take the tray from her. "Is Kyle still here?" he asked her. When she nodded silently he asked her to send him to join them. As he turned to take the coffee to Gabi he found her sitting up flexing her shoulder experimentally. His eyebrows knitted into a small frown.

"I'm sorry," he said. "I know I wasn't particularly careful of your other injuries earlier. The surprise of seeing you in the Rage drove everything else from my mind."

"Apparently you don't have too much to apologise for," she said, continuing to rotate her arm. "My collarbone feels like there's nothing wrong with it, and the ache is even gone from my ribs." She continued her evaluation. "Look," she gasped, showing him her wrists and hands. "The bruising is gone and my knuckles are almost healed."

It was true; there were only faint greenish yellow remnants of bruising where the vivid red and blue imprints of his hands had been and only pale pink marks where her knuckles had been split, grazed and bleeding. She looked up at him in amazement.

He put a steaming coffee cup and a donut into her outstretched hands and smiled at her astonishment.

"I told you that Vampire blood heals," he said wryly, but without a hint of condescension. He was obviously playing it safe.

"Hmmmm," she snorted, burying her nose in the warm steam rising from the coffee. "Maybe I should've listened. Then you and my traitor of a best friend wouldn't have felt that you needed to leave me behind tonight," she said grouchily as Kyle loped into the room. He was carrying Nex and her leather jacket which, miraculously, seemed to have survived unscathed.

"Whoa," Kyle said in mock astonishment. "Did she just say she should've listened to somebody?" When Gabi just glared balefully at him he turned dramatically overacted awestruck eyes on Julius. "Man, I never thought I would hear those words come out of that mouth."

Julius saw the irritation flash across her face. "Gabrielle, keep calm, he's just teasing. Kyle," Julius said in a warning tone, "getting her angry right now isn't a good idea. Grab yourself a drink and I'll attempt to explain."

As Kyle cracked open a beer, Julius turned to her.

"What you just experienced is known in the Vampire community as Red Rage. It's fairly common in recently turned Vampires. It's usually triggered by anger or irritation, occasionally even by fear or a shock, but the root cause is usually a lack of blood. It sometimes takes a young one a few months to figure out exactly how often they need to feed, those who have been underfeeding are more susceptible. The Rage initially builds slowly until the physical need to release the rage is so great that they have to act on the impulse or feel they'll explode. Unfortunately, the physical release does little to calm the rage, and far more to incite it. In this state, nothing and no one near them is safe. The only way to halt the progress of the Rage is to physically restrain them until they've calmed down enough for the Red Rage to dissipate. Feeding helps, but that usually isn't a good idea for the donor. It sometimes requires at least three or four Vampires to restrain one in this state, depending on the strength and skill of the young Vampire. It's called Red Rage because when a Vampire is in the grip of this rage their eyes turn blood red."

Gabi caught Kyle glancing surreptitiously at her eyes. Both of them were so engrossed in Julius's explanation that they didn't even notice Alexander enter the room until he spoke from his position leaning against the door frame.

"So she was in full blown Red Rage?" he asked, sounding incredulous.

Gabi actually jumped.

"Shit," she swore almost spilling her coffee. "Damn freaky Vampire. Breath next time so we know you're there," she scowled at Alexander.

He walked forward to join them, amusement twinkling evilly in his cornflower blue eyes.

"Alexander," Julius said warningly.

"Yes, yes, I know," he said, "no pissing her off if we don't want another demonstration of her destructive capabilities." He folded himself into the couch next to Julius, looking thoughtful. "What do you think this means?"

"I'm not sure," Julius said slowly, but it was clear that he had some idea.

"Are you thinking what I think you're thinking," Alexander asked him with barely disguised excitement.

"Will you two stop talking like telepathic twins and just spit it out?" Gabi ground out tiredly.

The two Vampires looked at each other and with a kind of awed reverence and said, "Dhampir," at the same time.

# CHAPTER 16

"What?" Gabi and Kyle asked in synchronic confusion.

"A Dhampir," Julius repeated slowly.

"What is a Dhampir?" she asked, carefully enunciating the unfamiliar word.

"It's a creature from Vampire legend. A bit like the Vampire equivalent of the Yeti." Julius suddenly broke off when he saw the disbelieving outrage on Gabi's face and rushed on to explain. "Er, that came out wrong, I don't mean in appearance or behaviour. I mean that there are stories of them in Vampire folklore throughout the ages; theories on exactly what they are and how they came to be, descriptions in old books, but no one has ever been able to definitively prove their existence. The young ones dismiss the reports as pure fantasy, but many of the old ones believe there is a thread of truth to the stories."

"What exactly are they supposed to be, and why would you link the word to Gabi?" Kyle asked with a large dose of suspicion in his tone.

"Legend says they're the offspring of a Vampire and human union." Julius could see Gabi's indignation rising again. He held up a placating hand. "Just let me finish."

"Fine, go on," Gabi subsided with a slightly disgruntled snort and set to devouring a chocolate covered donut.

"This half-breed was assumed to come from the mating of a male Vampire to a human female, as it's physically impossible for a female Vampire to become pregnant or bear a child. Her body is in stasis once she's turned, unable to make the changes necessary to sustain a new life inside it. The theory is that a recently turned male Vampire still has viable er, sperm in, er… well…. you know."

Gabi bit back amusement at Julius's discomfort.

"His nutsack," Alexander finished dryly for him, obviously having no aversion to using coarse language in front of a woman.

"Thank you, Lex. I think I had the picture already," she told him quellingly.

Alexander smiled with feigned innocence.

Julius cleared his throat and continued. "A bit like when a human male goes for a vasectomy and there's still a chance he could get a partner pregnant for a few weeks after the operation. Thus it was considered possible for a 'young' male Vampire to impregnate a human woman, and the child of that conception would be born with a combination of human and Vampire traits and abilities. Legend calls this child a Dhampir. They were reputed to grow quicker than normal, and be almost as fast and as strong as a Vampire, have better hearing, smell and eyesight as well as faster healing than a human, and would often have the same special ability of their sire, if their sire had one, though the power would be somewhat diluted."

"You're talking about an ability like yours to control Vampires, or Danté's to control Demons, right?" Gabi asked.

"Yes," Julius affirmed. "There are some other powers as well; such as the ability to completely bend a human to their will, not just the 'stock-standard' ability of ours to wipe or alter human memories or make them look the other way, a skilled Vampire like that can make a human commit suicide or murder their own child. Then there's telepathy, telekinesis and the ability to control animals."

Gabi bit her lip.

"Legend says a Dhampir can subsist on a diet of either human food or blood but is healthiest on a combination of the two. They age slower than humans, but do age, and are resistant to sicknesses and diseases that affect humans. They are not limited by the day and can walk in sunlight like a human without sustaining the damage that full Vampires do. They are also reported to be susceptible to the Red Rage throughout their lives."

Under the sudden intense scrutiny of all three men Gabi felt like a virus under a microscope, she glared back at them each in turn. Julius plunged on with his story.

"Many Vampires have tried to create Dhampirs in the belief that they could produce an army to protect them during the day, or loyal staff to run their businesses without drawing undue attention from humans and Magi. In fact, there are still those who are trying to find a way to create them. As far as any of us know, no one has ever done it successfully. There have been a number of reported pregnancies from these attempts, but most of the children have been born perfectly normal indicating a human sperm donor rather than a Vampire one. A few have been stillborn, and some have had horrible physical birth defects and mental deficiencies and have not survived long. These latter ones seem more likely to have been progeny of a Vampire donor. It seems that the change does somehow affect the pre-existing sperm, but not in a good way."

Julius paused and Alexander took over the story.

"So for decades there's been speculation on how else a Dhampir could be created. Within most myths and legend there is a kernel of truth, you know the old adage 'where there's smoke, there's fire'."

"And now you think you've found the fire," Kyle said in a flat voice.

"Gabi," Julius said softly, "do you know the circumstances of your conception and birth, what gave you your unusual abilities?"

"If I knew and I told you, what would you do with the knowledge?" she demanded, her eyes narrowing in suspicion. "Would you try and create an army of Dhampirs? Would you go around doing horrible things to unwilling human women?"

Julius leaned forward and looked her straight in the eye. "I swear to you, we wouldn't do anything like that. We need to protect this knowledge, keep it from others. Not all Vampires have the same moral code that we do. This is a part of the reason we have to have the facts; we need to be ready and able to spread disinformation about your abilities and your birth. It's only a matter of time before someone else questions your Vampire-like characteristics and works out the truth like we have."

"Will that make other Vampires more likely to try and harm or kill her?" Kyle asked.

"No," Julius said without hesitation. "You need to understand that if she is what we think she is, then she is like our version of the Holy Grail. Everyone would want to possess her, especially the oldest and most powerful." He looked pensively across at Alexander. "This is going to complicate things."

"Not if we can keep it quiet," Alexander disagreed. "We *have* to keep it quiet."

"It means we can't let any of Danté's entourage leave the country," Julius said in a deadly serious voice. "They must never get to report back to the Princeps."

A cold sliver of fear trickled down Gabi's spine at the fervency in Julius's voice when he said 'never'.

"Alright," Gabi said suddenly. "Order us some pizzas, and I'll tell you."

While Kyle placed their order for pizza and went to tell Gregory about the delivery, Gabi began retelling the story as she'd heard it from Byron. Gabi reiterated that she only had the story third hand; her mom had always been reluctant to talk about it with Gabi. She recounted her mother's attack in the alley, and how she'd swallowed a large quantity of the rescuer Vampire's blood, while she was only weeks pregnant with Gabi. The two Vampires were enthralled; they seemed unable to get over how simple the answer to their mystery turned out to be. Julius questioned her about the two Vampires involved in the incident, but she didn't have much to tell him, her mom had been the only one to clearly see both Vampires, and she wasn't talking about the details to anyone. The rescuer Vampire had apparently been sturdily-built with dark brown hair and a beard and moustache but that was as much as her dad had told Byron. They had hoped to see him again one day, to thank him for the rescue, but had never come across him after that and assumed he'd left the area. Then she described her birth and early years through Byron's eyes, briefly, as there wasn't much of noteworthiness in the early years.

Pizzas arrived then; Gregory came in holding them at arm's length, as though he were carrying boxes of live rattlesnakes, and deposited them on the table in front of the non-Vampires with a repulsive shudder. Julius dismissed him with an amused grin, and Gabi wasted no time opening the offering and shovelling mozzarella and Parma ham laden slices into her mouth ravenously.

Alexander and Julius curbed their impatience for the rest of the story and began throwing names at each other in an attempt to identify the Vampire who rescued her mother and who would ultimately be considered her 'sire'. They seemed to know a lot of Vampires. Kyle ate slower than normal, uncharacteristic disquiet hanging over him like a persistent rain cloud.

Gabi cleaned her hands and mouth on a napkin and downed a can of Coke before continuing. She moved onto the years when her 'differences' started showing up, much of the story was from her own memories, but she also filled in things Byron had noted. She relayed everything about the amazing connection she had with animals, as well as her enhanced senses, and the weird ability to sense Vampires and other supernaturals, and when someone was using a supernatural power. She told them about her incredible, by human standards, physical abilities and growth spurts. Then she paused for a moment, a little uncertain about telling them this next part, but then she realised that Julius may actually be able to explain some of her abnormalities. His input may enable her to finally solve some of the mysteries of her own body. She drew a deep breath and plunged on.

"As I reached puberty, my non-human abilities increased enormously. All the usual stuff, just enhanced. Then the negative stuff started as well. My appetite became erratic, I started suffering periods of trembling and weakness in my muscles, my temper was always only a spark away from igniting," she glared warningly at Kyle as his face lifted in a sardonic grin, "and I craved sugar all the time. My mom eventually gave up trying to

255

feed me normally and allowed me to eat whatever I
wanted, but the symptoms just got worse. There were
days I couldn't get out of bed.

Finally, Byron took me to a doctor he could trust, this
guy wasn't a member of the SMV, but he helped out when
he could. It was much easier back then to get blood tests
done without anyone knowing who they were for. So they
took a chance and sent them to a regular laboratory. The
test results showed severe anaemia, an unusually high
antibody count and several other anomalies. The
anomalies were so pronounced that the doctor had to
make up a story about the blood being contaminated to
stop the panic at the laboratory. You'd have to ask Byron
for the exact details of the anomalies, medical stuff all
goes over my head. We've pretty much been working on
controlling these symptoms ever since. I need large
doses of iron on a regular basis, and my blood sugar
levels never quite seem to stabilise. My metabolism
seems to run at hyper speed, chewing through energy like
a shark through sardines, hence my unwomanly appetite.
As a teen I was obnoxious about taking my iron pills, so
Byron eventually found a pharmacist who devised a way
to make lollipops containing the iron supplement. They
satisfied some of my sugar craving at the same time, so I
gave in and ate them. It's become a habit now, and
Byron still has the lollipops made up for me, I think he
sneaks other things into them, but I pretend not to know,"
she said with a rueful smile.

The three men waited in silence for her to continue in
her own time. Alexander got up and went to the bar,
coming back with a bottle of South African Merlot, a bottle
of Jack Daniels and four glasses. Sitting down, he
poured two glasses of wine and two bourbons. Kyle
grabbed one of the bourbons, adding ice and the
remainder of his can of Coke, grinning when Alexander

shook his head in dismay. Gabi picked up a glass of wine without really looking at it and took a large fortifying gulp.

"There is also an odd problem when I get injured," she finally continued. "For two or three days after a serious injury, I lose a lot of my extra speed and strength. My acute senses stay about the same, including the ability to sense Vamps and Demons, and my ability with animals doesn't seem affected either, but I'm not much faster or stronger than a normal human."

"How bad do the injuries need to be to affect you?" Julius asked.

"It's usually worst if I've lost blood, though badly broken bones aren't good either. Bumps and bruises don't worry me much," she told him. "Byron has a theory that my body sends all available energy to heal the injury, withdrawing energy from other physical activity until the initial danger period is over. The weakness doesn't set in immediately; usually only some time after I'm out of whatever situation caused the injury, I suppose once the adrenalin has stopped pumping."

"Hmm," Julius mused, "The theory does make sense. It would explain why your other senses and control over animals doesn't diminish, those don't require physical energy. So the weakness doesn't last until you're fully recovered?"

"No, usually only a few days at most," she answered.

"You obviously heal faster than a full human, but nowhere near as fast as a Vampire or Werewolf, is there a norm to the time it takes you to heal?"

Kyle lightened enough to crack a smile at that question.

"Sore point," he drawled, grinning at Gabi. "She hates that I heal quicker than her, as I have far less down time and rarely need hospital treatment. It just pisses her off no end."

Gabi mock growled at him, looking around for something to throw. Fortunately for him, there was nothing close at hand.

"Kyle," Julius said warningly. "We don't need another Rage incident right now."

"Right, sorry," Kyle replied with mock contrition. "She does heal quicker than normal though. Usually Ian, our resident doctor, works on about one third of the time it would take a full human to heal, but if she doesn't rest and eat properly in the first few days it can take longer. And pretty stubborn about resting," he said with a resigned glance at her.

She gave him a sarcastic pretence of a smile.

"And the Rage?" Alexander asked, "Has she ever been in that kind of rage before?"

"No," both Gabi and Kyle said emphatically.

"I mean, she loses her temper on a regular enough basis," Kyle went on. "Sorry Gabs, but you know it's true," he said with a brotherly smile to her narrow eyed glare. Then he turned back to the others. "But she's never gone to the degree that you were talking about, and I've never seen her eyes turn red or anything. Not even in a fight with Demons." He turned back to Gabi. "Unless there's something you're not telling me?"

"No," Gabi growled, "I can't remember experiencing anything like that before. I've never been so angry that I've lost control of my own actions."

"That's interesting," said Julius. "I wonder what triggered it now? There must be something that's changed to make you susceptible to the Rage. I'll give it some thought, now that I have all the pieces of the puzzle. Alexander and I will also have to discuss what information to allow to leak to explain your abilities. Fortunately, many of them could be explained by a regular intake of Vampire blood. Some Vampires take, what we call, a 'human servant'. This human will serve the Vampire in many ways, often including feeding the Vampire, and in return, the Vampire will share blood with the human, not enough to change them, but enough to ensure they never get sick, they age slower and they heal quicker. They also get enhanced speed, agility and strength, and heightened senses." He glanced at Gabi. "Your mother would have experienced some of these after she ingested the Vampire blood."

Gabi nodded in agreement, Byron had mentioned something like that.

Julius continued. "The effects only last a few weeks, so regular intake is needed to maintain them. I think this is a good basis for a story about your abilities. Alexander and I will throw some ideas together and come up with a feasible story and pass it by you and Kyle. You can also discuss it with Byron before we let the red-herring-cat out of the bag," he said with a small smile. "But you also need to understand that it is important to keep the extent of your ability with animals and your Vampire sense as quiet as possible, even amongst my Clan members, and especially from any non-Clan members. My immediate guard and my household staff I trust with my life, and so with yours too, but beyond that anything is possible. Danté has already infiltrated my Clan, so it's impossible to know who else we can trust with this." He turned to Alexander. "You need to make sure the story of the Red Rage doesn't filter through to the rest of the Clan. Go and speak to the guard now, as well as to Gregory and anyone else who was in the house, I'll reinforce the order later."

Alexander gave a short nod, knocked back the rest of his drink and rose gracefully to do Julius's bidding.

"Now," Gabi drawled as she reached for the wine bottle, "you two are going to tell me what you got up to tonight without me."

Kyle and Julius filled her in on the discovery that Sebastian had found e-mails between Stephan and a source outside the Clan, leaking sensitive information about the Clan's activities. The e-mails also confirmed that they were supposed to kill Gabi. Sebastian had traced the IP address of the e-mails sent to Stefan's private computer, and the evening's mission had been to search the address that the IP was registered to. While they'd hoped to find some occupants in the apartment, it was obviously only being used as a computer access point. They'd lifted all the computer equipment to bring back for Sebastian to go over and had left monitoring equipment to let them know when anyone entered the apartment again. A small contingent of guards would be waiting nearby every night to grab them when they returned, though it was possible they wouldn't go back if they knew that Stephan and Genevieve had died the true death. This would rest on whether there were any other traitors in Julius's Clan, and so far Sebastian hadn't been able to find anything to indicate that. The computer hard-drive from the apartment may hold something new, and Sebastian was working on it at that very moment. He was under orders to let Julius know immediately if he found anything relevant.

"I still do not appreciate being left out of the loop," Gabi grumbled, sounding nothing more than peeved. Somehow she just couldn't get herself anymore more riled up than that. A strange, warm lethargy seemed to have taken hold of her, and she couldn't shake it.

"We're sorry," Julius said, sounding anything but. "You know why we did it though. You needed to recuperate, and we know you put in a full day on a film set; it wasn't that big a deal. We were going to call you as soon as we returned to discuss what we discovered; you just jumped the gun a little."

"Did you drug my wine?" Gabi asked distractedly.

Julius raised his eyebrows in surprise at the abrupt change in topic.

"No, why?" he asked, his body coming to attention as his eyes ran over her, assessing for danger.

"I feel strange," she said, "weightless, and languid."

"Drowsy, confused?" Kyle asked, concern colouring his voice.

"No," she replied. "Not even tired, and I should be by now. In fact, I even feel quite calm and relaxed. I would say maybe it's how humans would feel when they talk about feeling mellow after a few drinks."

Julius suddenly relaxed his anxious pose and smiled ruefully.

"I think you're dead on Gabrielle," he told her, "you are intoxicated."

She frowned at him.

"Impossible, I've only had two glasses of wine, and I've never managed to get drunk, no matter how hard I've tried in the past."

Kyle nodded in agreement with that. "Yep, she's right, she's tried hard. She can outdrink me with ease."

But Julius just shook his head. "I don't mean on alcohol, I mean on my blood."

"What?" Kyle demanded, startled.

Gabi felt her mouth drop open in shock, and then form into a little 'O' as comprehension hit.

"Well, a combination, really, of coming down from the Rage as well as my blood," Julius continued. "I know you didn't take much, but we may find that Vampire blood will have a different affect on you than it would have on a full human. Quite often a Vampire will collapse after a Red

Rage incident; they'll sleep off the effects for up to two days. You haven't passed out, so it may be that my blood has helped forestall that, but it hasn't completely eliminated the effects, and at the same time your body is reacting to having the blood it's craved for years." Kyle was still looking at Julius as though he was speaking Aramaic, but Gabi found that she was unable to form the words to explain it to him, so Julius went on. "Think of it like a teetotaller suddenly having two or three shots of tequila one after another. It would be a huge shock to their body; the teetotaller would be blind drunk in moments."

Kyle still stared at him like things just weren't making sense.

"What do you mean, by her body craving blood?" he asked, glancing between Gabi and Julius suspiciously.

"Ah," Julius said. "Well, you remember I told you that a Dhampir could survive on either blood or human food, but did best on a combination of the two?"

Neither of them responded, but a kind of horror was beginning to dawn in Kyle's eyes.

"So, if we take what Gabrielle told me about her blood deficiencies, it sounds to me as though her body needs something more than human food. Taking into account the severe iron deficiency it would make sense that her body is craving blood. What we need to find out is whether it's craving human blood or Vampire blood." He said it in a calm, unemotional way, as though they were simply talking about taking a vitamin supplement, but Gabi could still feel the shock frozen on her face.

"Hold on a second," Kyle protested shaking his head. "I'm missing something here. When did Gabi get some of your blood?"

Gabi noticed Julius drop his eyes from Kyle's with the slightest look of guilt.

"During the Rage, I cut him with Nex," Gabi explained.

"Yes, when I was holding her down, my arm was bleeding practically into her mouth, "Julius said chivalrously.

Gabi sighed. "No, don't prettify it," she said with resignation. "Your blood just called to me on a level I've never experienced before. I couldn't resist the urge no matter what my personal thoughts were on the issue. I've never come across anything so enticing in my life."

"You've smelled human blood before, I imagine," Julius asked her, "didn't it smell enticing to you at all."

"Well, I've never understood the human aversion to the smell of blood. Blood doesn't smell bad to me, I guess. But I've never been tempted to taste it, or thought of it as appealing."

"Could it have been a side-effect of the Rage?" Kyle asked.

"Well, I guess the rage could have intensified the craving, but I doubt it would have created the craving," Julius mused. "In full Vampires the only side-effect is the need for sleep, but Gabi is rather unique, so anything I say is merely conjecture or educated guesses at this point."

"Well, there is one positive aspect to tonight's little escapade," Gabi mused.

"And that is?" Kyle asked.

"Jules' blood fixed all my injuries, so I can be back on patrol tomorrow night," she said smugly.

Kyle looked sceptical, so she pulled away the collar of her shirt to show him the place where Genevieve's bite had been. It was completely healed with a small, shiny, slightly puckered scar. "And I can tell you that my ribs and collarbone are good as new. Look, even the bruising has gone." She pulled the bottom of her shirt up to just under her bra to show them the flawless skin over her ribs. Alexander re-entered the room just then.

"No one will talk. They understand the repercussions," he informed Julius.

"Good," Julius said shortly, then filled him in on what they'd discussed while he was out.

Gabi sat listening for a while as the men talked things through, she knew they were talking about her, but she couldn't really bring herself to care. She shifted her body, curling her legs up underneath her and resting her head on Kyle's shoulder, then she decided to close her eyes for a moment until what the guys were talking about started to make sense. It must have been hours later when she felt someone lift her off the couch and her warm Werewolf pillow, and settle her comfortably against a solidly muscled chest. Her sleepy senses told her it was Julius who was holding her; she breathed in his cool, masculine scent and let herself drift back to a doze. She barely felt the mattress and pillow that Julius put her down on, or the warm comfortable weight of a thick, fleeced blanket that he gently threw over her after taking off her boots and knives. But somewhere deep in her subconscious she was aware of the fact that he spent a long time standing near the bed, just watching her sleep, with something like wonder on his face.

# CHAPTER 17

When she opened her eyes, it was just past sunrise. She knew she wasn't in her own bed, but the memories of the previous night were so fresh in her mind that she knew immediately where she was. She sat up in the large, unfamiliar bed, stretching luxuriously. She felt wonderful. There was no other word for it. The pain in her ribs and shoulder was a distant memory. But it was more than that; she felt 'right', like her skin and bones and muscles had just not fitted together correctly until this moment. Now everything was absolutely as it should be. The world was in sharp focus, and she felt warm and energised.

Wow, could that all be attributed to the small amount of Julius's blood she'd taken? It seemed ridiculous, but it had to be, there was no other explanation. Pizza sure didn't have that effect on her. If it had, she'd have bought a pizza restaurant years ago. The thought of pizza woke her stomach up, and it growled impatiently. Well, that hadn't changed, she thought wryly and threw the blanket off to get up and look for a bathroom. She realised her breakfast was going to have to wait until she drove to the nearest bakery or take-away, not much chance of finding breakfast in a Vampire house.

Nex and her other weapons lay on a chair near the door, and her car keys and mobile lay on the nightstand. Force of habit made her pick up the phone to check it. She frowned and blinked, and then padded to the window on the opposite side of the room to pull the curtains back. She peered out at the semi-dark sky in alarm.

"Damn," she breathed. "Sunset, not sunrise. Bloody hell! I've slept the whole day."

She spun as she heard the almost noiseless opening of the bedroom door. Julius filled the doorway with his wide shoulders, his head just brushed the top of the door frame. She realised she could smell his scent from across the room; it was a delicious mix of new leather, cinnamon bark and the air after a summer storm. She could also smell the latté in his left hand and the bag of pastries in his right.

"Is that your idea of a peace offering for leaving me to sleep all day?" she growled huffily.

"If you want it to be," he replied. "Would it work as one?"

"Not until after I've used a bathroom." A sudden feeling of panic swept over her. "You **do** have a bathroom, don't you?"

Julius restrained a grin, nodding his head towards a door on the far side of the antique dressing table.

"Yes, they came with the house. We do use the baths and showers, so it seemed unnecessary to remodel completely to our own specifications. The toilets are still in place. Claudia said to tell you that anything else you may need is in the vanity cupboard. I'll leave you to your ablutions," he said, moving to set his offerings on the dressing table. "I'll be in the entertaining room when you're done, my office is still in the process of being refurbished," he said with a deadpan expression.

Gabi stamped down on the guilt that threatened to surge through her—it was his own fault.

"Don't rush," he added over his shoulder as he headed back out the door, "Kyle said he'd go past your house and make sure the rabid animal was fed and watered, and Byron knows where you are." He closed the door behind him as Gabi hurried for the bathroom.

After devouring the coffee and pastries, she'd intended to take a quick shower, regardless of Julius's reassurance. She really wanted to get home; she needed a change of clothes and to check on Razor and Slinky. She also needed to get back on patrol, she'd had enough nights off, and she didn't want to put too much pressure on the new recruits. But once she stepped into the huge shower with its multiple shower heads and enormous array of gels, body scrubs and shampoos, she couldn't help herself. She pampered her skin and hair and then stood in the jets of hot water and let them massage the last of the stiffness from her muscles.

As she luxuriated in the heat and gentle pressure, her mind whirled through the revelations of the previous night. While many things didn't make sense, one thing was abundantly clear; her body wanted blood, and not just any blood, Julius's blood. That was really going to complicate matters.

By the time she got back into the bedroom, a fresh set of clothes was lying on the bed. They were her own clothes, the sort she'd wear on patrol, so she guessed that meant Kyle was back. She grabbed the hairdryer from the dresser and gave her hair a brief dry using her fingers. She dressed quickly and grabbed her keys, mobile and weapons on her way out the door. She realised, as she strode down the corridor towards the large staircase, that she'd need to grab some more food somewhere before starting her shift, the coffee and pastries had hardly touched sides.

Several male voices were coming from the entertainment room and found she could pick out most of them individually. Julius was obvious, as was Kyle and Alexander. Two other deeper tones she identified as Liam and Nathan, and then she felt her heart skip in shock as she recognised Byron's milder tone. She covered her unease and strode into the room confidently, nodding to each of the Vampires and going to give Byron a peck on the cheek.

"What are you doing here?" she demanded in an admonishing tone, throwing a questioning glare at Kyle.

"Don't glare at me Hellcat," Kyle said, throwing his hands up in a defensive gesture. "Not my idea."

Byron caught her hands, bringing her attention back to him.

"It wasn't Kyle's idea, Gabi," he agreed, "you can stop blaming him. I felt I needed to talk to Julius and Alexander myself after Kyle told me what they revealed to you last night about their Dhampir legends."

When Gabi's grim expression didn't soften, Julius said evenly, "He has my protection Gabi, he is safe here, and no one in this house will speak of his presence here or his association with you or the Society. I have made absolutely sure of it."

He emphasised the last words enough for Gabi to know how he'd made sure of it. She relented slightly, and her angry stance eased.

"Gabi," Byron said evenly, "it's not just the Dhampir legends that have brought me here. We've had some disturbing news, and I wanted to discuss this with Julius as well. I've waited for you, so that we can discuss it together.  I've asked Julius to include his most trusted lieutenants," he nodded towards Liam and Nathan.

Byron was keeping his voice calm and moderated, but Gabi could detect the underlying stress in it.  She took a deep, steadying breath; this wasn't going to be pretty.

*************************

Gabi was in the mood for a good fight.  She was still trying to be mindful of the possibility of the Red Rage returning; Julius had said there was a good chance it would, and she wasn't going to let it claim her again.  It rankled that this was supposed to be simply a reconnaissance mission.  When Byron had told them about the Magi Seers picking up a sense of evil emanating from this particular building, he insisted that they were only to find out what was inside and not go rushing in until they knew what they were facing.

She and Julius were being trailed by three of his personal guards; Nathan, Fergus and Marcello, as they stalked silently through the dark alleyway.  From the alley on the far side of their targeted building, Gabi heard a cat hiss and the sound of its claws on rough concrete as it took flight.  Those were the only sounds that gave away the location of Kyle and Alexander's group which was closing in from the other side.

A slight breeze eddied through the narrow street making Gabi wrinkle her nose at the array of malodorous smells it stirred up as it passed. Ugh, her ultra sensitive sense of smell she could almost do without.  She moved forward cautiously, trying to resist the urge to check that the Vampires were still behind her, they were so quiet and moved so smoothly that, to her normal senses, she felt utterly alone.  Only her supernatural ESP told her they were all less than five metres from her.  She held up a hand and brought the group to a halt, while she opened her senses to feel what was waiting for them inside the building. It was a relatively modern warehouse in an industrial area, and there was some kind of Magical protection around it. She still wasn't getting anything from it, her senses were just picking up the whole building as a solid supernatural being, she couldn't penetrate the shell to find out what and how many waited inside.

"This is SO off," she said low in her throat.

They were all wearing digital comlink devices, state of the art, and only barely available to the military elite. Lord and Lady only knew where Byron had managed to get them. They consisted of a small plastic patch, the size of a plaster, stuck on each of their necks near their voice boxes, as well as a smaller, barely visible patch placed behind each ear. They each also had a titanium encased microprocessor, the size of half a credit card, taped to their bodies somewhere, that was up to personal preference, and Gabi had hers (much to the amusement of the males) taped inside her bra. She knew it would be safe there and had little chance of falling off.

"Still nothing?" Kyle's quiet voice came through so clearly it felt like he was speaking directly into her skull.

"Nothing but a really bad feeling," she murmured back.

"So, are we agreed then?" Julius chimed in, "We wait for your Magus?"

Gabi sighed. "Yes, we wait for Athena," she agreed irritably. "She'd better hurry up."

Gabi was officially 'top dog' on this mission, something that the Vampires had agreed to surprisingly easily, apparently Demons made Vampires as nervous as anyone else. But she was treating it more as a collaborative effort, it seemed pointless to her to ignore the input of men who had been in more conflict than she would ever see in her lifetime. She tried not to have an ego when it came to that sort of thing, ego could get you killed quicker than anything else in this game.

Gabi's group moved back down the alley to where a large dumpster offered protection from the weak moonlight filtering through the clouds and hunkered down to wait. The Vampires were eerily still, Gabi had to restrain herself from fidgeting; staying still with the adrenalin pumping was not usually an option for her. Her restless energy needed an outlet.

"Kyle," she said softly, "you'd better go and meet Athena and bring her in. Don't forget she doesn't know much about being quiet so you'll have to give her some pointers. Get her to try it from a distance first; the closer she gets the higher the chance they'll hear her."

"Gotcha," Kyle's voice came back, "on my way."

"Do you think we need to check the rear section?" she asked no one in particular but Julius replied.

"It was reported as having no exit points, but it can't hurt to be sure," he murmured softly.

She suppressed a small, delicious shiver.

"Marcello," he said, the order clear.

The slightly built Vampire gave a quick flash of teeth and was gone.

Gabi chewed on her lower lip and ran her fingernails up and down the ridged hilt of a dagger strapped to her side, her eyes constantly roving over the darkened windows and doors on their side of the building.

Julius smiled as he watched her; he could see it was taking every ounce of her control to keep from pacing. Being still was not a natural state for her, he'd come to realise. Even when she was sitting or sleeping, she wasn't still for more than a few seconds at a time. Constantly in motion. He'd spent a long time watching her sleep today. He couldn't explain why he hadn't been able to drag himself out of the room; watching her had given him both a strong sense of peace and calm as well as an intense, protective anxiety as he replayed his recent premonition over and over again in his mind, determined to find a way to change it. Eventually the sun had risen well above the horizon and the brightness in the room had become uncomfortable. All the rooms in the house had blackout blinds, but he'd thought she would feel better if she woke to sunlight rather than utter dark, so he'd left hers open and retired to his own room to muse. It had been mid-morning before he fell asleep, and then Alex had roused him an hour before sunset to discuss some business. Most Vampires would have felt sleep deprived with that little sleep, but he'd developed the ability to handle it and could even go the entire day without sleep, something few Vampires ever mastered.

"Athena's here," Kyle reported in a low voice. "She's starting the counterspell now; she says it will take a few minutes."

"Oh. Shit." Marcello's accented voice came softly but fervently over the comlink.

"What?" barked Julius, even as the four shadows crouching near the dumpster reared up and sped towards the rear of the building.

"There's an underground opening here," Marcello said tersely. "It's been made to look like a manhole cover, but the scents around it indicate recent use by Demons and some other creature I've never smelled before."

"Fall back, get out of sight," Gabi hissed. "We don't want them knowing we're here."

"Too late," Marcello grunted, and they could all hear the sound of his sword clearing its sheath.

The other four followed suit, drawing their respective weapons, abandoning stealth and running full tilt down the alley.

"Kyle," Gabi shouted, "spread out your men and keep the other exits covered, and keep Athena working on the counterspell. We need to know what we're dealing with."

They leapt an eight foot wire fence at the end of the alley without pausing and rounded the corner into a grimy, unlit parking lot. Marcello was backing towards them, his sword out, swinging menacingly in front of him and a wicked looking dagger in his left hand. Pouring out of the ground were hulking, misshapen human forms, hissing, grunting and snuffling. As the pale moonlight bathed them in an eerie, blue glow, it was clear that there was no consciousness behind their flat, dead eyes, no thought behind their jerky, uncomfortable movements, simply mindless hunger.

"Ghouls," Gabi breathed in horror, "dozens of them."

"What the fook?" Fergus' revulsion was clear in his voice as the smell of rotting meat rolled over them like a tangible cloud.

"They're Ghouls," Gabi repeated, "humans who've been bitten by Demons, they become mindless, hungry…things. I've only come across two before. They're very hard to kill. They'll eat anything that comes near their mouths, so keep your body parts away from them. Not very clever but they don't bleed out and they don't seem to feel pain."

"How do we kill them?" Julius asked tersely, sizing up the horde that was spreading out and lumbering towards them. He'd heard stories of Ghouls but he'd never encountered any, they were enough to make even him shudder.

"Only one way I know of for sure. Kyle?" she called, "We need Lance here and as many flame throwers as Byron can find. Now!"

She addressed her small group without looking at them, once again the cold, hard Angeli Morte. "We'll have to fend them off as best as we can until the flame-throwers get here. Chop off limbs and heads, but be aware that chopped off bits keep moving; they can still do damage, especially the mouths."

Alexander's voice came over the comlink for the first time. "We're on our way," he said, but Kyle's voice broke in before he could say any more.

"Athena's almost done, Byron's got the message about Lance and the flame-throwers. Lance should make it here in about fifteen minutes; the flame-throwers will be closer to twenty."

"Oh," Gabi gasped and swayed on her feet.

Julius caught her arm and steadied her without taking his eyes off the Ghoul army.

"The warehouse," she said shortly by way of explanation. "Lex, stay where you are. The warehouse is full of Demons, I count five, no six, and at least three Vampires. Ahhh," she shook her head in frustration, "They're moving too much. They're heading for the street-side entrance. We'll hold the Ghouls here, you and Kyle need to stop the Demons inside getting away, keep Athena with you to banish them if you can't kill them."

She didn't hear whether Alexander agreed or not as the first of the Ghouls rushed them and the onslaught began.

The Demon-infected humans might have been ungainly, uncoordinated and lacking in anything except the most basic of intelligence, but they made up for it with speed and strength and a complete lack of reaction to pain. Gabi and the Vampires were faster and stronger but hugely outnumbered. The small group set their backs to the wall of an adjoining building and began chopping limbs, stabbing, spearing, beheading. Their world narrowed down to a blur of hands and mouths and crude metal weapons. The Ghoul army soon began to look like something out of a cheap horror movie, cuts and gashes, missing limbs and gaping wounds as the defenders set about cutting them to pieces.

Gabi found herself sparing regular glances at the rough tarmac looking for groping hands and gnashing mouths. She was intensely glad that Ghoul saliva didn't affect like Demon saliva did as she already had several sets of tooth marks on her calves, and her ruined boots would have to be binned after the fight. It was all out slaughter of the Ghouls, but for each one they cut down another took its place and the arms and hands of the first began moving towards them or moving towards the bodies they'd been severed from. Headless, limbless bodies careened around crazily, bumping into others or rolling around on the ground. Gabi noticed some of them picking up the severed pieces, and it looked as though the pieces were trying to reattach themselves. They didn't spout blood when you dissected them but oozed thick, red gore instead; the ground was gradually being coated in it and was becoming slick and slippery.

Through the comlink she could hear the occasional sound of grunts and groans as well as Kyle and Alexander shouting orders but pushed it all to the back of her consciousness. She'd hear if something had gone horribly wrong on their side, and she and her band of Vampires were just barely holding their own.

Nathan was the most silent of the Vampires, fighting with a single-minded intensity, always casting glances to see where Julius was, trying to be close enough to defend his sire. Fergus fought like a madman. A controlled madman, she corrected mentally as she ducked to avoid a metal fencing stake being used like a baseball bat. Fergus looked like a man who loved battle, he was grinning from ear to ear and picking up body parts to fling across the parking lot as he bellowed insults and dared the Ghouls to get him. Gabi was relieved that his voice transmitter had been turned off or broken. He appeared to be having the time of his life. Marcello was quick and agile, darting in and cutting a Ghoul down before it even knew he was close enough; he was utterly intent on his objective, but hadn't seemed to lose the initial horror of what they were fighting. He shuddered every time he got close to one of them and had a permanent, horrified grimace on his handsome face. Julius was poetry in motion; his swordsmanship was consummate, his movements quick, lithe and confident, his expression intense and focused. He spared a quick glance her way, throwing her a ghost of a grin as he effortlessly decapitated another Ghoul and set to chopping its groping arms off.

Gabi and the Vampires were keeping to a tight, defenders formation, leaving each other room to swing but watching each other's backs and gradually moving around the edge of the parking lot, keeping the solid walls of other buildings to their backs. They needed to keep moving to avoid standing on the bodies, limbs and entrails littering the ground they'd been fighting on. As they went, the small group fell into a routine of fight, dismember, kick and throw body parts as far away as possible, then fight, dismember, kick, fight.

At some point the waxing moon broke through the barrier of cloud and lit up the combat zone, and Gabi found her eyes drawn to the mass of attackers, she tried to count heads, well, attached heads anyway. Dozens of dead eyes glittered at her in the pale light; she gave up counting at twenty as the horror of the number of 'turned' humans began to dawn on her. This couldn't be accidental, Demons weren't often capable of leaving a human alive once they attacked; this had to be an orchestrated event.

As yet another Ghoul rushed her, she realised that it wasn't only men who had been infected, she'd seen some women amongst them, only recognisable by longer hair and daintier bodies, but the one rushing her now was barely more than a child. It seemed to have been a young girl. Once. Her ragged denims and dark, grimy T-shirt were sexless, but her features were refined and her hair longer than was fashionable for a boy, her body hadn't even had time to develop curves. Gabi suppressed a shudder and shoved down her feelings of guilt and horror as the dead eyes fastened on her. The Ghoul child bared its teeth and lunged for her. She dispatched the youth as quickly as possible and kicked the arms and head away to the side of the fracas. She spun away, scanning for her next victim.

"Shit!" She cursed as she almost fell over something in the dark. Righting herself, she found a head rolling on the tarmac: mouth open in a macabre grin, tongue waving hungrily. She aimed a boot at it and sent it flying through the air and into the chest of a newcomer just entering the edge of the fray.

"Thanks," the newcomer said with a grimace. The Vampires all spun towards the voice; none of the Ghouls had said an intelligible word throughout the entire fight.

"Lance," Gabi yelled with relief. "Sorry about that," she grinned as he kicked the head away from him back into the carnage. She wiped at a smear of gore across her face as she slashed Nex across the throat of another Ghoul. "Feel free to help out, but keep the flames," she broke off for a moment to duck under a swinging crowbar and then spun to finish off hacking the head from the burly shoulders, "away from our allies." She nodded towards the Vampires, who'd returned to the fight once they realised Lance was on their side.

"Sure thing, Hellcat," Lance replied, lazily kicking away a Ghoul who rushed towards him.

In the next instant, a Ghoul near the back of the fray emitted a loud unearthly yell and began smoking. Within seconds, he was engulfed in flames. The rest of the mindless creatures didn't seem to even be aware of one of them standing burning in their midst; they simply moved around him, though they seemed to take care to avoid the flames.

"Holy fook," Fergus exclaimed, pausing to look at the suddenly burning Ghoul in astonishment. He glanced back to Lance with gleeful amazement. "Now that's a handy talent to 'ave," he shouted with approval.

Lance gave the imposing Vampire a self-mocking bow just as another Ghoul burst into flames.

Fergus roared with laughter and renewed his attack on the ragged remains of the Ghoul army.

Gabi could feel the muscles in her arms beginning to burn. It wasn't often they had to fight such a sustained battle, usually by this stage whoever they were fighting would've backed off to regroup giving both sides time to catch their breath, but the Ghouls simply kept coming, and would until the very last one had been cut down and burned.

"Kyle," she called, "what's happening on your side?"

His voice came back, sounding a little breathy. "One Vampire made a run for it; Liam and Alex are chasing him down. We're dealing with the last of the Demons, the other two Vamps are dust," he reported.

"Alexander," Julius's voice didn't betray a hint of the fight he was in the middle of. "Take that one alive."

"Yes, Boss," Alexander replied with mild sarcasm, "we're trying. But he's not making it easy. Ahh, I think we have him cornered now."

The first of the burning Ghouls collapsed onto the tarmac and disintegrated, another five or six were burning where they stood. Gabi glanced around, assessing how many were left. They seemed to have stopped pouring from the hole in the ground but she couldn't know if there were more inside. Ghouls didn't show up on her radar like Demons and other supernaturals did apparently. She started making her way to the underground entrance to try and look inside.

"The flame-throwers are three minutes away Gabs," Kyle's voice echoed in her head. "We've cleared the warehouse. Charlie is going to stay with Athena out front and wait for the flame-throwers. Quentin and I are on our way to you."

"Watch your step when you get here," Gabi warned with a grunt as she kicked another head away into the darkness. Then she ducked into the shadows away from the main fight, grateful for the clouds that once more obscured the moonlight as she rounded the dwindling horde and made for the gaping hole in the ground. She heard Julius curse suddenly, as he realised she had slipped away.

"Gabrielle, what are you doing?" he demanded over the comlink.

"Don't worry," she replied, "I'm just going to see if that's the last of them. I'm sure you'll hold your own without me for a minute or two."

She rubbed briefly at a numb spot on her left shoulder where she had taken a hit from a crowbar. She'd hardly felt it at the time, but the numbness was wearing off, and a deep ache was creeping in. She reached the entrance and peered inside. It was dimly lit, obviously Ghouls didn't have the best night vision, and she could see a short flight of rudimentary wooden steps leading down into a narrow passageway crudely dug out of the earth. She couldn't see further than a few metres where the passage hit a T-junction, one side heading straight towards the warehouse, the other leading away from it.

"Damn," she swore softly; realising she was going to have to go down and check. She looked up to see if the rest were holding their own and flinched as a shadow moved next to her.

"Just me," Julius said quickly as Nex came up.

"Don't you know better than to sneak up on a girl in a Ghoul fight?"

"You're not going down there alone," he said, his tone brooking no argument. Which only made Gabi want to argue, of course.

Fortunately, common sense prevailed and she simply said, "Fine," and started down the steps before he could get in front of her. She heard his faint exasperated growl as he followed her. She peeled the small voice receiver off the skin behind her ear and tucked it into a pocket; the litany of shouts and commands was becoming too distracting.

The corridor was just wide and high enough for her to move comfortably, meaning it was too narrow and too low for Julius. It didn't make him move any less gracefully, but it did make him hunch his shoulders and try to pull his head in like a tortoise. Her self-satisfied smirk lasted until she cautiously peered around the first bend. The corridor to the left ran for another few meters and ended in a short flight of steps leading up to a solid looking metal door; that would lead into the warehouse she was sure.

The corridor to the right grew slightly wider and extended in a straight line as far as she could see in the dim light thrown from a few make-shift fluorescent lanterns hanging from the ceiling. On either side of the corridor, crude doorways were hacked into the hard-packed earth walls. There were dozens of doorways, spaced about four metres apart, each sporting a rough, wooden door. Most of them stood open but a few were still shut tight. She felt the cool, muscled weight of Julius's body as he pressed close to her to peer around the corner too. She felt her mouth fill with saliva and the now almost familiar ache in her canines as his scent enveloped her. She forced her mind back to the dank, earthy passageway and its closed doors.

"What do you think?" he asked quietly. "More of them behind the closed doors?"

She looked back at him. "Let's go find out." They moved cautiously into the wider passage and crept to the first door, which was standing open. They peered in, assessing for danger with all of their senses.

"Seems clear," Julius murmured softly.

Gabi nodded agreement and they warily entered the underground room. It had also been hacked out of the bare earth, it was damp and cold and lined with rows of what looked like crudely made bunk beds. There was an open hole in the ground in one corner, and Gabi and Julius could tell what it was for without going to check. The stench was almost enough to be a physical force. The floor was littered with bones and small skulls, nothing looked human, probably dog, cat and rat, Gabi thought with shiver of revulsion. Having quickly established that there was no threat in the empty room, they moved to the first closed door. It was bolted shut from the outside by a thick steel rod. They paused to listen carefully. Gabi knew Julius's hearing would be better than hers, so she looked at him expectantly after he'd pressed his ear to the roughened wood. Gabi could hear sniffling and what sounded to her like quiet moaning.

"How many?" she mouthed at him.

"At least three," he mouthed back.

"Ready?" she whispered, settling Nex comfortably in her right hand and pulling another knife from a thigh sheath.

Julius pulled her hand from the bolt. "My turn," he said, putting his own hand on the bolt and drawing it back before Gabi could do more than roll her eyes. They burst though and shifted into defensive crouches either side of the door, ready for anything.

Nothing happened.

There were three figures huddled on two almost bare pallets. None of them moved to attack. One whimpered in fear and another began crossing itself repeatedly, muttering what sounded like the Lord's Prayer. The others just sat still like the proverbial deer in the headlights. There were two bodies lying in a far corner of the room, well into decomp by the smell of them. The live ones were sitting on a couple of filthy, threadbare blankets and were dressed in dirty tattered clothing. Their hair was dishevelled, matted and all three were male if the ratty facial hair was anything to go by.

"They're still human," Gabi whispered, not sure if she was speaking to herself or Julius.

"They could still be infected," Julius warned. "Maybe they haven't had time to become fully Ghoul yet. How long does the transformation take?"

"I don't know." Gabi replied.

"How long have you been here?" Julius demanded of them.

They all just looked at him in utter terror, not one of them could get a word out, and the one who had been moaning began to cry softly.

"Bugger, they're scared shitless," Gabi cursed roundly. "We'll leave them here for now. Byron will know what to do with them. Let's carry on and see what other horrors this crypt holds." They backed out of the cave-like room and Julius shot the bolt back in place.

As they headed towards the next doorway, the acrid stink of burnt flesh, hair and clothing came wafting down from the entranceway. Apparently, the flame-throwers had arrived.

They checked three more open rooms and found all of them in much the same state as the first, give or take a body or three. Gabi had begun holding her breath whenever they entered one — the stench was stomach churning, she was sure she wouldn't feel like eating for a week.

The next door they came to was closed. The sounds from the other side seemed familiar, almost identical to what they had heard from the other occupied room. If anything, the sniffling sounded more like crying. They didn't let up their guard and entered the same way as before, quickly and ready for anything.

On the pallets this time was a woman holding a small body in her lap. She was facing away from the door, her shoulders hunched protectively as she sniffled over the limp bundle in her arms. Gabi froze in shock. A mother and child, in these conditions? Her stomach rolled nauseously but her anger burned white hot. She unfroze and moved closer to the pair, wanting to see if there was any hope of saving the child, though she could only hear one heartbeat besides her own.

As she bent towards the woman, she heard Julius say, "No Gabi, I don't..." and in that instant the woman struck. Hurling the body of the child off her, she spun and plunged a splintered shard of wood straight into Gabi's side.

"No, you can't have her!" the woman shrieked. "Child of Satan. She's mine. You can't have her." The woman was raving now, screaming as she gathered up the pitifully small body and backed into a corner like a brutalised animal.

"Gabrielle," Julius shouted in alarm. He reached her before reality did and caught her as she swayed towards the dirt floor, her hand clutching at the crudely made stake protruding from just under her right ribs.

"Fuck," she said slowly as she felt hot, sticky blood seep onto her hand.

# CHAPTER 18

"No," thought Julius desperately, 'this can't be it, this isn't right; it's not the same as the vision."

"Gabrielle," he breathed, gathering her up with infinite care, his mind torn between knowing it was better to leave her where she was so as to limit the damage, and needing to get her out of that filthy hole with its dreadful inhabitants. He looked into her eyes as the reality of what had happened registered in them. He could see the emotions lick over her face: confusion, shock, pain and then indignant anger. When he saw the anger, he knew he would take the chance and get her out.

"Kyle," he yelled, louder than necessary for the comlink, "Gabrielle's been injured, we need a stretcher and medics."

"Shit," Kyle cursed, then, "Charlie, send the medic back here fast, we're almost done so it'll be safe enough. Julius, do I need to send men down there? How bad is she hurt?"

"No, don't send anyone, we can clean up down here later," Julius replied. "I'm going to need some help getting her out the last section of the passage. It's very narrow, and I won't fit through carrying her."

He stopped at the intersection and glanced up to see Kyle already manoeuvring himself sideways down the narrow passage. Alexander was at the top of the staircase peering down into the gloom. Gabi was lying quietly in his arms, but he could feel the tension in her body as she braced herself against the pain, one hand clenched around the offending shard of wood. He was thankful that she knew enough about penetrating injuries not to try and pull the stake out. Kyle slowed and worry filled his eyes as he got close enough to scent the blood and see the stake protruding from her bloodied fingers.

"There's a door here I think leads to the warehouse," Julius snapped at Kyle. "See if you can find a way to open it, otherwise we'll have to take her out through there," he nodded back down the tight space behind Kyle.

"I can walk," Gabi said irritably, starting to wriggle in Julius arms, but a sharp, hissed intake of breath said clearly she wouldn't be.

"Hellcat, just lie still and behave," Kyle grumbled, as he squeezed through the cramped space of the intersection and worked his way to the metal door. "How the fuck did you get yourself staked anyway?" The surface of his tone was mildly admonishing and slightly exasperated, but Julius could hear the genuine concern underlying his teasing.

Gabi flicked him the bird with her free hand, knowing he would see it even in the gloom.

"What? Now I'm not Vampire enough to get staked?" she asked snarkily, and then coughed; a hoarse, rattling sound. She wiped her hand across her mouth and tried to hide the evidence of the blood smear as she tensed her body trying not to cough again. Alexander had reached them now, his slighter build making it easier for him to navigate the narrow space than other two men.

"Clever Vampires learn how to **not** get staked," Alexander retorted, "your basic training seems to be sorely lacking." He had his face set in a disapproving frown, but his eyes betrayed his own concern. He gave Julius a look loaded with meaning.

Julius shut his eyes and sighed. "Let's get her out first and see the damage," he told his second in command.

"Are you two talking like Siamese twins again?" she asked a bit breathlessly. "Do you know how annoying that is?" She ran out of breath after that, and the three men could hear the gurgle of fluid in her lungs as she tried to draw her next breath.

"What's with that door, Wolf?" Alexander asked.

Kyle snorted in disgust. "No fucking way in from this side, it's smooth as ice, no way to even wrench it from its moorings.

"It might cave the place in if we tried." Julius pointed out.

"I could go around, try to find a way to open it from the other side," Kyle suggested.

"Give her to me," Alexander said, "I'm smaller than you two, maybe I can get her through.

Passing her to Alexander proved difficult to do in the narrow space. Julius couldn't hand her directly across without driving the stake further into her body. It took Gabi a full minute of arguing to get Julius to set her on her feet so Alexander could take his place. He only gave in to stop her from talking; they all knew her right lung had collapsed and she was fighting for every breath. She was on her feet for less than a second before Alexander took her weight in his arms, every bit as gently as Julius himself had held her. Then he put his back to one side of the narrow passage, holding her as close to his body as he could, keeping one watchful eye on the stake, and began to smoothly crab-walk her out of the underground house of horrors.

"Still want to knock my fangs out?" he teased her with a toothy leer as Julius heard her painful, rasping breath becoming more laboured.

She smacked Alexander around the head half-heartedly with the hand that was draped over his shoulder. "Anytime Lex Boy…… just give me a few minutes……..to recover."

It was only seconds later that they all reached the open air and saw that the medic was already there with a stretcher. Alexander laid her on it with utmost care and then backed off as Kyle rushed to her side, crowding the human medic who was trying to assess the damage. Julius moved to her other side.

"Gabrielle," he said taking her hand, he paused until she drew herself out of the haze of pain and focused on him. "Let me give you blood. You've seen now how it can heal; you'd be back on your feet tomorrow." He could see in her eyes that she wanted to say yes, but there was still a trace of fear in her expression. He wondered if her apprehension had less to do with the physical effects of his blood and more to do with the fact that she craved it. She'd be terrified of the consequences of allowing herself to taste it, knowing it could make her an addict. "I swear it will not bind you to me in any way you do not wish it to. I offer it freely and without obligation."

Pain tightened the skin around her eyes as she concentrated on dragging in another rasping breath. "I'm not sure," she said, shaking her head, "can't think clearly." The loss of blood and oxygen was starting to affect her; her hand felt cold in his.

"Gabi," the medic interrupted, "I really need to get you to the hospital, you need to go directly into surgery." He looked a little wild-eyed at the group of Vampires surrounding them and edged closer to Kyle. "I'm sorry, but I have to move her now." He made a gesture to get the Vampires to move out of his way and looked to Kyle for help.

Then Gabi sighed, closing her eyes. "No," she said, softly but clearly, opening her eyes to look at the medic. "We're going to try this his way," she whispered, turning her head back towards Julius.

The medic began shaking his head, looking determined and tugging on the stretcher, but the Vampires closed ranks around them, and the man bit his lip, torn between doing what he thought was the right thing and putting his own life in jeopardy.

Kyle came to the rescue, quickly put a calming hand on the man's shoulder. "It's ok, Harry. They know what they're doing." Kyle reassured him. "I think you might be about to witness something close to a miracle."

The stockier man subsided, but his worried expression didn't ease.

Julius felt the choking tension ease from him and he held her eyes with his as he began to give orders.

"Harry," he said, his voice smooth and calming, "I'll need your help."

Harry bit his lip, his anxiety still tangible in the air, but he stepped back towards Gabi's side.

"Whatever I can do to help, of course," he murmured.

"Good," Julius said shortly. "I'll need you to carefully remove the stake when I tell you to. You'll only have a few seconds to do it, and you'll need to make sure there are no large splinters left behind in the wound. We don't want her flesh to heal around the pieces or we'll have to cut them out later. Can you do that?"

Harry's eyes were as round as saucers, and his pattering heartbeat was clear to everyone standing nearby, but his nod was sure and his hands were steady as he reached for a pair of scissors and began to cut Gabi's shirt away from the wound site.

"Kyle, Alexander," Julius called the other two closer; "I need you to hold her still when Harry pulls the stake free."

They moved to either side of the narrow stretcher, Kyle opposite Julius near Gabi's shoulder and Alexander next to Julius near her thighs. They nodded they were both ready. Julius pulled a small switchblade from one of his pockets and bent close to Gabi.

"I'm sorry, Lea, this is going to hurt," he murmured in tight voice, then he dug the blade into the flesh just at the base of his thumb and sliced deeply, through flesh and vein and tendon. As the blood welled up, as bright red as any human's, he crouched down to her eye level and held his hand to her lips. He used his free hand to turn her head in towards his bleeding palm, cupping the side of her face with his fingers, shielding her from seeing what Harry was doing, and holding her jade green eyes captive with his own.

The world around her had been blurring in and out of focus. The air was thick with an oily smoke that stank of burnt flesh and hair and other things. Getting air into her lungs was like trying to breathe in water. She knew she'd just made some kind of life-altering decision, but it was difficult to remember through the haze of pain and blood and smoke and spinning. A pair of deep sapphire pools gilded with golden halos caught her gaze and held her in place. The world seemed to stop shifting focus, and she heard his velvet voice, it sounded... regretful. She felt his cool, smooth skin press against her face and his eyes swooped closer as his other hand slipped into her hair and turned her face towards him. She found herself wondering who Lea was, and why she was going to hurt. The thought was barely formed when a cool, thick liquid touched her lips, it was delicious in scent and she opened her mouth to lick at the wetness. She closed her eyes in relief. It was intoxicating, heavenly, it chased all the pain and anxiety. She suckled, trying to draw more of the liquid into her mouth. She heard a voice and opened her eyes again, the beautiful face surrounding the sapphire pools gave a slight nod, and her world exploded in pain.

There was a horrible, ripping, tearing agony in her side. She closed her eyes and tried to scream, tried to twist away from the torture, tried to find a way to end the pain. Firm bands held her in place, some cool, some warm, and a gentle vice held her mouth to his hand and the warm sticky liquid oozing from it. Black spots and glittering specks danced in front of her closed lids as a calm, velvety voice spoke, trying to soothe her. She forced her eyes open, fighting the darkness trying to pull her down. She didn't want to be drawn into the abyss, but the voice was hypnotic, encouraging her to let go, assuring her they would take care of her. Who would take care of her, her confused mind wondered. As the flow of liquid at her mouth slowed, she felt a trickle of annoyance, nuzzling into his flesh for more, licking at the last few smears. The pain had begun to ebb slightly, narrowing down to an aching burn in her right side. The hand was pulled gently away, but tender fingers stroked her hair and her face; she could hear excited murmuring around her, could feel someone covering her with a blanket and tucking it in around her, but the mesmerising eyes still held hers. Her lids felt heavy, her body felt heavy and the darkness pulled at her again.

"The worst is over, Lea. Sleep now and heal. We'll take it from here." The soothing voice told her. And, in a rare moment of blind obedience, did as she was told.

When she opened her eyes, she was in a room, on a bed, under a luxurious blanket, and it was dark. It took her a few seconds to remember what had happened at the warehouse. Where was she? Had she slept only a few hours or an entire day? She had no idea. She definitely wasn't in a hospital, unless they'd started designing hospital rooms to look like something straight out of a five star hotel suite. As she took in her surroundings in the flickering light of a glass-fronted fireplace, she felt an eyebrow rise in reluctant appreciation of the beautiful decor in the room. The huge four-poster bed was solid wood, and the soft furnishings and bedding were in dark, masculine colours. As she lay curled on her side, she faced a wall boasting a magnificent oil painting of a rearing chestnut warhorse in strong shades of red, orange and black. Large pieces of dark wood furniture filled the corners of the room, and two large over-stuffed armchairs sat close together near heavy, velvet curtains, drawn back from French doors to reveal a clear, star-studded night sky. A man sat in one of the chairs, his pose relaxed but attentive. One of his legs was propped up on a tapestried foot stool and one hand cradled a large, half-filled wine glass. He watched her with calm interest.

"How are you feeling?" his voice purred, vibrating down her spine.

She felt like a cat that had just been stroked in exactly the right way. But that probably wasn't what he was referring to, she thought with a suppressed smile. She breathed deep and tried an experimental stretch, bracing herself for the pain. Surprise drenched her as the stretch yielded nothing but a mild stiffness. No pain at all. She threw the blanket off and pulled up the silk shirt covering her, then craned her neck to look at the site of her wound, her fingers reaching tentatively to probe the area. There was no wound at all; the area was completely healed over, not even a scab, just a dark pink area where new skin had formed. Her probing fingers told her the healing wasn't just skin deep, the flesh felt whole and undamaged underneath too, and completely pain-free. Not even a hint of bruising or swelling remained. And her lung, she thought worriedly, remembering the awful feeling of not being able to get enough oxygen. She drew another deep, experimental breath and felt it come easily, no fluid rattling, no need to cough. She'd either been out for weeks, or something miraculous had happened.

"The blood seems to have had the desired effect," Julius murmured. He'd removed his leg from the stool and sat forward facing her while she made her assessment, but he made no move to come any closer. "I hope you'll forgive me for forcing your hand while you were confused and in pain." He looked down into his wineglass, waiting for her reaction.

She could feel his tension now, radiating through the room. She remembered the thick, delicious liquid that she'd sucked from his hand; she'd been so far gone that she hadn't even made the connection at the time. Of course, it all made sense now. She felt a lazy smile turn up the corners of her mouth as she settled back onto the mattress, propping her head up on one hand.

"Somehow I think I might find it in me to forgive you for that one," she said, absently rubbing her other hand over her newly healed flesh. The same languorous, sensual lethargy that had affected her the first time she'd tasted Julius's blood cocooned her now. A strange, urgent need welled up inside her, and she realised she wanted him closer to her. "Why don't you come over here?" she asked him casually, patting the space on the bed in front of her. "By the scent in here this must be your bed?"

Julius paused for a heartbeat before answering. "I don't think that would be a good idea right now."

The flames in the fire-place suddenly surged brighter, as though hit by a blast of oxygen, and in the brief surge of amber light Gabi saw Julius's eyes flare with their own dark flame. He quickly dropped his gaze from hers and turned his head to stare out into the night. "In fact, I think it's probably a good time for me to leave. I just needed to know that you were alright."

The need inside her flared more insistently, resisting the thought of him leaving, and demanding she act to draw him closer.

"Why should you leave, it is your room isn't it?" she asked, trying to keep her voice from betraying her desperation.

He turned his face back towards her, a strange kind of anguish sharpening his features. "I," he began, then broke off, as his eyes stroked down the length of her body and legs, lying sprawled across the bed.

Gabi realised she was wearing only a loosely buttoned man's silk shirt and nothing else. All her clothes must've been covered in blood.

"I'm not sure I could… resist," he continued finally, "if I come any closer to you. You call to me like a Siren."

She watched him swallow convulsively.

"I said come here," she enunciated the words slowly and forcefully.

He closed his eyes, shaking his head slightly. "I'm not sure exactly what's happening right now, I've never felt anything like it, but I don't want you regretting your actions in the morning and hating me for it." He forced out the words through a tightly clenched jaw. "I need to go." He set the wineglass on a low table and stood up abruptly, as ungracefully as she'd ever seen him move, and headed towards the closed bedroom door.

"No," she said low and fervently. Before he could reach the door, she was standing in front of it. Moving quicker than she'd ever moved before, she turned the key in the lock and spun to face him, leaning back against the handle so he'd have to go through her to open it.

"Last chance, Gabrielle," he ground out warningly as he placed his hands against the door on either side of her face. "Last. Chance."

She answered him by slowing beginning to undo the buttons down the front of the silk shirt she was wearing.

As she let the soft material fall open to show teasing glimpses of her breasts and the soft tangle of auburn curls further down her body, she saw as well as felt his surrender. A low growl issued from deep in his throat as he drank in the sight of her firm curves licked by firelight. His eyes were slowly changing colour again, from almost entirely black back to sapphire and then the gold halo reappeared and gradually began to swallow the blue, his eyes taking on a hungry, molten glow. He was breathing hard and fast, his mouth slightly open, his canines lengthening as she watched. He leaned in towards her, dipping his head to get closer to her height and brushing her mouth with his lips. First, a feather-light touch of lips, and then, as she lifted her chin, straining to keep the contact, he deepened the kiss, plunging his tongue into her mouth, savouring the taste of her as he threaded one hand into her hair to hold her closer and the other began a slow, sensuous exploration of her body.

Her own hands had started off planted firmly against the door, but they soon found their way to his chest, where they encountered the barrier of cotton shirt and buttons. She tried to undo the buttons but soon lost patience and simply pulled the shirt open, sending buttons plinking across the floor. When she was finally able to lay her hands against his cool, smooth skin, she felt a slight easing of her intense need to be near him, but as she began to run her hands over his hard, muscled chest, pausing with interest at his small, rock hard nipples, making him groan into her mouth, and then skimming over his perfectly defined shoulders, she felt a wild, clenching desire building inside her. She tore her mouth from his and began to explore his body with her mouth, kissing, licking, nipping her way down his neck, across his shoulder and down the flat planes of his chest.

Suddenly, she was lifted and just as quickly she was on the bed, his cool, hard body half covering hers. Then she felt him move, heard his boots hit the floor, and his full attention was back on her. The shirt she'd been wearing was gone, and she couldn't remember removing it.

"Lea," he purred, "My Lea." And she suddenly felt the slightest wash of his power against her skin. It was like a million caressing fingers stroking her already sensitive skin. She shivered with pleasure, revelling in the sensation. He smiled down at her, a thoroughly male smile of pleasure, passion and possession. His hands roamed her body confidently, playing over her breasts, skimming down her taut stomach, and tangling into the russet red triangle of curls between her legs.

"I am going to make you scream for me tonight," he whispered, as he bent his head to take one of her nipples into his mouth and smoothly plunged his fingers into her tight, moist core.

Her body arched off the bed in exquisite, unbearable pleasure. A scream tore from her throat as his fangs grazed the hyper-sensitive flesh of her nipple and his thumb found the nub of her clit at the same time. Her hands, where they had been restlessly tracing the contours of the muscles on his arms and shoulders, reacted instinctively as an orgasm tore through her body. She raked her fingernails down his arm and back and fought an insane need to bury her teeth in his flesh.

As she desperately tried to get him to bring his mouth back to hers, tried to gain some semblance of control over her need to touch and taste him, he looked up at her face and grinned a wicked smile, then slowly began to kiss and nibble his way down her body towards the place where his fingers were buried, causing her to cry out again and again. When his tongue replaced his fingers she screamed again, arching off the mattress and clenching the sheets so hard she felt them rip in her hands. When he skilfully used the tip of a fang to gently rasp over her clit, another orgasm hit her like a tidal wave.

It could have been minutes or hours later that she came back to earth to find him licking and kissing his way back up her stomach. In a move that startled both of them, she flipped him onto his back and straddled him. She grabbed both of his hands and forced them down on the bed above his head, bending to run her tongue across his lips and then nip at his lower lip teasingly. He growled and tried to capture her mouth with his, but didn't use his strength to break her grasp.

"Uh, uh," she said warningly, "my turn now."

He sank back and allowed her to explore his body with her hands, her lips, her teeth. As she moved lower, tracing the dips and grooves formed by his sculpted muscles with her tongue, grazing her nails roughly down his ribs, his breathing grew rougher and faster, his hands clenched into fists. When her warm hand finally moved to cup his balls and her hot, moist mouth moved to cover the tip of his erection, she closed her eyes in satisfaction, and his body bucked against the bed, a hoarse groan ripped from his throat.  She moved to take more of his smooth, silk-over-steel shaft into her mouth using her tiny fangs to graze the edges, and he let out another guttural moan and pulled her away, flipping her over back onto the bed and trapping her body with his own. He was breathing in short, sharp pants, his eyes completely gold in colour.

"I'm sorry Lea, I need to be inside you now," he gasped.

She smiled wickedly and opened herself to him.

"I think that can be arra…" before she could finish her sentence he plunged inside her and her sentence ended in a shout of pleasure.

He started out slow, retreating completely and then plunging inside her deep and hard. Her hands and nails bit into the skin on his back, trying to draw him closer and keep him inside her.  As he finally capitulated to the speed and rhythm she demanded, her pleasure became a never-ending torrent, rising higher and higher with each thrust; she felt like she would splinter into pieces before she reached the crescendo.  Through the haze of ecstasy, she felt him dip his head to her exposed neck and nuzzle at her jugular, felt his breathing become more irregular and then he fastened his mouth over hers again, drinking her in, pillaging her mouth with his tongue, and increasing the rhythm of his thrusts.  She knew instinctively what he wanted, what else he needed in that moment.  She pulled her mouth away from his, throwing her head back and exposing her neck.

"Take what you need," she managed to gasp, and as he hesitated, she grabbed his head and pulled him to her neck.  She felt his tongue run over her skin once, twice, and then twin points of pain for only a fraction of a second.  There was a slight pulling sensation and then she screamed again, clawing at his back.  Each pull from his mouth on her neck sent a spear of erotic sensation shooting through her veins, tightening her already hard nipples, turning her inner core to molten liquid and blotting out every other sense in her world. Her body clenched around his erection as the next mind-blowing orgasm took her. She was barely aware that he had stopped drawing blood from her, but felt it as he came with her into the prolonged climax.

Gabi wasn't sure how much later it was that she felt him move away from her and rise from the bed. She followed his movements with her eyes; though her heartbeat had slowed to a steady canter and her breathing was almost normal, she couldn't seem to make her body or her limbs respond to commands. Not that she felt any pressing need to be anywhere else, but she probably could've done with a trip to the bathroom. He moved to the curtains, pausing in front of the gently lightening skyline before pulling down a blind and drawing the curtains closed. Sunrise couldn't be far off, she thought idly. He turned towards her again; his pale, perfect body catching the dying light from the fire and making things clench low in her core when she thought she couldn't possibly have it in her to feel like that again for at least a decade. Something in his expression cut through her post-orgasmic haze and made her frown.

"What is it Julius?" she asked, trying to keep the worry out of her voice.

He was as still as a glorious marble statue and then finally said in a voice barely a whisper, "I think I should go and find another room." As she opened her mouth to protest, he continued. "Our sleep during the day," he paused, searching for the right words, "well, it can be rather... disconcerting for someone who is not accustomed to seeing it. I don't want to make you uncomfortable."

299

She blinked slowly, still fighting the languor that threatened to overtake her mind and body. "Come here," she said in a voice that brooked no argument. "This is your room, in your house. If I'm uncomfortable I will leave. But at this moment in time I have no intention of going anywhere, even if my body would listen to a single command I gave it," Then she rolled over and stretched, making a space on the bed behind her and patting it. His eyes showed his doubt, but he obeyed and slid back into the bed with her, scooping her up in his arms to hold her close against him and pulling the blankets over them both. She sighed contentedly and snuggled against him, and then suddenly stiffened.

"I do have a question for you though," she said in a slightly indignant tone.

His body stilled, waiting.

"Who the hell is Lay-ah?" she demanded, her tongue tripping over the unfamiliar pronunciation. She felt his chest muscles move in a slight chuckle, and he laid a cool kiss on her shoulder.

"You are, my dear Gabrielle," he said in his velvet purr. "Lea is a Latin word. It means lioness." She relaxed again with a soft snort and then let sleep drag her down into its blissful depths.

# CHAPTER 19

The insistent phone woke her. She blinked drowsily, forcing her eyelids open and trying to work out where the phone was. Her sleepy brain finally processed the fact that she wasn't in her own bed, and a cool arm was wrapped around her waist. Oh, Lord and Lady! She only barely managed to resist the compulsion to leap out of the bed. The events of the past few hours bubbled back to the surface of her consciousness. She calmed herself with a few deep, cleansing breathes. The room was still in darkness, but she could make out the gleam of daylight around the edges of the thick velvet curtains.

The phone beeped again. "Shit," she swore softly, wondering what time it was, and hoping it was still the same day she thought it was. She carefully moved Julius's arm and pulled herself away from his oddly warm embrace. He didn't stir at all as she placed his arm on the bed, and Gabi was reminded of his statement that the way he 'slept' during the day could look disturbing.

She studied him for a moment. He lay on his side, his eyes closed, and his thick sweep of dark eyelashes resting, in striking contrast, to the pale pearlescence of his skin. His face was entirely relaxed; something she'd never seen before. It lent a certain vulnerability to his features; she found she could picture him as a young boy in her mind. He must've been absolutely angelic looking. It was startling to realise how much he schooled his features when he was awake, how the pressure of his responsibilities and the weight of decades of existence hardened and etched the contours of his face. She could see why a person may be perturbed by his sleep. He lay like someone in a coma, add that to the total lack of vital signs and she could see how he may appear dead to some. But he didn't appear dead to her; there was still an essence of him in the room. She'd seen plenty of dead, of all varieties, and she knew the difference, she could see and feel when the spark of life was gone. With Julius the spark was alive and well, and his presence enveloped her.

She sighed as the phone beeped a third time, intruding on her inner speculations. She found it on a dresser and scooped it up as she began cautiously opening doors in the room, hoping one of them led to a bathroom.

The date and time on the phone eased Gabi's anxiety; it was a little after ten on Wednesday morning, so at least she hadn't slept another whole day away. The fight with the ghouls had gone down only nine or ten hours ago, so she couldn't imagine there was wholesale panic about her state of health just yet. And yet, between Kyle and Byron, there were seven missed calls and five new messages. She sighed with relief when the second door she opened led to a huge modern bathroom complete with robes and huge, fluffy towels. She slipped into the smallest of the robes, it was miles too big for her, but warm and comfortable, before calling Byron. She felt a stab of guilt

302

as she heard the relief in his voice when he answered her call. She assured him she was fine, that she was healed and didn't even need to go and see Ian. It was only as she spoke to him, answering his worried questions that she realised she wasn't hungry. She hadn't eaten since the couple of pastries the previous night, before the mission to the warehouse, and normally she'd be absolutely ravenous by now. She dealt with Byron's concern as quickly as she could, promising to pop in at his house later in the day to prove she was fine and answer the rest of his questions.

Her second call was to Kyle. He was a little less concerned about her injury, he'd seen the wound close in front of him, and more concerned about any other side effects. She side-stepped the questions as best she could, she wasn't ready to tell him what had gone down a few hours ago between her and Julius – she hadn't quite figured that one out herself yet. He was also calling to say that Razor had threatened to rip him into little shreds when he'd gone to her place this morning, and even Rose was having a hard time keeping him from destroying the house.

"I'll be there just as soon as I can grab a quick shower and find some clothes to wear. I assume mine were unsalvageable, as I can't find them anywhere in J..... uh, the room I was sleeping in." She hoped Kyle didn't notice the slip. "Drat, I also need to find my car keys."

Kyle was chuckling into the phone. "I'm on my way to the Estate now, I have some clothes for you, as well as coffee and breakfast. I was hoping you'd be conscious sometime soon."

Gabi could hear the roar of the van's engine as he started it up. "Thanks, Wolf," she said, grudgingly appreciative. "Sometimes you prove to be surprisingly useful to have around."

Kyle's chuckle grew evil. "I should warn you that I have ulterior motives this morning," he told her.

Gabi drew in a breath. "What now?"

"Oh, I don't know," he tried to sound casual, but failed miserably, "I'm just interested to know why Gregory refused to call Julius or you to the phone just before sunrise this morning, even though he insisted that you were, and I quote, 'definitely not injured or unconscious'. He sounded rather uncomfortable, in fact. Just what were the two of you up to?"

Gabi growled low into the phone and found herself in front of the bathroom mirror checking the state of her throat where she'd made him bite her. She was relieved when she couldn't find any sign of puncture wounds or bruising.

"None of your business, Wolf." She hit the disconnect button. "Shit," she cursed softly, belatedly realising that Julius wasn't going to hear her anyway. Bloody Gregory, surely he could have come up with some better story to cover for his boss. Kyle wasn't going to leave her alone until she gave him an explanation. She just hoped she could put him off until she figured it out for herself. She started the shower and stepped in, a hundred thoughts whirling in tiny, confusing circles through her brain.

She drank her latté in silence and picked at a croissant as Kyle relayed what had happened at the warehouse after she passed out. Athena had gone down into the 'Ghoul Hole', as it was now being dubbed, and declared that they needed to seal off the inhabitants until it became clear whether the rest were going to turn or not. So food and water had been taken in to those still alive, under heavy Vampire guard, and corpses had been removed and burned. Hunters with full field teams were supposed to return that night to see what had developed. Magi were working hard today trying to track down anecdotal evidence or records of how long it took for humans to complete the change to Ghoul, or how to prevent the change. No one was holding out too much hope there, though. Julius had 'questioned' the Vampire that Alexander had managed to capture alive, but he hadn't known anything of use, he was just a hired hand who was supposed to watch that the Demons did what they were supposed to. He didn't have any idea where Danté was hiding out. The only contact he had with Danté was a phone number, which Sebastian was following up.

The two of them were sitting on the tiled veranda just off the entertainment area they usually converged in, soaking up the morning sun. The house had been quiet and empty except for two women (Werewolves, Gabi thought) who were cleaning the house. They'd looked a little quizzically at the two newcomers but hadn't tried to make any conversation, just nodded politely and carried on with their duties. Kyle confirmed that there were Weres on duty at the front gate too, they'd buzzed him through with no problems.

"Have you eaten already this morning?" Kyle asked suddenly, changing the topic.

"No," Gabi said, confused by the odd question. "Why?"

"Well, I've never seen you pick at food first thing in the morning. It just struck me as odd. Are you sure you're feeling alright?" He hadn't yet started interrogating her about what was going on with her and Julius, but Gabi realised he was heading that way now.

"I think it's the blood, you know?" she answered a bit hesitantly. "I feel great, better than I can remember feeling for a long time." She paused and chewed on her bottom lip for a moment. "I don't feel hungry at all, and that's a new experience for me," she tried a smile, but she knew he could tell it was forced. She buried her nose back in her coffee.

"And the place you were staked, it's completely healed?" he asked, "You don't seem to be stiff or sore when you move."

She stood up and pulled the edge of her T-shirt up to show him her ribs where the terrible wound had been. He leaned forward to run his fingers over it.

"Wow, that's amazing," he breathed. "I'm not sure I would believe it if I hadn't seen it with my own eyes. That's faster than I heal."

Gabi flashed him an impudent grin as she sat down again and resolutely finished off the croissant in front of her.

"And something more happened between you and Julius?" He made it more of a statement than a question.

Gabi flashed back to half an hour ago when she'd emerged from the shower, clean and awake, but no less confused by what had happened between her and Julius. She'd gone back to the bed, brushed his tousled blonde hair back from his angelic face and resisted the urge to place a kiss on his slightly parted lips, then had pulled the blanket up to cover him before she gave in to the compulsion to climb back into the bed with him and go back to sleep.

"I'm not ready to talk about it yet," she said flatly.

Kyle's eyes flashed darkly, and his expression became grim. "If he tried something that you weren't ready for —" he started to say.

Gabi cut him off with an annoyed glare. "I'm a big girl, Wolf, I can take care of myself. Whatever happened between us was by mutual consent. I wasn't forced into anything."

Kyle backed down a little at her fierce glower, but not entirely. "It didn't have anything to do with you taking his blood?" he asked, still a harsh edge to his tone.

"I don't know, alright?" Gabi almost shouted in irritation. She stood up abruptly and paced out into the garden. "I don't know if it was the blood, or just a natural animal-based reaction to adrenalin, or some weird chemical connection we have. I haven't figured it out yet."

Gabi allowed her normal anger free rein; anger was a good way to deal with stuff she couldn't figure out. It made people leave her alone and stop poking at her. "So just leave it alone. I'm not in the mood for discussing it!"

Kyle studied her with a pensive frown, as though watching a car fire; not quite sure if it was going to peter out by itself or explode any second.

"Ok," he finally said. "But when you want to talk...." He left the sentence hanging.

Gabi drove home, chafing at having to keep to the speed limits. She wanted to put her foot down and feel the engine roar under her. When she finally made it home, Razor was waiting out on the porch for her. Apparently, he'd heard her car turn up the driveway. He watched her walk up the stairs and then pointedly turned his back on her and stalked off into the garden without any kind of greeting.

"Oh, dear," she sighed and went inside to find Rose busy in the kitchen.

"What's the matter," Rose asked, hearing her.

"Razor has the sulks," she explained.

"Ahh, yes, he's been throwing temper tantrums all over the house this morning," Rose agreed. "He's worse than having a jealous boyfriend waiting at home, hey?"

Gabi snorted in amusement. "It'd be far easier to break up with a jealous boyfriend than to re-home Razor.

Guess I'll have to find something special to tempt him with before he tears my whole house apart." She gave Rose a quick hug and turned on the coffee maker, more out of habit than any real desire for coffee.

"Are you hungry?" Rose asked. "I can whip up something quickly."

"No, I'm fine, thanks. Kyle brought food when he brought my clothes."

"Are you alright after last night?" Rose asked, worry colouring her tone. "The rumours are flying like locusts in the Community this morning. Kyle filled me in on a few of the details. Demons and Ghouls on the loose in the city. I wish you weren't caught up in the middle of all this my sweetling, it worries me so."

Gabi gave her reassuring smile. "I'm fine, honestly. I have a lot of people watching my back." Then she backed away to look into Rose's eyes, still keeping her hands on Rose's shoulders. "I can't back away when the City needs me, I'm my Father's daughter, and I have special gifts that will help keep the people of the City safe. We'll get through this nasty war, and we'll send those Demons right back to the deepest pits of Hell."

Rose patted Gabi's hands. "I know. If anyone can do it, you and Kyle can. I've heard the way the Community talks about your Father. He's spoken so highly of, he was so respected. I know he would be so proud of you."

Gabi silently gave Rose a fierce hug. "Now I could do with a good workout, but best I make up with Razor first."

Gabi pulled up outside SMV HQ a couple of hours later, having done sufficient grovelling to get Razor to quit sulking and having dealt with her urgent business e-mails and phone calls. She'd meant to go straight through to see Byron but his secretary told her he was busy in a meeting, so she headed instead to the practice hall — a specially laid out area the size of football field, partly undercover and partly open to the elements, which the Hunters used for training. It was extremely well equipped with a full gym, an area for weapons practice and, Gabi's favourite, a brutal obstacle course. Gabi quickly changed into spandex leggings and a tight-fitting crop top and went to warm up. The hall was empty; just the way she liked it. She spent a few minutes warming up in the gym and then eyed the obstacle course. The course was interactive; it had pop-up dummy enemies, hidden booby traps and was redesigned on a daily basis to keep the trainees on their toes. She was looking forward to seeing what it had to throw at her today.

It felt amazing to let rip after days of taking it easy, of freedom from the constant companions: pain and stiffness. It was incredible to experience her enhanced abilities and capabilities. Julius's blood had done more than just heal her and curb her appetite; it had made her faster, stronger and more agile. Her reaction time was infinitely quicker, and she blew through the obstacle course like a bottled hurricane — destroying the dummies set out to catch her, leaping the climbing walls almost without touching them, barely registering the blunt darts shot at her at irregular intervals and nimbly leaping over the floors that fell away from her feet. She swung herself onto an overhead cat walk with one hand and worked her way into the rafters, only to leap down from the height of two stories to instantly decapitate two dummies waiting for her on the ground. She was laughing with sheer pleasure and barely breathing hard when she rounded the last corner and nearly crashed in Byron who was waiting for her to finish.

"Gabi," he said in delighted greeting, catching her around the waist before she knocked him over. "That was quite a display."

There was a smattering of applause from the viewing deck above where she and Byron stood. Normally, it was where tutors and assessors stood to review performances of the Trainees, but today Lance, Doug and Athena were standing on it watching her. Lance and Doug were giving her a reluctant round of applause, Athena was simply standing with a disdainful look on her face.

"I think you've just blown your previous best time away completely," Byron said in proud amazement. "I guess there's no reason to send you to Ian for a check-up after all."

Gabi threw a challenging wink at the other two Hunters and gave Byron a quick hug, trying not to get sweat all over him.

"I told you I was fine," she said in mock exasperation. She didn't really expect Byron not to worry about her, she knew better. "In fact, as you can see, I'm a bit better than fine." She grabbed a towel from a pile on a nearby bench and used it to wipe the sweat from her face and neck. "I take it you're not all here just to watch me do the course."

A chuckle erupted from Lance. "Well, we weren't gathered at HQ to watch you," he drawled, "but once Melinda saw you heading for the hall she came to call us. She'd heard about you being staked from Harry and didn't put much stock in his story of your miraculous healing. They wouldn't believe me either, so we came to check that you weren't overdoing things." He had an enigmatic smirk on his face which Gabi was sure had something to do with Athena, if the sidelong glance Lance gave her was anything to go by.

Gabi bowed dramatically. "It's good to know I have so many people watching out for my best interests," she pretended to smile sweetly at them. Then her smile disappeared and a long-suffering look took its place. "Now, if you will all just go back to what you were doing and leave me to my exercise for the day, I'll be a happy person."

Lance and Doug took the hint and left with mock salutes. Athena stubbornly stayed where she was, arms crossed and staring haughtily down at her, until Byron cleared his throat. She finally broke eye contact with Gabi, pursed her lips and flounced off the platform. Gabi turned back to Byron. "I was coming to see you once I finished here," she said.

"Yes, Hazel told me you'd stopped by at my office," he replied. "I was in a meeting with Irene."

The mention of the Senior Magus' name snapped Gabi to attention. The members of the Council didn't often meet outside of Council sessions, unless it was a matter of extreme delicacy or dire emergency.

Byron nodded, seeing the dawning comprehension on Gabi's face. "She had some urgent news for us. Athena, Doug and Lance were already here to discuss going in to clean out the Ghoul Hole later. Kyle and Matthew are on their way here so I can tell you all together. Get finished here and join us in the small conference room, okay?"

Gabi nodded; she knew Byron's moods, so she knew he wouldn't discuss this with her until everyone was together. She leant forward putting a hand on his shoulder and gave him a quick peck on the cheek.

"Ok, see you in fifteen," she said and headed for the showers.

# CHAPTER 20

She poured herself a cup of coffee and took the empty seat next to Kyle at the large oval conference table.

He gave her a quick, assessing grin. "I hear you tore up the obstacle course today," he whispered. "Fastest time on record." He nudged her with his elbow teasingly.

"I didn't know anyone was watching or timing it," she hissed back in annoyance.

Byron cleared his throat, preventing further discussion. "As you all know, Irene came to us with some urgent information from the Magi Council this morning," he said without preamble. He steepled his hands in front of him on the mahogany table.

Gabi thought he looked troubled but determined; whatever was coming was bad but not insurmountable. Athena was watching the rest of them rather than Byron, so apparently she'd heard the news was already. Gabi supposed that, as one of the High Councillors for the Magi Council, she'd been privy to the information before Byron was. She wondered why Athena hadn't been the one to bring them the news. It seemed odd that the older Magus had come into the offices to tell Byron.

Byron continued, "One of the Oracles had a vision this morning, and it seems to relate directly to our current situation."

There was a collective intake of surprised breathes. The Oracles were a trio of the Magi Council's most powerful Clairvoyants. Their true identities were a closely guarded secret, more closely guarded than Byron's was. When they had a clairvoyant vision, it was invariably accurate, as long as it had been interpreted correctly. They also had an uncanny knack of knowing what to do in order to alter the outcome of a vision. Of course, it was frequently impossible to interpret their visions; many of them were hopelessly obscure and often, by the time the meaning of the visions became clear, it was too late to do anything about them. To the Oracles credit, they did manage to help prevent dozens of catastrophes, both minor and major, each year. None of them had any control over what they saw and couldn't be asked to look for something specific. It was theorised that if they meditated over a particular subject they would get some kind of insight on the subject, but there was no way to ensure it was the insight they wanted. Many of their visions were not about bad or dangerous events; many were not warnings at all, just glimpses of the future, sometimes happy and bright. There was a team of Magi who spent their days trying to work out what the visions actually meant and if they required any action to be taken.

"They have 'seen' what Danté and Mariska are planning, and when they plan to do it," Byron continued. "Athena, you can probably explain this better than I can, why don't you continue?"

She nodded curtly and stood up to address the rest of them. "The visions were unusually clear, so we've been able to decipher them relatively easily. From what the visions have shown us, Mariska has been declared Maleficus."

Gabi felt her eyebrows shoot up in astonishment and saw confusion on the faces of the others; it seemed she was the only one of the Hunters who knew what this meant.

Athena seemed to realise she'd lost most of them, so she impatiently explained, "Maleficus essentially means criminal Magus. It's extremely rare for one of us to be so labelled, it's not done lightly. Even those who are Dark Magi are not often branded as such. It means instant death on capture; the trial has already been held, and the Magus has already been found guilty of evil deeds. It's now only a matter of catching up with her to mete out the punishment." She paused to allow this news to sink in and for the murmurs of surprise to die down.

"Summer solstice is almost upon us," she continued, "and this year it'll be a particularly powerful day and night as it coincides with a full lunar eclipse. The ley lines will be overflowing with power, almost any magic would be possible on a night like this. Mariska and Danté are going to be harnessing this unusually potent force to try to open a permanent gateway through the Void, allowing Demons an unobstructed pathway into our City." Athena's eyes were brimming with suppressed fury, she jabbed a finger into the table. "The Oracles say they will get it right, that Mariska has enough ability and has found the right spells to do it. Unless we can find a way to stop them." She almost growled the last sentence, then her voice dropped to a whisper. "We *have* to find a way to stop them." She dropped back into her chair, seeming exhausted by the prospect.

Gabi found she had no patience with the annoying woman; they had work to do, things to plan out,

314

information to find, sitting in a sorry-for-yourself heap wasn't going to get them anywhere. "So when exactly is the summer solstice this year?" she asked the Magus irritably. "And did the Oracles have any idea where to find Mariska or Danté, or how we can stop them?"

At Gabi's sharp words, Athena tried to pull herself together, sitting up straighter and flicking back her hair. "Four days time, and no they didn't get any clues as to where the Vampire and the Maleficus are hiding out," Athena answered tonelessly. "The best way to stop them is to capture Mariska or kill the Demon Master. Mariska cannot control Demons, so she wouldn't open the gateway if he wasn't there to control them."

"I'm assuming the Demon Master is Danté?"

Athena nodded curtly.

"So the long and the short of it is that we have less than a hundred hours to find them and put a stop to all this," Gabi summarized when no one else seemed capable of speech.

"Where do we even start?" Matt asked in a voice that spoke of the sheer enormity of the task.

"We start with the only direct link we have to them," Lance spoke up, steely determination in his tone. "The warehouse and the humans left behind in the Ghoul Hole. There has to be a clue somewhere in that place."

"You're right," Doug spoke up now, "it's the only lead we have."

"I agree," Byron said, nodding. "We need to get everyone we can spare out there." He turned to Athena. "Magi would be particularly helpful there, especially Diviners or Clairvoyants, anyone who can pick up on psychic energy or life-force. Maybe we can pick up some idea of where they've set up base."

Athena's natural business-like attitude kicked in. "Yes, of course," she replied. "I'll contact Irene and coordinate to have everyone we have available join us at the warehouse. I'll be there myself as well, as soon as I've made arrangements." She stood and briskly left the room.

"Doug, will you collect one of the trainees and head to the warehouse as well?' Byron asked. "We may need your expertise in case any of the humans have turned. Take a couple of flame throwers with you." Though he sounded brisk and detached, Gabi could see how much the thought of having to take human lives was affecting Byron. He took a deep breath to steady himself. "I'll contact the Werewolf pack leaders and ask if they can spare us some additional muscle."

Doug nodded agreement and left the room.

"Lance, Matt, I need you two to go home and get some rest." Byron put up a hand at their immediate protests. "We'll need you tonight. We've seen what can come at us in the dark, we'll use the daylight to do our investigations, gather information, and at night we need to have as many as possible fresh and ready to take down whatever is sent our way. So go home, rest, recharge and report back here before sunset."

They reluctantly agreed and departed for home, after Byron assured them he'd call if anything happened during the day.

"Are we going to head out there, too?" Kyle asked when just the three of them remained in the room.

Byron ignored the question. "I would prefer you two also went home to rest, but I know better," Byron said with a rueful attempt at a smile. "You can go and help for a while at the warehouse if you both promise me that you'll take time off for a few hours this afternoon. I need you both at your best tonight."

As it turned out, Gabi found it easier than she'd anticipated to go home for a catnap after lunch. She'd felt relatively useless at the warehouse, the Magi were doing the most good; Healers trying to help the humans, Mediums trying to reach the spirits of the dead, Clairvoyants trying to pick up traces of energy and Athena concentrating on tracing the source of the impressive wards that had hidden the place from psychic sight. Another two humans had turned into Ghouls, and Gabi was secretly relieved that they'd already been dispatched by Doug when she arrived. It looked as though the rest of the humans would pull through without turning, as least that's what they were telling themselves.

Byron had arranged secure and far more humane facilities for the remainder of them, and the first task of the evening would be for Gabi, Kyle and whatever Vampires Julius could spare, to transport the pitiful bunch to the new facilities where they could be monitored and cared for. After that, they'd be splitting into three groups with a mix of SMV staff and Vampires for a patrol through areas where strong ley line convergences occurred. As there was still a fairly large cloud of suspicion and enmity surrounding the inclusion of the Vampires in the Patrols, it was decided that a 'referee' would be needed in each group. Kyle would go with one group and Gabi with another. Lance had worked with the Vampires the previous night and didn't seem to have any problems with them, so he was their natural choice to lead up the third, Matt could take his pick of groups to join.

Gabi knew this would be her time to make a contribution, not wandering around the warehouse during daylight hours pretending to know what she was looking for. So she and Kyle drove back to her house for a nap until sunset.

Gabi had texted Julius before going to sleep, asking him to meet her at the warehouse with as many of his guard as he could spare. His reply woke her just before dusk. He and his guard would meet them at the warehouse at 8 pm. She rose, stretching, still enjoying the absence of pain, and went to kick the guest bedroom door, rousing Kyle. As she changed into fighting gear, she wondered how long her new speed and strength would last, if it would disappear in slow increments or vanish abruptly. She sincerely hoped it wouldn't vanish in the middle of a battle. That could prove disastrous.

The two of them stopped at a burger place to fuel up on the way. Gabi caught the nervous stares that were being directed their way and had to suppress a grimace. She glared at the diners, thinking they were lucky she'd decided to remove the knives and swords before she walked in. Still, at least they weren't going to be harassed by anyone. The heart rate (which Gabi could hear quite clearly) of the freckle-faced teen who was serving them ramped up to dangerous speeds as he stammeringly confirmed their order and took the cash Gabi held out to him. He dropped the change onto the counter and looked up with nervous eyes as he stuttered his apology. Gabi rolled her eyes as Kyle tried not to snicker.

"I told you we should've used the drive-thru," she grumbled, briskly scooping up the scattered money and going to sit at a vacant table in a dimly-lit corner, leaving Kyle to collect the tray of food and drinks. When the food arrived, Gabi found she was hungry, though still not starving as she would normally be; she actually had to make an effort to finish the three burgers and extra large fries.

Kyle was contemplating her lack of appetite a few hours later while sitting holed up in one of three secure vans transporting the wretched looking humans. Facilities had been set up for them in an abandoned mental asylum on the outskirts of the city. It'd been earmarked for demolition in a few months time but was still mostly functional at the moment. Byron never ceased to amaze Kyle in his ability to source absolutely anything. Between Byron, Irene, and Ian they'd set up everything in less than twenty-four hours.

His Vampire companion for the journey had surprised him. Somehow, he'd ended up in the van with Julius, though he assumed that was because Kyle chose the lead on the van that contained the woman who'd tried to attack Gabi; obviously neither of them were prepared to let Gabi anywhere near the woman again. He'd seen the loaded looks being traded back and forth between Gabi and Julius and had assumed Julius would take the first opportunity to get Gabi alone, but instead, as the Hunters each chose a van to guard, Julius had joined Kyle, Alexander had teamed up with Gabi and Fergus had eagerly joined Lance. As there was only space for two guards inside each van, the rest of them were following in separate vehicles, two of these assigned to each van in case of trouble.

The driver of the van sat in a separate cubicle, completely protected by thickly armour-plated steel. The steel was embedded with silver, as the vans were frequently used for bringing in renegade Werewolves. The only communication Kyle and Julius had with Rory, the Werewolf driver, was by intercom. Julius and Kyle were in small, cramped seats in a separate, barred area at the front of the van which afforded them a clear view of the grieving mother and another male huddled in separate heaps on the floor in the rear of the van.

Kyle didn't foresee any problems with the male; he was so scared as to be almost catatonic. He hoped the

Magi would be able to erase the horrors of the past few days if they didn't turn, but he secretly thought it was a vain hope. Nobody could go through what they'd just been through and walk away unscathed, and no one could give the woman back her dead daughter. Of course, first they had to stay human.

Kyle tried to shake himself out of his morose thoughts and turned to study Julius instead. He assumed that Gabi and Julius had got 'down and dirty' the previous night. He was pretty sure Gabi would've discussed anything else with him and was well aware of Gabi's physical attraction to the Vampire. Gabi wasn't easy to read on that score, unless you knew her particularly well, or had supernatural senses. He had both. He spoke without changing the direction of his gaze; he looked straight into Julius's soul-swallowing eyes.

"If you hurt her, I'll be forced to make you bleed," he said with a calm matter-of-factness.

Julius was silent for two heartbeats; there was no question he knew who Kyle was referring to. "You love her," the Vampire stated, "I understand that."

"I've always known the best match for her would be a supernatural," Kyle tried to explain. "It's always been hard for her to hide her non-human side. She couldn't keep it up in a one-on-one relationship, not and still be happy. She manages it in her business but even that takes a toll on her; she has to be careful in so many ways. At least her gift with animals, though generally seen as remarkable, is never suspected by humans to be anything supernatural," he paused for a moment lost in thought but then continued. "But I guess I'd always thought of her with a Werewolf or Shapeshifter, possibly a Magus if she could find a really tough one," he said with a slight lift of his lips. "I'd never considered her with a Vampire. I know that probably sounds terribly prejudiced, but then we hadn't met any Vampires to actually form relationships with." He finally looked away from Julius's gaze. "The more I think about it the more it begins to make sense. You understand her in many ways better than anybody else does; even me, her closest friend for nearly half her life. I realise now that she has more in common with Vampire nature than either of us ever thought possible."

It was Julius's turn to look away now; he looked down, as though studying his hands. "You understand her just fine. The two of you would make the perfect couple. Have you ever considered that?" he asked still looking at his hands.

Kyle actually barked a short laugh. "Yeah. Yeah. The idea did certainly occur to us." Kyle acknowledged. "It definitely seemed like the perfect solution for both of us. When she turned seventeen we gave it a shot," he felt his eyes go distant, remembering. "But you can't make chemistry work by ordering it to. If it's not there it's just not there. For me, it was there; she's not exactly unattractive after all, but Gabi just couldn't get into it. I think I was too much like a big brother to her, too familiar." He snorted now. "And with senses like ours you can't even fake it, can you?"

Julius nodded rueful agreement, looking up now but staying silent, allowing Kyle to continue his discourse.

"Anyhow, after a couple of tries, we gave it up and decided the sibling relationship worked best for us. So, we rib each other about our romantic flings and help each other pick up the pieces when things fall apart. I've never seen her lose her heart though; she never makes herself that emotionally vulnerable to anyone. She's seen her mother go through losing her father, and then she watched her mother nearly make a catastrophic mistake with a violent boyfriend. You're the first person I would be worried about truly hurting her emotionally, because I can

321

see that she's become emotionally entangled with you already. As a man who cares deeply about her, I ask you to think carefully about becoming more involved with her. If you're not serious about her, you need to distance yourself from her now, before she gets in so deep that she can't untangle herself." He said this last bit in a deadpan rush. He didn't relish taking on the stern big brother role, but he'd do just about anything to protect her. He also knew that if she found out about this conversation they'd both be bleeding.

Julius finally spoke. "I'm not a Magus, so I don't like to make predictions about the future, and I have no idea whether it can actually work between me and Gabrielle, but I can assure you that I also have her best interests at heart. I find myself feeling extraordinarily protective of her but not in a brotherly kind of way," he said with a slight smile. "If anyone else tried to hurt her, I would rip their throat out without a second thought, so I understand your feelings on the matter, I would expect nothing less from you if I were to hurt her myself."

There was silence in the space as Kyle tipped his head in acknowledgement of Julius's statement.

"Tell me about her mother's violent boyfriend. I was under the impression her mother was happily remarried," Julius asked, steering the conversation away from the original topic.

"She is happily remarried, now, at least. The guy is very pleasant and comes from a line of Shapeshifters, but isn't a Shifter himself. So at least her mom doesn't have to cover up for Gabi all the time; it makes it easier for Gabi and her mom that way. The violent boyfriend came when Gabi was still at school. I guess it would help you understand the story if you have a bit more background to it. I'm going to vehemently deny ever telling you this if she finds out that you know about it though."

When Julius wryly nodded his acceptance of the conditions Kyle continued, "Gabi was only ten when her dad was killed. Her mom went into a serious depression and was almost catatonic for weeks afterwards. Byron and his wife helped look after Gabi and cover things up from social services. If the social workers had any idea how bad it had actually been they would've hospitalised her mom and put Gabi in foster care. Anyhow, they eventually managed to get her onto medication and she was able to function almost normally, but a lot of the household responsibility fell on Gabi's shoulders. She had to grow up fast and in a way the mother/child relationship became almost reversed. Gabi felt responsible for her mom, and although their relationship wasn't exactly plain sailing, she was very protective of her mother. I guess we also have that in common," he mused, half to himself.

"Several years later, her mom met a man in the local book store, and they began dating. When I met Gabi, the man was pushing to move into the house with them. Gabi was dead set against it, she had some sixth sense about this guy, she didn't trust him or like him one bit. I have to admit, at the time I felt it was simply the fact that she didn't want her dad replaced, perfectly understandable under the circumstances. The only reason her mom hadn't let the man move in was because he was full human, and she wasn't sure how he'd react to Gabi's supernatural abilities, which would become obvious once he spent enough time around her." He gave a brief snort of laughter. "Gabi absolutely delighted in giving him a hard time; she'd even ask me for ideas on how to annoy him further. She mouthed off to him every chance she got, she pushed every one of his buttons, and was rude and obnoxious every time her mom was out of earshot. She even encouraged her gazzilion pets to give him a hard time. They'd bite him, peck him, shit on him, trip him up, scare him."

Julius echoed Kyle's smile, as though he, too, could picture the scene of a young, short tempered, foul-mouthed Gabi trying her damnedest to annoy a human without giving herself away.

Kyle continued, "But though she did seem to get to him, none of her efforts actually deterred him. I think now that she may have been spot on with her idea that he was only there to get his hands on the large inheritance her dad had left for the two of them. A few months later, he was becoming increasingly insistent that he should move in with them, bringing up news reports about house burglaries and crime in the area and how they needed him to protect them. Gabi thought her mom was close to cracking, but she got home early from school one day to hear them arguing in the house. This ignorant asshole was screaming and hurling verbal abuse at her mom, Gabi opened the door on the scene and saw her mom standing across the room with a terrified expression; she had a puffy red mark across her face and blood trickling from the corner of her mouth." He noticed Julius fists clench. "She didn't even hesitate," Kyle said with all the gloating of a proud big brother, "she walked straight to the hall closet and took out her father's nine iron." He felt a dark-humoured smile creased his face. "She never described much of the scene to me; I don't think she remembers much of it, but I can picture his cockily confident face as she approached him. He would've been thinking he was quickly going to take that golf club away from that dainty, little fourteen year old and put her in her place at long last. He could never have imagined how she was about to let loose on him with it." He saw Julius's hands relax from their tendon-straining clench. "Her mother finally managed to pull Gabi off of him; he was still alive at that point but just barely. They called Byron, not wanting to involve the police and not knowing what else to do. He arrived quickly and threw the man in his car, helped them clean up the mess in the house and told them they'd never have to worry about the man again, and for Gabi that was the end of the story. Her mother was far more cautious about going out with men after that, and Gabi, for a time, had a severe distrust of all men."

"What happened to the boyfriend?" Julius asked calmly and without apparent interest, but not fooling Kyle in the slightest.

"Gabi has still never asked Byron what happened to him and claims she doesn't want to know. But I asked him one day, I wanted to be sure that he could never try to reappear in their lives, or that's what I told Byron anyway," his expression turned chagrined. "I obviously didn't fool him because he wouldn't tell me anything beyond that the man's memories had been wiped, and he would never get the chance to hurt another woman again. I'm guessing he was made the scapegoat of a vicious crime, made a full, magi-induced confession to police and is now serving a long prison sentence somewhere in the world."

Julius eyebrows rose in surprise.

Kyle chuckled. "Don't forget that Byron is at least as protective of Gabi as I am, and he's a downright crafty old fox when it comes down to it. Don't ever make the mistake of underestimating him."

Rory's voice crackled over the intercom as the van's engine cut off. "We're here guys."

It didn't take them long to unload the humans and leave them in the capable hands of a group of dedicated Magi Healers. Gabi was secretly very relieved that the woman who'd staked her was under heavy sedation, mainly because she'd continued to react with violence toward anyone who came near her, but the rest of them gave no trouble, following orders with numb obedience. She was intensely glad to be done with that part of the evening's work.

They quickly split up into three groups as planned, this time Julius joined Gabi's team and Alex took up his habitual position alongside Julius. Fergus and Nathan had a brief, silent squabble about which of them would be the fourth member of Gabi's team, and it was Nathan who backed down in the end and joined Lance, along with Marcello and Matt, who was still trying to get used to the idea of working with Vampires. Kyle's team consisted of Charles and Quentin, who'd both fought with them in the train station, and a Vampire Gabi recognised as the dark complexioned Vampire from the bar a few nights ago. His name was Tabari, Alexander had told her, explaining that Tabari was something of a rarity in Vampire society, being of black, African descent. For some reason, Alexander didn't know exactly why, there were very few black Vampires in existence. The paleness of Vampirism sat strangely on him, turning his skin a dusty ashen hue. When he spoke, his fangs were unashamedly visible and his accent was strong enough to bring Gabi vivid memories of her time in Southern Africa.

Kyle pulled out and map and spread it over the bonnet of a car. They quickly divided the City and its main ley line areas up into sectors and chose their sectors. They agreed to check in with each other every hour, then piled into the cars and vans and headed out on patrol. Gabi's Mustang had been left at the warehouse so she knew she'd have to join Julius in his car. This time he'd arrived in a less conspicuous Audi. A quick glance from Julius had sent Alexander and Fergus to join the driver and medic in one of the SMV vans specially equipped with weapons and medical supplies.

The tension in the car when she climbed in was almost palpable. Julius was obviously not comfortable around her. She was fairly certain he would've noticed that she took a shower before leaving this morning, which should've told him that she hadn't bolted like a startled lamb when she woke up and found him comatose next to her. He probably even knew that she and Kyle had stayed long enough to have breakfast before they left the estate. She wondered why he still seemed so tense. Was he regretting what had happened last night? She couldn't stand the silence a moment longer.

"I feel like I owe you an apology," she said, breaking the silence first.

"What?' he asked; shock clear in his tone.

"Well," she swallowed, "I, uh, didn't give you much choice in the matter last night. I should have controlled myself a little better." She looked down at her hands, trying to make herself unclench her fists.

Julius let out a loud, masculine laugh, the tension in the car dissipating in an instant. He looked at her side-long with a mischievous twinkle in his eye. "And I was fending you off with a bargepole." he retorted. He caught her chin with his fingers, not bothering to pay attention to the road, and tilted her face to look at him. "It was an amazing night," he said in a deep purr, ensnaring her eyes with his. Then he sighed and broke her gaze. "Can we save this conversation for later?" he asked, sounding regretful. "If we start talking about it now, I'm not going to be able to concentrate on the task at hand." He ran the back of his fingers softly down her cheek as he withdrew his hand. "Perhaps we can discuss it at your house after we finish up here?"

327

Gabi felt a rush of sensation flood her, and she had to clamp down hard on her self control. "I might owe you another apology tomorrow if we do that," she warned him, trying to keep a blush from her cheeks.

A slow, pleased smile lifted the side of his face that she could see, the tiniest hint of a dimple appearing as he tried to keep the smile from becoming a smirk. And then their conversation was brought to an end. They'd arrived at their first ley line convergence.

# CHAPTER 21

They'd been at it for over four hours and they'd found absolutely nothing. Between the three teams, they'd covered almost every square inch of the City areas with the strongest ley line activity. They'd unearthed a few things of interest, but there'd been no scent of a Demon, Ghoul or unknown Vampire anywhere. Kyle's team had found a group of homeless humans staying in an abandoned warehouse who told them that half their number was missing, at least twenty of the people who usually crashed in the place had disappeared three nights ago and not been seen since. The unspoken consensus between the Hunters and their company was that they weren't the only group who had lost members. Danté was obviously picking the easy prey, taking those who wouldn't be missed. There'd been a very slight scent of Demon left near the squalid warehouse, which only Kyle had been able to detect, but it ended a few blocks down the street, so it seemed that they'd left in a vehicle.

At 1:30 Gabi got a call from Byron. She was incredibly frustrated that there was absolutely nothing to report. Byron told her to send two teams home and leave on one patrol. It was pointless exhausting everyone when nothing was happening, the other two teams would still be on standby if things went pear-shaped. He assured her that SMV staff were monitoring the emergency call lines as well as the police frequencies, if anything strange went down anywhere in the City, they'd know about it. Gabi reluctantly agreed that roaming the streets aimlessly seemed a waste of resources, so she called the other two teams to meet at a late night coffee bar.

She sent Marcello and Matt in to get coffee while the rest of them gathered in the parking lot, as all of them traipsing into the small café would've scared the shit out of the handful of late-night patrons. When she told them Byron's orders to head home while her team continued the patrol, there was a huge uproar. Nobody wanted to go home. Kyle finally made the point that she was the only one of the Hunters with a day job, so it would make more sense for her to go home. Eventually, she agreed to draw straws to see who stayed and who went home. Kyle grabbed some plastic coffee stirrers and broke them into different lengths. Fergus got to hold them and the three leaders chose. Kyle drew the shortest straw, so he and his team would stay on duty until just before dawn; the rest would go home but stay close to the phone.

Julius drove Gabi back to the warehouse to collect her car. Then he followed her as she drove back to her house. Gabi could feel little tendrils of pleasurable anticipation curling in her stomach at the same time that anxious tension knotted her shoulder and neck muscles. She didn't know where things were going between her and Julius, but she did know she felt more strongly about him than she'd ever felt about a man in her entire life.

She was almost unnaturally drawn to him, and she worried it wasn't real, and then she worried that it was real, was she falling in love with this man? This man who was a Vampire? Is that what the incredible urge to be with him, near him, a part of him was all about? Love? And even if she could figure out her own feelings, what about him? Was she just an amusing fling, a roll in the hay, a notch in the bed post? Something new and different and therefore interesting, for now, something he'd grow bored with in time?

She'd like to think she could sit down and have a conversation with him tonight, try to work out where their relationship was going, if they even had a relationship, but she knew better. She knew that the moment they were alone together the lust would flare between them. That she wouldn't be able to keep her hands off of him. She'd spent the whole night keeping a tight rein on her actions, all the while wanting to find a dark corner and kiss him into insensibility. The strength of her need for him scared her. She realised she had two options; to not invite him into her home tonight, to tell him that she didn't want a repeat of the previous night, to send him back to his estate and to keep away from him as much as possible until the war with Danté was over, and then to never see him again. Or she could give in to her desire. She could let fate take her where it may, to open her door and her body to him and see where it led them, knowing that she may have to pick up pieces of a shattered heart in the future. When she stopped the Mustang outside her front door, she'd made her decision.

She got out of the car and steeled herself, taking a deep calming breath as he unfolded himself gracefully from the driver's seat of the Audi. She knew the next few minutes were going to be difficult.

"Let me go inside and try to 'talk' some sense into Razor first," she said. "I'm sure you don't want a repeat of the other night." She allowed a small, teasing smirk to escape.

"I'll just wait out here while you tame the monster," he agreed with a slight growl. "But don't take too long," his voice became a sexy purr, with a hint of the accent he got when his fangs were extended. A delicious shiver ran down her spine as she turned and hurried into the house, leaving him in the dark, lounging against the Audi.

It took her a while to convey what she expected from Razor to the huge cat's mind. Cats' minds worked so differently to a human's, and they saw the world in much more basic principles. The way she worked with the animals was by using pictures and emotions. Emotions were the easiest for her to control: she could force calm over a panicked or violent animal, she could encourage bravery in a timid animal, she could soothe a disturbed animal. Positive actions were also fairly easy to convey. She could visualise what she wanted to animal to do and give it a mental 'push' to do what she wished. Negative actions were the most difficult; the 'don't do this' instruction was quite complicated, as she first had to show the action and then find a way to show the reverse of that action and convey that the animal was *not* to do the action. It wasn't the way their minds tended to work. So telling Razor to *not* attack Julius was a tricky undertaking. She could feel his fierce resistance to the whole idea. Finally she showed him that if he attacked then Julius would leave and so would she; Razor had a fairly well developed understanding of cause and effect, so that ultimately led him to give in, though he did so with very poor grace. He stalked off to sulk in the lounge, and Gabi had the feeling that her brand new lounge suite was going to need some repairs in the morning.

She was still in a crouch on the floor in the hall where she'd been conversing with Razor when Julius appeared in the doorway behind her.

"Amazing," he breathed, "I can sense your power when you use it like that." His eyes held a kind of wonder. "I could taste the emotions you were projecting to him, and then there's a kind of pressure, like velvet brushing against my skin. I've never felt anything like it."

He stepped into the hall, put his hand out to draw her to her feet and laced his fingers with hers. As she straightened, he pressed close to her, crowding her until she was backed up against a wall. His free hand flew to the back of her head, and in a fraction of a heartbeat, he'd pulled the fastenings from her hair, and it tumbled down around her face in gentle, chestnut waves. His fingers wove into the strands at the back of her neck and pulled with enough force to tilt her head back, raising her mouth to where he could capture it with his own.

"I can feel yours, too," she said in barely a whisper, as she watched his lips part to reveal his fully extended canines. "When you call to others, it feels like the tingle in the air before a summer storm."

And then his lips were only millimetres from hers, he paused there and drew a slow lungful of air into his chest through his nose, as though relishing the scent of her. She unlaced her fingers from his and plunged both her hands into his hair dragging his head forward so his lips finally met hers. She felt him try to temper the joining of their mouths, try to take her mouth gently, but she was too far gone, and as their lips met, tongues tangling in a hard, desperate kiss, she felt his sharpened canines nick her tongue and pierce her bottom lip. His body shuddered against hers as the metallic taste of her blood swept through both their mouths. He groaned, plunging his tongue more roughly into her mouth, sucking at the small injuries, his hands now running freely over her body, removing weapons and sheaths with hurried dexterity, and then starting on her clothes.

The difference in their heights made kissing an almost gymnastic feat, so once he'd removed everything but her lace panties he lifted her up, and she curled her legs around his waist, luxuriating in the feel of his tautly muscled body close against her bare skin. The coarse fabric of his shirt chafed pleasurably against her nipples, bringing them to hard, aching points. She realised she needed to get rid of the material between them and only barely stopped herself from ripping his shirt off again. She managed to control herself enough to pull the shirt over his head, and then pulled herself as tightly as she could against him as she pressed little biting kisses along the line of his jaw towards his ear.

"Bedroom?" he asked hoarsely.

"Down the corridor, second door on the left," she whispered as her lips found his earlobe and her tiny canine teased the tender flesh. He tightened his grip on cool air brushed across her skin, his muscles undulate under his smooth, cool skin but she kept her eyes closed and started nipping her way down his neck. A moment later, they were falling. She blinked her eyes open as she hit the carpet, the softness of her fake fur rug beneath her back. He was above her, his body half covering hers. His arms had completely cushioned her body as they fell, she'd hardly felt the impact. They'd made it to her room, but not to her bed. She was vaguely aware of her bed a few feet from them, still mussed from her catnap earlier, but as Julius lowered his head to her body and she felt him rip apart the lace of her panties with his teeth, everything else in the world ceased to exist.

They did make it to the bed at some point, Gabi realised as she finally became aware of her surroundings again. They were both entangled in the sheets, her head on his chest and his arm was wound tightly around her waist holding her close to him. The bedside clock told her it was a few minutes before 3am. She'd lost track of an entire hour. She was still breathing heavily, and her heart was pounding like she'd run the obstacle course twice. She knew they both could do with a shower, but she wasn't sure how long it would be before her arms and legs would obey her commands. She could still feel the burning tingle where his fangs had pierced her inner thigh, and she felt a blush trying to rise in her cheeks at the memory, though her traitorous body clenched in recalled ecstasy. His arm tightened around her.

"Shower?" he asked, kissing the top of her head.

"When I regain some control of my muscles," she agreed. "You can go first, while I recover," she suggested, knowing what was likely to happen if they got into the shower together.

"Or," he said in a seductive purr, "I can carry you."

She chuckled weakly and struggled to a sitting position; his arm released her, but his deft fingers began to trace a path up and down her spine.

"So many scars," he said softly, as he traced a jagged one about three inches long across her left shoulder blade.

She snorted softly. "Goes with the territory, as they say."

"I wish I could erase them for you," he said, sitting up behind her and kissing the imperfection.

"Each one has a story," she said thoughtfully, "Many of them are lessons I had to learn the hard way. I'm not sure I'd be willing to give them up."

"Lea, my warrior," he said, and she could hear the smile in his voice.

"And you?" she asked him. "How many battle scars do you have?"

"No visible ones,' he said enigmatically, but continued before she could interrupt. "Vampires don't scar unless the injury is inflicted by silver, or the wound comes into contact with salt water."

"Oh," she said, surprised. "So Fergus' face?" she left the question hanging. Julius took a breath and she could feel a sense of sadness surrounding him now. She wondered briefly at her ability to feel his emotions, she didn't think for a moment that she was imagining it, it was simply too strong to ignore.

"He poured salt into the wound before it healed," he answered slowly, "like you, he wanted to remember the lesson."

She knew that was all he was going to say on the matter and that whatever the sadness was about, it was old and deep-seated. She wouldn't push him now; she would pry it out of him some other time. She peeked at him over her shoulder.

"Shower?" she asked with a raised eyebrow, then dragged herself off the bed and sauntered naked into her en-suite bathroom. As she turned on the water, she heard a phone ring. Her pulse leapt, even as she realised that it wasn't her phone ringing. She moved back to the doorway and watched as Julius scooped up his pants from a pile on the floor and found his phone. He was glorious naked, she thought. He checked the caller's number.

"It's just the Estate," he told her, "go and shower, I'll join you as soon as I'm finished."

She nodded and retreated to the steamy warmth of the shower cubicle. When she heard the shower door open, she scooted over to make room for him but instead of joining her he was already dressed.

"I'm sorry," he said, "I have to go. There's been some kind of accident at the Estate."

"Do you need some help?" she asked, all business now. "I can be dressed in a few minutes."

He reached into the shower, putting his hand behind her head and drawing her close enough for a kiss, heedless of the water soaking his shirt sleeve.

"Thank you, Lea," he breathed, "but no. It's probably better that I deal with this one without any distractions. Get some sleep, I'll call and give you an update before I crash for the day."

And in the next instant he was gone, just the memory of the feel of his lips remained in the shower with her. She unhurriedly finished her shower, pulled on some loose cotton pyjamas and then went to make a cup of hot chocolate and soothe Razor's ruffled ego. The thought of her bed without him in it was strangely unappealing, but eventually with nothing else to do and at Razor's insistence she went back to bed and crawled under the covers making sure her phone was in reach.


The atmosphere was grim when Julius strode into the manor house. Alexander was waiting for him, and the rest of the guard, except for Charles, Quentin and Tabari, who were still on patrol with Kyle, were milling uneasily around on the ground floor. They came to attention when Julius entered, and the house went silent.

"Come," Alexander said shortly and started up the stairs.

Julius followed him wordlessly. At the top of the stairs, Alexander turned and headed towards Julius's newly refurbished office. The door had been re-hung and most of the display cases and shelving had been fixed and refitted. The mess of glass and metal and wood had been cleared away, and a new desk stood in exactly the same position as the old one. Julius had left instructions for Sebastian to set up his new computer in the office tonight and to make sure his internet was running and the firewalls were in place. The computer was ready on his desk. Everything looked in place, exactly as it should be, except for the blood. And the smashed glass. And the decapitated body. And the head. Julius felt an almost physical punch in the chest as he took in the sight. If he'd had air in his lungs, it would've left him in a whoosh.

"It's Sebastian," Alexander said quietly, when Julius didn't speak. "I came up to check if he'd made any progress on tracking our traitors. I said he could work in here once he finished setting up your computer."

Julius could feel a cold, dark rage building inside him. He moved to the head, crouching down to turn it so he could see the features. Sebastian's frightened eyes stared back at him unseeingly. The head hadn't deteriorated yet, Sebastian was such a young Vampire that his body would decompose like that of a human. At least it made identification easier. The scene in the office showed that Sebastian had tried to fight his attacker or attackers off, but he hadn't been able to put up much resistance.

"Who could have done this?" Julius asked in a tight voice.

Alexander sighed and slumped against the wall near the doorway. "I don't know. I've kept everyone away from here. No one else has been in the room since I found him except me and you. I haven't told them it was murder, I gave them the story I gave you on the phone." He paused, tension tightening the muscles along his jaw. "I think it was someone on the inside, Julius. There are no unknown scents in here or anywhere else in the house. Not that I can detect anyway."

"It can only be one of a handful of people then," Julius said. "Most of the guard was with us tonight. That leaves us with the household staff and the Werewolves." Julius moved across the room to inspect his weapons collection.

"The Jambiya Dagger is missing," he said shortly. "That means the murderer didn't come prepared, so it's unlikely it was an outsider."

"There are two more things," Alexander told him. Julius braced himself as Alexander continued. "Gregory is missing. No one has seen him since midnight, when Claudia heard him take a call on his personal phone."

"And the second?" Julius asked flatly.

"Sebastian's computer is gone."

Julius sank into his new office chair, only vaguely aware of the splatters of blood smearing against his pants and shirt. There was only one reason someone would murder Sebastian and steal his computer. Sebastian had found another traitor in the Clan. The traitor had killed him before he got a chance to tell Julius, and everything Sebastian had found would've been on his computer.

"I think maybe we should get Kyle in here," Alexander said cautiously. "He'll be able to scent things you and I can't. His nose is so good he can tell how many hours it's been since the scent was left. It would help to know who's been in here in the last few hours. The scent is particularly muddied in here with all the workers who've been in and out fixing the room up over the past few days."

"Call him," Julius said shortly, "It would be best to have the rest of the guard back here anyway after this. If he only finds Vampire scent in here, I will personally be questioning everyone who's been in the Estate in the past twenty-four hours."

Alexander pulled his phone from his pocket. Kyle answered almost immediately. Once Alexander explained the situation, Kyle agreed to pack up and get to the Estate as quickly as he could. They'd encountered nothing of excitement since the others had left.

"Eerily quiet," Julius heard Kyle describe it to Alexander, "as though something big is being planned which has called in all their resources. I'm just hoping it's too late in the night to start something." Alexander muttered his agreement and disconnected the call.

"Call down to the guard station and ensure that Kyle and the guard are let in. Tell them that no one is to leave the Estate without my express permission. Then send the household staff and any off duty Wolves to the gymnasium and make sure they are kept there under guard. Tell them nothing."

Alexander nodded and left the office.

Julius swivelled his new, now blood-stained, office chair and bent to open a cupboard, taking out a wine glass and a bottle of red wine. He put both on his desk, avoiding the pooled, drying blood and de-corked the bottle with a quick twist of a corkscrew from his top desk drawer. As he poured the burgundy liquid into the crystal glass, his thoughts turned back to Gabi. He wondered if she was asleep. He resisted the urge to call her, it wouldn't be fair to wake her if she was getting some rest, but the urge to hear her voice was almost overwhelming. He'd thought that his draw to Simone was the strongest thing he'd ever felt for a woman, that he'd never feel such an insane urge again. In fact, he'd schooled himself to never let another woman have that kind of hold over him again. Look what the affair with Simone had gotten him. But his willpower just wasn't enough to rescue him from Gabi's lure. She was his Siren call. His resistance was a pile of breadcrumbs.

He still didn't know how she would react to the thought of a relationship with him. The physical chemistry between them was as obvious as the lean on the tower of Pisa, but he had yet to introduce her to the reality of his life. She'd seen the girl, his feeder, being escorted home a few nights ago and had apparently realised what she was, but Gabi hadn't actually seen him feed, except for his feeding on her.

His groin tightened at the thought of the taste of her. The taste of her blood was almost addictive, far more deliciously potent than the blood of a normal human. He hadn't told her that he'd woken at midday after taking her blood, which was unheard of for a Vampire who'd crashed for the day. Julius was able to keep himself awake through the daylight hours if he needed to, but once he let himself sleep he had no control over when he woke, and he rarely woke more than an hour before sunset. He had never woken at midday. It was the anti-thesis of what he'd expected.

As she had a certain amount of Vampire in her DNA, he'd expected her blood to be less potent, less nourishing for him. Vampires couldn't feed each other. They could take blood from each other, it gave an amazing edge to sex, or it could be used as a way of showing dominance, but it didn't actually provide nourishment. Something contained in human blood was needed. But her blood had been his version of Red Bull, it was incredible. It would probably scare her to know how incredible he found it. But in reality, even if she was willing to let him feed from her, he'd still need to take blood from other feeders. Even though he didn't need to feed every day, at times he could stretch to every third or fourth day, over time it would weaken her, and there would be times when she couldn't come running when he needed blood. She had her own life, and he wasn't going to interfere in that.

He also knew how he would feel if he would have to watch her have that kind of close interaction with another male, the jealousy would be hard to contain.

At that thought, he wondered if any feeders had been brought to the Estate tonight, he'd have to get Alexander to check. They had two or three resident feeders; people who lived on the Estate and worked there or studied during the day and were available to Julius and his staff for feeding when necessary. Julius encouraged his staff to go off the Estate and find donors in the clubs and bars of the City. He enforced a strict code of conduct when it came to feeding; donors had to be willing, there was to be no violence in the act and the donor's memories had to be cleared of anything to do with being bitten and fed on. But occasionally someone needed blood urgently or didn't have time to go 'hunting', and this was what the feeders were for. He only allowed the feeders to stay for a few months at the most; they usually left with some memory about undertaking a medical experiment and a decent bank account, so it worked for all parties concerned. Julius wasn't sure what Gabi would make of that, but they did have to feed somehow, he was trying to do it in the most humane way he could.

Kyle's voice downstairs pulled him from his contemplation, and he drained the last few drops from his glass as Kyle walked into the office and stopped to stare at the head and body on the floor.

"Time to change office I think," he said to Julius with an eyebrow raised in surprise. "This one seems to attract violence."

Julius refilled his glass and looked enquiringly at Kyle.

"No, thanks Julius. I'd rather not dull my senses tonight. I have a funny feeling there's more going on than we realise." He paused, closing his eyes and drawing in a deep breath through his nose. "Alex said you want me to see what scents I can trace in here?"

"Please," replied Julius, "there are so many in here at the moment. Though our sense of smell is enough to identify most of them, it is hard to tell how long it's been since they were actually in the room. It would help us immensely if you could tell how many were in here in the last few hours."

Kyle nodded. "I can probably do that, though if I haven't been close to the person I may not be able to tell you who it was, but I can tell if it was human, Were or Vamp. Do you have any idea when Sebastian was killed?" Kyle started moving around the room, his eyes half closed in concentration, carefully avoiding the pools of drying blood.

Julius could see his nostrils flaring as he breathed in the air and all its scents. "He was still alive at a little before midnight, Claudia heard him making some kind of noise and went to check on him just before she went off duty. She said he looked pleased about something but wouldn't discuss it with her. She incidentally heard Gregory on the phone on her way out, and that was the last anyone heard from either of them."

Kyle completed a circuit of the room and began a second round. "So the scent you're after will be less than four hours old," he mused, mostly to himself, so Julius didn't reply but drank his wine and attempted to keep a leash on his rage.

"There are only four scents newer than Claudia's," Kyle said as he got back to his starting point again.

Julius held up his hand to stop Kyle from continuing as they heard soft footsteps approaching.

Alexander entered the office again. "Everyone is under guard in the gymnasium," he informed Julius, giving Kyle a nod in greeting.

"That's probably not necessary," said Kyle. "Unless you or Alexander killed Sebastian, your killer is Gregory."

Julius saw the shock hit Alexander as hard as it hit him, it felt like some kind of spell had been cast at him, freezing him in place, not allowing his body to move while his brain tried to comprehend the impossible. Kyle seemed to sense their anguish and he walked over to the desk and refilled Julius's half empty glass. Minutes must have passed before Julius finally unfroze, a bone-deep sadness dragged at him as he finally picked up the wine glass and drained it in a single swallow.

"You're absolutely sure?" Alexander asked in an emotionless voice.

"Yes," Kyle said, there was sympathy in his voice. "Sebastian must have scratched or cut him with something, I can scent small traces of his blood in here."

As the shock wore off and reality returned, Julius realised that they were holding pieces of a puzzle that wasn't making any sense. They needed more puzzle pieces before the whole picture started to emerge.

"What did Sebastian find that had him excited?" he demanded from no one in particular, banging his fists on the desk in frustration.

"If it was on his computer, we'll never know," Alexander said bleakly, "Gregory must've taken it with him."

"So, whatever he found was worth killing for," Kyle prompted. "Do you think he found other traitors in your Clan?"

"That's possible," Alexander conceded bleakly.

Kyle started pacing, on the far side of the room from Sebastian's body. He mused as he paced. "He was a computer geek, right?" He looked to the Vampires for their affirmations. "Have either of you two checked your e-mail or intranet to see if he forwarded you anything?"

Julius could've kicked himself that the idea hadn't occurred to him. His hand twitched and the new computer purred to life. A few quick clicks and he'd found what they were looking for.

"You're right, there's something here from Sebastian."

A feeling of dread washed over him as the other two rushed around to watch as Julius opened the first of several video and audio clips.

Kyle knew there was trouble brewing seconds into the first clip; Julius's face was a mask of undiluted rage, Alexander's was pinched with disbelief and betrayal. It was clear now that Gregory had been working with Stephan and Genevieve as well as a Werewolf in Julius's employ. They'd all been feeding information to Dante's Clan and taking orders on ways to undermine security and stir tensions in Julius's Clan. Somehow Gregory had known that his cover was blown, so he'd killed Sebastian, grabbed his computer and run to Dante. As Julius and Alexander looked at each other in rage and horror, a sudden thought occurred to Kyle.

"Sebastian was the one who tracked Gabi's details for you, correct?" he asked, tension locked his jaw, making it hard to form the words.

"Yes," Alexander replied, slightly confused.

Kyle knew the moment that Julius caught up to him, as the wine glass Julius was holding exploded, fracturing into thousands of tiny shards, the remaining wine splashing onto the desk to mingle with the drying blood.

"Her address is on that computer," he said hoarsely.

Before any of them could react further, a phone rang. Kyle recognised his own ringtone and patted his pocket before pulling out his phone. He glanced at the call ID.

"It's her," he breathed.

# CHAPTER 22

Gabi's mind hit full consciousness the moment she heard Razor growl. Her hand instantly flashed to the 9mm strapped underneath the bed, and she ripped it free of its mount. Yes, it was highly illegal, and yes, it had cost her a fortune to have smuggled into the country, but she figured if anything nasty enough to require the use of it was in her home she would happily take the legal consequences. If she was still alive when the cops arrived. It was a small, compact Glock 19 with an extended 19 round magazine, and it had been a long time since she last fired it, though she made sure it was cleaned and oiled at least once a month, and Glocks were renowned for their unfailing reliability.

In the darkness, Gabi could see Razor fuzzed out to his fullest size, on his tiptoes and glaring at the bedroom door, the low growl in his throat continuous and menacing. Gabi didn't doubt him; she could feel the Vampire presences and smell the sulphuric stench of Demon. She released the safety on the Glock, eased herself quietly out of bed and hit speed dial 1 on the mobile next to the bed without picking it up. She grabbed Nex from the dressing table and shoved the scabbard into the waistband of her pyjama bottoms. When she heard the click of Kyle picking up the call, she yelled at the phone while keeping the gun trained on the bedroom door.

"Three Vampires, unknown number of Demons. Get back-up and get here. Now!"

Kyle's panicked reply was drowned out by the sound of the bedroom door exploding inward. Gabi ducked to avoid the bigger splinters of wood and threw herself into a diving roll, landing in the corner of the room nearest the door, out of the direct line of sight of anyone, or anything, entering. She flattened herself against the wall and steadily took aim, waiting for the first head through the shattered doorway. Slinky, shocked by the noise and commotion, beat a hasty retreat off the bed and into Gabi's laundry basket, while Razor emitted an ear-piercing shriek and launched himself at the first Vampire through the door. The Vampire was tall and thin and fairly old if his aura was anything to go by. He entered somewhat casually, obviously not expecting any kind of resistance, let alone an attack. The onslaught of an animal the size of a half-grown tiger, with teeth and claws to match and shrieking like a banshee, completely threw him off his stride.

A second Vampire was directly behind him, though so much shorter than the first that he was all but invisible in the darkness. Shorty, in his haste to get in on the action, shoved Lanky straight into Razor's attack. Razor took Lanky at face level sinking teeth into the Vampire's cheek and clawing at his eyes and nose. The tall Vampire lurched backward screaming and batting at his furry attacker. Shorty simply leapt over his beset companion and headed for Gabi's bed with a long knife and a coil of rope in his hands. Gabi could only imagine the confused look on his face when he suddenly looked down and found the tip of a curved blade protruding from his chest. She wondered briefly if he had any idea that he was already dead when he fingered the sword tip dazedly. She didn't bother waiting to see his body shrivel, she put a bare foot on his back, kicked him forward onto the bed and yanked Nex free, then spun to face the Demons now pouring through the door. They were only slightly distracted by the Vampire rolling around on the carpet, screaming, with a large cat attached to his face. She switched the gun to her right hand and smoothly began pulling the trigger, aiming at the eyes gleaming maliciously in the darkness. Her heart was pounding and adrenaline was screaming through her bloodstream, but her mind remained calm and clear. She knew she was hugely outnumbered, and Kyle wasn't going to make it with reinforcements in time.

"Raz," she screamed at the huge cat, pulling at his mind to let the Vampire go and backing away to one of the large bay windows that looked out over her garden. Escape was the only option now. She knew the woods and surrounding farmland like the back of her hand, if she could get out of the house, she could lead them a merry chase across country and bring them back for Kyle and company to finish off. She was running out of bullets fast. Damn, why did Demons have to have so many fucking eyes?

Four of them were lunging around the room blindly, making wild grabs for her, but more had appeared in the doorway. The room was a seething mass of grotesque bodies, skeletal arms and dank, acrid breath. She put more bullets into their faces, trying to dodge sprays of blood, and used Nex to hack at arms, hands and fingers reaching for her. Razor was still wrestling with the first

Vampire, Gabi tripped over the bones of Shorty as she backed away from a rotting arm and tried to get close enough to Razor to pull him away. She slammed Nex into the throat of one of the smaller Demons who'd spotted her in the gloom and made a lunge at her, she leapt clear of the acidic blood and heard the carpet and floorboards hiss as the Demon fell forward and began trying to crawl towards her.

"Raz," she yelled at the cat again and threw a mental order at him to let go and get out. He paused briefly, hissing at Lanky, and reluctantly began backing away towards Gabi. He never took his eyes off the Vampire, who was screaming and trying to hold flaps of skin and flesh in place on his face. Gabi noticed he was missing an eye and a couple of fingers, too.

The bedroom was fast becoming too crowded for Gabi to avoid all the searching arms and hands. They'd closed off her escape from the bigger windows— there was only one option left. She leapt onto the bed and aimed a flying kick at the small window above her bed. The glass and wood gave way in a muffled explosion. She yanked the curtain out of the way, kicking at a scaled hand which latched onto her ankle, and fired another shot into the Demon's face — it was her last bullet. She pulled herself up onto the window ledge and threw the gun at the Demon's head, slashing Nex down onto another groping hand. Razor jumped up next to her as the hand, with six black-clawed fingers, began tightening inexorably on her ankle, compressing the bones together excruciatingly, claws digging into her flesh. She hacked at the toughened skin on the wrist, desperately sawing with Nex's keen edge until she managed to sever the hand from the arm.

As the second clawed hand reached for her out of the dark, she grabbed Razor and pulled him with her as she tumbled backwards out the window, landing in a defensive crouch in a muddle of azalea bushes, soft earth and bark. She grimaced at the sting of dozens of glass and wood splinters embedded in her back. Her cotton pyjamas hadn't been much protection. She let Razor go, giving him an order to hide, and praying to the Lord and Lady that Slinky stayed hidden. She took a second to pry the Demon hand off her ankle, suppressing a shudder as she unhooked the claws from her flesh.

Then Gabi and Razor spun as one to face the third Vampire materialising out of the darkness at the edge of the garden. He was tall and muscular and walked with confidence and controlled tension. Although he had nothing of Julius's easy grace, something about the third Vampire brought Julius to mind. Gabi could just make out a cruel smile playing at the corners of his mouth. Then she realised what the similarity was to Julius; the Vampire's power was colossal, it radiated around him like a tornado on a leash. She breathed in, allowing her body to flow into a natural, battle-ready position, Nex comfortable in her right hand.

Razor reacted before she could stop him, hurtling towards the powerful Vampire in a ball of angry, claw and tooth filled rage. To Gabi's horror, the Vampire took Razor's attack in stride, allowing him to get just close enough and then flicking out his arm, hurling Razor back against the side of the house with a sickening, bone-snapping crunch. The cat let out a feeble hiss and immediately tried to pick himself up. Gabi sent him a sharp order to lie still and play dead, and he subsided. Her temper, ignited just minutes ago by the assault on her treasured sanctuary, now roared into a howling inferno.

"Let me guess," she said in a deadly calm voice, "you would be Danté."

Without turning to look, she could hear some of the Demons trying to climb out of the window, she needed to do something fast. If she could take out Danté the whole war would be over, but could she do it before the Demons took her down? Only one way to find out. She sprang at Danté almost before his name had finished passing her lips, rushing him, but instead of going for the obvious kill she flipped herself lightly over his head spinning as she came down to face his back and leaping to drive Nex into his chest as he spun to find her. But he was no longer there; he moved faster than her eyes could track; he'd done one of Julius's disappearing tricks.

"Yes," said a balefully amused voice to her left. "I am Danté. You'll have to excuse my appalling manners. It's been a long time since I've found a need for them, and I'm rather rusty."

His voice was condescending in that nasal, upper class kind of way but also strangely hypnotic. Gabi realised that he was trying to control her mind, and once again thanked the lucky star she lived under for her immunity to Vamp mind control. She moved to face him where he stood several metres away and fell into an offensive position. Damn, he was fast. Could she draw this fight out long enough for reinforcements to arrive? Maybe if she kept him talking.

"Is there a reason you're disturbing me in the middle of the night, Danté?" she asked in a bored tone. As she spoke, she was searching the garden for other things to use as weapons. Aside from the bird bath and few sun-faded garden gnomes, there wasn't much to work with. If she survived this, she vowed she'd be hiding weapons in the garden from now on. She was going to have to take this fight slower than she liked and wait for the right opening.

"I would have thought it would be obvious, my dear," Danté replied. "I can't have Julius getting the upper hand in our little war, now can I? You'll make a good little pawn to control him with. He always did have a stupidly soft spot for women and children. Terribly chivalrous is our Julius." He sniffed disdainfully.

"What makes you think he gives a shit what happens to me? I kill Vampires after all," Gabi asked in feigned confusion.

At that point, Danté swept closer to her again in one of his untrackable moves, coming to an abrupt halt less than three feet away from her. She steeled herself against the natural urge to flinch away from him. He leaned in towards her, lowering his face to the same height as hers. She could actually see the insanity swirling in his eyes. He had a chilling, unnatural smile on his face.

"Because I can smell him on you, and, more importantly, in you, my little beauty," he breathed rancid breath into her face.

Gabi nearly gagged.

"Julius doesn't share blood readily. Oh, sex he will do casually, but not blood," he said, dragging the last word out and reminding her disturbingly of Jack Nicholson's portrayal of The Joker. All he was missing was the absurd make-up.

Gabi kept all movement from her muscles until the quarter second before she sprang at him, Nex aimed straight at his heart. He leapt back, actually caught by surprise, but still quick enough to deflect Nex from his heart. There was a ragged slice across his left hand and arm, the sleeve of his dress shirt falling open. He didn't seem to feel any pain as he made a grab for her throat, forcing Gabi to dance back out of reach cursing herself; he wasn't going to make that mistake again.

"You're a vicious little vixen," he said through gritted teeth, as he inspected his bleeding arm. "You'll pay for that." Then, abruptly the rage left his face and an oddly innocent curiosity seemed to fill it. "It's not like Julius to hook up with a spirited woman. He always liked them quiet and docile. He must be going senile in his old age." He said this last in a hushed, slightly conspiratorial voice.

Gabi couldn't keep up with his mood swings. She knew that Julius was right about Danté being utterly and certifiably insane. There was only one cure for this particular Vampire, and that was healthy dose of death. Gabi risked a quick glance around the garden and realised that she was completely surrounded by what amounted to a small army of Demons, she lost count at twenty; there was no hope of escape. Come on Kyle, she thought anxiously backing away, trying to put her back to the partially crumbled garden shed and wondering if the roof would hold her. A ruction drew her attention to the front of the house. The Vampire that Razor had attacked stumbled out into the night, cursing inventively.

"Where's that fucking monster?" he all but screamed.

"Something wrong, Errol?" Danté asked mildly, his eyes never leaving Gabi.

"That fucking demonic cat ate my fingers, and look at my face, I think I've lost an eye. You didn't tell me there would be a fucking demon cat in there," he ranted.

"Calm down, Errol, I'm sure they'll grow back. The cat is over there. Perhaps if you cut it open you can retrieve your fingers from its belly," Danté said, flicking his fingers in the direction of Razor, who was lying panting where he had fallen after hitting the side of the house. The tall Vampire's eyes gleamed evilly as a satisfied smirk replaced the anger on his ravaged face, and he drew a long knife as he stalked over to the cat.

"No!" Gabi screamed and darted back towards Razor, ignoring the slowly undulating mass of Demon forms trying to surround her.

"Sssstop," ordered a darkly familiar rasp as the Wraith floated into the middle of the melee, placing itself between Gabi and the other Vampire.

Gabi froze unwillingly.

"Enough of thiss nonsenssse," it declared. "The Baron iss coming, with plenty of reinforcementss. Unless you want to meet him on thossse termsss, Massster," it spat the word, "then we musst leave now."

"Fine," barked Danté with a sulky edge to his voice. "Bring the girl. Errol hurry up with the cat."

Gabi unfroze and dived past the Wraith, springing into an aerial flip she came up just short of Errol and used a roundhouse kick to send him flying into a nearby group of Demons, then she placed herself in front of Razor protectively, Nex firm in her hand. Julius was on the way, all she had to do was hold out for a few more minutes. Then the Wraith filled her vision, its ghostly arm extended towards her head. The last thing she saw was Errol, having picked himself up out of the mass of Demons, move around behind her with his knife gripped in his right hand. She heard Razor hiss weakly and then scream in agony, and then pain and darkness swallowed her whole.

Kyle was out of the van before it came to a complete stop, Julius was one step ahead of him, but they froze as one at the stairway in front of the house. The door stood ajar and there was only deathly silence inside.

"They've gone," Julius managed in a strained voice. "There are no Demons or Vampires here now."

The other twelve Vampires flowed around them, weapons out and battle ready.

"Search the gardens," Julius ordered tersely, but he already knew they wouldn't find anything. He looked at Kyle bleakly and then at the house.

Kyle nodded and closed his eyes, as if he knew what Julius was thinking, if Gabi was still here, she would be inside and she wouldn't be alive. In silent agreement, they stepped forward to search the house together. They quickly made their way through the house, noting the destruction that had taken place. Julius felt something tighten inside him; he knew how Gabi felt about her home, her sanctuary. Even if she was still alive, it would never be the same place of solace and comfort to her again.

They checked her room, taking in the broken window, the Demon blood, the Vampire bones, the gun and spent bullet casings on the floor, signs from the rest of the house indicated a large contingent of Demons, not even Angeli Morte could've taken on that many Demons single-handedly. A small noise made them both react instinctively, weapons drawn. The rustle came again, and Julius realised it was coming from Gabi's laundry basket.

Kyle sighed and called out, "Slinky?" The rustle came again, and the clothing writhed until a little masked face poked out. Kyle sighed again and walked over to pick up the little creature, draping him around his shoulder. "Hey, Stinks. Where's your Mama? She'll be glad that you were clever enough to hide and keep yourself safe." His voice cracked on the last word.

Julius felt as though a sharpened stake had just been rammed into his chest. In fact, he would have preferred a stake to the pain that ripped through him. What had he been doing letting her get involved in all this? Only one thing kept him from collapsing to his knees; if they'd wanted her dead, they would've killed her and left her here for him to find. The fact that she wasn't here meant they'd taken her and wanted to use her as leverage, and for that they needed her alive.

"Stay alive, Lea," he whispered, "stay alive, and I'll find you. If it's the last thing I do."

A shout erupted from just outside the small shattered bedroom window.

"Julius." It was Alexander calling him with a touch of regret in his voice.

Julius felt liquid nitrogen pour through his veins as he leapt nimbly out the broken window, not wanting to see what Alexander had found. It wasn't what he'd expected, but it wasn't much better. Razor lay in the cold soil of a flower bed, a piteous sight. His fur matted with blood, his mouth slightly open and his eyes flat and lacklustre. The normally large, vital body now lay gaunt and limp. A laboured breath rasped through his damaged lungs. It looked as though someone had stabbed him repeatedly with a knife.

Most of the Vampires had gathered in a sombre semi-circle, and Kyle pushed his way through to fall on his knees next to the dying cat. He threw his head back and howled, long and mournful. Razor focused his eyes for a brief moment on Kyle and then began a painful, stuttered purr. Julius felt himself collapse to his knees beside the cat, he guessed the cat must have been trying to defend Gabi, it just didn't seem right. He knew if Gabi was here right now, and she had the power to fix one thing in all of this chaos and destruction, it would be Razor. He had to try.

"Alexander, help me," he ordered brusquely, trying to lift the cat without damaging him further. "Give us some room," he barked at the rest of them. "I want to know how many were here, how they got here and how they got in. I want answers, now move."

His guard knew enough to hurry to their duties without further questions.

Only Fergus hung back for a moment. "Good luck," he growled softly, "I hope it works." Then he disappeared into the darkness.

Alexander and Kyle helped lift Razor into Julius's arms, and then they all walked back into the house, Slinky sniffing the air anxiously from Kyle's shoulder.

Byron arrived a half hour later. Julius had already dispatched most of his guard back to the Estate. Sunrise was only a few minutes away, and while he and Alexander could withstand sunlight through the additional UV protection on the windows in the Aston Martin, the others could not. Just before they left, Fergus came to Julius and pressed something into his hands, when he looked down he realised it was Gabi's Kris.

"She'll be wantin this back when we find er, Sire," he rumbled, his unscarred eye steady on Julius face. 'And we'll find er, Sire, doncha be doubting that." The huge Scotsman bowed his head briefly and was gone.

Julius had never regretted his inability to go out in the sun more than on this particular day. How could he possibly go back to the Estate and do nothing while Gabrielle was in Danté's maniacal clutches. He knew better than anyone else what atrocities Danté was capable of. The rage tore at him. When his phone chimed a few minutes later, something made him pause and check the message. What he read caused his anger and anguish to solidify into something cold, hard and terrifying. Wordlessly, he held the phone out to Kyle and Alexander so that they could read the message. It had been sent from Gregory's personal phone.

*"Your inside man has proved so valuable to me in the past few weeks, it was a great pity that he got himself*

*discovered. It meant I had no further need of him. I'm
sure it'll give you comfort to know that I didn't make his
passing easy. Traitors don't deserve mercy, do they?
Your new lover has real spirit, she's not your usual choice
at all. I think I may have to try and tame her for you. I
feel like I no longer know you, Julius. I trust you will still
do anything to save those you love, surely that soft-
hearted part of you hasn't changed? If you want her to
see another sunrise, you will surrender to me. This is the
last time I'll be so generous. You'll get details of our
meeting at sunset."*

"Byron," Kyle said urgently, "get a trace on this phone
number," and he read the mobile number to the older
man, who immediately picked up his own phone. "If the
phone is still on we'll be able to trace it." His voice held an
edge of urgency and fear.

Julius could smell the Wolf on Kyle stronger than it had
ever been before. If he'd been any other Werewolf, he'd
be on four legs by now, the strain on his face and the
sweat beading on his forehead told Julius that it was a
battle he could lose at any second.

"They'll call me back in a few minutes," Byron said.
The strain was showing on the older man's face as well.
He took a deep breath as he looked around at the
destruction of Gabi's kitchen and living area. "I've called
Rose," his tone said that it had been a difficult call, "She'll
come in at first light to help with," he paused, "to help with
Razor. She'll know what to do. What Gabi would do."
He swallowed, exhaling and fighting for emotional control.

"We'll get her," Kyle said fiercely, gripping the older
man's shoulder with one hand. "She knows how to
survive, she's tough and she's smart, she'll know we're
coming for her."

"He's right," Alexander put in, "We have no control
over what's happening to her now, but we know he's not

going to kill her while he still thinks there's a chance Julius will surrender. Let's focus on what we can do. If we can find where he's holding her before sunset, then the upper hand is ours."

"Yes." Byron nodded, his eyes had grown hard and the set of his shoulders showed his renewed determination. "We have the backing of one of the biggest networks of Magi, Weres and Shifters in the world. We'll find her. And then we'll put an end to this threat. Julius, you and Alexander are welcome to join us at HQ. Most of our conference rooms are in areas without windows for security reasons, and there are sleeping quarters should you need them."

Julius nodded curtly. "We'll collect a few things from the Estate and then meet you there." He knew that with a day of no sleep and some kind of battle looming tonight, he and Alexander would need to feed. Then he and Alexander and the dark brooding air that surrounded him swept into the Aston Martin and sped off, leaving Kyle and Byron to calm Rose when she first arrived and to show her to where they'd put Razor.

# CHAPTER 23

Consciousness returned to Gabi in a painful rush. The instant she realised she couldn't move, a spike of adrenalin shot through her, clearing her mind and bringing back memories of the invasion and attack at her cottage. She stilled her body and opened her senses, checking with both the supernatural and the physical. There were over a dozen Vampires within a few hundred metres of her and at least double that number of Demons. None of them were in the same room as her, in fact, they seemed to be somewhere above her. She could hear water dripping and her nose told her she was underground; the smell of damp earth and decaying wood was strong, but it was overlaid by an old scent of...was that wine?

She opened her eyes a tiny crack. At least the Wraith hadn't taken her sight this time. Hard, uneven floor boards pressed uncomfortably into her shoulders and spine. She tried to turn her head and found that it was the only part of her that she could move except for her fingers. She was being held spread-eagled to the floor by U-shaped metal rods driven deep into the wooden floor boards over her wrists, upper arms, ankles, thighs, torso and neck. She was pinned to the ground like an insect in a display case. The bars were just tight enough to ensure she had no free movement while still allowing blood flow. There was no room for her to get enough leverage to pull the bars free. She began trying anyway, as she scanned the dim room she was trapped in. She realised that it had once been a wine cellar. Rows of wine racks lined the walls lit by a single candle burning in a crudely made holder on a table in the centre of the room. Dust coated every surface and spider webs adorned every niche and crevice.

When she noticed the large oak barrels piled on top of one another in a corner, she realised that this wasn't just the kind of wine cellar that you found in the basement of a house or a restaurant, this was the kind of wine cellar that you found on a vineyard. It was the kind of wine cellar that was used to age wine before it was bottled and shipped off for sale. She was being held on a winery. She gave a small snort, no wonder they hadn't been able to find any trace of Danté, Mariska or his cronies in the City. He wasn't hanging out in the City; he was hiding out in the countryside – the last place any of them would've thought to look.

***********************

Kyle met Julius and Alexander at the underground security door and led them to a small elevator, pressing the button for the top floor. No one spoke as they left the elevator, there was a tense, agitated air surrounding them. If a full human had walked past the trio, they would've found themselves inexplicably moving well out of their way. Julius was the only one of them who knew what Gabi was likely being subjected to, and he wasn't about to enlighten the others. He'd let his anger rise when he was taking blood from a feeder earlier, and Alexander had had to pull him off the poor man before he took too much. As it was, the man was being looked after by Jonathon in the medic wing at the Estate. He would have to keep a throttle hold on his rage today; he knew that calm, clear thought was what was needed until they found her. Then he could unleash the fury. He wasn't fool enough to think that his own surrender would make the slightest difference to Gabi's life or stop Danté and Mariska from trying to open a permanent gateway to the Etherworld. That was one ace they had up their sleeves; Danté would have no idea that they knew his true intentions for Solstice night. Gregory had run before he found out about that.

As the three of them entered the small conference room, there was a quiet hubbub. Anxious excitement tainted the air as about a dozen people sat around the dark wood table. Julius recognised all of the faces except for two younger males and one older one. All the other Hunters were present, as well as all the members of the SMV Council and a Magus who'd been with them at the fight in the train station. As they entered, the conversations and discussions cut off abruptly.

"Julius." Byron stood to greet the late-comers. "You remember the Council members; Irene, Margaret and Alistair?"

Julius nodded a curt greeting to them.

"And you of course know Athena, Lance, Douglas and Matthew."

"Yes," Julius acknowledged shortly.

"The two young men next to Douglas are our Hunter Trainees, James and Timothy. They've been fast-tracked in order for us to have a few extra weapons specialists with us. The gentleman on the left of Margaret is Stewart, he is the best Magus Tracker that we have, and the one on his left is Neil, one of our most experienced defensive Magi."

Julius barely afforded them a nod. "Is there anything to work with yet?"

"Yes," replied Byron with the faintest trace of hope in his tone.

His reply brought Kyle up short from his beeline to the catering table.

"What?" Kyle and Julius demanded at the same moment, in the same don't-mess-with-me tone of voice.

*************************

She was mentally keeping track of the vile, turbulent presence that she knew to be Danté and realised he was moving closer to her. Seconds later, she heard a key turn in a rusty lock and his dark aura swept into the room. He was followed up by a slightly built woman with shoulder-length, mouse brown hair and dark, pitiless eyes. Mariska, Gabi guessed. Her appearance was so plain, so nondescript as to be disconcerting. She was dressed in a worn looking beige skirt with an equally well used cream blouse and dark brown cardigan. In a crowd, no one would give this woman a second glance. She would simply fade into the background. Exactly what a Maleficus on the run needed, Gabi thought sourly.

"Ahh," Danté sighed dramatically, "Julius's little vixen is awake."

He walked towards the table that stood between the door and where she lay on the floor, laid several items on it, and almost lovingly positioned them in a neat row. Gabi couldn't see what the items were, but the satisfaction on his face was enough to send a thrill of fear though her.

"Now, don't worry too much," he said, turning his calmly deranged gaze on her, "I promised Julius I wouldn't kill you if he surrendered himself to me tonight. So I do have to keep you alive, but that doesn't mean we can't have a little fun in the meantime." He paused and took a few more steps towards to her, cocking his head and studying her. "Gregory told me some interesting things about you. I'm very interested to know if they're true."

Gabi felt ice course through her veins; she knew pain was coming. She began deep breathing and imagined pulling her mind into a small tight sphere of protection as her meditation coach had been trying to teach her for years.

*************************

Byron made a calming, placating gesture with his hands. "Take a seat and we'll fill you in on what we know," he told the trio, "it's not all good news, I'm afraid."

Kyle completed his trip to the catering table and returned with a cup of coffee and two donuts, taking one of the remaining empty seats and wrapping his long-fingered hands around the cup. Julius could see they were trembling against the Styrofoam. Julius and Alexander took seats as well, once Julius realised that their presence was making most of the room nervous and that sitting would make them look less frightening. He knew that by calming the situation the previous free flow of ideas and information would restart, hopefully resulting in something positive on Gabi's location, but both Vampires (and Kyle apparently) were finding it hard to rein in the need to be doing something violently physical.

"Yesterday, a number of objects were found at the warehouse that Werewolf noses assured us had been

364

touched by Vampires or Demons," Byron said once they had taken seats. "Magi spent the entire night trying to track the owners of the objects or the source of the magical power they could feel in the wards on the warehouse. Some of the stronger trackers could get a general direction but nothing else. The creatures that touched them or owned them are being magically protected, obviously by Mariska. This morning, Stewart tried tracking Gabi from personal items that I brought him from her home. He had a small measure of success." He indicated that Stewart could tell the newcomers what he'd discovered.

Stewart cleared his throat nervously under the intense stare of the two Vampires. "I, uh, felt a pull. A definite draw to the north east and a feeling of distance. I'd swear to the fact that she isn't in the City anymore, and at this stage she's stationary. But, beyond that, I can't tell you much more. The clothing that Byron brought just wasn't quite a strong enough bond for me to close on her essence through the layers of magical protection." He sighed and shook his head, looking slightly dejected. "It was like trying to catch little wisps of mist in my hands; it kept slipping through my fingers."

"The good news," Irene spoke up now, "is that the pull Stewart felt is in the same direction the others who tried tracking the objects from the warehouse felt. So we're confident that they're somewhere to the north east of the City, probably in the countryside."

Stewart sat forward, putting his head in his hands. "Maybe if I had something of Gabi's that she'd touched while fighting them, or something that one of the," he shuddered, "one of the Demons or Vampires who took her touched at the same time she did, it could give me a better connection to her."

"If we can get a better idea of the where to look, narrow down the search area," Irene said, "then Athena would be able to track the source of the protective Magic."

Athena, silent until now, nodded and then added, "I've tried scanning for Dark Magic, but my range for picking up traces is no more than nine or ten kilometres. Further than that I can't sense it, and there's nothing that close to us."

A quick movement by Julius and the glint of metal made everyone jump and drew a few gasps of shock from those around the table. Julius held out a calming hand as he turned the hilt of the short sword towards Stewart and pushed it across the table in the Magus' direction. Nex stopped just short of the man's elbow.

"That is Gabrielle's Kris. She would've been wielding it against her attackers this morning. It was found in her garden shortly after she was taken. Will that help?" he asked the disconcerted man.

Stewart's eyes went wide with disbelief, and then a spark of hope seemed to ignite in them. He jumped up, carefully picking up the sword in two hands and holding it almost reverently. "Excuse me," he whispered, "I need a quiet space." And with that he rushed from the room.

*************************

Danté seemed particularly intrigued by her rate of recovery; she didn't bother trying to tell him it was only as a result of Julius's blood that she was healing so fast. But as the morning dragged on and the punishment continued, her rate of recovery became slower and slower, as if the effect of Julius's blood was being drained away with the healing of each new round of abuse. She'd fought when Danté had pulled the bars free, she'd flown for his throat with her bare hands. When he caught and held her arms, crushing the bones until she heard them snap, she'd screamed but then had tried to use her legs and feet and teeth to hurt him back. Eventually, he'd commanded Mariska to 'do something to hold her still'. The Maleficus had begun to chant and in a few moments Gabi had felt her mind lose control of her body.

As she lay, unable to stop what was being done to her body but still able to experience every exquisite pain, still able to smell the blood and the burnt flesh, her mind took flight, trying to find relief from the relentless agony. As it fluttered helplessly, seeking some kind of distraction, she linked into the psyche of a flock of ducks in the sky outside, flying in a loose V formation and heading for a nearby lake. Through their minds, she could see a holiday resort along the edge of the lake. Holiday-makers were making the most of the warm, sunny day. A small, detached part of her mind latched onto a new and exciting thought, and if she could've, she would've smiled.

***********************

The wait for Stewart to return with news seemed interminable. The others gradually fell back into the tense conversations they'd been having before the Vampires joined them, much of it arguing over what the best way was to scan the whole of the north east area with just one Magus who was strong enough to sense Dark Magic from any kind of distance. It was close to an hour later when Stewart finally returned carrying a map of the City and its outlying agricultural land. He was tense and excited.

He laid the map on the table, smoothing it out with shaking hands. "I still can't penetrate the protection to get an exact location for her," he warned them, sensing their rising hope and expectations. "I have a much better general direction and distance though."

He pulled a red marker and a ruler from his jacket pocket and began taking measurements on the map. In a few minutes, he'd drawn a curved block around an area of agricultural land to the north east of the City. She is more than 20 kilometres from us as the bird flies, but less than 30 kilometres. I know it's not perfect, but if we get Athena out to that area, she should be able to track down the source of the protective ward. Gabi is definitely in the middle of that ward."

"Well, it's better than I nothing I suppose," grumbled Athena peevishly, "but you've still left me a lot of ground to cover."

A moment later, one of the internal phones beeped. Byron stood up and answered it. He listened for a moment, his face showing surprise and then a hopeful gleam as he thanked the caller and disconnected.

"Turn on the TV to local news coverage," he directed Kyle. "It sounds like our search area has just been narrowed."

Everyone turned with interest to the TV as Kyle flicked it on. A roving reporter was standing on a grassed area next to a lake surrounded by a throng of people who were dressed casually, as though on holiday.

"I'm standing here at the Pine Lake Marina where a flock of ducks have been exhibiting some bizarre behaviour this morning," the reporter was saying into his microphone. "We've been filming for at least ten minutes, and the ducks have been flying in this formation for the entire time the cameras have been rolling. It seems that ducks are trying to learn their ABCs. Holiday-makers at the Marina say the ducks got people's attention at around mid-morning by dive-bombing a group of water-skiers and then flying high into the sky, not in their usual V formation, but in another letter entirely." At that point, the camera panned up into the sky where a flock of large ducks was lazily flapping around beneath a light smear of cloud in the very distinctive shape of the letter H.

Julius felt a wry smile twist up the corner of his mouth, and when he glanced around the rest of the room, there were a few full grins on the faces of those watching the report. The reporter was now droning on about duck experts and their theories, but nobody in the conference room was listening anymore. Kyle actually whooped.

"Forget the Bat-Signal," he yelled with delight. "Our Gabs has got the Hellcat-Signal!"

Alexander snorted next to him. "Go Hellcat," he said, shaking his head with reluctant admiration.

All heads turned to Athena. "Alright, alright," she said. "I'm going. Do I have to drive or can I use the helicopter?"

The Council members looked at each other in indecision, so Julius spoke up, "If I may make a suggestion," he asked, when they waited for him he continued. "The sound of a helicopter will be very audible to any supernatural. If Alexander and I can keep ourselves from sleep during the day then Danté can too. If they realise their hideout has been discovered, they may try something desperate. It would be safer to do the recon as inconspicuously as possible."

There were lots of nods of agreement, but Athena just looked annoyed.

"I would also suggest that at least some of the team leaders go with her, so that once Athena pinpoints Gabi's exact location they can do a proper survey of the area, aerial shots are helpful, but eyes on the ground will enable us to isolate the best points of attack." Julius's military training may have taken place over two centuries before, but certain things didn't change much over the years.

"Yes, that's an excellent point," said Doug. "Athena, I'll join you. Kyle, you want to come along?"

369

SHARON HANNAFORD

Kyle gave him a 'was that a trick question' look and went to raid the catering table before they left.

"Neil," Byron said to the older Magi standing quietly out of the fray. "I think you would be an asset on the trip in case Athena needs to call on extra power."

The man nodded and hurried to join the small group getting ready to leave.

"Keep in contact and let us know your every move," Byron said to the departing team, "and Kyle?" he waited until the Wolf looked back at him, "don't try anything stupid. We do this as a clean, strong, united attack. Gabi can hold out until the full contingent arrives."

Kyle nodded, a little reluctantly, and turned back to follow the others out, gripping Julius's shoulder briefly on his way past, an ocean of unsaid things flowing between them.

Elements of the remaining group left to take care of their own specific tasks; Irene and Margaret were going to prepare a team of offensive Magi as well as a team of Medics and Banishers; Matt and Lance went off with the rookies to organise the weapons and gear needed for the attack; and Stewart was sent off to get some rest — he was looking grey and haggard after the last session tracking Gabi. As Alistair started to leave on his assignment of gathering the Werewolf contingent, Julius called to him.

"Patrick will be here in a few minutes," he said, referring to the Werewolf who headed up his daytime security. "He's also a dominant Wolf, but he's had the kind of military training which will prove invaluable tonight. Do you think the two of you can work together in this?"

Alistair thought for a moment before replying. "Yes, I know Patrick's reputation," he nodded, "His input will be very useful. I'm sure we can find a way to work together.

370

I'm assuming you're bringing in a team of Werewolves of your own to assist in the rescue?"

"Yes," Julius nodded, "Patrick was just rounding them up and getting them organised. What we need tonight is a coordinated, precision attack, so we need to have everyone on the same page. I'll make it clear to mine that other rivalries are to put aside for tonight."

"I can do that, too," Alistair agreed. "Though it may be safer to keep the two teams on opposite sides of the fray."

Julius gave a wry smile of agreement. "I'll leave the details to you and Patrick to sort out." Alistair took his leave, agreeing to meet back in the conference room in an hour. That left Byron, Julius and Alexander in the room.

"You have a keen understanding of military operations, Julius," Byron remarked. "You've done this kind of thing often?"

Julius bit back a smile as he moved back to study the map. "I was a lieutenant in the army of King George the 2nd and fought in the Seven years War against France in the 1750s. I cut my teeth against the Scottish in the Jacobite Rebellion of 1745," he said casually to Byron. Then he looked up and speared the older-looking man with his deep blue gaze. "The technology may have changed in that time, but the tactics remain very similar."

He'd spoken mildly, but he could see the effect his statement had on the man. Byron was used to being the most mature person in the organisation he'd helped to found, being almost venerated for his wisdom and experience, and he'd just had to think about the fact that Julius was more than four times as old as he was, had actually experienced the history that had been written about by hundreds of noted historians.

Byron collected himself, closing his slightly gaping mouth and wiping the astounded look off his face. "One of these days you and I need to have a long conversation," he said to Julius finally, muted awe in his voice.

Alexander rolled his eyes and started making small marks on the large aerial photo of the area someone had laid on the table.

"You're not gonna believe this," Kyle said, his voice slightly tinny over the speakerphone.

"Just spit it out, Kyle," Byron said with an unusual hint of annoyance in his tone.

"They're holed up in an old wine estate," Kyle informed them. "The story from the locals is that the original owner died a few years back without an heir, while the lawyers have been trying to track down any living family the place has been left to go to ruin. No one had any idea that it was being occupied again." The listeners could hear a car engine in the background. "There's a strong 'go-away' ward placed all along the boundary fences of the vineyard, so that would explain why none of the locals noticed anything odd. Athena said she's not going to bring down the wards now, as it would probably alert the Maleficus. Between her and Neil they were able to worm though the protective ward and pinpoint Gabi's location without disturbing it. She'll be able to bring it down when we're ready to strike."

"Alright, well done," Byron said. "Have you finished driving the area?"

"Yes," came Kyle's reply, "Doug and I have run most of the boundary, the place is surrounded by the old, overgrown vineyards. It'll give us a lot of cover going in, but it'll be easy to lose them if they make a run for it. We're on our way back now for a full debriefing. See you in half an hour."

\*\*\*\*\*\*\*\*\*\*\*\*\*\*\*\*\*\*\*\*\*\*\*\*

Danté and Mariska had given up their torture sometime after midday; apparently they did have other things to do besides play with Gabi. She'd stopped healing at some point and Danté seemed to have grown bored with his sport. Gabi had enjoyed her sojourn with the ducks; she wondered if her message had been received.

\*\*\*\*\*\*\*\*\*\*\*\*\*\*\*\*\*\*\*\*\*\*\*\*

The logistics of involving the Vampires in the attack made timing very tricky. Though the best time to attack would've been while the sun was still up, everyone agreed that the Vampire contingent was essential. Julius knew most of his guard would be awake well before dusk, but they couldn't withstand the light outside until the last few minutes before full sunset. They countered the problem by calling in two military helicopters that Byron had access to. By using blackout on the windows, they could get twenty Vampire guards to the vineyard at sunset, and the first wave of the assault would commence the moment his guard could leave the helicopters.

Athena knew Gabi was being held somewhere in the centre of the manor house, but the team hadn't been able to lay their hands on a copy of the blueprint for the house on such short notice. The advance team, who was responsible for ensuring Gabi's safe release, would be going in blind to the layout of the house. Kill teams and sweep teams were in place and ready, Medics and Banishers were in position away from the main points of assault.

As the dying light of the sun turned to burnt amber, a precision, military-style assault descended on the decaying vineyard. Four ranks surged into motion from different directions. Doug and Lance each led a large contingent of Werewolves, coming in from the east and the west, the majority of them in their Wolf form, but a few had managed to keep their human shape and were armed with flame-throwers. The Wolves were shaggy-coated and massive; their flanks reaching Doug and Lance's shoulders, saliva dripped from their mouths and their strangely human eyes gleamed, intent and battle-ready. Two black-clothed Magi brought up the rear of each group, like dark, silent ghosts. A smaller group moved in from the north, covering the rear of the buildings. The two rookies led this team, backed up by some experienced SMV Werewolves, Shape-shifters and Magi; their main goal to catch and eliminate anything trying to flee into the overgrown vines. Just as the sun touched the edge of the horizon a deep thrumming filled the air and the fourth team poured from helicopters in a silent, black torrent; leaping out as the helicopters hovered twenty meters from the ground, fifteen Vampires in dark clothes, lead by Liam and Nathan, landed lightly in the dust, drew their weapons and surged towards the front of the main building to meet the Demons, Ghouls and Vampires pouring out of every door and window.

A fifth team followed in the wake of the main attack. Julius, Alexander, Kyle and Athena had only one purpose — find and free Gabi. They hung back as the opposing sides met in a clamour of shouts, howls and unearthly shrieks. Within moments, the attacking forces set to achieving their first objective, drawing the fighting away from the main building and out into the open, dusty, unkempt gardens, allowing the small rescue team to slip inside unnoticed. Once inside, they ducked into a small side room which was empty except for some dust covered furniture and a few paintings and the men kept watch as Athena concentrated on pinpointing Gabi's location. She came out of her trance in a few moments and pointed north east.

"That way," Athena whispered and they left the room on swift, silent feet, making their way towards the rear of the house. They followed Athena though the kitchens into some storage rooms and came to a blank wall. There was no door or window nearby, Athena looked confused and frustrated.

"She must not be in this building, but she's really close, almost under our feet. It's not an exact science," she hissed at Julius's angry glare.

As they spun to retrace their steps, looking for a way outside, a pair of unknown Vampires materialized from the gloom. One of them gave a startled shout but before they could run or attack they were frozen in place by the force of Julius's will. At a glance from Julius, Alexander and Kyle moved to take up watch positions.

"Where is the woman?" Julius growled at the two captive Vampires. He watched dispassionately as the two buckled under the weight of his power, agony contorting their features.

"Cellar," they both gasped immediately.

"How do we get there?" he demanded.

"Door is inside….. ne.. next building," one of them gasped.

Julius didn't bother putting his next question into words, he simply exerted more pressure.

"Behind you, behind you," the other one shrieked. "There is a secret passageway, open the cupboard."

Julius eased the lash of his power and the two slumped forward on the ground as Kyle hurried to open what appeared to be a door to large built-in cupboard. When he opened it, the musty smell of old wine and oak barrels seeped out. Julius turned back to the other Vampires, already recovering from their ordeal and dragging themselves to their knees. "Who is your Sire?" he asked in a deadly voice.

There was a short pause and then defiance filled the eyes of one. "Danté. The King of Demons," he spat at Julius. "No one can overcome him. HE is our Sire."

At his words, the other Vampire also straightened his spine and his face took on a sneering insolence. The sneer was still on his face when Alexander's sword severed his head from his shoulders.

A moment later, they could hear human voices coming from the far side of the kitchen, the SMV contingent was cleaning up from the rear, so the men sent Athena to join the newcomers before making their way through the dank, underground passageway to the wine cellar. The far side of the passage tilted upward again as though it came out at ground level. They slowed at the other end, preparing for whatever was waiting for them on the other side of the door. As they burst through the door, a group of five stood guard around a large trapdoor cut into the wooden floorboards. The Vampire and four Demons spun as one at the sound of their arrival and immediately launched into an attack. Julius heard a ripping noise to his right and spared a glance to see Kyle explode into Wolf form, his clothing falling in torn strips around him. It was the first time Julius had seen him in this form, and at any other time he would've taken a moment to drink in the sight of the magnificent Wolf. Kyle gave a toothy grin and launched himself at the foremost Demon, while Alexander engaged the Vampire. He threw a look at Julius as he spun to block a blow from one of the Demons.

"Go. Find her," he shouted and chopped the arm off the Demon before spinning back to his Vampire opponent.

Julius didn't hesitate, he dodged the fight and sped straight for the trap door, throwing it open and jumping down into the dark, landing soundlessly on the hard-packed earth floor. A door stood closed at the end of a short, narrow corridor.

# CHAPTER 24

Julius sped towards the door, his boot covered feet barely touching the ground. He could feel Danté's and Gabi's presence in the room beyond the door. He wasn't sure how many non-Vampires were in the room with them, but it didn't matter. He didn't bother to check if the door was locked or not, he simply threw his power and his weight at it and it shattered into a confetti of wooden splinters. He plunged into the room, prepared for anything — except the scene that faced him.

It took him a half second to scan the entire room and realise that there was no one else in the large, dank room except the two people on the floor near the far wall. A lighter and candles lay on a table, amid a collection of knives, wooden stakes and pieces of silver chain. There was blood on most of the knives, and it wasn't Danté's. Julius forced himself to drag his gaze from the contents of the table to the target of his rage; the Vampire now hunched over the much too still form of the woman he would do anything to protect. He knew before a second had fully passed what Danté was doing crouched over

Gabi's motionless body. He was doing the one thing that would hurt Julius the most. He was taking Gabi's blood, draining her, so that he could Turn her. Change her into a Vampire. Danté's Vampire. If Danté managed to get any of his own blood into her at the right moment, Gabi would become a Vampire and would be inescapably tied to Danté; by Vampire law she'd be his to do with as he pleased.

Julius saw the same thoughts fly across Danté's face as he swept across the room towards them, Danté had counted on having more time, but he would try it now if he was forced to. His mouth ripped from Gabi's neck to his own wrist.

"NO!" Julius roared, flying at Danté. His rage afforded him speed and strength he'd never experienced before. Before Danté could withdraw his fangs from his own vein, Julius was on him. Julius didn't even bother trying to hold the deranged Vampire with his power; it was too much of a risk with Gabi lying so close and Danté's blood already welling from the puncture wounds in his arm. He simply launched himself at Danté with the power of a speeding train. The other Vampire flew backward through the air to hit the bare brick wall several feet away. The force of his impact cracked the wall and shook the room, bringing a cloud of dust and debris raining down on them all. Danté leapt up from the floor, flicking his long, dark blonde hair out of his eyes and dusting off his clothes. For a moment, the two Vampires simply stared at each other, their memories peeling back the years.

"Julius." Danté's voice was calm and genteel, but still held the usual tinge of arrogance. "It's been too long."

As Julius stalked towards the other Vampire, placing himself between Danté and Gabi's still form, he found himself looking into the face of someone he had once loved unconditionally; someone he'd respected and adored.

"Yes, it has Danny," Julius said, only barely conscious of using the old nickname. The other Vampire let out a peal of manic laughter.

"Sorry, Julius. In case you hadn't noticed, Danny doesn't live here anymore. There is only Danté, Demon Master and soon-to-be Master of the City," Danté declared, wiping at a smear of blood at the corner of his mouth and sneaking a hungry look at Gabi around Julius's shoulder.

"You're not getting anywhere near her again," Julius said in low warning. "This is going to end here and now!" His words didn't seem to register on Danté, and he continued as though Julius hadn't spoken.

"I must say, I can see why you've kept her around. She tastes awfully good, even if she was a bit too spirited for my liking. I think I've solved that problem though," his voice dropped to a conspiratorial whisper, "pity you won't get to enjoy the new, broken-in Angeli Morte."

Julius's chest tightened and rage washed through him in a cold wave.

"But there is only room for one of us in this world." Danté's voice trailed off as his eyes suddenly turned devious, and he took a step towards Julius. "Unless, brother mine, you are willing to join with me." A new plan seemed to be blossoming in his mind. "Come, Julius, give me your blood oath. Stand beside me instead of against me. Demon Master and Vampire Master - we'll be unstoppable. Even the precious Princeps will be running for cover. The world will be ours to do with as we please." His eyes were alight with excitement and fervour.

As Julius stared into Danté's demented, grey eyes, he knew he was finally doing the right thing, and it gave him a small measure of peace. Danté had given him an opening, and he took it. His eyes softened, his body relaxed, and his eyes closed in apparent submission. "Brother," he whispered, almost stumbling towards the other Vampire, reaching out his arms as though to welcome him.

Danté froze for an instant, his expression suspicious, and then he smiled beatifically. He moved towards Julius, reaching out to him in welcome as well.

Julius moved willingly into that embrace. "Danny," Julius whispered again, "I love you." And then he plunged Nex into Danté's back, straight into his brother's heart, twisting the blade viciously to make the death quick and final. He watched the shock flash across Danté's face as he held his brother's body against his own for a moment. Then the shock left Danté's face, and in the last moment of life, his brother's human eyes stared into his, and they looked… grateful, then the light was gone.

Julius took a deep breath. "Goodbye, Danny," he said, still whispering, and he let his brother's body drop to the floor.

He didn't watch as the body began to whither and shrivel but rushed back to where Gabi lay utterly still on the floor in a spreading pool of her own blood. He desperately moved her head to get a better look at the bite wound on her neck. The blood was still pulsing out of the open carotid artery. A movement in the doorway brought Julius back to his feet in a swift motion, immediately on the defensive. Kyle and Alexander surged into the room and stopped dead at the sight in front of them. Kyle had switched back to human form and was wearing Alexander's overcoat.

"Danté?" Alexander asked urgently, eyes darting around the room.

Julius indicated with a toss of his head the pile of decaying skin and bones lying a few feet away.

"Gabi!" Kyle cried, horrified as he took in the sight of her. Besides the blood pooling around her shoulder, she had obviously been beaten, stabbed, cut and burned. One side of her face was a black and red swollen mess, her eye swollen shut, blood trickling from her mouth and nose.

Julius looked down at her, and then at the blood covering his hands, her blood, her body lying crumpled in a heap at his feet, his head swam as he realised that this was his vision come to life. This was what he had seen would happen so many days, was it only days - it felt like months - before.

"No. No! No! NO!" His voice rose with each denial, until the last was a kind of roared keening.

"Stop that," Kyle yelled at him. "She's still alive, can't you feel her heartbeat? Listen Julius, she's still got a chance. We must stop the bleeding."

"Julius," Alexander's voice cut into his moment of insanity, sharp and reproachful. "Kyle's right. She's still alive. Either help us or get out the way."

Julius felt a semblance of sanity return, felt the red tinge to his sight fade a little, and realised he was crouched over her in a protective stance, daring anyone to try and get near her. He blinked and mentally shook himself, trying to calm his inner sense of utter hopelessness.

"Get the medics. Now," he growled at Kyle.

Then he knelt in the blood close to her head. He leaned down to brush away her blood matted hair and fastened his mouth to the terrible wound. He sensed more than saw Alexander keep Kyle back when Kyle saw what he was doing; reassuring him that Julius was only stopping the flow of blood, not feeding. He heard Kyle speak quickly and urgently into the phone telling the medics where to find them. He kept pressure on the wound with his tongue, not even tasting her blood in his mouth as he did it. He worked his mouth making himself produce more saliva, forcing it into the rip in her artery with his tongue. Once he felt the pulsing slow and could sense the wound coming together, starting to close, he unfastened his mouth from the area. He continued to lick over the wound again and again, cleaning the blood away from her torn skin and flesh, and beginning to seal the outer wound. He prayed to whatever God was listening that he'd done enough to stop the flow of blood from the artery.

Kyle let out a relieved breath when Julius moved away from her neck, and they could see that the blood flow had stopped. Kyle knelt down on the other side of Gabi and was now trying to assess her injuries and do something to help.

"I'm not sure the artery is completely sealed," Julius said, lisping slightly as he tried to speak around his extended fangs. "We need to get her to a hospital, her heartbeat isn't strong or steady, and she's lost far too much blood."

"The medics are at least a few minutes away, they have to be escorted through the fighting," Kyle said. "Ian is on his way in a chopper, and he has bagged blood with him, but his ETA is about ten minutes."

It was a clear indication that all of them were monitoring her condition closely when all three of them looked at her simultaneously as her heartbeat faltered for a terrifying second, and then started up again in an unsteady, hiccupping rhythm.

"Julius," Kyle said anxiously, "you gave her blood to heal her when she was staked. Give her some now, enough to stabilise her until the medics can get here."

Julius turned tortured eyes to Alexander's briefly, acknowledging Alexander's brief shake of the head, before looking back at Kyle.

"I wish I could," Julius whispered hoarsely, "but it's too dangerous."

"What?" shouted Kyle in disbelief. "You're the reason she's lying here. Now you can't do anything to help her." His anger, quick and hot, burst across the Vampires' senses, the smell of Wolf suddenly filling the room. Neither of them had ever seen Kyle lose his temper, never even seen him come close.

"Kyle," Alexander said, putting a calming hand on his shoulder, "you need to understand what happened before we got here. Julius didn't say he didn't want to help; he said it was too dangerous."

"What's that supposed to mean? What happened before we got here?" Kyle was still furious. If he was any other Werewolf, he would've been sporting fur, fangs and four legs already.

"Danté was trying to turn Gabi." Alexander explained calmly, but Julius could hear the edge of fury in his voice. "That's why she was on her way to bleeding out. He wasn't just feeding; he opened her artery so he could drain her. He was in the process of turning her into a Vampire. A Vampire who would've belonged to him in every possible sense of the word."

Kyle shuddered, but persisted in his angry frustration. "So why does that make it dangerous for Julius to help her."

"To finish turning a human a Vampire has to give his own blood to the human after he's almost drained the human of their own blood."

"Do you understand now?" Julius demanded, angry again himself. "She's lost enough blood that if I give her any of mine, or Alexander's, it may finish what Danté started. It may turn her into a Vampire. Do you think she wants that? Do we have the right to make the decision for her?" Julius could no longer contain the profound turmoil inside him. Pain seared across his face, his eyes burned with fear and torment.

"Shit!" Kyle slumped down beside her, taking her hand, bringing it up to his mouth to brush the back of it against his lips, and closing his eyes as though in prayer.

There were brutal black and blue marks circling her delicate looking wrist, interspersed with bleeding chafe marks, and a blade-shaped burn stood in sharp contrast to the rest of her perfect, pale, ivory skin along the length of the inside of her forearm. Julius purposefully avoided taking an inventory of all her injuries, concerned he might lose his tenuous grip on sanity if he saw all the evidence of the brutal abuse she'd been subjected to. Alexander moved to a position near the door, on full alert as sounds of fighting drifted down to them.

"Hang in there, Babe. Come on Hellcat, you gotta hold on until help gets here," Kyle murmured to her, almost crooning.

One emerald green eye, the unswollen one, fluttered open and tried to fix on his face.

"Gabi, Gabi," Kyle shouted excitedly, "can you hear me?" He leant over her anxiously.

She didn't respond, just kept her eye trained unsteadily on Kyle.

"Gabrielle?" Julius tried now, gently running the back of his fingers down the less injured side of her face. "It's alright, you're safe, medics are on the way."

Her only response was to move her eye from Kyle's face to Julius.

"Uh, Julius," Alexander interrupted, moving closer to them again. "Something isn't right. If she's conscious she should be reacting to the pain of her injuries. She's too still. Can you taste something strange in the air around her?"

"Shit," Julius cursed, "you're right Alexander; I can taste magic. How did I miss it before? Someone has bespelled her. It must have been the Dark Magus. What has that bitch done to her?"

"We need Athena," Kyle spoke urgently; "her speciality is counter-spells, if anyone can release Gabi, she can."

Alex moved in a rush of wind and was out the door before Kyle finished his sentence. The other two men both turned their attention back to Gabi as her breathing faltered and her heartbeat became a stuttering staccato.

"Gabi," Kyle said sharply, as her eye began to drift shut. "Stay with us, Sweetheart, we need you to stay here with us. Someone has to help us nurse that vicious cat of yours back to health. Julius might have saved him but that doesn't mean he'll be allowed anywhere near him again." He was grasping at straws, trying to find reasons to make her fight to stay with them, but incredibly it seemed to help.

She opened her eye again, they both saw the pain in her wavering gaze, and they both knew she didn't believe Kyle that Razor was still alive. She obviously thought her captors had killed him.

"It's true Gabs," Kyle insisted. "We got to your house minutes after the fight had gone down. Raz was still alive; if only barely, I don't think a vet could've saved him, but Julius gave him some of his own blood. You wouldn't have believed it if you didn't see it yourself. That bloody cat got up and started trying to track the bastards who took you. We had to restrain him and lock him in one of your steel cages out in the garage to keep him from coming with us." Kyle was babbling now, but it seemed to be holding Gabi's attention. The emotional pain in her gaze had eased.

Alexander arrived back in a whoosh of air, unceremoniously depositing Athena down in the room and pushing her towards Gabi and the other two men.

"Wha?" Athena said in confusion, trying to regain her balance and get over her shock of being swept up by the stunningly handsome English Vampire and rushed through to this dungeon of a room at the speed of lightning. She was thankful she'd borrowed a pair of jeans and a sturdy pair of boots for this mission instead of wearing her usual attire. Then she saw what Kyle and the arrogant Master Vampire were hovering over, and she caught her breath in horror. Gabi? Could that body lying slashed, burned, bruised and broken in a pool of blood possibly be Gabi? The way the men were stroking her face and hands, talking encouragingly to her, it had to be her. Athena couldn't believe that she was still alive.

Alex suddenly gave a frustrated sigh and grabbed her hand to drag her closer to the group on the blood-splattered floor.

"We think there's a spell on her. She isn't acting right; we can smell magic on her. Do something," Alexander ordered her in a tense snarl. "And try to wipe the horror off your face, we need to try and keep her calm," he growled the last warningly.

Athena took in a few quick, gasping breaths, trying to master the expression on her face. She'd thought the battle outside was horrific, watching the violence and destruction, but seeing someone she knew lying in that state wasn't something she'd prepared herself for. She may not particularly like Gabi, but she now had a far greater understanding of the strength and tenacity of the other woman, of what Hunters went through in the line of duty. Managing to gather herself she walked around Kyle and knelt at Gabi's head, the knees of her borrowed jeans quickly soaking up the congealing blood.

"I need the two of you to back away a bit," she said to Kyle and Julius.

Both men turned defiant glares at her.

"Please," she tried again, "I can't get a clear idea of the spell with you touching her."

Kyle gently put Gabi's hand down and moved back a foot or so, Alexander had to come over and put a hand on Julius's shoulder before he did the same. Athena closed her eyes and moved her hands slowly back and forth over Gabi's head and shoulders.

"It's a spell of compliance," she said without opening her eyes. "Well, a twisted version of the spell of compliance, designed to paralyse her." Athena gave a horrified little shudder and opened her eyes. "I can remove it, but once I lift it she will probably flail around in pain, you'll need to be ready to hold her steady, but do not touch her until I say so." She looked at Kyle and Julius with her own warning glare. "Do you understand me? This is going to be a difficult spell to lift and if you interfere you could do her permanent damage."

"Yes, we understand," Julius answered angrily, "just get on with it!"

Athena took a few deep breaths, centering herself and calling on the Lord and Lady to assist her, then she laid her left hand on Gabi's forehead, her right laid flat over her own heart. As she opened her mind to search for Gabi's essence, a wall of physical pain crashed into her with enough force to knock her sideways onto the bloodstained floor; she caught herself painfully on her left elbow, gasping for breath, a sweat instantly breaking out on her forehead.

"What's wrong?" all three men demanded simultaneously. Julius lunged for Gabi again, catching himself a millimetre from touching her, strain and worry etched into his face. Kyle's hands clenched into tight fists, and he was breathing hard, like he was fighting to keep himself calm.

"Her pain," gasped Athena, "When I merge with her mind, I can feel her physical pain. Lord and Lady, how can she stand it?" She pushed herself back into position and got ready to start again. She hoped she was prepared for the onslaught this time. Alexander moved closer to her and took up a position just behind her. Athena wondered if he was there to stop her from making a break for it. "She's in a world of pain, once she can move she will probably react to it quite strongly, be ready."

The men all nodded.

"Is it alright for me to catch you if you collapse again?" Alexander asked.

She nodded quickly, barely thinking about how, an hour ago, she would have cringed at the thought of his cold touch.

"Yes, just don't touch Gabi until the spell is lifted." She laid her hand back on Gabi's forehead and plunged back into a world of fire and agony. She knew Gabi could feel her presence, she felt Gabi relinquish what was left of her battered mental defences and allow Athena free reign over her essence to begin unravelling the complicated spell.

A small commotion at the door captured her attention for a second, but as soon as she realised it was only the Magus medical team, her focus was back on Gabi. She ignored the gasps of horror and hushed whispers, and concentrated on unravelling the complex, twisted spell. She barely noticed Alexander motion the newcomers to stand still and not approach. Her breathing was coming in short, sharp gasps, and she could feel the sweat beading on her face and neck as she continued her silent chant. As the spell began to break down, the air was suddenly thick with the feel of the dark energy rising around them, a sickly sweet odour intertwined with the fetid stench of the long dead, it lifted the hairs on her arms and sent shivers down her spine. Obviously, she wasn't the only one feeling the effects as the Magi Medics quickly began a low, murmured chant and soon a crisp, clean breeze swirled around them fending off the vile touch of the dark magic. Finally, she felt the last thread of the spell snap, and her chant broke off.

"Now," she whispered hoarsely, and she slumped sideways as though boneless.

Alexander caught her limp body and carried her over to the medics. Kyle and Julius both leapt into action as Gabi gave a low, agonised scream and tried to curl into a protective foetal ball. Each of them tried to hold her shoulders and hips gently in place, crooning to her, as she brought the hoarse screams under control.

"Watch out for her ribs and right leg," Athena warned them urgently. She was in a sitting position but still panting as if she had run miles and was feeling distinctly light-headed. "I think she has a cracked skull and a broken jaw on the left, too." The two female Magi near the door now rushed forward.

"Let us help," Melinda said, "we can ease some of her pain and try to repair some of the damage."

Athena knew that while Melinda looked barely out of high school, she was an accomplished healer who'd been involved with the SMV for many years already. If anyone could help Gabi right now it was her.

Kyle moved away from Gabi a little to allow the Medic access to Gabi's side. "Be careful Melinda, I can see you're exhausted already, don't over do it, just the life-threatening stuff," he said firmly.

Athena felt an unexpected frisson of respect for the semi-Werewolf, and, for the first time, a twinge of guilt that perhaps she'd been treating the non-Magi a little unfairly.

Melinda was already running her hands over Gabi's body about an inch above her flesh. Tarryn; another darker haired and slightly older Magus knelt down near Gabi's head, trying to avoid the blood. Julius flashed a dark, antagonistic glare at her. She cringed back slightly but didn't move away.

Julius could feel Athena's annoyance as he glared at the Healer crowding him away from Gabi.

"I can heal the burns, so they won't scar," she said in a tiny squeak of a voice, before Athena could interrupt and berate him.

Julius's glare softened, and he sighed.

"Sorry," he muttered, backing down and feeling the other Magi relax, "Do anything you can to ease her pain." Then he turned his attention back to Gabi, ignoring the gathering crowd.

"Go ahead Tarryn," Kyle encouraged gently, "just don't exhaust yourself, there are others injured outside who'll also need your attention."

She nodded and set to work centering herself.

"She has a slight tear in one lung from a splintered rib," Melinda said, "and there is some other internal damage. I'll try and repair as much as I can." She settled herself closer to Gabi's body and placed both hands on top of one another over Gabi's right lung and began chanting.

As the chanting grew between the two women working over Gabi, the others at the doorway started to chant too, and soon the air was filled with a warm radiant energy that seemed to caress the skin and to soothe and calm troubled thoughts. Suddenly, Gabi took a deeper, easier breath and seemed to sigh in relief, her body relaxed a little under Julius's touch, and he didn't need to fight so hard to try and keep her still. He could see full consciousness return to her as her gaze caught his, and she really looked at him for the first time since he entered the room.

"Lea, I'm so sorry," he whispered to her. "I can't tell you how sorry I am that he did this to you. I can't tell you how sorry I am that I wasn't able to protect you from him." His eyes filled with all the pain and torment he was feeling.

She weakly lifted her fingers to his mouth and laid them over his lips, wincing as something hurt her. "Shh," she hissed, through her teeth, obviously unable to move her jaw. "I'm ok."

He gently pressed her fingers closer to his lips and kissed them, closing his eyes against the grateful tears that threatened to spill down his face.

"Raz?"

Julius smiled weakly. "Yes, he's going to be fine. Probably more dangerous than ever for a few weeks until the Vampire blood wears off."

"You hope the effects wear off," teased Alexander from somewhere near the door. He and another Magus were hovering over Athena, trying to get her to sit down in a chair and drink something. She wasn't playing good patient and looked ready to collapse at any minute.

"Danté?" Gabi drew his attention back.

"He's gone. Dead," Julius said in a toneless voice. "I destroyed him. He will never touch you again." He could hear the steely protectiveness in his own voice.

Gabi closed her eyes, looking grey and exhausted.

A phone rang somewhere in the room. Kyle reached into one of his pockets. "Ian is here, I'm going to lead him in," he said quickly and rushed out the door.

"Stay with us Lea," Julius said sternly to Gabi when it looked like she may slip back into unconsciousness, "Ian is almost here with blood and pain meds for you. It's going to be alright. Just try and stay with us."

The two Magi who'd been working on her slowed their chanting and took deep, steadying breaths as they moved away from her. They both looked pale and tired.

"We've done what we can," Melinda said, "she needs blood and fluids now more than anything."

"Thank you," Julius said gratefully. "I can feel how you've eased her pain. I am in your debt."

As the Magi medics melted away, taking a still trembling Athena with them, Ian, Kyle and a human medical team burst into the room. Ian rushed straight to Gabi and Julius, shouting orders at the two human men who were setting down a stretcher and other medical supplies nearby. Ian gave Julius a cursory nod of greeting and set to work fastening a pressure cuff around Gabi's upper arm, trying to avoid a partially healed burn, and a heart rate monitor onto one of her fingers. He was keeping his expression carefully neutral and business-like, but Julius could taste the doctor's anxiety and horror at seeing Gabi in this condition.

He calmly asked Gabi a few questions, but when Julius could hear how hard it was for her to speak he broke in and told Ian what Athena and the other Magi had said about her injuries. Ian listened carefully to the list of her worst injuries as he deftly set up two IVs, one with blood and one with saline, with Kyle acting as IV stand. Ian tried to find a vein in her hand, and then in her arm, growling in frustration as the needle didn't find what he was looking for. The heart monitor bleeped erratically, warning them that her heart was beginning to fail; the lack of blood was taking its toll with each passing second.

Julius suddenly put out his hand. "Let me try."

Ian hesitated for a second and then handed the needle to Julius. Julius took the needle and lifted Gabi's arm in his large, pale hand. He closed his eyes and ran his thumb softly over the crease on the inside of her elbow, once, twice, a third time. Then, in a blur of motion, he sank the needle home; he was rewarded almost immediately with a drop of blood from the other end of the needle. Ian let out a breath he probably didn't know he'd been holding and quickly injected a full syringe of Morphine into Gabi before hooking up the blood and saline.

As the Morphine and the blood slowly helped steady Gabi's heart rate, and her blood pressure began to normalise, the rest of the world came back into focus for Julius. He realised he had no idea what was happening above-ground. Kyle had reported that the worst of the fighting seemed to be over, and since Danté's death many of his followers, the Vampire ones anyhow, had surrendered and were throwing themselves on Julius's mercy. Julius was only interested in finding Mariska and making sure they'd eliminated all the Demons. He gave Alexander a look and his second in command left on quick, silent feet to check what was going on.

The other two medics helped Ian splint her broken ankle while Kyle and Julius helped keep her still. Julius closed his eyes and breathed deeply when she screamed in pain, reminding himself to keep his grip on her gentle. At that moment in time he could have destroyed Danté a hundred times over without a single moment of regret. Finally, Ian allowed Julius and Kyle to lift her onto the stretcher. As they were preparing to leave, Julius stooped down and picked something up; he put it on the stretcher with Gabi, tucking it in against her thigh, in reach of her right hand. She noticed the movement and moved her hand down to touch the object. An almost contented smile lifted one side of her mouth as she closed her fingers around the familiar shape of Nex's hilt. Then they left the horror of the underground cellar and headed for the helicopter as fast as they could without jostling her.

# CHAPTER 25

Voices in the dark. That was all. No sight, no smell, no feeling, no pain. Just murmured voices. Soothingly familiar voices. Nothing to worry about. She didn't need to leave the dark numbness. She could put names to the soft voices. She could hear words, but she couldn't make sense of them, yet. For now, she was content to absorb them, she'd process them later.

"How is she?" Alexander's voice.

"Ian and Jonathon say she's stable." Kyle's voice. Stressed, tired.

"She hasn't come around yet?"

"No, they're keeping her in a coma for a few days so the head injury can heal."

"She's strong, she'll be alright."

A snort. "Yep, she's Hellcat."

The voices were quiet for a moment.

"Have they found her yet?" Kyle's question.

"The Maleficus?" Alexander's hard-edged query. "No." Sharp, annoyed. "They're looking under every rock, but it's like she simply vanished."

"The Magi will find her. Eventually. What about the Demons and Ghouls?"

"Obliterated. None left. The Magi even found a way to damage the Wraith. They don't think it will be back in a hurry. There were a few more humans who'd been bitten or just held captive; they've been taken to the asylum with the rest. We found Gregory's remains."

"How is Julius?"

A heavy sigh. "I've never seen him like this. He's been questioning the Vampires who surrendered. I had to get away for a while. He's not himself. Nathan and Fergus are trying to reason with him." These words made something tense inside her.

"Has he found out anything of value?"

"Gregory claimed to have interesting information about Gabi. None of the Vampires know what it was or whether he told Danté. None of them were high up in his Clan, they were just following orders."

"Do you think he told Danté about her being Dhampir?"

"We don't know. It seems that at least one of his commanders wasn't at the vineyard when we attacked. We don't where he is now, or what information he may have."

"Shit."

"Why don't you take a break, Wolf? Get some food, a shower, some clothes," a trace of amusement in Alexander's voice. "I'll stay with her."

Darkness and silence.

"I don't think that's......." A louder voice that took her a moment to find a name for. Ian. Yes, Ian's voice. An edge of panic in it.

"Don't worry, he won't hurt her." Kyle's reassurance. "He's going to hurt himself if we don't let him at least see her. Not even Rose can keep him calm anymore."

"It's alright Ian," Byron's voice, soothing. "Razor won't hurt Gabi. Let him see her, and be near her. It will do them both good." Muttered grumbling. Then a bone deep, soul massaging purr enveloped her.

Darkness and peace.

"What's the news, Wolf?" Alexander's voice.

"Jonathon just left. They're going to bring her out of the coma tomorrow." Kyle's voice. Lighter, happier. "I'm just trying to work out how we're going to keep her in bed for the next few weeks. She's a terrible patient when she's conscious." A wry chuckle.

"Good luck with that."

"So, do you think this thing is really over?"

"Well, the influx of Demons and Ghouls should come to an end without Danté around to control them. But with Vampire politics there will always be power struggles. If Danté knew about Gabi and managed to get word to the Princeps......" A deep sigh. "Only time will truly tell."

"Well, they'll have a lot of people to get through first if they come after her." Kyle's voice. Hard, resolute. A mutter of agreement. "There is some good that came out of this mess. The Werewolf packs have called a truce and are trying to work together to form their own Council and play a more defined role in the SMV. Byron has had seven promising Hunter Trainee applications. The Magi High Council is overhauling its systems and looking at ways to prevent others like Mariska slipping through the cracks."

A long pause, then Kyle spoke again. "The Council will welcome Julius and the Clan to the table if he wants to be a part of it. They are trying hard to understand your kind. Now would be a good time to cement alliances and formalise boundaries."

Alexander's voice. Heavy, weary. "Julius will need some time. Vampires....." A pause. "Older Vampires don't react well to emotional turmoil. His feelings for Gabi, the betrayal by his Children, taking Danté's life, these are harder for him to cope with than you might expect. It would be helpful if you could try to explain this to the Council. Buy him some time to recover."

"Okay. Yeah, I can do that." Kyle's voice dropped to a whisper. "What about him and Gabi?"

"I don't know," Alexander's voice. "I guess that's up to the two of them."

Darkness and disquiet.

Consciousness returned to Gabi in stages. The first stage was an awareness of the pain. Not the acutely blazing pain which was her last real memory, more of an all-over, dull hum of ache. She yearned to slip back into the warm, dark pool of oblivion where the pain didn't exist, but her mind was inexorably making its way to the surface. The need for information stirred her to the next level of consciousness. She could hear the faint, steady beeping of a heart rate monitor, the hum of other electronic equipment and the almost inaudible drip of liquid. She could feel a cool sheet touching parts of her body, other parts felt cocooned and warm. She could smell antiseptic, but not as strongly as she would've expected in a hospital. Her next level of awareness told her it was too quiet to be a hospital, and curiosity broke the final layer of oblivion. She heard her own groan and held her breath while she learned how to cope with the sudden assault of a hundred different hurts.

She knew he was there. Without opening her eyes, without hearing him move, without smelling his scent in the air, she knew he was in the room with her.

"Julius?" she tried to say. Her voice came out a hoarse rasp. She swallowed, trying to work some moisture into her dry mouth. She opened her eyes finally as she felt the faint disturbance of the air near her. The room was almost dark, lit only by the monitors that surrounded her on two sides and the moonlight streaming in the window. He was a dark, silent shadow near her right hand. She could feel the tension and anxiety rolling off him like a palpable wave.

"Water?" she croaked, lifting a hand to search for a cup. As she started to lift her shoulders to sit up, she could feel stitches pull and muscles and tendons scream in protest. A cool hand pressed her down.

"Wait," his voice was a mere whisper.

A moment later, the top half of the bed gently tilted upward with a slight hum. A loud purring started from somewhere in the vicinity of her feet, but the cat didn't move. Some dim memories of voices in the darkness clicked into place.

Julius leant in close to her, and with infinite care, slid his hand behind her head, holding her upright enough to take a sip from the glass of ice water he was holding to her mouth. "Slowly," he cautioned. "Not too much."

She nodded minutely but was finding it hard to control herself when her mouth felt like a long abandoned salt pan.

He allowed her three small sips and then settled her back on the pillow. "Do you need more pain relief?" he asked. "We weren't sure how much to give you, Ian had a general idea, but we were being cautious. I can up it." He moved to reach across her to the dripline.

She raised her right hand to catch his; it made her wince. "It's fine," she rasped, her voice a little stronger. She grasped his fingers and pulled his hand to her face, waiting. Finally, he turned his face and looked down into her eyes.

She didn't know where exactly she was, or how many hours or days she'd been unconscious, but none of that mattered when she looked into his face. Grief, horror and guilt were etched into every line. His eyes were coal black and dark shadows underlined them. He opened his mouth to speak, and she knew what he was going to say and interrupted him.

"Sit," she said, indicating the edge of the bed. "We need to talk."

He pulled his hand away from hers, gently but firmly, his features hardening into a controlled mask. "I need to call Kyle. I promised I'd let him know the moment you woke."

"Is it true?" she asked him. "What Danté told me, is it true?" She heard his broken sigh and then a chair being moved to her bedside. She turned her head to see him collapse into it, his head in his hands.

"If he told you I was his brother, then yes," he answered roughly, "it is true."

She waited; she knew he needed to say more.

"My Maker's name was Simone; she seduced me, pretending to be human, and later turned me without my consent. She expected me to forgive her and join her in a life of eternal, sadistic fun. I couldn't find it in myself to forgive her, and I didn't want to become like her, so I walked away from her to find my own way in my new and difficult life. Simone didn't like to be thwarted, and like the petulant child she was, she sought revenge. She went back to my family's estate a few years later and seduced my younger brother. Unlike me, Danté willingly joined her cause. He was the baby of the family and his lack of maturity made him easy to manipulate. When I discovered what she'd done, how the two of them were travelling the world committing atrocities in the name of 'fun', I hunted them down. I'd grown strong over the intervening years, and I killed Simone: a true death. Danté was under my blade, and I could've killed him, too. I should've killed him, too." Julius's voice had dropped to a whisper. "I looked into his eyes, and I couldn't do it. I warned him to change his ways. I offered to help him. He ran from me, spitting curses and swearing vengeance for Simone's death. I should've killed him then." Centuries of despair and regret made his last words leaden.

"But you did kill him," she said softly. "You had to do something life should never have asked of you." She reached for him; compassion warring with anger and hurt. Anger that she hadn't been able to help, hurt that he hadn't trusted her enough to tell her the truth.

"I could only do it because of what he'd done to you, because of what he was trying to do to you," he growled, his hands clenching into fists so tight that his knuckles looked ready to burst from the skin. "If it had been anyone else lying there, I'm not sure I would've been able to do it. I might have let him live."

"I'm sorry," she whispered.

"SORRY?" he roared, lurching out of the chair, storming to the window. "Sorry?" he asked, still loud but not yelling. "What have you got to be sorry for? Danté tortured you to within millimetres of your life; he was trying to turn you into a full Vampire. I could kill him a hundred times over for what he did to you." He was breathing hard and his hands were clenched in his hair as he stared at her incredulously.

"I'm sorry I wasn't strong enough to kill him for you," she said quietly. "No one should ever have to take the life of blood kin. I wish I could've done it for you."

Julius collapsed to his knees on the floor, his head hung, and in the pale light of the full moon Gabi could see his tears splash down onto the floor tiles. They left tiny dark specks where they fell. She wished she could go to him, take him in her arms and comfort him, hold him until his grief was spent, help ease the weight of his guilt. But even if she hadn't been confined to the bed with plastercasts and plastic tubes, she wasn't sure she could comfort him. Not yet. Her own spirit felt like it had been shredded into a million tiny pieces; her confidence in herself was shattered, she was bleeding on the inside as well as the outside. How could she offer emotional support when she was so deeply in need of it herself?

And so, she watched him in the light of the moon, until he finally stood and came to her. Without looking at her, he bent and kissed her forehead, a featherlight touch of lips and then he was gone.

She closed her eyes against the sting of her own tears, then she felt a movement on the bed. She opened her eyes to see Razor sitting next to her, simply gazing adoringly into her face, his joy at seeing her vibrating through his entire body. Gabi laced her fingers into his lush coat and felt some cuts on her face crack open as she smiled at him. Suddenly, it felt as though a few of the tattered slivers of her spirit had just healed into a larger, more robust chunk. She remembered Kyle calling her back from the welcoming darkness with the words that Razor was still alive, but she hadn't actually believed him. Seeing the cat sitting next to her, whole and uninjured was a priceless gift, a caress to her battered soul.

She must've drifted back to sleep because when she opened her eyes again, the faint grey light of dawn was colouring the room. She turned, looking for the water glass, and found Kyle slumped in the chair a few feet away. He was asleep, but at the sound of her movement, he cracked one eyelid. A warm, relieved smile lit his face, and he sprang up to go to her.

"Thirsty?" he asked, seeing her eye the glass. He helped her sit and drink. "It's so good to see your eyes open," he enthused. "I want to hug the breath out of you, but I don't know where to touch you." He settled for ruffling her mussy curls and dragging the chair closer to sit where she could look at him without straining.

"Where are we? It doesn't sound or smell like any hospital I know."

"You're in Julius's private hospital wing at the Estate. It's fully equipped, set up for his Werewolves, and Ian has been liaising with Julius's Vamp doctor about your treatment. Ian really wanted to get you to his hospital but Julius wouldn't budge, and he's not really in the kind of mood where anybody is keen to argue with him."

"Oh," she said lifting her hand to her hair. "Ugh, what a mess." Her hair was heavy with sweat and dirt and blood.

"Yeah, the nurse didn't want to wash your hair until the major wound had closed a bit. It was a nasty one," Kyle explained.

"What's the rest of the damage?" she asked, suddenly realising she had no idea and lifting the sheet to peer down at herself underneath it. She catalogued the braces, bandages, burn dressings and stitches as he filled her in.

"Broken left arm, broken right ankle and shattered knee, fourteen broken ribs, a cracked skull, fractured cheek bone, and I didn't bother trying to count the stitches. Ian might know the final count." He tried to sound unaffectedly jovial as he listed the injuries, but Gabi could hear the concern underlying his cheerful tone. "They pumped five or six bags of blood into you as well."

"Ian's going to book me off for weeks isn't he?" she asked in resignation.

"Hmmm, I'd go with months," Kyle replied. "And, if Byron has anything to say about it, it could well be years."

She made a rude noise in her throat.

"We'll just see about that," she declared, a gleam coming into her eyes as she stroked Nex's hilt where she found it tucked between the bed railings and the mattress.

# ABOUT THE AUTHOR

I've been calling myself a writer since I was 8 years old, and wrote my first autobiography at age 10. As a teenager I wore lots of black and owned a black cat, who travelled around on my shoulder. At school it was rumoured that I was a lesbian witch. I never tried very hard to dispel the rumours. If I wasn't at school or working on our local tourist farm I was either reading or horse-riding.

Born and raised in South Africa, I've been living in New Zealand since 2008 with my little family. While I call myself an author, in reality I wear many hats (housewife, mother and cat slave are my other job titles). I'm an avid reader of fantasy, PNR & UF and a passionate animal person. My life has always been filled with animals of all shapes and sizes. If I ever give up writing I think I'll study animal behaviour or start my own menagerie.

Keep up with Gabi and the gang at:
www.hellcatseries.com
Twitter @ShazFly
Find me on Facebook
www.facebook.com/pages/Author-Sharon-Hannaford/244568828958484

or look me up on GoodReads.

Love my book cover?
See more work by my awesome graphic artist, Erin Kuhle at http://laschae.deviantart.com/

Printed in Great Britain
by Amazon